THE VIATOR CHRONICLES BOOK 1

JANE RALSTON-BROOKS

First printing, 2015

Purple Thistle Publishing

ISBN-13: 978-1519674418
ISBN-10: 1519674414

Cover art and design by Trevor Smith

Printed by CreateSpace

For
Roger

Table of Contents

Acknowledgments

My thanks to my husband Roger, who pushed me on and believed in my dreams, to Kathleen Shaputis, whose cheerful encouragement at the Olympia Writers' Group was a great inspiration, to my daughter Claire Frank for her hours of creative, editorial and objective help, to my editor Mimi, the Grammar Chick, to Trevor Smith for the amazing cover art and design, to Rebecca Durkin, who has seen me through this whole process, to friends and family for their encouragement, and to my parents, who continue to gift me with dreams.

"Deep into that darkness peering, long I stood there,
wondering, fearing, doubting, dreaming dreams no mortal
ever dared to dream before."

Edgar Allan Poe - The Raven

VIATOR

Prologue

Late afternoon sunlight shimmered through the birch trees and evergreens, and a dense undergrowth of ferns crowded the trail. Sean quickened his pace. He'd been following for hours through ever more treacherous territory, and he still hadn't found his charge. *Where was that man?* A chill breeze from the north rustled through the leaves, and he heard the gurgle of water ahead. Scanning the small stream that cut across his path, he wiped the perspiration from his forehead with the back of his hand and searched the far bank. When he saw the telltale tracks and loosened stones, he leapt over the stream and scrambled up the far slope. Broken branches marked the path, and he followed these signs as he ran through the forest.

The path curved around a tall boulder, and Sean was unable to see ahead. He slowed his pace and slipped a knife from its sheath on his belt. He jogged around the turn and found the right edge of the path sheared off, exposing a high precipice. A short distance beyond the cliff the narrow path widened again and wound down to the forest in the valley below, where it forded a river far ahead. Along that path he could see the figure of a man, and he knew he had found his charge. He breathed a sigh of relief, tucked his knife away, and edged along the bluff until the path widened again. Then he ran full speed, knowing he was on target.

Brown mud stained Sean's black pants and jacket from the hours of the long chase. No one had ever run from him for so long. Why this time? Didn't the man realize Sean was there to help?

The sun had set and a waxing moon glowed in the sky by the time Sean had reached the valley floor. He shivered from a sudden cold breeze. The hair rose on the back of his neck as he caught the scent of carrion reek, and he slowed and loosened his sword. The man must be close by, but the stench was alarming.

"Where are you?" Sean called.

"Here. I'm here," a man answered from the direction of the river.

"Wait for me … stay where you are. I can help you."

Sean took off as fast as he could, racing along the path. The trail grew wet and slippery as it sloped downhill toward the water. He slid in the mud but caught himself before he tumbled.

The path was paved with slick stones leading to the bank of the river, and Sean took the wet steps more carefully. Bushes and reeds grew thick, blocking the river from view. When he reached the water's edge, he saw the rocky beach open out. The river widened in this spot, becoming shallower, allowing for large stones to make a ford across to the opposite shore. But he sensed this roaring river was a border of some kind—once across, it might not be so easy to return. He looked across and groaned. The man he needed to help was on the other side.

Sean stepped close to the water's edge and called out, "Come back."

The man was already heading into the forest on the opposite shore, but he stopped and turned. He hesitated, and Sean could see doubt and confusion in the man's eyes.

"Come back," Sean shouted again.

The man looked directly at Sean and took a few steps toward him. He rubbed his hands over his face and through his blond hair.

"I can't. Help me," he called.

Sean frowned and took another step closer to the river, calling again, "Come here."

The man shook his head and pleaded, "Help me."

Sean sheathed his sword and stepped out onto the nearest stone in the river. His foot slipped into the icy, rushing water. He tried again, and this time his footing held. He crossed the river from rock to rock slowly, and with great care he finally reached the opposite shore and scrambled up the slippery bank. The moon was high, and the birch trees on this side of the river were dense. Sean stood and looked around.

"Where are you?"

"Here."

The answer came from just to the left. Sean turned to go that direction when the air grew icy and foul. He almost gagged from the stench, but he walked into the darkness of the forest.

The shape of a man rose from the ground in front of Sean—an enormous black shadow, cold, dark, and cruel, but so much more—a mortifer. Sean drew his sword.

"What have you done with the man?" Sean demanded.

The shadow laughed, a high hollow sound that was eerie in the night air. "Nothing—he is ours."

The bushes rustled behind him and Sean whirled with his sword, striking another mortifer as it crept up from the forest. The sword pierced its side, and it fell, rolling in agony. The first mortifer leapt and slammed Sean across his back with its staff, throwing him forward. Sean's sword fell but he caught himself, stumbling forward a few steps.

He whirled around. It was hard to see well in the darkness under the trees, but his night vision was keen, and he knew he could handle one or two mortifers, even as tired as he was.

The first mortifer stood nearby—what was it waiting for? It knew Sean didn't have his sword.

A blast of icy wind blew through the forest again, and the rotten stench grew overwhelming. Sean gagged, and then he scrambled for his sword.

A blow from a staff struck him hard across the back again just as he grasped his blade, and he fell to the ground but with his sword still in hand. He leapt up.

A horde of mortifers stood before him, the flaming ice of their eyes froze him, and he groaned. How many were there? They were countless. They loomed over him, growing taller, and wavered in the breeze like wispy phantoms. But they were all too real. How had they known he was here?

Where was his charge? Sean cried, "What have you done with him?"

Again the shadow mocked Sean with its hollow laughter. It pointed to the right, and under the shadows of the dense trees Sean saw the man he was supposed to help—he was standing, waiting. Watching. Sean's eyes widened. He knew he had been betrayed. This was a trap.

He had to warn the others of this danger, but a mortifer drew a long sword from its scabbard and attacked. Sean dodged that blow and countered with a swing that severed the shadow's sword arm. It screamed its rage, and the others, some armed with tall staffs and some with swords, leapt forward. He dodged one but another struck him. They attacked him with sword, staff and knife. He destroyed one mortifer after another, but there were always more. He stumbled, and they descended on him, battering him with their staffs, but he rose up again, finding more strength. He swung his own sword to hit one of the shadows in the chest, destroying it. A sword struck him in the shoulder. He was weary, and he was in agony, and still he tried to fight them off. He felt another gash to his back. He was struck in the chest, in the arms, on his back over and over, and he sank to his knees. His clothes were wet with sticky blood.

The mortifers scoffed at him. "You are ours now, viator."

For a moment there was silence in the dark forest.

A crow cawed as it flew overhead, and Sean looked up.

He struggled to stand and swung his sword at another mortifer, striking and felling it, its blackness oozing out over the wet forest floor. Another shadow stepped forward and pierced Sean once more with a long knife blade to his chest. He fell to the ground, his face in the dirt, the taste of blood in his mouth.

The crow landed on the ground nearby, and Sean whispered, "Betrayed."

The crow cawed again and flew away.

Chapter 1

Erin sipped her champagne and studied the dagger. The copper handle was decorated with intricate swirling designs that were smooth and polished, while the edge of the blade glittered like fire in the lamplight. It rested in an ebony case on a cushion of green silk inside the glass display cabinet. It seemed familiar, from long ago, and she puzzled about where she may have seen it before. She could almost feel it fitting comfortably in her hand.

The gallery was full of an eclectic group of people, some edgy and modern, while others were dressed in elegant evening clothes and jewelry. Each piece of art on display was lit from several directions in the darkened rooms, casting distorted shadows on the walls and ceilings, the light sometimes catching a person's face and highlighting it at an odd angle. Most of the people were talking and laughing in groups, and the wood floors and open spaces amplified the sound. Erin turned just as her friend Aleesha sashayed across the room leading a heavy man wearing a creased taupe suit.

"Erin, you must meet Kenneth." Aleesha beamed, her slim silver skirt and jacket shimmering in the light.

Erin smiled at the man. His shaved head was covered by a turquoise blue fedora and diamonds glittered in his ears. He bent forward and kissed both Erin's cheeks.

"Aleesha's told me so much about you and your gallery." Erin pressed her hand into his.

Kenneth looked ecstatic. "I'm so thrilled to meet you. Aleesha has told me all about you, too. Welcome to the gallery. What do you think? Look around and tell me. Besides being in the best location in Seattle, I think we've been able to put together some of the best collections of any of the galleries in Pioneer Square. Please tell me what you think."

"I love it," she said.

"Can I get you anything?" he continued, clasping her hand and looking her up and down. "You look gorgeous—so classic. When the music starts be sure to tell me your impressions. I'd be honored if you'd play a song or two."

Erin felt her face grow warm as she smiled and tried to answer, but he kept up a stream of comments and questions. He finally paused to take a breath, and she said, "Thank you for inviting me to your exhibit. I'm already enjoying it immensely. I'm sorry, though, I won't be able to play tonight. But Aleesha tells me you have some excellent musicians to entertain us."

Kenneth glanced at Aleesha, a small pout on his face. He turned back to Erin. "Oh, my dear, and I have my grand piano here all ready for you."

"I'm sorry," Erin stammered.

"Erin hasn't performed in a couple years," Aleesha said.

Kenneth patted her arm. "Well, don't give it another thought. I can always hope, can't I? But you're my guest, dear! Enjoy."

He grabbed a couple more glasses of champagne from a nearby tray, handed them to Erin and Aleesha, and when he noticed some new guests enter the gallery, he ran to greet them.

"He's a kick," Erin laughed.

Aleesha put her hand on Erin's shoulder and grinned as they both watched him. "Yes. He's really a dear man. And he's right—you do look gorgeous. I love that dress on you."

"Thanks. It was one of William's favorites."

Erin wore a short, dark blue dress and had pulled her brown hair up into a French twist to show off her pearl earrings. She thought about the last time she had worn the dress—she and William had been celebrating their tenth wedding anniversary. A sob caught in her throat. She took a quick sip of champagne and forced a smile back onto her face.

She and Aleesha filled a couple of plates with hors d'oeuvres and walked through the rooms, admiring the art and looking at the people. Aleesha knew many of the other guests, and she stopped to chat with them or compare impressions of the art. The musicians soon began to play, and Erin and several other people gathered around them. Piano, fiddle and bodhran accompanied a young woman whose haunting soprano voice gave Erin goosebumps.

As she listened to the music, Erin glanced around the room and noticed an attractive man who stood alone by the door. He looked familiar. He was stirring his drink and staring at her, so she quickly looked away. A few minutes later she glanced back, and he was still studying her, even as he gulped his drink and set the glass on a tray. Feeling embarrassed, she retreated into the next room where she pretended to examine a dark painting of ancient Celtic shields while she gathered her thoughts. She was sure she had met him before. Blond, blue-eyed, wearing a finely tailored charcoal suit, obviously went to the gym regularly. He was probably around her age. Did he recognize her? Could she have known him in school?

A man spoke quietly right behind her. "What do you think of the shields? I prefer the next painting—the one with the swords. Seems more proactive." She turned around, and he was smiling at her, dimples in both cheeks, eyes laughing. She blushed.

"Aren't you Erin Holley?"

She nodded. "Yes ..."

"I thought so. It's been about two years. I'm Gary Arthur. I was a friend of William's. I almost didn't recognize you with your hair up."

"Oh, yes. I thought I had met you before."

His voice grew quiet and serious, his eyes clouding over. "I was sorry to hear about William. I had just seen him the day before the ...

accident. It was such a shock. I had left the country when I heard. I felt I should come back, but I couldn't—I couldn't get away." He paused, frowning, and looked down at his hands. "I'm sorry I wasn't there for you."

Erin was taken aback and shook her head. "No, it's okay. It would never have occurred to me you should be here."

"Really?"

She smiled at him. "Of course not. I'd only met you a few times. But thank you."

He leaned against the wall and sighed. "William was an old friend." His eyes grew more intense. "And how are you doing? You look great. And the kids—you have two, right?"

"Right." She nodded, her head tilted to the side. She studied his face. He wasn't smiling but his dimples still creased his cheeks. "We're okay. Matt's almost twelve now, and Gwen's seven. They're really growing up."

"Good. And you still live in Anacortes?"

She nodded. "Still in the old house on Puget Sound." She paused a moment. "Did you say you saw William the day before the accident?"

Gary glanced at his watch and looked at the doorway. A line of sweat trickled from his hair beside his ear. He bent his head and nodded. "Just briefly. I'll never forget what he said that day." He shook his head. Then he looked back at Erin, his eyes sparkling. "I remember your little house on the water."

"We love it there … but what did William say?"

Gary drew a breath just as a stocky middle-aged man entered the room. His tan trench was dripping, and water ran from his thin gray hair down his thick neck. He wiped his face with a handkerchief and frowned at Erin before he glanced at Gary and nodded his head. Gary nodded back, turned to Erin and said, "My business associate's here. I've got to run. We've got a meeting."

He grabbed her hand and gave it a squeeze, then turned and followed the other man out of the room.

Erin stood still for a moment, staring at the door after they had left. She was surprised and a little shaken—she hadn't run into someone from William's past in a long time. What a coincidence they had both been at this gallery tonight.

She wandered back toward the musicians. The crowd had become quiet as they listened to a slow ballad, and Erin grew more thoughtful. She remembered Gary from the few times they had met. He had come to a couple social events hosted by William's company. A picnic and a Christmas party. She remembered him playing ball with Matt at the picnic. He had brought a date to the Christmas party—a tall, beautiful woman with long, dark hair.

She stopped and stood still as a statue, her heart suddenly filled with grief and uncertainty. These memories brought images of William to her mind so clearly—dancing at the Christmas party with the glow of firelight on his face, playing checkers with Matt at the kitchen table, laughing as they ran on the beach together. She missed him so much. And then the day of the accident—she remembered it as if it had just happened, and the pain hit her again like a sharp blow. She hadn't known William had seen Gary the day before. What did William say to him that long-ago day, something so memorable Gary would never forget it?

The room was too hot and too loud. She needed to get out. She found Aleesha and convinced her to leave, and they drove the long way home to Anacortes in the wind and rain.

Chapter 2

GRAVEL crunched under the tires as Aleesha turned the car into Erin's driveway and drove past the apple trees. Wind blew through the branches, scattering the blossoms. As they stopped in front of the little house, Erin leaned over and hugged Aleesha. "Thank you, Leesh. I'm so glad you invited me." They said goodnight, and as Aleesha drove away, Erin unlocked her front door.

"Edna?" Erin spoke quietly so she wouldn't wake the children. She walked to the living room and saw the older woman sitting on the couch, snoring softly with a closed book on her lap.

Edna opened her eyes. "Oh, you're home." She sat up straight and smiled. "Did you have a nice time?"

Erin sat beside her and patted her arm. "Yes, a great time. How were the kids?"

"Good as always."

Edna had been a close friend and neighbor of Erin's grandparents years ago when they had owned Erin's house. After Erin had inherited the house and she and William had moved in, Edna had become a generous babysitter.

Erin walked Edna the short distance home, and after returning she climbed the stairs and peeked in on the children. Matt and Gwen were sound asleep, so she went to her room and closed the door. She approached the corner of her bedroom and lit both candles on the small, cloth-covered table, and kneeling on the floor, she gazed at a photograph illuminated by the flames. The photo showed a smiling man sitting in a sailboat, a captain's hat on his head. She touched it and whispered, "I'm so sorry, William." She bowed her head and sank to the floor. After several minutes, she blew out the candles and climbed into bed.

***

Erin raced over the moors, her dark hair streaming behind her as the wind and rain tried to force her back. She could hear nothing but the wind. Lightning streaked across the sky, flashing brightness across the wild land, and there, a little way ahead, she could see the shadow. A scream, and she knew she was close. She raced on, forcing her way against the storm.

Suddenly all was black. Where was that girl? Erin slowed her pace. The lightning blazed again, and she saw the precipice at her feet. She caught herself, stopping at the ledge. The sound of the waves from far below roared even louder than the wind. Leaning over the edge, she called out, "Where are you?"

"I'm here. I'm stuck," the girl answered from below.

"I'll help you. Look—I think the moon is rising," Erin called.

A little moonlight gleamed through the streaming clouds showing the face of the cliff and the figure plastered against the wall below. Her wide eyes stared up at Erin, her pale face streaked with mud.

"No, look out, behind you," screamed the girl.

Erin felt the icy darkness behind her and caught her breath. She turned and drew her sword. The mortifer loomed over her, the shape of a man shrouded in gloom. Its piercing eyes gleamed with hunger; its stench of decay nearly gagged her. She raised her sword. The shadow struck first, smashing her right arm. Erin fell, pushed down to her knees into the mud, her sword arm pinned by the dark creature's foul blade. With her other hand she reached for the knife in her boot. It glittered in the moonlight as she pulled it from its sheath, and she thrust upward with all her strength. Her hand and arm froze as she struck, but her knife sliced through. The mortifer lurched backwards howling, and Erin leapt up, grabbing her sword.

The shadow swung its blade hard, but she dodged and it missed. She thrust her sword full force into its shrouded darkness. With her frozen hand, she struck with her knife again. The mortifer dropped its sword and collapsed into the mud. Its wail shot through the night, piercing through the sound of the wind and waves. Its cold blackness and stench poured out like vapor, faded, and were gone.

Moonlight brightened the moor, and Erin dashed to the cliff again, searching for the girl. She rubbed her cold arm and called out, "It's gone—you can come back."

The girl below didn't answer, but Erin could see her form against the face of the cliff. "Try to climb. It's gone now. You can come up."

"I can't climb. It's too slippery."

Erin stretched out her arm and rubbed it again, sensation creeping back into her fingers.

"Hold on, I'll be down."

She eased over the edge of the cliff. The slick rocks were muddy and treacherous, but Erin found many small handholds, and with care, she climbed to the spot where the girl clung. When she reached her, the girl asked, "What happened to that thing? What did you do?"

"It was an evil shadow, nothing more, and it's faded away now," Erin said. "Let me help."

"I'm afraid to move."

Erin took her by the hand, placing it carefully upward a little, then moved the other hand and guided her feet. They slowly made their way back to the top.

The rain had stopped, and they both scrambled over the ledge and lay on the muddy grass. Erin stood and helped the girl to her feet. She stood as tall as Erin, and she wiped her hands on her clothes and smoothed her hair from her eyes.

"Think of a place you love—a place where you feel safe," Erin said.

The girl looked at her with questioning eyes. "What do you mean?"

"Do you remember a favorite place, somewhere with good memories?"

The girl nodded, and the sky slowly brightened. The sun broke through the clouds, which rolled away to the horizon. The girl's eyes opened wide, and she looked around as the moor became a meadow. Willow trees lined a small creek. The wind softened to a light breeze, barely stirring their hair, and they heard the creek bubbling over its stony bed.

They walked to the creek and sat down on soft grass dotted with buttercups. The sunshine warmed their hair, and Erin closed her eyes and inhaled the fresh, clean air.

The girl trailed her hand in the water, and a smile crept over her face. "I know this place. This is where I came for picnics when I was small."

"This is beautiful. It could be my safe place too. What's your name?"

"Carolyn."

"Remember this place, Carolyn. If you are afraid a shadow is coming, think of this place."

Carolyn scrambled to her feet, fear in her eyes. "I thought you killed that thing. Can it come back? What will I do?"

Erin stood up beside her and put her hand on the girl's arm. "You tell it to be gone, and it will. You think of this place, and you'll be here, safe."

"I just tell it to be gone? But why didn't you do that? Why would that work for me?"

"Because this is your dream, not mine."

Carolyn nodded and lay down on the grass, and Erin lay down beside her. When she looked toward Carolyn again she was gone, and Erin relaxed, knowing the girl had wandered into an ordinary, restful dream.

She closed her eyes and enjoyed the warmth of the sunshine. A breeze rustled the leaves overhead, and Erin opened her eyes again. She had left Carolyn's place and was lying on the grass in front of the library near Aleesha's shop. The sunshine was still bright, and the wind blew a few white clouds across the sky. The street in front of Erin was empty—no cars, no people. Not even a seagull flew overhead. All she could hear was the wind and distant waves.

The sudden approach of footfalls made her sit up straight. A man was walking along the sidewalk on the opposite side of the street. He was tall, dressed in black with a long sword hanging from his belt, and he hadn't noticed her. *Who could he be?* She kept still. He walked past, and Erin relaxed. Just then he stopped and turned, looking directly at her. He brushed his dark hair from his forehead and slowly drew his sword from its scabbard.

***

Erin jolted upright and found she was in her own bed. Closing her eyes again, she lay back down and tried to drift back into the dark dream that had awakened her, hoping she could remember some of it. She'd tried hundreds of times already, but rarely could she remember more than glimpses of cold, dark shapes in the shadows.

A vague memory reached toward her. She heard the sound of ocean waves crashing against rocks and saw the glint of a sword. Her skin grew cold, her breathing became short and shallow, but the memory soon faded away.

She climbed out of bed into the dark of the room, her feet sinking into the comfort of the thick wool rug, and slipped on her kimono. The fine blue silk was soft and light against her skin—a gift from William.

She walked barefoot downstairs in the dark. Slipping out the kitchen door, she gasped at the brisk air, then ran on her toes down the narrow path over smooth, well-worn stones, through the fragrant garden to the beach.

The last stars faded with the approaching dawn, and Erin listened to the lapping of waves against the rocky shore. Her bare feet were cold on the rocks. She stooped to pick up a stone and threw it into the water, releasing some of her tension.

These dreams had been tormenting her for nearly two years, dreams that disturbed her so much they shocked her awake, but still she could barely remember them. She felt surrounded by fog, and her anger flared.

She gathered more stones and threw them hard, one by one into the water. The familiar activity soothed her, and she started skipping the stones over the water's surface. The sun, although still hidden behind the hills, had risen, and Erin took a deep breath and gazed out over the smooth, dark water.

She turned away from the beach and walked back to her house, made some coffee and went upstairs. In her room, she touched the photo of William, bowing her head. These early morning hours were when she felt the most alone. She sighed, walked into the bathroom and turned on the shower, ready to begin another day.

Chapter 3

Matt was almost finished with his breakfast. "I need some money for my school lunch account today."

"You're down to zero already? It seems like I just gave you forty dollars," Erin said and sipped her coffee.

"That was a long time ago. I've been out for a few days, but I borrowed from Jacob. I need to pay him back, too."

Erin wondered if she had anything left in her bank account. "I'll give you some cash today. How about ten dollars? Then I can give you a check to take to school when I get paid Friday."

"Okay." Matt ran upstairs to get dressed.

Gwen pushed her cereal around in the bowl with her spoon.

"Hey, you," Erin said. "Why don't you eat some of that?"

Gwen put a spoonful of cereal in her mouth. After she swallowed, she said, "Can I be done?"

Erin looked at the half-empty bowl, sighed, and said, "Sure. Go get dressed, sweetie."

She walked into the living room and looked out the window toward Puget Sound. A breeze was blowing, scattering blossoms from the trees and raising a few white caps. After finishing her coffee, she pulled her purse out of the closet. She looked at her checkbook, subtracted a few numbers, and shook her head. Only twenty-three dollars left until Friday. She counted her cash—twenty dollars. She pulled out ten for Matt and put the rest back. That would go for lunch with her friends Hannah and Aleesha today. She'd be brown bagging it for the rest of the week.

They all went out to the small carport and climbed into Erin's white Explorer. A small plaque on the visor read, "Guardian Angel by your side, through your travels, protect and guide," and Erin brushed her thumb across it before starting the engine. She glanced at the back seat.

"Tonight I want you two to bring your trash and water bottles inside. There's barely room for you to sit."

"This is mostly Matt's mess," Gwen said.

Matthew laughed. "Those Hello Kitty wrappers aren't mine."

"You both have some cleaning up to do."

Erin dropped the children off at school and drove several miles to the music store in Anacortes where she worked. The shop smelled like polished wood and old books, the oak-framed cabinets overflowing with sheet music and instruments. Between helping customers, she sat at her tall, upright piano and played a few songs.

At noon Ed, the storeowner, arrived, and Erin left for lunch. She threw on her coat and raced down the street to the Marina Café. Hannah met her at the door, and they entered together.

Erin slid to the inside of the booth, and Hannah brushed some flour off her jeans before sitting down beside her. The restaurant hummed with chatting patrons, and the clatter from the kitchen added to the homey atmosphere. The walls were sunshine yellow, and each table had a vase holding a yellow flower. Inside, it was easy to forget the steady drizzle outside.

"What were you baking this morning?" Erin asked.

"Scones." A strand of Hannah's blond hair had escaped its braid, and she tucked it behind her ear. "All the tourists want scones in the afternoon these days. I made some dried cherry and hazelnut ones today."

"Mm, sounds good," Erin said. Hannah and her husband Carlos owned a small bakery. Erin enjoyed stopping by their shop and watching them together: Carlos with his Latin good looks, dancing around tall, blonde Hannah. Erin was glad to see Hannah today for lunch; her gentle, easygoing nature was soothing.

Aleesha pushed the door open and strolled inside. Her short dark hair was sleek and curled under, and she wore a royal blue skirt with a matching embroidered jacket. She entered the restaurant with a wave to them and blew a kiss to the owner behind the counter.

"Ladies, it's wonderful to see you today." Aleesha sat down and crossed her legs, then reached across the table to grasp each friend's hand in one of her own. She looked from one to the other, smiling with her mouth closed, as if afraid her words would spill out.

"You look pleased with yourself," Erin said, laughing. "What's up?"

"They say good things come in threes. I just had two this morning."

"Tell us," Hannah said.

Aleesha grinned. "I sold the Capoeman."

Erin gasped. "The original? The one of the raven?"

"Yes. The buyer has been eyeing the painting for weeks, and he finally came through."

"Leesh, that's wonderful."

The waitress came with glasses of water and took their orders.

"What was the second thing?" Hannah asked.

Aleesha glanced at Erin. "I had a call from Kenneth."

Erin explained to Hannah, "He's the gallery owner who had the exhibit we went to last night. What did he want?"

"It was kind of surprising. The man you were talking to last night—the one who knew William? He's one of Kenneth's friends. I've met him a couple times before, too. Anyway, he called Kenneth today. He wants to get in touch with you, Erin. He wants to see you again, and he didn't know how to reach you."

"Really?" Erin picked up her water glass and took a long drink. "What did you say?"

"I told Kenneth that I was already planning a dinner party next Saturday and you were coming, and I'd be happy to invite Gary too."

Hannah looked from one friend to the other. "Who is this Gary?"

Erin felt her face turn red. "He's an old friend of William's who was at the gallery last night."

Aleesha continued, "He's single, attractive, and has a great business. And from what Kenneth says, he was quite taken with you last night, Erin."

Erin shook her head.

The waitress brought their food, and they started eating.

"Do you want to see him again?" Hannah asked.

"He seems very nice, and he was William's friend," Erin said.

A smile spread across Aleesha's face. "Then it's settled. Dinner at my house Saturday. I'll invite a few more people, and we can have a party. What fun!"

Erin took another bite, wondering if she really wanted to see Gary again. She knew she'd retreated into her own quiet part of the world after William had died, but her friends kept pushing her to socialize more. Maybe she should. Gary's face darted into her mind, his blue eyes shimmering with laughter. He had certainly intrigued her. Despite the nervous flutter in her stomach, she suddenly found herself looking forward to Aleesha's party.

Chapter 4

THE doorbell pulled Michael away from his writing, and he walked down the stairs and opened the front door. "You made it," he said.

"I almost didn't think I would, after all the traffic. I-5 was stop and go almost all the way from Portland," Bruce said as he stepped inside and dropped his suitcase to the floor.

"Well, this is it. My new castle," Michael said as he looked around with satisfaction. "What do you think?"

The deep burgundy and forest green of his overstuffed furniture along with the dark oak tables and Persian rugs made the rooms feel plush and warm. Several antique weapons hung above the fireplace: a halberd and Celtic spear, and two Claymore swords. On the far wall were a double-headed war axe crossed with another spear. A full suit of armor stood in the corner. Sunshine streamed through the open curtains, highlighting a large gargoyle standing guard on one side of the oak mantel.

"I think you're nuts," Bruce said. "It's a nice house, but I still don't know why you moved all the way out to this godforsaken town."

Michael shrugged. "I told you. I need a change of scenery. Besides, this place has been in my dreams lately."

The men walked through the house to the kitchen. Michael pulled two beers from the fridge and handed one to Bruce.

"You know, Elizabeth thinks you're sinking into one of your dark spells," Bruce said.

"She always worries. That's what sisters do." Michael grinned.

Bruce took a long drink. "You're already settled. You've made good use of the last two weeks." He scanned the weapons. "This place suits you."

He walked into the living room where several photographs sat on top of the piano and picked up one of a small boy. After studying it, he set it back down and turned toward Michael. "You're doing all right?"

Michael nodded. "Yeah. I am."

Bruce sat down in the overstuffed chair and took another swallow. "I saw Marie last week."

Michael coughed. "Where did you see her?"

"I ran into her on campus. She's taking a couple of classes. We got together for lunch the next day."

Michael nodded and sat down on the sofa. "She always did like you. You would have made her happier than I ever did. So, how is she?"

"Good. I told her you moved up here. She thought you might be slipping into one of your dark spells, too."

Michael laughed. "She would."

"She's married."

Michael's eyebrows shot up as he looked at his brother. He nodded his head and turned to look out the window. "Good. She deserves all the happiness she can get. I'm happy for her."

"Yeah? You're okay with this?"

"It's been four years. Five since Colby died. Of course I'm okay with this."

They drained their bottles. Michael didn't want to talk about his ex-wife or about Colby. Wouldn't the pain ever go away? He tried changing the subject. "And what about Julie? You still seeing her?"

"No, not for a while," Bruce said with a grin. "A flashier guy came along, I guess."

"She was too young for you anyway."

"Yeah, I know. Fun though." He looked around. "So, where's your work space?"

"Upstairs. Come on. Bring your bag. The guest room's up there, too."

Michael led Bruce to the first room at the top of the stairs. An old oak desk stood under the open window with a worn black leather chair in front of it. A small oak table in the corner was covered with books, all by Michael Woodward. The laptop on the desk was turned on, and a breeze stirred the curtains.

"How's the new book coming?" Bruce asked.

"Good, finally. It's starting to flow. I'm having a book signing here in town in a couple of weeks for the last book. You ought to come."

"Meet some of the locals?"

Michael shrugged. "Yeah, sure."

Bruce rubbed his chin. "I know you felt a change of scenery would help you over your slump. I suspected there was more to this move than you were saying, but I thought there might be a woman here."

Michael leaned with his hands on the back of the chair and looked out the open window. "No, that's not happening. There's no woman here."

"You've been dreaming of this place? What about?"

"Simple. Walking down the city streets, the beach, the ferry."

"Any viator dreams?"

Michael drew in a slow breath. "Just the other night I dreamed of a woman on a street in town. I think she was a viator. The rest of the dreams have been ordinary."

"You don't know who she is?"

Michael shook his head. "Never seen her before. At first I thought she was a child, but on second glance I saw she was a small woman with a sword at her side. She'd been watching me. Her eyes had the wariness of a viator on the hunt, but she was startled when I looked at her, and she vanished. I thought it was odd."

"It could be the set up for a trap. Remember how Sean was having dreams about Seattle before he went there? And he ended up betrayed."

"We don't know for sure if there was a connection. Besides, everything has risks. I want to know why I've been dreaming of this place. And I like it here. It's quiet, picturesque, and the San Juan Islands are just a short ferry ride away. I can write here."

Bruce shook his head. "At least you're getting out of your slump."

"Well, I'm glad you came. When you go back to Portland you can tell Elizabeth I'm fine."

"I'll wait to make that judgment until after I've been here a while," Bruce said.

Chapter 5

TALL firs swayed in the wind overhead, and the sunshine weaved flickering patterns of light and shadow across the ground. Erin lay back on the grass and gazed at the treetops. She'd been waiting in that pleasant spot for a while but knew better than to relax; the dreamer would need her soon enough. White clouds hurried across the deep blue of the sky, and she watched an eagle soar high overhead.

She wore her usual black pants, shirt and boots. The day was warm, and she took off her jacket, putting it under her head.

He called. She scrambled to her feet. It was nothing Erin could hear; she could only feel it. The dreamer cried out. She ran to the narrow road below and paused—which way? To her left. She bounded up the road, leaving her jacket behind.

His urgent call led her onward and she ran faster, the road leading her uphill through a forest growing more dense and dark with every step. The fir trees became taller and crowded closer together, shutting out the sunlight. The road wound around huge boulders and across the face of a precipice. She ran faster, and even in her desperate rush she felt joy in her speed as the wind whipped her hair away from her face, and the muscles of her legs strained to go faster still.

She burst out of the forest and sprinted through a deep meadow. Without the trees, the wind blew in fierce gusts. As she slowed to follow the road around another huge boulder, a gaping chasm in the mountainside opened before her. The road crossed it over a narrow bridge.

Erin stopped. The dreamer stood on the bridge.

The young man leaned over the rail as he looked down, and then turned and saw Erin. His eyes widened, face twisted, and he cried out, “No, get back.”

Erin opened her arms, palms out. “It’s all right. Come to me.”

He shook his head and yelled, “No.”

She took a small step toward him, and he waved his arms, “It’s going to fall. Don’t come out here.”

“Come to me. You’ll be safe.”

He shook his head. “I have to stay here. But not you. Go away.”

Erin stepped closer. “Why?”

“Don’t you see it? There’s a crack right there.” He pointed to the edge of the bridge.

“Then come off.”

He shook his head. “I can’t.”

“Why not?

“I have to do this,” he whispered.

“What did you say?” Erin asked.

He looked at the ground. “It’s what I have to do.”

Erin gazed at him. He was young, early twenties, with brown hair and eyes, but terror twisted his handsome face. His eyes darted around the ground, and he groaned.

“What’s your name?” Erin called.

He looked at her as if he didn’t understand her question before answering. “Paul.”

“Paul, there’s no need to do this. Come with me.”

A roar like thunder broke from the bridge, and Paul dropped to his knees. Dust rose from the center of the bridge, and a crack grew at its edge. Erin dashed toward him and pulled him up by his arm, but the ground shifted under her feet, and she fell, landing face down in the dust.

Paul screamed and Erin grabbed hold of his shirt. The bridge was crumbling underneath them. She tried to crawl away, but he was too heavy for her to drag. The outer edge of the bridge was gone, and dust rose up, blocking her vision, but she could hear the rumbling as, piece by piece, the rest of the bridge collapsed. She thrust one arm around Paul's chest and tried to haul him back. The last of the bridge gave way, and her feet dropped out from under her. They both screamed, and she reached out wildly with her free hand and seized the edge of the shattered road. She found herself dangling in the air, still holding tight to Paul.

He clung to her. She yelled, "Hold on. We can make it."

She couldn't see through all the dust. Paul had wrapped his arms around her waist. She coughed. "Are you all right? I need to let go of you and use both hands."

He tightened his hold, and she slowly loosened her grip on him. She reached up with her other hand and got a firm grasp on the pavement. A sharp stone cut her palm as she tried to pull herself up, and her arms ached. Paul groaned.

"We've got to pull ourselves up to the road," she said.

"I can't let go of you."

"I'm right here. I'll hold you again—see the ledge?"

He moaned just as the ledge under Erin's hands gave way and crumbled. She fell backwards and reached out blindly as they plunged into the gully. Erin wrapped both arms around him, and he clung to her waist. The fall took her breath away, and she looked down. Trees raced up to meet them.

She closed her eyes and said, "Paul, we'll float—in this dream we can float."

"What?"

"Think. We're like feathers, floating. We're flying."

The ground below was closing fast when Erin felt the change. The wind slowed. They were no longer plummeting to the earth. Like feathers, they floated lazily toward the earth and the creek below.

Paul still held onto her, and his eyes were squeezed shut. They slowed even more, and Erin whispered, "Look."

He opened his eyes and gasped. Their feet touched the ground on a grassy knoll beside the stream. Their knees gave way, and they both collapsed onto the grass. Paul rolled onto his back and lay there staring upwards, breathing hard. Erin sat up.

"You're all right." She sat still for a few minutes and her heart began to calm down. She laughed.

Paul stared at her and began to laugh, too. A few tears streamed from his eyes.

Erin touched his arm. "How many times have you fallen from that bridge?"

He frowned. "Maybe five."

"Why? Why do you keep doing that?"

He sat up. "How did you do that?"

"Make us float? You did it. This is your dream. And since it's your dream, you can change it. I just made a suggestion. And you did a very good job of making it happen." She patted his arm, then stood up and brushed herself off.

Paul stared at her for a minute and rose to his feet beside her. Erin rested her hand on his shoulder. "You're punishing yourself. Why?"

His face clouded and he shook his head. "I can't tell you."

She gripped his shoulder and shook him. "How can you say that to me? Didn't I just fall with you? I deserve to know why."

He looked up at the mountainside, then his eyes darted to Erin. "My brother fell from that bridge."

"And was that your fault?"

"He died in that fall."

Erin heard the water bubbling in the nearby creek and the wind stirring the branches of the trees. Paul sat down on the grass again and put his head in his hands. Erin sat next to him. She knew enough about grief and guilt. Her own pain was always close to the surface, but she pushed it back down.

Paul lifted his head and looked at Erin's face. "Who are you?"

"My name is Erin."

"Why are you here?"

"You called for help."

He sighed. "Look, I asked my brother to go to the store to pick up some beer. He didn't want to go, but I talked him into it. The bridge was icy, and his car went over the side. He died because of me." He covered his face with his hands.

Erin wrapped her arm around his shoulders and said, "You had no control over that event, and you couldn't have foreseen your request would result in your brother's death."

"Oh, don't give me that bullshit! I know all that. But if I hadn't asked him to go, he'd still be alive. I would have been the one to die. I should have died, not him."

Erin was silent and rested her hand on the back of Paul's head for a few minutes.

"We all die someday," she said.

He nodded.

"And there's no guarantee you would have died had you gone to the store that night. Your brother might have died that very night by some other means if he had not gone on that errand."

He frowned at her.

"You have your life for now. Live it for your brother's sake," she said.

She saw her clothes had changed to a long white dress that gleamed in the sunshine, and her feet were bare.

She kissed his forehead. "Sleep now. When you wake, you will be refreshed. And remember, you can always float like a feather in your dreams."

He lay down on the grass. Erin stood and watched him, and he faded from her sight. She sighed and walked toward the creek. Her former black clothes returned, and she was dressed as before.

She'd left her jacket where she'd been lying before Paul had called her, and she wanted to go back and get it while she was still in this place. She leapt over the creek and made her way through the forest, heading back toward the road. Sunshine glimmered through the trees, and it was easy to find her way through the scattered brush. She wondered if she would see Paul here again sometime, or if he'd be able to put his guilt behind him. Sometimes it took a dreamer many visits to move past such a traumatic event, even when no mortifers were making things worse.

When she reached the road she turned left and followed it down the slope. A crow landed on a tree branch overhanging the road and eyed her. A short distance further, Erin heard voices arguing up ahead, and she slowed her pace. Two men were shouting in the forest. Erin paused in the shadow of the trees and listened.

"Out of my way—you can't stop me!"

The second man's voice was quieter but just as angry. "You fool. Do you know what you're doing?"

"Go to hell."

The first man crashed through the trees and sprang out onto the road right in front of Erin. He stopped when he saw her. He was blond, a very good-looking man. Was it Gary? The other man rushed out of the forest, grabbed his arm, shoved him up against a tree and held him there by the throat. He was tall with dark hair, dressed in black. Erin stepped backwards into the shadows under the trees, her hand on the knife at her waist. But the tall man let the other go and nearly threw him to the ground with a snort. "You're right. I can't stop you," he said.

The blond smirked and took off running down the road, while the tall man stood like a sentinel, his back still turned to Erin. She didn't move. The crow flew past her and let out one loud caw when it was overhead. The man turned around and looked directly into her eyes, and his own dark eyes widened with surprise. He scanned her up and down, a faint smile creeping over his features. In an instant, he turned away and ran back into the forest. Erin heard a twig snap where he had gone, and the forest became silent, with not even the sound of a bird.

She stood in the protection of the trees, relieved he was gone, and tried to determine who these men could be. She'd never met any others, besides the dreamers and the mortifers who hunted them. Was the blond man a dreamer? And this tall, dark man some new kind of malicious creature? Perhaps the same man she had seen in a previous dream who had drawn his sword when he saw her? He frightened her, and the blond, who looked so much like Gary, had certainly wanted to get away from him. She shivered and walked back to the knoll where she had left her jacket, put it on, and lay back on the grass until she faded into dreamless sleep.

Chapter 6

Erin looked through her closet. Her green dress was pretty, but missing a button. The black dress, too formal. A skirt and blouse seemed too frumpy. Her wardrobe definitely needed some help. She finally settled on navy blue pants and a lacy white sweater. After curling her hair and adding some lipstick, Erin went downstairs.

The day had been beautiful, and the children had been on the beach with some friends, long since gone home. Erin had taken advantage of the good weather to clean up her yard: mowing, weeding, and planting bright primroses. As she had worked she kept thinking about the chance meeting with Gary, and she was looking forward to talking with him again. Their conversation had brought memories of William back so painfully, but Gary was one of William's old friends, and it would be good to share some memories. She also felt a vague sense of unease, and even though she couldn't remember it, she knew she'd had another disturbing dream.

Gwen was packing toys into her backpack as Erin entered the kitchen.

"Are you ready to go to Mrs. Edna's house?" Erin asked.

"Sure," Gwen said as she put another doll into her pack.

Matthew called from his bedroom, "All set." He came down the stairs with his backpack. "Let's go, kid," he said to Gwen.

They walked across their gravel driveway and through a gate in the hedge to the small white house next door. Baskets of blue and yellow flowers hung from the eaves, and small stone statues of rabbits and birds clustered in the gardens. They knocked on the door and Edna greeted them, her white hair in tight curls.

"Already had dinner, kids?" she asked.

"We sure did," said Gwen. "We're ready for dessert!"

"Well, come on in and have some snickerdoodles and ice cream."

They stepped into the little house.

"Thanks so much. I shouldn't be later than eleven," Erin said.

"Have a great time, dear."

Erin climbed into her SUV and drove to Aleesha's house in Anacortes. Several cars were already parked in front when she drove up, so Erin parked on the street and hurried up to the door.

"I'm so glad you're here. Come in," Aleesha said as she opened the door. She handed Erin a glass of champagne.

The old house was filled with people. Candles glowed, casting a soft light on the white furnishings. Although it was May, a small fire burned in the fireplace. White carnations and roses spilled over vases on several tables, filling the house with a subtle, sweet fragrance. Past the living room, Erin could see the dining table sparkling with crystal, roses, and silver. Soft jazz filled the room, and the atmosphere breathed relaxation.

Aleesha introduced her to several other guests, some local artists and gallery clientele. Hannah and Carlos were there, and Erin knew several of the others already.

"Gary's not here yet," Aleesha whispered.

Erin chatted with Hannah while she sipped her champagne, and Aleesha glided among her guests chatting until a knock at the door took her back to the entry. Erin watched as she opened the door and let Gary inside. His appearance was more striking than it had been in the gallery's uneven lighting. He was tan, muscular, and his blond hair was freshly trimmed. His pale blue sweater matched the color of his eyes perfectly. Aleesha handed him a drink, and as he looked across the room directly at Erin, his eyes brightened, and he raised his glass briefly toward her. His grin showed off the deep dimples in his cheeks. He continued talking with Aleesha, and Erin slowly made her way toward them.

"Gary, you met Erin Holley the other night? Here she is." Aleesha turned to Erin as she approached.

"Yes, hello," Gary said. He reached out his hand to her. "Erin and I are old friends."

Erin shook Gary's hand. "It's good to see you again."

"You too." His eyes sparkled and lingered on hers.

Another guest drew close and asked Gary to settle a little dispute about a gallery in Seattle, and he turned to Erin. "Would you mind?" He squeezed her hand and walked away.

Erin wandered through the room listening to different conversations. Hannah and a few other women stood together in one corner of the room when Erin joined them.

"I heard he's been all over the world," said one woman. "A friend of mine was at a party in the American embassy in Turkey and danced with him there."

Another guest leaned forward. "I hear he goes scuba diving in the Caribbean every year."

"What does he do for a living?" asked Hannah, glancing behind her to try to get a glimpse of Gary.

"I'm not sure. Some kind of imports, I think," said the other guest. "He makes a lot of money. He met his girlfriend skiing in the Alps."

"He has a girlfriend?" someone asked.

"Not anymore. He left her a month ago. Actually left her in Spain. Rented a house for her, packed his bags, and left. I heard he paid for the house a year in advance."

"Really?" said a couple of the women in unison.

"Well, I would love to dance with him in Istanbul … or anywhere," said a guest. "He's a very attractive man."

Erin looked across the room at Gary, where he was talking with a couple of men about, what? About tropical fish. Yes, he was a very attractive man. What kind of life he must live, traveling all over the world.

Aleesha called everyone for dinner, and they strolled through the house, chatting and laughing. When Erin sat beside Hannah, Gary set his drink down at the seat next to her.

"May I sit here?" he asked as he pulled out the chair.

"Of course." Erin sipped her water as he sat down.

"I'm sorry I dashed off like that the other night," he said.

"That's all right. I hope your meeting went well."

He laughed. "I survived. I was surprised to run into you there. It's been so long. How have you been? Are you getting along all right?"

"I'm doing okay."

He frowned and shook his head. "William was a good man."

"He was wonderful," she said quietly.

Gary picked up his drink and took a swallow. "I've really missed William's friendship. I can't imagine how it's been for you."

Erin felt a moan begin to rise inside. "I've missed him so much."

He frowned and put his hand on her arm. "I'm sorry. I'm just causing you more pain."

She pushed her emotions back down and shook her head. "No, I'm all right. I never knew you and William were such good friends."

"Well …" Gary stammered a little and took another drink. "We saw each other a lot the year before he passed away."

"I didn't realize …"

"I was traveling a lot … but he helped me with some work issues."

Erin sipped her champagne. "The other night you mentioned you saw William the day before the accident and that you'll never forget what he said."

Gary leaned back in his chair and let out a long breath.

She looked at him earnestly. "I'd really like to know what he said that had such an impact on you. William had been distracted for a few days, like something was bothering him. He didn't tell me what it was, but I know something was on his mind."

"And you think what he said to me might be connected? Why?"

She shrugged and shook her head. "I don't know. When you and I talked the other night, it just struck me. I would feel better if I knew what had been bothering him. It might be nothing at all. I know it was a long time ago, but ..."

He took another drink. "William had a meeting with someone right before he saw me, and I don't think it went well. Whoever he met with must have said something to really piss him off. I'd never seen him like that. He said he smelled the stench of carrion, and ... it better stop. He said someone was going to have to pay."

"What? What does that mean? The smell of carrion?" She shook her head. "I don't understand."

"I don't either. He didn't explain it to me. And he didn't tell you anything at all?"

"No."

Gary shrugged. "Well, it's old history now."

"I guess." Erin sighed, and they both ate a few bites in silence. Why would William say such a thing? It reminded her vaguely of something, but she didn't know what. She could see that Gary had been disturbed by the incident and didn't want to talk about it.

"You're probably right," she said. "It was so long ago."

They were silent a few more moments. "What about you?" she said. "I hear you travel a lot, but I don't really know much about your business or where you travel to."

Gary hesitated. "Did William ever talk to you about what I do?"

"Not really."

He smiled. "I import goods: clothing, furniture, machine parts, lots of different things. I spend a lot of time in Asia, some in Eastern Europe, too. Always looking for new suppliers. It has its ups and downs. What do you do? Do you work with Aleesha in her gallery?"

She laughed as she passed the rolls and butter to him. "No, I play piano. I majored in music, and I work in the local music store and give lessons."

"You're a musician? Are you good?"

She blushed. "People have said they enjoy hearing me play."

It was Gary's turn to laugh, his dimples deepening and eyes sparkling. "Even the worst musician could say that. It's obvious you're too modest. I'll just have to ask Aleesha. No, better yet, I'll have to hear you play and judge for myself."

"You might be disappointed."

He studied her face for a moment and leaned close to her. "I don't think so. You're more beautiful than I remembered, and I don't think you'd disappoint with your music either."

He was so close she felt his warmth. "I haven't performed in over two years. I just give lessons now."

"Why?" he asked. "Why don't you perform anymore?"

Erin looked out the window into Aleesha's garden. The pink rhododendrons were in bloom and a finch splashed in the nearby birdbath. "I just haven't felt like it anymore—after William died." She shrugged.

He finished his soup and broke off a piece of roll, buttered it, and took a bite. They were both silent. Gary poured more wine into her glass and leaned toward her so she could feel his warmth again. "It will get better," he said.

Erin wondered if she could possibly be a more depressing dinner partner. Every topic she raised seemed to make him feel sorry for her. She tried to think of a happier subject, but Gary spoke first.

"So, do you go to a lot of art exhibits with Aleesha?" he asked. "Are you familiar with Ian MacKenzie?"

"Yes, I love his work. Aleesha had some of his paintings in her gallery not long ago, and I even got to meet him."

"If you like Ian's art, you obviously have good taste. What else do you like?"

His eyes flickered with amusement, and she felt her face flush.

"I meant, what other kinds of art do you like?" he said.

"Of course. From the exhibits I've seen, there are fewer still that I really enjoyed. I like the old masters best. William and I saw the Leonardo da Vinci exhibit in Victoria a few years ago, and I was awestruck."

Gary nodded. "I saw that, too. It was wonderful. I enjoy many styles of art, and … I like many other things too."

Erin laughed. "So I've heard."

His eyes widened, and he leaned closer to her whispering, "What have you heard?"

She pulled back a little, but a smile crept over her face. "Nothing much, really, just that you dance in Istanbul, scuba dive in the Caribbean, and keep girlfriends in Spain."

"Ohhh, I see. Where did you hear that?"

"I guess it's common knowledge. So do you?"

His eyes hardened. "Not exactly. She's no longer my girlfriend. I have been known to dance and scuba dive, though. Among other things."

"Sounds like you lead an exciting life. I've never been out of the U.S., except to Canada. I haven't even been to Mexico. Is your travel all for work, or is some of it for fun?"

"A lot of both."

Aleesha invited everyone to bring their coffee into the living room. Erin sat on a couch next to another woman who chatted aimlessly about her sister's new house. Gary wandered over to the fireplace nearby where he stood by himself, sipping a glass of brandy, his arm resting on the mantel. Erin only half listened, her eyes flitting to Gary every few minutes. Another woman approached Gary, and Erin watched the two of them as they went outside onto the deck.

The mantel clock chimed and Erin looked at her watch, surprised to see that it was already ten thirty. She started to get up from the couch. "I promised my babysitter I'd be back by eleven, so I'm afraid

I've got to go. It was great to see you again," she said to the guest next to her.

Erin found Aleesha to say goodbye, and Aleesha pulled her into the hallway. "Did you have a good time?" she asked.

"Yes, I did. Thank you for doing this. And it was nice to see him again."

"Where is he, anyway?" Aleesha peered around the room.

"He went outside a while ago. But I've got to get back home. Thanks so much. I've really had a wonderful time."

She retrieved her coat and purse from the hall closet, looking around one last time for Gary. She walked out to her Explorer and unlocked the door, but turned around when she heard the sound of footfalls behind her.

"Do you have to go so soon?" It was Gary.

"Yes, my babysitter's expecting me," Erin said. "She's my neighbor, and getting older, so I don't like to keep her up too late."

"Of course."

Erin couldn't see Gary's face in the dark, but she could feel his warmth. He was standing so close to her they were almost touching.

"I should really go. It was good to see you again," she said. She started to turn toward the car, but he put his hand on her arm, and she stopped.

"I'm staying in Anacortes for the weekend."

She caught her breath. "What?"

"I'd like to see you again. Dinner tomorrow?"

"I'm sorry, I can't. Gwen's having friends over for pizza and a slumber party. I have to stay home." She was almost relieved to have a genuine excuse but felt a twinge of disappointment, too.

"Could I come over? I'd love to see the kids again. I could help."

"What? You wouldn't want to do that. Three seven-year-old girls? It won't be fun. It'll be exhausting."

"I want to. And I always get what I want."

Erin laughed. “Really? Well, if you really want to. We’ll have dinner about six.” She searched through her purse for paper and a pen. “Here’s my address. It’s easy to find. I’m on Dewey Beach. My driveway is the long one through the apple trees. But don’t feel like you have to do this.”

Gary took the paper and said, “I don’t. And I remember where your house is.” He stood still for a moment as if waiting for her to do something.

“I don’t remember you coming to our house.”

He laughed. “You weren’t there.”

“Oh. Well, good night,” she said.

“Good night, Erin Holley,” he whispered.

Erin watched him walk back to the house, her knees shaky. The moon shone between the clouds and cast a cold glow on the street, and she felt a sudden chill. She climbed into her SUV and drove toward home. Her heart was pounding. She hadn’t been attracted to anyone for so long, and here she sat, trembling. Was she really that lonely? What would William think?

Chapter 7

THE phone ringing pulled Erin out of her sleep, and she rolled over and answered.

"Hello?"

"It's Aleesha. Are you still in bed? Sorry, but I just had to find out how everything went with you and Gary. What do you think?"

"He's all right," said Erin, still half asleep. She looked out her open window at the scattered clouds. "He's coming over tonight to help me with Gwen's slumber party."

"What? He's coming over to your house tonight? For a slumber party?"

"He's not part of the slumber party. He's coming over tonight, and we'll have dinner with the kids. He's not staying."

"But when did you talk to him about this?"

"He followed me out to my car," Erin said.

"Really? That's great."

"Maybe." She sat up in bed. "Don't get too excited about it. I don't know what he's really like, except that he was one of William's friends. I only met him a couple times before. I don't really know him."

Aleesha's voice was reassuring. "If he was friends with William, you know he must be a good man."

"Yes." Erin hesitated. "Last night I heard all the women talking about what a fast life he leads."

"That doesn't mean anything. Kenneth knows him pretty well, and I gather he has had a few adventures. But I'm sure there's no truth to the story about him killing a man. I think that's all made up. You know how people exaggerate."

"He killed a man? Why didn't you tell me this before?" Erin hopped out of bed and grabbed her robe.

"No, no, I don't believe a word of it and neither does Kenneth. Besides, the story is that it was self-defense. So, you see, it's fine."

"Fine? Good grief. What's the story?" She went downstairs, hit the button on the coffeemaker, and walked over to the window to look at the beach. The wind was blowing a few clouds across the sky, but it looked like it would be a gorgeous day.

"What I heard is that he was on a boat with friends somewhere in Asia," Aleesha said. "Someone came on board, threatened them, and Gary shot him first. I don't know if he actually killed him."

Erin shivered. "Anything else you know about him?"

"His old girlfriend is definitely out of the picture. She's in Spain, and he doesn't even talk to her anymore." She paused. "Don't overthink this, darling. Just have some fun and see where it goes. Spread your wings a little."

Erin sighed. "I'm just kind of nervous."

"Of course you are," Aleesha said. "It'll be fine, though, you wait and see."

"Yeah."

"One more thing. Different subject, and this is too much fun. Have you ever read any of Michael Woodward's books? He writes thrillers."

"No, I haven't."

"You should, they're very good." Aleesha paused. "But anyway, I found out Michael Woodward just moved here to Anacortes. He moved into a little house just two blocks away from me."

"You're kidding."

"No. And Blue Heron Books is having him there to give a talk in a couple of weeks. We've got to go."

"Sure. I'll have to read one of his books."

"Definitely," Aleesha said.

They said goodbye, Erin took a quick shower, and then woke up her kids.

***

"Let's put sprinkles on them. Lauren likes sprinkles," Gwen said as she spread chocolate frosting on the cupcakes.

"Sure." Erin dug around in the cupboard until she found some blue and yellow candy sprinkles. "Here you go."

"Thanks. Why aren't Lauren and Rose here yet? I think they're late."

"It's only five o'clock. They're not late, but I'm sure they'll be here soon."

Earlier in the day, Matthew and Gwen had helped clean the house, and Gwen had picked a bunch of fresh lilacs from the garden. Their fragrance mingled with the aroma of freshly baked cupcakes, and the whole house smelled delicious.

The doorbell rang, and Gwen ran to answer it. Erin followed and greeted Rose and her mother. Lauren and her mother followed behind them.

"You both got here at just the right time," Erin said. "Come in, and you can help Gwen put the sprinkles on the cupcakes."

When the girls finished decorating the cupcakes, they ran upstairs to Gwen's bedroom, and Matthew and his friend Jacob walked into the kitchen.

"When's that guy going to get here?" Matt asked.

"I told him dinner's at six, so he could be here any time soon," Erin said. "Can you stay for some pizza, Jacob?"

"I'll call my mom and ask," he said.

Erin pulled out the dishes and glanced at the clock again. She wondered if Gary had changed his mind and would cancel, and the thought gave her a dull ache in the pit of her stomach.

Matt stepped in front of Erin. "Is that guy your boyfriend?"

"What? My boyfriend? I don't know him well enough yet, Matt. I need to get to know him better before I could even think about that."

The doorbell rang.

Erin put down the plates and walked to the entry hall while Matt and Jacob went upstairs. She paused for a moment, suddenly anxious about how Matt felt, then she opened the door to Gary.

"Come on in," she said. "I'm glad you found us again."

"It was easy," Gary said as he walked inside. He was wearing khakis and a blue polo shirt, and Erin felt a bit underdressed in her worn jeans, T-shirt, and bare feet.

"I had forgotten how far you are from town. Here's a bottle of wine to go with dinner." He handed her the bottle and walked to the living room window to look out at the Sound. Erin followed him.

"Come outside and see the beach—it's the best part." She led him back through the house to the door in the kitchen and set the bottle on the counter.

"Mmm, cupcakes," Gary said, and he scooped frosting from the bowl onto his finger and licked it off.

"We go all out when we have company. Dinner will be my world-famous homemade pizza, so you're really in for a treat."

Gary's eyes shone as he looked at her. "Wow, I'm impressed."

Erin laughed. "I'm exaggerating. I mean it's good pizza and everything, but it's simple."

"Yeah, sure."

"Let's go down to see the beach for a minute, then I'll put the pizzas in the oven." Erin kept a pair of flip-flops at the back door, and she slipped them on her feet.

They walked down the stone pathway. The wind blew and whitecaps dotted the water, but the tide was out, and the air smelled of seaweed. Erin led him onto the rocky beach and pointed out Whidbey Island and the direction to Deception Pass and to Seattle. The wind was brisk, and Erin's arms were covered with goosebumps.

"You're getting cold," Gary said.

"Let's go back inside. I'll open that wine you brought."

"Sounds good."

A sailboat glided close to the shore, and Erin stopped to watch. Gary wrapped one arm around her shoulders and rubbed her arm to warm her. They gazed after the boat until it was out of sight, then looked at each other and smiled.

Back inside, Erin put the pizzas into the oven and poured two glasses of wine. Gary helped her set the table and paused several times to look out the window. "This view is spectacular."

"Thanks. The house is old, and I don't have the means to do any remodeling, but it's comfortable. My grandparents used to live here."

"I like the house the way it is." He looked around at the worn but comfortable furnishings. "And here's your piano. You've got to play something tonight."

"We'll see. I'm not sure if I want to. I might not live up to your expectations."

"You're not getting out of it so easily." He looked at the books on the shelves, and stopped when he saw a small, ornate silver flask. He picked it up and turned to Erin. "This is interesting."

"The flask? It belonged to my grandparents. It's very old."

He put it back on the shelf and sipped his wine.

"The pizza will be done soon. I'll call the kids down," Erin said.

"Okay."

The girls giggled as they filed down the stairs, and Matt and Jacob followed close behind.

"My children, Matt and Gwen, and their friends, Jacob, Lauren, and Rose. Kids, this is Gary."

He said hello and offered to show them his car. Matt and Jacob exchanged glances, shrugged, and said sure. When they walked out to the front, Erin heard the boys. "Wow! Is that a Porsche? This is your car? Can you give us a ride?"

The boys came back inside, laughing, and Gary followed them, a wide grin on his face.

"Did you see Gary's car, Mom? It's so cool," Matt said. "Can we go for a ride with him?"

"You'll have to ask him," Erin said. "But it'll have to wait—pizza's ready. Go wash your hands, kids."

They ran off to the bathroom. She leaned against the counter again, and Gary picked up his wine glass, still grinning.

"I'd love to take them for rides."

"They'd be talking about it for days."

They all sat down at the table, and it wasn't long before the pizzas were devoured. Matt asked if Jacob could spend the night, and Erin said that would be fine, so all the kids went back upstairs to play.

Gary refilled their glasses with the last of the wine. They sat in silence for a minute, enjoying the calm. Erin ran her finger around the rim of her glass. "What do you think of the kids?"

"They're the best. This is the most enjoyable dinner party I've been to in years." He looked into his glass, and his smile faded into a frown.

"Tell me more about what you're doing now. I really don't know that much about you," Erin said.

He shrugged. "I've been lucky. You know I'm in imports. That's how I ran into William again after college. I was handling some parts for the navigation systems his company was building."

"Yes. I remember now. About five years ago?"

"Right." He drained his glass, walked into the living room and sat on the sofa. "We were good friends in college. After running into him at work we stayed in touch. We used to play basketball when I was in town. He was a great friend."

Erin used to love watching William play basketball. She got up from the table, not wanting her feelings to get the better of her. "Would you like some coffee?"

"No, thanks. Why don't you come sit down?" He patted the seat on the sofa next to him.

Erin sat down in the overstuffed chair facing him. She looked at the designs in her rug, tracing the patterns with her mind.

"These last two years have been hard for you," Gary said quietly.

She nodded.

"I always thought William was especially lucky," he said.

She looked at him with questioning eyes and shook her head.

"You," Gary said. "He had you." He stood up and stretched his arms over his head, walked to the window and looked out. They were both silent a few minutes. He turned around and looked at the floor with a frown while Erin studied him. Fine lines fanned out from the corners of his eyes in his golden-tan face. His blond hair was neatly trimmed but a curl formed around his ear, and his shoulders and arms looked powerful under his shirt. As she watched him, a flicker of memory from her last dream came back to her, when she thought Gary had been there. She shuddered. He looked at her, and his brow creased.

"Sorry, I didn't mean to get all quiet."

"No, not at all—it's fine," she said.

"Let me help you clean up the kitchen."

"All right. Then I plan to put on a movie for the kids. I hope you can stay and watch it with us."

"Sounds good."

They cleaned up the kitchen and Erin made popcorn. They joined the children watching the movie, and by the time it was finished, Gwen, Lauren, and Rose were sound asleep on the floor. Matt and Jacob climbed the stairs for bed, and Erin woke the girls and went upstairs with them to help them set out their sleeping bags as Gary stepped out the kitchen door.

After the children were in bed, Erin went outside and saw him standing at the edge of the lawn where the rocky beach began. The air had grown still, and stars were bright in the sky. He turned as she approached.

"Beautiful night," he said. "I always thought I was lucky, but do you realize how lucky you are?"

"Sometimes good things happen. Sometimes bad things happen. I've had my share of both."

"I'd like to see you again."

Erin was quiet for a minute. "I'd like to see you again, too."

He slid his arm around her waist. She pulled away a little and said, "Gary, I like you, but I need to take it slow."

"No, you don't." He wrapped both arms around her and pulled her to him, bent his head to hers and kissed her. His kiss was smooth and intoxicating, almost overwhelming. She had missed this so much. Every thought she had was driven from her mind. All she could feel were his arms holding her tight and his mouth on hers. When he let go of her, she stepped back and took a deep breath.

"I'd like to see you next weekend," he said.

She nodded.

"How about Saturday night?"

"Sure."

"Good." He touched her cheek and trailed his fingers down her throat, then pulled his hand away. "I've got to go." He started back up the path, and she followed. They walked around the house to his car.

"I never did give those boys a ride. I'll have to do it next time," he said.

"They'll love that," she said, and then remembered about the next weekend. "Oh, no. Saturday won't work—we have plans. It's Matt's birthday, and I'm taking the kids to Orcas Island for a bike ride."

He grinned and leaned against his car. "I could come."

"You'd want to do that? … I'm not sure …" *Would Matt want to have Gary join them for his birthday?*

He reached into his pocket and handed her his business card. "I like biking. Call me this week, and you can tell me all the details." He held her shoulders and kissed her again.

When he stepped back, his eyes searched her face. Even in the twilight she could see the intense blue of his eyes.

"Good night," he said. He slid into his car and drove down the gravel driveway to the street. His lights soon faded.

A gust of wind stirred the trees, and Erin shivered. She turned back to the house, but a shadow moved in the trees nearby. She stopped and held her breath. The shadow fluttered in the wind and grew taller.

"Who's there?" she called, unable to move.

The shadow shrank to the ground. Erin told herself it was just an old garbage bag, caught in the breeze, and she ran back into her house, her emotions a tumult of pleasure and apprehension.

CHAPTER 8

EXCEPT for a bit of moonlight that found its way through some gaps in the heavy curtains, the huge old house was shrouded in darkness. Erin sat in the center of an old velvet-upholstered sofa in the center of a large room. The polish was worn away from the wood floor, and the room was strewn with delicate tables, sofas, and chairs. In the darkness all the colors were muted gray and black. Soft footfalls approached from the hallway, and she turned to see who was coming in the gloom.

A small, frail woman tiptoed through the door. She carried an unlit candle, but Erin's night eyes could see her. Her white hair was caught in a tight bun at the nape of her neck, and her face was deeply lined. The collar of her long dark dress reached to her chin with small ruffles, and the bodice fit snuggly before flaring out full at the waist. She squinted as she peered into Erin's face. "So good of you to come, my dear," she said.

"I'm happy to be here with you," Erin said.

"The others are all upstairs, but they'll be down shortly."

"That sounds fine."

The old woman started to walk out of the room, but stopped and whirled around to face Erin. "But you know—Franny isn't here," she almost shouted.

"Are you sure?" Erin asked.

The old woman spat out the words. "Of course I'm sure. She's the one this is all about, and she won't come anywhere near this house. It's all a waste of our time, and I don't like it one bit."

"Ma'am, please sit down. I would love to hear more about this. What is your name?"

"My name? What do you mean? You don't know my name? Wait a minute." She backed away from Erin. "You're not Michelle. Who are you? I thought you were Michelle. Get out of my house."

Erin stood and looked directly into the woman's eyes. She reached out and tapped her cheek and said, "*Videre.*"

The old woman sucked in a breath. "What? Of course you're not Michelle. How could I have thought that? I get a little confused lately. Michelle is upstairs. Yes, I am glad you could come. Can you help us find Franny?"

Erin heard several people whispering and walking quietly in the hallway, as if they were afraid to make any noise. In a moment the three of them glided into the room: two young men and a young woman. Erin stepped forward and held out her hand. "Please sit down."

The first man, who was tall, thin, with a narrow face, and dressed in an ill-fitting dark suit, reached toward Erin. "I'm Roland, this is my sister, Michelle, and my brother, Lawrence." Erin shook each of their icy hands. "I see you've met Mother already."

"She was just asking me about Franny. Do you want to find Franny, too?"

"My lord, no. Why would we want to find Franny? Whatever she's doing is her own business," scoffed Michelle, who plopped herself into a chair, her long skirt flouncing as she landed. Erin could see that Michelle was very pretty, perhaps even beautiful, but her face was twisted into a severe pout.

"That's so true," Lawrence said. His black suit fit quite well. He turned and walked toward one of the windows, pulled open the curtain, and looked outside. Silvery moonlight streamed into the room, and Erin could see the pale faces of these people more clearly.

The mother sat down. "Nonsense, you two. You just don't know how important Franny is to this household. We've got to find that girl and bring her back. We need her to stay with us. Dear, what did you say your name was? You've got to find that young woman right away and talk some sense into her."

"Yes, we do need to find Franny. Can you help us?" Roland asked.

"I might be able to. But why do you want to find her so badly? Why is she so important?" Erin asked.

"Because without her, we're all dead," Roland said.

"Roland." Michelle stood up. "How dare you say such a thing."

"Really," Lawrence said.

The old woman sat quietly and looked down at her hands. She shook her head.

"You know it's true," Roland said, looking from one to the other. "We're nothing without Franny."

"Where do you think she is? Erin asked

They glanced at each other and shrugged.

"What does she look like?"

"She's much taller than you, and she's got lots of black hair," Michelle said.

"All right. Why don't you go upstairs and wait while I look for her," Erin said.

They got up to leave the room and slowly made their way up the stairs. Erin sat still on the sofa, and when they had all closed their doors, she stood up and walked over to the fireplace. An unlit candle rested on the mantel.

"*Scintillare*," she said, and the candle burst into flame, casting flickering shadows around the room. She picked it up and walked to a window. Holding the candle high, she pulled aside the heavy curtains and looked behind them. Standing there was a tall, beautiful young woman, with long, dark curly hair. She shrank into the corner, her eyes wide, staring at Erin.

"Franny?" Erin asked.

"Yes." She breathed a deep sigh.

"Please come out."

Franny bent her head and came out from behind the curtains. She walked to the sofa, collapsed on it, and covered her face with her hands, sobbing quietly. Erin sat down in the chair opposite her, put the candle on the table nearby, and leaned forward. The light from the candle wasn't much, but it seemed to warm the room a little.

Franny lifted her head and looked at Erin. Her face was smeared with tears, and her eyes were pleading. "They keep me here in this house. All the time. And they are so cold. I have to get away from them."

"You've got to let them go," Erin said.

Franny looked at her sharply. "What?"

"They will go, if you let them. I know how hard it is, but they need to go. Tell them goodbye. They don't belong here anymore."

"What are you talking about? They're the ones keeping me here."

"It feels that way right now. But you know they're only staying because of you. Please let them go." A tear rolled down Erin's cheek. Franny reached out and touched it with her warm hand, then sighed again.

"It's hard to let them go when you love them so much," Erin said.

Franny nodded. "You understand? But when they're gone, I'll be so alone."

"Each of us is alone. But your place is with the living, and theirs is not. Free them."

Franny rose, her long skirt rustling and shimmering in the moonlight, her dark hair like a cloud around her face, and she walked back to the window. She gazed outside and shook her head.

"I miss them already," she said.

"I know."

Franny came back and stood before Erin. "Will you help? Will you come back?"

Erin nodded. "If you need me."

"I will let them go."

They both rose. Franny squeezed Erin's hand and walked to the door. Erin heard her climb the stairs and call out to her mother, sister, and brothers. "Come, my loves, I have something to tell you."

Erin walked to the front door and went outside into the moonlight. She walked down the steps and along the flower-lined path to the narrow street, where she turned and looked back at the big, old house. "Goodbye," she whispered.

From the corner of her eye she glimpsed a dark movement in the shadows of the shrubbery. She drew her sword from its sheath and was on it in two steps, but the mortifer rose from the bushes and swung his staff. She blocked his blow with her sword, and he stepped back, his fiery eyes gleaming with harsh laughter.

She stood straight and faced him. "You've lost this one."

His hollow voice sent shivers through her body. "For now. But we will have her. Her loneliness will bring her to us." He laughed and whispered, "Just as yours will."

Erin lunged forward with her sword, but the shadow had already turned and fled into the forest.

***

Erin woke with a start. Her heart was pounding, she was shivering, and she knew she had to hunt something. What? Something frightening, and she had to catch it. She climbed out of bed but was too agitated to do anything but pace in her room. The floor was cold, and her skin was like ice, but she didn't care.

The white light from the moon shone through her window as it moved across the sky. She stopped pacing to gaze at the moon above and its reflection in the water below. Her garden shone with a silvery glow, and she leaned her forehead against the windowpane. *It was just a dream.* She went down to the kitchen and poured herself a mug of milk. She microwaved it and sat at the kitchen table, taking small sips until her heart slowed. When she finally climbed the stairs to bed, she lay awake until morning.

***

A few days later Erin drove to work through a steady rain, the big drops splattering on the windshield. She flipped on the wipers and turned on the radio, thinking about the coming weekend. She hoped the rain would let up for their biking trip. Matt had been planning this trip for months to celebrate his twelfth birthday.

She'd slept fitfully every night for the last week, sometimes waking completely, sometimes just restless. The dreams disturbed her more than ever, but all she could remember were fragments. Every time she woke, she woke trembling. No details and no sleep. She looked in her rearview mirror and groaned at the circles under her eyes.

Five days had gone by since she had seen Gary, and she still hadn't called him about the weekend. She wondered if he really wanted to join them or if he was just being kind. He might have forgotten all about it by now. She decided to quit putting it off, call him, and find out.

She pulled into the music store parking lot and pulled out her phone. She searched her purse for Gary's card and punched in his number.

"Good morning. AB International," a pleasant woman's voice answered.

"Gary Arthur, please."

"One moment." Music came on the line.

"Gary Arthur's office," said a brisk female voice.

"Is Gary in?" Erin asked.

"Who's calling, please?"

"Erin Holley."

She was put on hold again, and the music was back. She looked at her fingernails and pushed back a couple of the cuticles.

"Gary is on the other line right now. May I have him return your call?" asked the woman.

"Sure." Erin gave her the phone number of the music store and went inside, wondering if he would call her back. She decided it was just as well she hadn't reached him. If he didn't call her back, she'd know he wasn't really interested.

By the end of the day, Erin collapsed into a chair and closed her eyes. She had given six lessons that afternoon, plus Ed had needed to run errands in the middle of the day, leaving her to attend to the customers, too. She was exhausted and had started gathering her things together when the phone rang.

"Anacortes Music. This is Erin."

"It's Gary. Sorry it took me so long to get back to you. It's been one of those days."

"I've had one like that myself."

"Is the bike ride still on?" Gary asked.

"Sure is."

"I'll be there. Should I meet you at your place?"

"My place is good. Say about nine o'clock?" Erin said.

"In the morning?" He sounded surprised.

"Of course."

"Do I need anything besides my bike?"

"Just your helmet," she said.

"See you then." Gary hung up the phone.

So Gary would be there after all. Erin touched her lips, remembering the feel of his mouth on hers, and her heart started pounding. *Was this the right thing?* She shook her head, chiding herself for making such a big deal out of a bike ride. They would have a fun day with the kids and get to know each other a little better. All she hoped for was good weather and a good night's sleep beforehand. The last thing she wanted was to look like a zombie on Saturday.

Chapter 9

Another wakeful night left Erin more tired in the morning than before she had gone to bed, but she drank an extra cup of coffee and got the kids off to school. Only two customers came into the store that morning, and Erin sat behind the counter, fighting to keep her eyes open.

"Are you awake?" Ed was looking at her with concern.

Erin lifted her head from the counter. "I'm so sorry. I guess I kind of drifted off. What were you saying?"

"I just wanted to let you know I'm going out for a bite of lunch now."

"Oh, no problem," Erin said.

"Good. Are you all right? You drifted off once last week, too."

"It's nothing. I keep waking up at night. I'm just not getting enough sleep."

"Hmm." Ed was heading toward the door. "I hope it gets better. See you in a bit."

Erin went over some of the music for her lessons that afternoon. After a while she called Hannah.

"Bakery De Oro," Hannah answered.

"Hi, it's Erin. Are you still up for our walk?"

"Sure am. What time?

"How about a little after one o'clock? I'll meet you at the bakery?"

"Sounds good."

At one o'clock Erin buttoned her coat, stuffed her hands into her pockets, and walked the three blocks into the wind to the bakery. A few dark clouds scurried across the sky. Hannah had decorated the little shop in a Mediterranean style with rich colors, grape vines and trellises painted on the walls, and creamy white pottery on decorative shelves. Three small bistro tables with two chairs each sat in a corner by the windows, where patrons could enjoy coffee and a pastry with a view of her petunia-filled pots outside.

"Hi, Erin," Hannah said when Erin pushed the door open. She pulled a worn leather jacket over her orange T-shirt and tossed her long, single braid over her shoulder. The two women hugged each other.

"Carlos, I'm going for a walk with Erin," she called out.

Her husband came out of the back room, wiping his hands on his apron. "Hola! Que tal, Erin?"

"Muy bien. Como esta? Do you mind if I take Hannah away for an hour?"

Carlos grinned at her. "Only one hour. Mi querida has to make a special order cake this afternoon."

"Okay, one-hour limit. Let's go."

As they walked down the street toward the waterfront Hannah said, "You've got to tell me all about your weekend. You saw Gary again? Tell me about him."

"He's a nice guy. He came over Saturday night and had dinner with us."

"That's what Aleesha told me. It sounds like you made a good impression on him. Does he have a chance with you?" Hannah said.

Erin gave her a sidelong look. "I'm going to see him again this weekend—we're all going for a bike ride on Orcas," she said. "I have such mixed feelings. I have to admit I do like him, though."

"Is there anything wrong with that?" Hannah asked.

"I feel confused. He'll talk about William, and I'll feel so sad, then he changes everything, and I feel, um, like all I want is for him to kiss me."

Hannah smiled. "And has he?"

"Yeah." With her head down Erin continued, "I told him I needed to take it slow, but he said no, I didn't. Then he kissed me. I was so surprised—it was so sexual."

"Carlos was very physical right from the beginning. And you know how wonderful he is."

Erin nodded. "There's no denying that it felt good to be kissed," she said, but she frowned as she thought about it.

Hannah laughed. "I'm not at all surprised."

"In fact, part of what I don't like about it is that it felt too good. I feel disloyal."

Hannah gave Erin a brief hug. "But you're not. It's okay for you to enjoy being with someone."

They continued their walk toward the water. The wind blew harder, smelling of fish and creosote, and they stopped a minute to watch the seagulls swooping over the bay. Two tall men ran past them, dressed in shorts and T-shirts. Erin and Hannah watched them until they turned a corner and were out of sight.

"I haven't seen them before," Hannah said. "I wonder if they're new here."

"Could be."

"Runners. That reminds me, you know my friend, Jill? Remember her daughter, Carolyn? The sweet girl who's on the high school track team?" Hannah said.

"I think so—a pretty, blond girl?" said Erin.

"Yeah. She told Jill she had a dream about you. It was so vivid that she almost thought it was real. I guess you saved her from some big bad monster."

"Really?" Erin stopped walking; everything around her seemed to stop moving.

"Yes. Isn't that funny? I wonder why she would dream of you? She was having nightmares for quite a while. Jill thinks it was because she felt too much pressure with school and sports. She didn't even want to go to sleep anymore she was so afraid. And not getting enough sleep made the stress worse, too. But then you popped into her dream and made the monster go away." Hannah laughed.

Erin felt shivery and a little weak. "That's a strange dream."

Hannah touched Erin's arm. "What is it?"

Erin kept her eyes on the sidewalk. She shook her head as if trying to shake her thoughts away, but a brief memory of Carolyn on a cliff-face flashed through her mind. "Nothing. It just made me think of my own dreams. They've been waking me more often lately. And I can't get back to sleep. I've been so tired I even fell asleep this morning in the shop."

"This has been going on for a long time."

Erin looked out over the boats in the marina toward the water and the horizon. A bench was nearby, and she walked to it and sat down. "These dreams started right after the car accident."

Hannah sat down, too. "That's right."

"The vision or dream I had in the hospital before I woke up—where I followed William across the river and tried to bring him back." Erin's voice dropped to a whisper. "There was a dark, evil shape that tried to hurt me." Her whole body shook, and she felt icy cold. Fine drops of sweat broke out on her face.

Hannah looked at her, concern in her eyes. "Erin, it's all right. It wasn't real."

She wiped her face with her arm and shook her head. "Of course not. It was so frightening, though. And even after all this time—just the memory is so scary—it's as if I saw that creature just last night." She shivered again and whispered. "Maybe that's what my nightmares are about."

"Oh, I hope not," Hannah said, but Erin saw that Hannah was thinking the same thing.

Erin took a deep breath and stood up. "We'd better head back."

"You're right. I've got to get started on that cake."

***

"I could use some water. Let's stop here," Michael said as he and Bruce turned back toward his house on the last leg of their run.

"Got cash?" Bruce asked.

"A little."

They stopped outside an ice cream and candy shop and paused to catch their breath. The wind picked up again, and some heavy raindrops splattered on the sidewalk. The two men went inside.

"Water and a rocky road cone, please—one scoop," Michael asked the clerk behind the counter.

"Make mine two scoops of rocky road," Bruce said.

Michael shook his head as he grinned at his brother. "You always try to outdo me, don't you?"

"Always."

"You'll never be able to."

"Hah!"

They sat down at a table by the window to eat their ice cream and watch the people outside as they rushed to get out of the rain.

"There's the two women you noticed by the water," said Bruce. "They just walked past."

"Yes," Michael said.

"What struck you about them?"

"The brown-haired one looks familiar. I think I've met her before, but I can't place where," Michael said with a shrug.

"She doesn't look familiar to me." Bruce stood up. "Ready to go?"

"Yeah," Michael drained his cup. "Let's go."

They ran out the door into the rain.

Bruce said, "There they are again—in the next block."

The brothers slowed to a jog and watched as one of the women called out goodbye and went into a music store. The blond kept walking. As they ran past, Michael wondered where he had seen the woman. *Small. Dark hair.* Something about her tickled his memory, and he couldn't get her out of his mind.

Chapter 10

Erin closed and locked the music store's door and walked the short distance to her car. The clouds had rolled away, sunshine warmed her face and hair, and the breeze smelled like the salty Puget Sound. She breathed deeply and felt a surge of contentment. Tomorrow would be a sunny day, and Matthew was going to have a wonderful birthday. She headed home.

As soon as she turned into the driveway, Matt and his friend Jacob ran to meet her from Edna's house next door.

She stopped the car and opened the door. "Hi, guys."

Matthew was the first one to reach her. "We've got Jacob's bike here now, but we need your help."

She laughed. "I'd better let Edna know I'm here first. Can it wait a couple minutes?"

"Oh, sure."

When they reached the house, Edna swung open the screen door as she dried her veined hands on her apron.

"Hello, dear," she said. "Gwen'll be right out—she's working on a project in the kitchen."

"Thanks." Erin gave Edna a quick hug. "How's everything?"

"Very well."

Gwen came out, and Erin and the children hauled Jacob's bike to their house. It needed a new tire and some other adjustments, so Erin helped the boys with the work, and it wasn't long before they were done.

"Thanks, Mrs. Holley," Jacob said. "See you tomorrow." He hopped onto his bike and waved goodbye as he left for home.

"We'll pick you up at nine," Erin called after him.

After dinner Erin and Gwen mixed up Matt's birthday cake. While it was in the oven, Erin checked over everything she had prepared to take the next day. She'd picked up little meat pies from Hannah's bakery, apples, cheese, grapes, French bread and butter, and bottles of juice. With the cake, a thermos of coffee, and some chocolate bars, Erin thought it looked like a perfect birthday picnic.

Matt sat on the stairs and watched Erin add some napkins to the basket. "Is Gary still coming tomorrow?" he asked.

"Yes, he is." She glanced at him, and then looked back at the basket. She felt like she was forgetting something.

"Do you think he'll give us a ride in his car?"

"I'm sure he will if there's enough time," Erin said. She checked to be sure she had plastic forks.

"Mom, I don't know about him," Matt said.

Erin looked at him sharply and her stomach turned over. "What do you mean?"

He shrugged. "Jacob says he's too smooth."

"Too smooth? Well, don't worry—I'm not rushing into anything."

"Yeah, I know."

Erin walked over and sat down next to him on the stairs. "I don't even know Gary very well. We can see how much we like him tomorrow, okay?"

"I suppose so."

"We're going to have a fun picnic and bike ride. It'll be a great birthday. We can do whatever you want."

Matthew smiled. "Whatever I want? I'll have to think about that." He ran up the stairs to his room, and Erin smiled after him. She didn't want him to worry. She did enough of that for both of them.

After the children were in bed, Erin wandered to the beach, scanning the shadows as she walked. The night was calm, so she sat on a log and gazed at the reflection of the moon on the water. Across the bay Skagit Island was black, but lights glimmered from two boats moored beside it. The water rose in small swells as the tide inched up the beach. She had sat on that same log and watched the same moon so many times with William.

The roar of a car speeding up the road jolted Erin upright, and she turned around to see a black SUV pull into her driveway. She was sure it was Gary. She looked back at the water and the moon for a moment, then got up and walked toward the house, feeling an odd mixture of anticipation and reluctance. Gary had already jumped out of his car and was knocking at the front door. She ran around the house to meet him. "Hi. I wasn't expecting you till morning."

"I know it's late, but I just got into town and wanted to see you."

"Come on in."

They walked in the front door and headed into the living room. Most of the lights were off, and the house was dim and shadowy. Gary sank down onto the overstuffed couch, leaned his head back and looked up at the ceiling.

"It was a long drive," he said.

"Would you like something to drink?" she asked.

"Yeah. What have you got?"

"Water, Coke, tea, brandy. Or I could put on a pot of coffee."

"I'll take a brandy."

Erin pulled out a bottle from a kitchen cabinet, picked out two small brandy snifters, poured hot water into them and swished it around. She dumped out the water and poured some brandy into each glass. Gary watched her from the couch.

"Here you are." She handed him his glass.

He raised his glass to her and took a large swallow. He leaned his head back again. Erin sipped hers. "Do you have a place to stay?"

"Yeah, my assistant made a reservation for me at a hotel in town."

Erin switched on a table lamp and sat down in the chair opposite him. "Everything all right?"

He gave a short laugh. "Just great." He looked away, then glanced back at her. "It was a rough day." He drained his glass.

"Do you want to talk about it?"

"No, it's really boring. Why don't you tell me about the plans for tomorrow?"

"Sure. The ferry takes about an hour and a half to get to Orcas. Matt and I already loaded our bikes on top of my car—there's room for yours and Jacob's too. Gwen's will have to go in the back. Once we get off the ferry, we'll drive to the state park and to the top of Mt. Constitution—there's a great old lookout tower there, and the view is amazing. Then we'll go have our picnic and ride."

"Sounds perfect." Gary leaned toward her, resting his arms on his knees. "Do you do this often?"

"Only once before. It was a lot of fun."

He stood up, stretched his arms towards the ceiling, and walked to the living room window. It was dark in that part of the room, and Erin was struck by how bright his blond hair was even in the shadow. She felt an urge to smooth her hands across his back. He turned around and grinned at her. "Are your kids here?"

"Of course. They're in bed."

He nodded. "I'm beat. I'd better go. We've got an early start in the morning, right?"

"Right." She stood up and walked over to him.

He bent down and kissed her lightly. His lips were smooth, and he tasted like brandy.

She stepped backwards a half step and said, "I'm cooking breakfast in the morning—you want to come? It won't be anything fancy."

"Yeah, I'd love to," he said. "What time?"

"Eight o'clock?"

"I'll be here." He walked to the door and let himself out. Erin followed him outside and looked at his SUV.

"New car?" she asked.

He shook his head, "No, I've had it. I needed to drive something that would carry my bike. Unfortunately, that means no rides in the Porsche for the kids."

"They'll be disappointed, but there was nothing else you could do."

"Next time. See you in the morning."

He climbed into the SUV. Erin watched until his taillights disappeared, and she shivered in a sudden cold breeze. She glanced around, scanning the shadows under the trees, and dashed back into the house, her skin covered in goosebumps.

Chapter 11

Erin dropped ten feet into the darkness below, curled up, and landed in a crouch on the floor of the cavern. She gasped. Her breath lingered as a cloud of mist in the bitter cold air. Up above a crow cawed, and then was silent. She stayed motionless for a moment, listening. The only sound was a slow drip, drip, drip of water far away, in the further confines of the cave.

She rose, and as her eyes became more accustomed to the darkness, she was aware of a deeper blackness against the wall in front of her. The hair on the back of her neck rose, and her stomach twisted as she smelled the sick stench. The mortifer turned, its cold gleaming eyes piercing as its hatred smashed into her. Three more stood beside it, black shapes in the dark, and their icy hunger reached out toward her.

In one smooth motion, Erin drew her sword, lunged forward, and sliced across the first of the mortifers. It jumped back, but her blade pierced through, and it collapsed in the darkness with a long shriek. It dissipated like a heavy mist, flowing out into the surrounding murkiness. The others stepped closer to Erin with their swords drawn and staffs raised; their blades glinted like ice.

"Leave this place," she commanded.

They laughed at her, hollow and mocking. "You have no power here."

"Where is the man?" she asked.

They laughed again. "We have eaten him. There is nothing left."

She stepped forward bracing for the attack, but her arm was grabbed from behind, and she was pulled back. Her head struck the stone wall, and she hit the ground. She tried to force herself to her feet but froze at the sight in front of her, and she could only watch.

A tall man dressed in black was attacking the mortifers with fury, his sword cleaving them, destroying them before their weapons could reach him. A fifth shadow had been hiding low in the darkness beside her, and the man whirled around and sliced through it. Its wail filled the cavern, its bitter cold flowing across the floor like hoarfrost. The man leapt in front of Erin and swung his sword, splitting the next in two, and its screech echoed as its darkness dissolved in the cavern. Another shadow struck the man with its staff, knocking him to the ground. He rolled and scrambled back to his feet, but it lunged toward him, flashing its long sword. The man blocked it and swung his own sword through the shadow's face as it screamed and fell backwards into the darkness of the cave. The last mortifer turned and fled, and the man followed it like the shadow of a phantom.

Erin jumped to her feet and tore after them. She knew the mortifer would be headed for the dreamer, and she had to reach him. But who was this man? What was he? What was he doing here?

She ran over the jagged rocky floor through the maze of caverns, trying to keep him in sight. They raced on and on until Erin no longer had any sense of how far they had gone, or in what direction the entrance lay. In nearly complete darkness, her night-eyes could still make out the wraithlike shape of the man running in front of her. He favored his right side, limping slightly—probably wounded from the mortifer's blow. Gradually he slowed, then stopped. Erin stopped behind him.

"Shhhh…" he breathed.

She froze.

They crept forward again without a sound, and then Erin could hear it: a low moan came from up ahead. They were close now. The man reached back and touched Erin's arm with his gloved hand.

They crept nearer, and the moaning grew louder. At last, around the next corner, they found the terrified dreamer.

A small chamber, lit by the red flame of a candle on the floor, opened off the passageway. Frost covered the walls, which glowed red like blood from the flame, and red icicles hung from above the door. Shadows grew and faded as the flame flickered. The stench gagged Erin, and she covered her mouth. The dreamer, maybe fifty years old, was naked and chained to the wall with his arms overhead. The mortifer loomed over him with his knife, tracing long lines across the dreamer's chest with its pointed blade. Blood oozed from the wounds and trickled down his body, dripping to the floor. Erin's heart beat hard in her throat, and her stomach lurched with every moan the dreamer made. He tried to shrink against the wall, but the shadow laughed deeply in its throat and began to slice his skin again.

Suddenly it stopped and stood up tall, nearly filling the chamber. Its gleaming red eyes turned toward them, and it swung its knife up to attack.

Erin clenched her teeth and reached into her boot. She pulled out her own knife and let it fly. It hit the shadow squarely in the chest and split it open, its hollow cry filling the cavern as it exploded into black mist. The dreamer screamed, and the strange man rushed to him. Erin's knife fell to the floor. The man touched the shackles, and they fell away from the dreamer's arms and legs, while he crumpled to the ground, trembling and sobbing.

Erin dropped to her knees beside him. "It's gone now—they are gone."

The stranger said, "Over there—a cloak." A brown cloak hung on a nearby peg. Erin grabbed it and wrapped it around the dreamer's shoulders; he sat up and pulled it tight around himself, still shaking.

"Where did they go? Why are they doing this to me?" he asked, looking up at the man.

"They won't hurt you again tonight, but we need to hurry," said the stranger. "We must leave while we have the chance."

The man shrank back again. "Aren't we safe here now?"

"No, we have to go," the stranger said. "They may return. We'll stay with you until you're safe."

Erin put her hand on the dreamer's shoulder. "What is your name?"

"Bagley. My name is Bagley."

"Give me your hand," she said.

"Who are you? I've never seen you before." Bagley looked up at the strange man. "I remember you."

"Yes, I've been here with you before. Now come, we need to go. We'll shine a light through all the chambers and tunnels so you can see which way to go."

But Bagley shrank back against the wall. "No, I couldn't. I can't. I'm so afraid."

Erin sat beside him and touched his face with both of her hands, like a mother soothing a frightened child. "Then just a little way. Come, I will hold your hand. We can go slowly, and I'll stay with you. Just a few steps."

He looked into her face. Erin took his hands into both of hers, and she felt her warmth flow into him. Bagley's face relaxed. They stood, and Erin picked up the candle and coaxed him down the hallway in the dark, shining the candle's light into every room they passed, while the strange man limped behind them through the cavern's maze.

The tunnels were vast and silent, and Erin encouraged him to choose their direction each time they came to a crossroads. He shivered and moaned, and Erin paused several times to soothe him. At long last, she heard a low hiss from up ahead. They came to an opening in the rock wall, and beyond, the wind blew across a field of tall grass in the starlight.

Bagley stopped and looked all around, breathing deeply. His form faded away, and Erin relaxed and sank to the ground.

The tall man stood beside her and said, "You have a healing touch."

She looked up at his stern face, and he slowly disappeared. "Wait," she called after him, but he was gone. *Who was he?* When he had tossed her against the wall, she had been sure he was her enemy. But he had fought the mortifers. *For his own purpose, perhaps?* She lay back on the soft grass and closed her eyes, thankful she had been able to help the tortured dreamer. That was the important thing.

Chapter 12

Erin slid into the booth beside the window, and Gary sat beside her. Gwen, Matthew, and Jacob took the opposite seat. Around them more ferry passengers found places to sit: families with diaper bags, college students with backpacks, and other people of all ages, many coming to ride bikes along the winding, scenic roads of Orcas Island.

Gary rested his arm over Erin's shoulders as they looked out the window. With the ride more than an hour long, Matt and Jacob decided to explore, and Gwen asked if she could go with them.

"Don't make me take her. It IS my birthday," Matt said.

"Just for fifteen minutes, then bring her back to us," Erin said.

"Oh, okay."

The kids left, and Gary and Erin watched as the ferry pulled away from the Anacortes dock and blew its whistle. He leaned over and kissed the back of her neck. "That was a great breakfast."

"Thanks." She looked at his face, right next to hers. Gazing past her out the window, his eyes were pale blue in the bright light. He glanced at her and grinned, showing his perfect white teeth and deep dimples. His smile almost felt like another kiss. She wondered how she had ended up on a ferry with this attractive man, a man she hadn't even remembered a couple weeks ago.

They sat back and watched the islands go by as the ferry plowed through the water. The sunshine glittered on the dark surface of the Sound, and steep rocky shores led to grassy hills and then to the pine and fir trees of the island forests.

Gary said, "I've lived in Seattle for ten years—been all over the world, but never here. It's beautiful."

Erin smiled. "Yes, one of the best places on earth."

Gwen bounced into the booth and announced, "There's a restaurant here, and they have cinnamon rolls. Can I get one? And Matt brought me back because I have to go to the bathroom."

Erin laughed. "Well, then, let's go find it."

They found the restroom and went to the café for a cinnamon roll. The ferry was pulling into Lopez Island, the first stop, so they strolled to the forward deck to watch. A little road wound up the hillside from the dock into the trees, and a few buildings lined the road. Erin pointed out the seals playing on the beach, and Gwen laughed at them and threw pieces of her roll to the swooping seagulls.

As the ferry pulled away and they turned to go back inside, Erin noticed a man lounging on the bench behind her. He was watching her, but he looked away when she caught his glance. She studied him; he was tall and lean, his legs stretched out straight in front of him, ankles crossed. He wore a black leather jacket, and his short, dark hair was combed back. His face was a little weathered and he had a couple days' growth of beard, but his dark gray eyes were bright as he gazed over the water. He seemed familiar.

He looked back at her with a questioning expression in his eyes. She realized she'd been staring at him and turned away. Redness rose in her cheeks, and she took Gwen's hand, pushed open the door, and went back inside. She picked up some coffee at the snack bar for herself and Gary before they went back to their booth.

Matt and Jacob got back just as Erin and Gwen sat down. The captain announced over the intercom that it was time for passengers to return to their vehicles, so they gathered their things and headed back to the stairs. Gwen needed to use the restroom again, so Erin rushed to guide her there.

They raced down the aisle, rounded a corner, and Erin slammed into the same tall man she'd seen earlier. Her cardboard coffee cup smashed into his shirt, gushed coffee down his front, and she lost her balance. He grabbed her to keep her from falling, then stepped back in surprise. He looked down at his white shirt and jeans, soaked with her coffee.

Erin stood staring at him and his clothes. "I'm so sorry. Here, let me see if I can clean it up—are you all right?" She pulled some tissues from her bag and started to dab at the coffee on his shirt.

He pushed her hand away. "No, don't, that won't help."

She looked at his face. "I'm sorry. Are … are you all right?"

His frown softened into a small smile. "Yeah, just wet. Are you okay?" He took one of her tissues and swiped at his pants. "I guess neither of us were watching where we were going." He turned to Gwen. "Are you all right, young lady?"

"I'm fine. You're the ones who crashed," she said.

He grinned.

"Gwen, we've got to go. There's the restroom—go ahead—I'll wait here."

Gwen ran into the nearby restroom, and Erin turned to the man. The left corner of his mouth was lifted into a smile.

"I've got to get down to my car, so I'll just say I hope we meet under better circumstances next time." He turned around and ran down the nearby stairs to the car deck. She watched his back until he passed through the door below. Shaking her head, she picked up her crushed cup from the floor and looked at the puddle of coffee.

As soon as Gwen came out of the restroom they dashed down the stairs to the car. Gwen said, "Mommy crashed into a man and spilled her coffee on him."

Gary laughed and said, "Was it still hot?"

"No, just warm."

"Good thing."

Erin groaned as they got into the car.

They drove off the ferry and wound up the hill, past the few shops near the dock, and on through a small forest of fir trees. Bright sunshine warmed the air. They wound their way over the island and drove through the pleasant waterfront village of Eastsound, heading to the other side of the island and the state park. They continued past the lake and picnic area, and started the long, winding climb to the top of Mt. Constitution. As the car struggled up the steep mountainside, Jacob and Matthew's eyes grew wider.

"I forgot how far it is to the top," Matt said.

They drove higher and higher. Gwen stretched her arm out the window and brushed her fingertips across the leaves of the trees; there were no shoulders on the narrow road. They crossed a one-lane bridge and kept climbing.

"How high is this mountain?" asked Gary.

Erin grinned. "About twenty-four hundred feet. It's the highest point in all the San Juan Islands."

"The view from the top must be amazing," he said.

She nodded. "There's a tower up there that we can climb, and we'll be able to see for miles."

They finally arrived at the top, and Gwen, Matt, and Jacob ran down the path to the lookout tower with Erin and Gary strolling after them. Trees shaded the parking lot, and as they came out of the woods into the clearing, the brilliant sunshine was blinding. Erin's eyes soon became accustomed to it, and she looked around at the view below.

The expanse of Puget Sound stretched out to join with the sky on the hazy horizon, and islands dotted the water with green. She looked east to see Mount Baker, and south to Mount Rainier, both mountains still snowy white. Two ferries in the distance were plowing through the water.

Gary said, "I had no idea. This is incredible."

The children had already climbed the stone steps to the top of the tower, so Erin and Gary followed them up the winding stairs. From the top they looked out in every direction.

"This tower was built in the 1930s, modeled after lookout towers from the 1300s," Erin told him.

"It does look medieval," he said.

Erin pointed out the mountains. "Sometimes you can even see Mt. St. Helens from up here."

They walked back down the stairs and looked into some of the small locked-off rooms they passed.

"Doesn't it make you think of a medieval prison cell?" Erin asked.

Gary laughed. "And torture."

"I think I've dreamed about towers like this."

When they reached the bottom, Erin gathered the children together again, and they made their way back to the car. Gary reached for Erin's hand. "I've dreamed of towers like that, too."

"Is that good or bad?"

He shrugged. "Neither, I guess. Just curious." He looked back at the tower behind them.

"Let's go find a picnic spot," said Erin. "It's high time for lunch."

"Sounds good to me," said Jacob. "I'm starved."

They piled into the car and wound their way back down the hill.

Matt said, "We should ride down this hill. It'd be awesome! We could probably go fifty miles an hour."

"We could go faster than that," said Gary. "This is some hill."

Erin glanced at Gary. "I don't think so, guys—this is just too steep and long."

They passed a group of bicyclists riding down the hill.

"Look—they're doing it," said Jacob.

Gwen said, "I'm not riding down this hill."

"No one said you had to," said Matt.

When they reached the highway, they turned right and drove to the picnic area—a large, flat, grassy spot beside the lake, with picnic tables, a concession stand, and a swimming area. They found a table near the lake under the shelter of a large maple tree and carried their picnic gear from the car. Erin spread a tablecloth on the table, then covered it with paper plates and the food. The cake was placed in the middle.

Gary said, "Wow, this is some picnic."

Erin surveyed the table with her hands on her hips. "We like to do things right."

"Good, you got the meat pies from Hannah," Matt said. He grabbed one and took a big bite.

They all sat down at the table and ate their lunch.

When they were ready for the cake, Erin lit the birthday candles, and they all sang "Happy Birthday" to Matt. He was able to blow out all the candles before the breeze did.

"What did you wish for, Matt?" Gwen asked.

"Can't tell," he said. "Then it wouldn't come true."

Everyone ate a big slice of the chocolate cake, and they spent some time tossing stones into the lake. The park had filled to overflowing by that time with families playing and picnicking.

"I've been thinking," Matt said, "we could drive to the top of Mt. Constitution, and me, Jacob and Gary could ride our bikes down the hill. You and Gwen could drive back down in the car and ride around here until we get back."

"That doesn't sound like fun to me," Gwen said.

"It's my birthday. And Mom told me I could do whatever I want today," Matt said.

Erin stood still, looking at Matt. "That's such a long, steep hill. I really don't think it's a good idea."

"But Mom, you said anything I want."

Gary put his arm around Erin's shoulders and kissed the top of her head. "I'd be with them," he said. "They'd be fine. It sounds like a lot of fun."

Erin looked at Gary's impish grin, and then at Matt's pleading eyes.

"Oh, all right," she said. "But you guys be careful. Remember to keep your gears low and your hands on your brakes."

"Yeah, we will. Thanks!" Matt said, beaming. He and Jacob did a high five. Then he did a high five with Gary. Erin shook her head.

They loaded their gear back into the SUV, and Erin said, "Let's go."

Chapter 13

Rays of afternoon sunshine splashed through the forest, sparkling on the ferns and huckleberries that lined the road. They wound their way slowly to the top of the mountain again and passed several groups of people coasting their bikes down the hill. When they reached the top, Erin parked the car in the shade, and they all climbed out. They got the bikes down and retrieved their helmets from the back of the car.

Erin handed out water bottles and gave Matthew a quick hug. "We'll meet you at the picnic area, okay? Watch out for cars—don't expect them to see you. Stay on the side of the road. And don't go fast. Got it?"

"Yeah, Mom. We'll be fine," said Matt.

"We'll be careful," said Jacob.

Gary kissed the top of Erin's head and whispered, "You're sexy when you're giving orders."

She pulled back a little and smiled as a thrill ran up her spine. "Stop that," she said. Gary grinned.

The boys and Gary hopped on their bikes and headed down the hill. Erin and Gwen got back into the car, drove slowly out of the parking area and waved as they passed.

"Why can't I ever do what I want?" Gwen asked.

"Today's Matt's birthday. When it's your birthday you'll get to pick what to do."

Gwen stared out the window, a pout on her face.

When they finally reached the bottom, Erin turned toward the picnic area.

"Do you want to ride your bike around here, honey?" Erin asked when they arrived at the park. "There's some kids swinging and climbing on the bars. We can go over there if you want."

Gwen looked around. "I want to swing, Mommy."

"Sure, let's go."

They walked over to the playground. As Gwen climbed onto a swing, Erin found a patch of soft green grass nearby and sat down cross-legged to watch. The park was crowded and noisy, but the warm sunshine made her feel drowsy. Lying down, she watched the white clouds in the sky. She was glad Matt was having a good birthday and that Gary's offer to ride with the boys seemed to be easing Matt's concerns, but she hoped Gwen wouldn't hold it against him. She wondered how the rest of the day would turn out. After a while she closed her eyes and relaxed into the soft grass.

She felt light and a little dizzy, as if she were going to float away. Like the clouds?

The sunshine grew brighter, and Erin sat up and looked around. The air was luminous. She sat on pure white sand beside a wide lazy river, and across the river in the distance nestled a small pastel village—buildings of soft blue, yellow, green, and pink. The intense light made the air glimmer, and on her side of the river people crowded the beach, all dressed in bright summer clothes. Erin looked down at herself. She alone was dressed in black—black pants, boots, and a tight black shirt. A sword at her side. Her brown hair was tied back in a ponytail. The clothes felt right for her, and she knew that she had worn them before. She looked across the river at the town again, and a sudden longing filled her to explore those pastel cobblestone streets and speak with anyone who might be there.

"Mrs. Holley?" said a distant voice. "Mrs. Holley?" It was insistent. Erin opened her eyes and saw the green grass and trees of Orcas Island.

"Jacob?" She sat up. "What are you doing here?"

"You've got to come. There was an accident. Matt got hit by a car." Jacob stood next to her astride his bike, sweating and pale.

Erin jumped to her feet. She couldn't breathe and her stomach lurched. She took a gulp of air and called out, "Let's go, Gwen. We've got to go!"

She stopped Gwen's swing, and they rushed back to the car while Jacob followed, pushing his bike.

"What happened?" she asked him.

"We made it down the hill and were on the road to the park, and Matt was hit from behind. We weren't going too fast, and we stayed on the side, just like you said. It was on a curve. He got thrown in the woods."

Erin felt every muscle clench. "Is he all right?"

"Mommy, what happened?" Gwen asked. "Is Matt okay?"

"Is he?" Erin asked Jacob, and she held her breath. She was afraid her legs were going to give out from under her. A car hit her son.

"He was talking—I think he's all right," Jacob said. "Gary told me to get you."

She let out her breath and ran. They jumped into the car and raced down the road as fast as Erin dared.

"How far?"

"Not sure," Jacob said.

Erin looked at him; tears ran down his dusty cheeks leaving streaks of dark brown. "He'll be all right," she said, and she glanced at Gwen in the back seat. Her pale face was staring out the window, and she held one hand tightly over her mouth.

"Gwen, he'll be all right," Erin said again, hoping it was true. A tear trickled down Gwen's cheek.

It took only minutes to reach the spot. A sheriff's car, a pickup, and a maroon car were pulled over to the side of the road as far as they could go, and several people huddled nearby. Gary was off the road sitting beside Matt, who was stretched out on his back among the trees and shrubs. Another man was kneeling there, too, talking to him. Erin pulled in behind the cars and dashed across the road.

Gary rushed to meet her, putting an arm around her shoulders. "He's okay. Maybe a broken arm, some cuts and bruises, but he's really okay."

"Thank God," she said. Her knees suddenly bent under her, and Gary caught her. She stood again and ran. She reached Matt and knelt beside him. He was pale, scratched, and dirty. A bandage covered part of his head.

"Matt, are you all right?"

"Mom," Matt said, and his eyes filled with tears. "My arm hurts and my head hurts, too."

Jacob and Gwen had climbed out of the car and stood across the street. Jacob walked over to join them.

The man kneeling beside Matt asked Erin, "Are you Mom? I'm Joe, EMT. I was nearby when I got the call. Your son will be fine. He banged his head pretty hard but doesn't have a concussion. He landed on his arm, but it doesn't look like it's broken. I'd have it X-rayed, though, just to be sure. How long are you staying on the island?"

"Just for the day."

"Where are you from?"

"Anacortes."

"Good. You should head back home and stop at the emergency room in Anacortes for an X-ray. Other than that and some cuts and bruises, your son should be all right. He'll probably be pretty sore tomorrow, though."

"Thank you." As relief began to replace the fear, Erin closed her eyes, and a few tears ran down her cheeks. She smiled at Matt.

"Hey, you. Tell me what happened."

Joe stood up and patted Erin's shoulder. He walked over to where the sheriff was talking to a man and woman. Gary joined them. Erin glanced at them: the man, in his late forties, dressed in jeans and a brown suede jacket, spoke urgently, and the woman listened and nodded her head. The sheriff stood still, his face stern.

"We were all just riding down the hill, Gary first, then Jacob, then me last," Matt said. "I was all the way over to the side of the road, but when we went around that curve up there, that car came up from behind and hit my bike. I went flying over my handlebars and landed here. I think I must have hit my head on something, because it sure hurts even though I was wearing my helmet."

"We were all on the side of the road as far as we could go, and Gary was making us go pretty slow," Jacob added. "I think the car was going too fast, and the guy couldn't see around the curve until it was too late. Or else he just wasn't paying attention."

Erin nodded. "Did you talk to the sheriff yet?"

"No," Matt said. "Gary did for a few minutes, but I haven't yet."

"Thank God you're all right." Another tear slid down her face and dripped onto her hand. "I'm going to talk to the sheriff."

As she approached the group, Erin heard Gary say, "You must not have been watching where you were going then—we were single file at the edge of the road."

"Yeah I was," the man said. "The kid just rode out right in front of me. There was nothing I could do."

The sheriff interrupted. "I've taken your statement. I'm going to talk to the boy now. Stay here." He walked toward Matt, and Erin followed.

"Well, son, how are you feeling?" the sheriff asked.

"Been better."

"Can you tell me what happened?"

Matthew told him what he'd told Erin, and the sheriff jotted it down. "Thanks. You're sure you didn't ride out into the middle of the road for a minute?"

"No, sir. I was being real careful. We all were. We weren't even talking. We were just riding, and there was no reason for me to go to the middle. I was on the side."

"Thanks. I hope you feel better soon."

The sheriff walked back to the couple and Gary. Erin joined them. After handing the man a ticket, the sheriff said, "I have to give you this, sir. If you want to contest it, follow the instructions on the back."

Joe and the sheriff got into their vehicles and drove away. The man who'd hit Matthew looked at Erin. "I didn't see him until it was too late. I'm sorry. Here's my card in case you need to get in touch with me."

"Thanks," Erin said.

The couple climbed into the maroon car and left.

"Let's get out of here," Gary said. He helped Matt to his feet and supported him as they walked over to the SUV.

Erin walked into the woods to get Matt's bike, and she almost cried when she saw how bent it was. She brought it back and put it into the back of the SUV, while Gary and Jacob loaded the other bikes. She looked around.

"Where's Gwen?"

They all stopped and looked around. "Where's Gwen?" Erin said again, louder. Blackness clouded her vision and she grabbed Gary's sleeve. "I only took my eyes away from her for a few minutes. Where could she go?"

He shook his head, mouth open.

"She was right by the car after we got here," Jacob said.

Erin closed her eyes for a second, then looked at Gary. "Okay. You go down the road in that direction, and I'll go this way. Surely one of us will find her. Just go for fifteen minutes, then come back. Matt, you and Jacob stay here in the car, and if she shows up, keep her here—we'll be back in a half hour."

The shadows of the trees stretched across the road as they headed out. Erin went in the direction of the park, thinking Gwen would most likely go back there, although she couldn't imagine Gwen leaving them at all. *Why had she left? Did someone take her?* Erin shook her head. She didn't want to think about that until all other possibilities were done away with. She looked beside the road in both directions and watched for a small girl's footprints in the dirt. Sweat dripped off her face and dampened her shirt as she approached the park. She called out, "Gwen!" several times and stopped to listen but heard no answer.

Noisy and crowded, the park was full of children laughing and playing. Erin looked at her watch; nearly fifteen minutes had passed, but this was the most likely place to find Gwen, and she wanted to search. She took the beach area first, peering into the face of every child there. She asked some older children if they'd seen her, describing her clothes, her size, her hair color, but no one had. When she reached the end of the park, she looked at her watch again—more than twenty minutes had gone by. She turned around and searched the picnic area as she wound her way back to the road. No success.

Each step back to the car became more difficult. She searched the trees beside the road for any clue. The car was a short distance ahead, and the boys must have been watching for her, because Jacob flung open the door and ran to where she was.

"Any sign of her?" he asked.

She shook her head. "No. Isn't Gary back yet?"

"We haven't seen him."

She looked down the road and glanced at her watch; she was so late getting back herself. When they got back to the car, she reached into the open window and squeezed Matt's hand. His face was pale, his eyes red.

"When Gary gets back, we'll drive to the police station," Erin said. She walked a short distance down the road and scanned the direction Gary had gone. She still couldn't see him.

She walked back to the car, and Jacob rushed past her down the road. Matt flung open the door of the car and stood watching. Erin turned to look after Jacob.

Far down the road Gary was walking toward them, carrying Gwen. A sob escaped Erin's throat and she raced down the road toward them.

"Gwen," she called as she got closer. "Are you all right?"

"She turned her ankle and couldn't walk back," Gary said.

"Why did you leave? Where were you going?" Erin brushed the tears away from her face.

Gwen looked at Matt, who had just reached them. "I thought Matt was going to die like Daddy," she whispered.

"Hey, I'm not going to die," Matt said.

Erin bit back a sob and took Gwen from Gary's arms. She hugged her close and said, "Don't ever run away again. Matt'll be okay. Now, what about your ankle?"

"I think I broke it."

Erin put her on the ground and looked at her swollen ankle.

"I'd say you sprained it," Erin said. "We can wrap it with the ace bandage I have in the car." She looked up at Gary. "Thank you for finding her."

"No problem. Glad to help," Gary said.

"Would you mind carrying her back to the car?"

"Of course not."

Gwen wrapped her arms around Gary's neck as he picked her up.

They all got into the car and headed back to the ferry. The shadows were growing long as they pulled into the line of cars at the terminal.

The ferry was on time, and the ride home was much more subdued than it had been in the morning. They were drained. Gwen sat curled up next to Gary, Erin on his other side, and Jacob and Matt sat nearby talking and reading comic books. Erin fell asleep with her head on Gary's shoulder until the captain announced their arrival at Anacortes.

The wait in the hospital emergency room didn't take long. The X-ray showed Matt's arm was broken, but besides some nasty bruises and scrapes that was his only injury. Once his cast was on, and the doctor and nurses had signed it, they were ready to go.

They trudged back to the car in the dark, worn out and famished.

Matt said, “It’s still my birthday. Let’s stop for pizza.”

“That sounds like a great idea,” Gary said.

The pepperoni never tasted better at Vince’s Pizzeria, and Erin felt better with food in her stomach. The drive home was much more cheerful than the ferry ride had been. They dropped Jacob off at his house and drove to Erin’s, where she helped the children into the house while Gary lifted the bikes down from the top of the car.

Stars were bright as Erin went back outside to find Gary waiting for her, leaning against his car, his form a silhouette against the streetlight in the distance.

“I’m so sorry about Matt. I feel completely responsible. If I hadn’t encouraged the idea, or if I’d ridden behind the boys, this never would have happened,” he said.

“Don’t be ridiculous. You’re not to blame—don’t even think that. It was Matt’s idea, and I’m the one who said it was all right. And what would I have done without you there?” Erin couldn’t help but catch her breath as she said this, and she wiped a tear from her cheek.

Gary took hold of Erin’s arm and pulled her close. He wrapped his arm around her neck, rested his head on top of hers, and said, “It must have been a terrible day for you.”

“Don’t, you’ll just make me feel sorry for myself.”

He pulled her around to face him and held her arms, then bent his head and kissed her lips softly. She wrapped her arms around his back and relaxed her body against his.

“Ohhh,” Gary moaned, turning his face away but holding her closer. “I’d better go before I’m not able to.”

“It’s so late,” Erin said. “I have a guest room. You can stay here if you like.”

He laughed. “No, I’d be in your bed for sure. And I know you’re not ready for that.”

Erin felt a thrill run through her, but she knew he was right.

His cell phone rang, and he looked at it and scowled, then glanced at Erin. "This'll just be a minute."

"Yeah?" he answered the phone and listened. "They won't budge?" Erin heard the angry voice of the man on the other end of the line. Gary walked a few steps away.

"Calm down. Look, all right. I'll get it cleared up at the meeting. I'm heading back right now," Gary said.

The other voice spoke more quietly; Gary's eyes traveled from the ground to Erin's face. He turned away. "There's no risk. I need to find out." He paused, listening again. "You're overreacting. Shit, I'll take care of it." He disconnected.

"Is everything all right?" she asked.

Gary put a smile on his face. "Yeah. That was my business partner—he always overreacts. Sorry about that."

He kissed her again. "Thanks for letting me come."

"I'm glad you did."

"Me too. I'll call you this week." He climbed into his SUV and drove away. A crow landed in the driveway where his car had been and let out one loud caw before it flew away. After that, the night was still.

CHAPTER 14

THE bell jingled above the door of the bookstore as Michael opened it and stepped out onto the busy sidewalk. He'd just made the final arrangements for his book signing to be held in a couple of days, and he started the long walk back home. A few scattered clouds dotted the sky, a light breeze stirred the blossoming trees, and it was a perfect day for a walk.

As he drew near the music store, he thought about the women he and Bruce had noticed the other day. One of them had gone into that shop. *Did she work there?* He opened the door and walked inside.

Instruments hanging from the walls and rows of sheet music crowded the store. A few customers were browsing through the music, one teenage boy was tuning a guitar, and the sound of a piano came from a back room. He glanced around but didn't see the woman anywhere. What was it about her that had seemed so familiar? He started looking at guitars against the back wall. A man with wire-rimmed glasses and a thin gray ponytail walked down the stairs and asked a customer if he could help her.

The piano music stopped and some muffled voices came from the back room. A door opened, and there she was coming out of the room, saying goodbye to a teenage girl. He recognized her—a petite woman with pale blue eyes and dark hair. She was the same woman they'd followed, and the same one who had spilled coffee on him on the ferry. His eyes widened; she was also the woman in his dreams—the one who'd watched while he and Gary Arthur had argued in the forest. She was the same one in the cavern with Bagley. She was a viator. He was sure of it.

He turned away and studied the guitar in front of him while watching her out of the corners of his eyes until she finished talking to the girl and went back into the room by herself. The sound of melancholy piano music came through the door. *What was it? Schubert?* He listened for several minutes to the gentle melody before walking out of the store and up the street. The music ran through his thoughts. He'd been having dreams about Anacortes for months but hadn't seen this woman in his dreams until recently. Seeing a viator during the day was unusual, yet he had been drawn here, right where this one lived. *Why?* He walked past a bakery and saw that it served espresso, so he turned around and went back.

He pushed open the door and went inside where the aroma of fresh baked bread made him realize he'd missed lunch. Another customer completed her purchase, and Michael asked the man behind the counter for a latte and a loaf of Italian olive bread to take home.

"Hannah," the man called toward the back of the store. "Por favor, make a latte for this gentleman?"

A tall blonde dressed in overalls and a T-shirt came out wiping her hands and smiled at him. "Hi," she said. "What size?"

"Grande, please," he said. "Or do you just call it a medium?" He smiled. He'd seen her before too—she was the viator's friend. He shook his head slightly, surprised at the coincidence that had brought him into her shop.

"Grande, medium, they both work for me," she said with a grin, and she brewed his espresso and steamed the milk. "Say, are you new in town? I've seen you around before, haven't I?"

"You may have," Michael said, "but I am new."

"Welcome to Anacortes. What do you think so far?" she asked and handed him his drink.

"I'm … intrigued." Michael sipped his latte.

She gave him a puzzled expression while she washed her hands and dried them on her apron. "Intrigued? With Anacortes? Why?"

"It's not what I expected."

She laughed. "Welcome anyway. My name's Hannah, and this is my husband Carlos." Carlos was on the other side of the room helping another customer, and he nodded his head toward them.

"Nice to meet you. I'm Michael."

Hannah squinted at him. "Michael Woodward the author?"

"Yes."

"It's so nice to meet you. I've read all your books—they're great—so suspenseful. My friend Aleesha is so excited you've moved here. I can't wait to tell her I've already met you. She'll be so jealous."

"I'm glad you like my work. Thank you," he said, surprised and flattered. He hadn't expected anyone to have heard of him here.

"Oh, yes. Aleesha first told me about your books, and I've read them all. Aren't you doing a book signing at Blue Heron soon? Aleesha said something about it."

"Yes, Saturday at two o'clock." He wondered who Aleesha was, if she might be the viator.

Three more customers came into the shop and looked at the display cases. Hannah glanced at them.

"Are you and your husband planning to come?" Michael asked.

"I will, but Carlos will be working. Aleesha and Erin are coming, though," Hannah said.

"Erin?" he asked.

She grinned. "Another friend."

One of the women who entered the store looked at Hannah. "I think we've decided," she said.

Michael lifted his latte. "Thanks for this and the bread. Hope I see you Saturday." He caught Carlos's eye. "Buenos tardes." Carlos smiled and nodded.

"Bye. Nice to meet you," Hannah called after him as he walked out the door.

Michael sipped his latte and walked slowly up the street toward home. *Coincidences? So the woman is a viator, and she lives here.* He wondered if he would meet her in their dreams again.

Chapter 15

Erin sat on a grass-covered hill above a wide, slow-moving river. The stars were bright in the darkening sky, the air smelled sweet, and she could see flickering lights from the village on the far bank. She felt drawn to those lights, but knew she had to stay where she was and wait for the dreamer's call. A breeze stirred the leaves on the trees behind her, and her skin prickled with a sudden chill. Beginning in the west, the stars disappeared as a coal black cloud advanced across the sky. The wind grew stronger, and Erin stood up.

Lightning lit up the western sky, and the roar of thunder traveled across the horizon like a log rolling downhill. The cloud had covered half the stars already when Erin heard the dreamer's voice.

"Ayaaaa!" Erin heard it in her mind, and she turned toward his call and ran. She raced to the northwest, heading toward the cloud and the lightning, into the woods and away from the river. She leapt over a creek and heard the dreamer's call again—closer.

"Where are you?" she called. The stars were nearly all covered now, and it was black under the trees.

She smelled the rotting scent of a mortifer and drew her sword.

"Where are you?" she called again.

"Here," the man's voice cried out. Erin heard a blow and a thud, and outrage filled her gut. The shadow had him. She rushed toward the sound and thrust her sword at the deep shade under a tree, but the mortifer stepped aside and swung its staff full force at her head. She blocked its blow and pushed it back against a tree, where the pressure of her sword against its staff held it firm.

"Where is he?" she demanded. The shadow's eyes gleamed, but it said nothing. She swung her sword around, freeing his staff for a moment, and the shadow whipped the weapon above its head with both arms for a deadly blow. Erin twirled, avoiding the full force of the staff, but it slammed into her shoulder, and she fell forward, dropping her sword with a gasp. She rolled, and the staff missed her and hit the ground hard. She leapt to her feet and pulled her knife from her boot, sweeping it toward the mortifer's face. It danced backwards while she advanced. When it lifted its staff overhead, she moved in closer with her knife. Its eyes glowed red flame. "You're lost, Viator. You are ours now." It swung its weapon again, and Erin reached up to block the blow with her left arm while she thrust her knife upwards. She heard a crack and pain shot down her arm, almost bringing her to her knees, but her knife pierced through, and the mortifer howled. It backed away, turned and fled.

Erin tried to follow but stumbled with pain. Her eyes blurred. She shook her head and slowly stood up, shivering with the cold. The words of the shadow and the pain left her shaken and dazed. She slid her knife back into her boot, and then looked around for her sword. It was a distance away—she picked it up and slid it into its sheath. She had to find the dreamer. With the mortifer gone, the forest wasn't as dark, and she called out, "It's gone now—where are you?"

"Here," said a muffled voice, and Erin moved in its direction.

"You are safe now. Come out," she called. "Look for a lantern—there should be one nearby."

A light flared from behind a fallen tree a short distance away, and a young man stood, holding the lantern. His eyes were wide, and he looked toward her expectantly. "Erin? Thank God—I hoped it was you. It's Paul, from the bridge."

"Are you all right?" She rushed to him.

"Just scared. Well, and I have a nasty bump where that monster clubbed me." He rubbed his head and whispered, "You were fighting that thing."

"Yes, it's gone now. Do you remember what I told you before?" she asked as she gently felt the lump on his head. She saw that she was now wearing a long, shimmering white gown.

He nodded.

She rested her hand on his wound for a moment and continued, "You should feel better soon."

Paul closed his eyes. "Thank you for coming again."

"Remember your own power in your dreams. You can change things."

"It's hard to remember that when a monster jumps in front of you."

"Nevertheless, it's true. I suggested you'd find a lantern, and you did. You believed me and made the lantern appear. And you see my dress? You imagine me this way. This is how I look to you."

Paul frowned and stepped away. "What do you really look like?"

She laughed. "Just like this, except I wear different clothes."

"Are you real?"

"Very real."

"What about those monsters?" He stepped over to where the mortifer's staff had fallen, picked it up, and examined it.

"They are real, but you can make them leave," she said. "You tell them to leave, and they will."

"Just like that?" he asked.

"You hold the most power in your own dreams. Don't let them frighten you so much you forget your own strength." She sat down on the log, and her skirt fluttered around her. "They are real, and they have power, but not as much as you have."

He nodded his head slowly as he stared at her.

"If it comes after you again, laugh at it, and tell it that it has no power over you. Then think of being in a beautiful, safe place—someplace you love."

His brow creased. "I'll try to remember. Will you come again if I need you?"

"Of course. Now, sit down and relax. Tell me about the most beautiful place you've ever been—a place where you feel safe and comfortable—maybe where something wonderful happened to you."

"That's easy," Paul said. "My childhood home in North Carolina. We lived in a huge white house surrounded by trees. There was a creek in the back where we played."

The sky grew lighter, and a creek bubbled at their feet. Grass grew down to the edge of the creek, and sunlight shone through the trees and sparkled on the water. Paul looked around with wide eyes.

"Come here anytime you want—just think of this place, and feel the peacefulness you're feeling now," Erin said.

Erin watched Paul as he relaxed and slowly faded away. She was pleased he could slip into a restful sleep so quickly, and she sat down on the warm grass to rest and heal. After only a few moments a stick snapped behind her. She jumped to her feet and spun around. In the deep shade under a thicket of trees she could see the mortifer; its eyes gleamed red as it watched her. Once again she was dressed as a viator, and she drew her sword.

"You're too late. I've sent him back," she sneered. It stood silent in the deep shade of the trees.

"I'm here for you," the shadow hissed. It glided out from the thicket, and the forest became dark and cold. "We are watching you."

Erin stepped forward to meet it and swung her sword, but the mortifer blocked her blow with its own blade. It pushed her back with an icy force that numbed her whole body. She yelled and lunged forward again, then twirled around, swinging her sword and striking it with such force that the shadow blew apart. The wind caught it, and it drifted away.

"*Miserere,*" Erin whispered. She stood with her sword in front of her, clasped with both hands. Her heart pounded in her ears, and her whole body trembled.

Chapter 16

Erin awakened slowly. It took several minutes to shift from her dream back to her bed, and even after she opened her eyes, she still felt the terror. She was covered with sweat, her heart pounding. She remembered the shadow of her nightmare, and what it had said. It wanted her; they were watching her. She lay shivering for nearly an hour before climbing out of bed and going downstairs. She knew that shadow creature, that dark monster—she remembered the one from the night William died. Why was she still dreaming about them? *Were they in all these frightening dreams?* Her stomach ached. She wrapped a blanket around herself on the couch and held tight to her knees, curled up close. *Get hold of yourself—it was only a dream.* At four o'clock in the morning, Erin knew she would get no more sleep that night, so she fixed a cup of tea and looked out the dining room window.

As the dark sky grew lighter it blended with the gray of the Sound, and thick drops of rain splattered on the water. Seagulls flashed white against the sky. After two cups of tea her trembling stopped, and at seven-thirty Erin went upstairs to take a shower. She tried to focus on the day ahead. In spite of the dream and the dreary weather, she was looking forward to it; she, Aleesha, and Hannah were planning to meet for lunch and go to a book signing at the Blue Heron.

She stood under the water for a long time, letting its warmth soothe her. She lathered twice and then smoothed Chanel No. 5 lotion all over her body. The enchanting scent made her feel like royalty.

Gary hadn't called all week. Each night she'd expected to hear from him, and each night she'd been disappointed. She wondered if the fiasco last Saturday had been too much. He'd been such a hero for her on Orcas Island, making it that much more painful that he hadn't called.

She dressed in jeans and a light blue T-shirt, and pulled her hair back into a low ponytail. No sense doing too much with it when the wind and rain would just mess it up. She went downstairs and found Gwen and Matt sitting in the living room watching cartoons.

"Morning," she said.

"Can we have pancakes today?" asked Matt.

"That's just what I was thinking."

She had just set the table when the phone rang.

"Hello?"

"Erin? It's Gary."

"Gary, how are you?" She leaned against the wall.

"Good. I'm in New York. Been here since Wednesday. I've been in meetings nonstop."

Erin flipped a pancake. "How's everything going? Has it been a good week?"

"I've run into some problems, but nothing I won't be able to work out. How's Matt's arm?"

"Fine. He's acquired new celebrity status with his friends." She glanced at Matt on the couch and gave him a wink.

"I'm not surprised. And Gwen?"

"Good. Her ankle is much better. We had a good week. I'm getting together with Aleesha and Hannah today for some fun. Are you going to be working in New York all weekend?"

"Most of it. I'll be seeing a few friends here tonight, though. Haven't seen them in a while."

"I'm glad you'll get a bit of a break."

"Yeah. I'll call you when I get back. I've got to run now."

She leaned against the wall again and closed her eyes, a smile on her face. She felt like she'd been holding her breath all week and could finally let it out.

After they ate breakfast, Erin cleaned up the kitchen while Matt and Gwen got dressed. She dropped the children off at their friends' houses and drove to Aleesha's.

"So good to see you. You look wonderful today," Aleesha said as she opened the door and pulled Erin into her house. "Come, let's have a cappuccino while we wait for Hannah. She just called. She's running late. Apparently Carlos couldn't part with her so early this morning, and she just got out of the shower. Mmm, you smell nice."

Aleesha brewed the coffee, and Erin sat down on a stool at the counter. She leaned over to smell a bowl of fresh carnations and closed her eyes, then took her coffee from Aleesha, cupping it with both hands.

"Have your children recovered from their harrowing weekend?" Aleesha leaned against the far counter in the kitchen and sipped from her mug.

"Yes. Matt's enjoying the attention he's getting with his cast, and Gwen was fine once she realized Matt would be all right." She shuddered at the memory.

"It must have been awful," Aleesha said, and she put her arm around Erin's shoulders, giving her a quick hug. She sat down on the stool next to Erin. Her mouth curled into a smile as she watched Erin out of the corner of her eye. "Is Gary coming out this weekend?"

"No, he's in New York. He called this morning."

Aleesha set her mug down with a clunk. "Is he there on business?"

"Yes, he's been there nearly all week."

Aleesha nodded and drank more of her cappuccino. She got up, rinsed out her mug, and set it in the sink. Then she turned around, crossed her arms, and leaned back against the counter.

"Now you've seen more of him—tell me—what do you think?"

Erin sipped her coffee. "I'm willing to see him again."

"You are so noncommittal."

Erin laughed. "What should I commit to?"

"I don't know," Aleesha said. "You never tell me what you really think."

Erin gave her a quick hug. "I like him, Leesh. He's smart, funny, and nice to my kids. He was great to have on Orcas. I'll see more of him."

"All right. I'm glad you like him."

A knock at the door, and Hannah bounded into the kitchen, her wet blond hair in a braid down her back. She was wearing baggy jeans and a yellow rain jacket that dripped water onto the shiny wood floor.

"Hey, you two," she said. "What a great day. Carlos made me eggs Benedict this morning, and it was fabulous. Do you think this rain'll let up soon?"

Erin and Aleesha smiled at each other.

"Probably not for a while, dear," Aleesha said as she grabbed a towel from a drawer in the kitchen and wiped up the water from the floor.

"You're dressed for it, though. I like your rain slicker," Erin said.

"Thanks. Sorry about the water."

"It's okay. Should we get going?" Aleesha asked.

They filed out of the house and drove the short distance downtown in Erin's car and parked. The rain had stopped, and a few patches of blue sky shone between the hurrying clouds. They strolled into an Italian restaurant where the wait for a table was short, and they were soon sitting by the window. Each ordered a glass of red wine.

"Remind me, who is this author we're going to see?" Erin asked.

"Michael Woodward," Aleesha said. "You still haven't read any of his books?"

"No, I meant to, but haven't had a chance."

"They really are good," Hannah said. "And the author's very nice-looking and charming."

Aleesha and Erin stared at her.

"You've met him?" Aleesha leaned forward and grabbed Hannah's arm.

Hannah grinned. "We chatted over a latte in the bakery just two days ago."

"Really? And you didn't tell me? What's he like?" Aleesha asked.

"He's tall, dark hair, and very pleasant. He said he's 'intrigued' by Anacortes."

Aleesha sat back. "I'll have to have a party for him. After all, he is a new neighbor. I should invite him to the gallery, too."

"Of course!" Erin and Hannah laughed together.

"Would you two be open for a dinner party in two or three weeks? Carlos too, of course, and Gary if you want, Erin."

"We'd love to come," Hannah said.

"I'm sure I can make it," Erin said. "I'll ask Gary."

Their food was served, and they each ordered another glass of wine. Aleesha nibbled at her salad, while Erin and Hannah filled their mouths with forkfuls of pasta. They talked and laughed throughout lunch, and it was nearly two o'clock by the time they were finished and had paid the check.

Sunshine had broken through the clouds and the air smelled like spring flowers. They put on their sunglasses and walked down the street to the Blue Heron Bookstore with their coats on their arms.

A table had been set out with about twenty folding chairs facing it. Another chair sat behind the table, and a few piles of books were stacked on top. No one was sitting, but people stood around the room in small groups, talking quietly. Erin recognized a few music store customers and greeted them. Two tall men stood near a bookshelf talking to Richard, the storeowner. Erin assumed one of them must be the author. They both looked familiar. One was a little younger with brown hair, blue eyes, and a smile that didn't stop. He looked around the room, his eyes lingering on each person, his smile widening if they happened to look back. The other, a taller man with dark hair and gray eyes, appeared more serious. He wore a French blue shirt and jeans and was slim, his shoulders well-defined. Erin was sure she'd seen him before. Richard said something to him, and he laughed. As his face lit up, Erin couldn't help but smile. Then her smile dropped from her face, and she turned her head away, wishing she could step back and hide behind a bookshelf. He was the man she'd spilled coffee all over on the ferry.

People began to take their seats, and the three friends found chairs in the middle of the room. The younger man walked to the back of the group and sat down, stretching his legs out in front of him. The tall man walked over to the side of the table.

Richard stepped forward. "Thank you everyone for coming. It's wonderful to see so many of you here. I'm Richard Shore, owner of Blue Heron, and I'd like to welcome you. Our guest today has written a variety of books and articles, from thrillers to philosophical essays to how-to articles. He has taught writing classes at City University in New York and at Portland College, and has made presentations at schools around the country. We are fortunate he has decided to make Anacortes his home. His latest book, just published, is called *The Course*. I finished reading it last night, and I can say confidently that you won't be able to put it down. It's excellent. With great pleasure, I introduce to you: Michael Woodward."

The man stepped forward while Richard took a seat. He took a deep breath. "Good afternoon. Thank you Richard, and thank you everyone for coming out on this rainy day. I'm Michael, and I'd like to introduce my latest book to you today—*The Course*. I can read a few excerpts for you, tell you a little of the story's background, and answer any questions you have. Does that sound good?" His voice was deep and soothing but carried easily to the back of the room.

Several people said, "Yes."

He looked around the room and his gaze lingered a moment on Hannah, then he glanced at Aleesha, and when he spotted Erin, his eyes locked onto hers, and his mouth curled into a smile. Erin felt the color rise in her cheeks. He smiled broadly, took a deep breath, and then looked away.

"*The Course* was conceived when I was in New York four years ago teaching a writing class. The class was full to overflowing, and several students were really struggling. One day I was walking home from the college carrying armfuls of papers. One of these students, John, was out for his daily run, and he crashed right into me. The papers went flying everywhere. Of course, he helped me gather them up again, but he felt terrible. He helped me carry the papers home, and we talked for quite a while. I learned a lot about him. John's a long-distance runner. He runs marathons. And four years ago he was almost killed in a car accident. He could barely walk after that, but now he's running marathons. This remarkable young man who was struggling so hard in my class, but could run marathons, was my inspiration for *The Course*.

"But the book is not an inspirational story about his ordeal. It goes beyond that. John had a very unusual experience while unconscious following his accident. I'm sure you're all aware of many people's near-death experiences?"

Several people in the audience nodded.

"His own experience was similar but went beyond that of most people's."

Erin wondered if John's experience had been anything like her own after the car accident.

The author continued, "John entered another world, a world with beauty and also dark, fearsome evil, before he was sent back to consciousness. And ever since, night after night, he continues to pass into that world through the doorway of his dreams, where he travels into other people's worst nightmares and fights the shadowy demons that seek to destroy them."

The hair on the back of Erin's neck tingled, and she felt a wave of dizziness.

He continued. "Who knows the depth of the human mind and what worlds it can enter once it crosses that first border?"

Erin sat as still as stone, her eyes fixed on Michael Woodward, her breathing shallow. *Is that what is happening to me? No—this is fiction.*

Michael looked into the eyes of the people as he spoke, and their eyes were on him; it was as if the audience held its collective breath—the only other sound was from the traffic on the street outside. He picked up a copy of the book, opened it to a page that was marked, and began to read. He was relaxed and read confidently in his deep, calm voice. Erin studied him as he leaned against the table, and each glance he gave to the audience seemed full of interest, almost amusement, as if he held a secret.

When he set the book down, the crowd applauded. People slowly got out of their chairs and walked forward to have him sign copies of his book. He sat at the table and spoke to each person in turn, asking what they thought and how they'd like him to sign their book.

Erin sat in silence for a few moments. She turned to Aleesha. "I see why you wanted me to read his books."

"When I'm reading one, I can't put it down," Hannah said.

"You see, I told you," Aleesha said. "Let's go get a book signed."

They got into line. Michael spent a lot of time with each person, so the line moved slowly. Erin felt eager to meet him but reluctant as well. She hoped he didn't remember her from the ferry, and she played with the idea of leaving before she got to the front of the line.

He was still signing the book for the woman in front of her when he glanced at Erin. "Did you have a good time on Orcas Island?" he said.

She groaned inside. "Actually, it was a disaster of a day. I should have realized that bumping into you was an omen." She took a step closer and held up both hands, palms out. "Don't worry. No coffee today."

He laughed. "I was concerned when I saw you coming. But I'm sorry to hear your day on Orcas turned out badly. Is everything all right?"

"Yes, thanks. We all survived."

"Good." They were both silent.

Erin felt her face begin to grow warm. "I'm very sorry about drenching you with my coffee. I hope it didn't ruin your day."

"Not at all. Don't worry about it." Michael stood up. "Would you like a book?"

"Oh, yes." She picked one up and held it out to him. "I haven't read any of your other books yet. But I can see I've been missing out. From what you read today, this sounds very good. In fact, it sounds, well, very intriguing," she stammered.

"Thank you." He took the book from her, and his hand brushed hers for a second. She shivered and pulled it back. "What's your name? Would you like me to write it to you or just sign my name?"

"Oh, my name's Erin. With an E. Please sign it to me."

He held her gaze briefly. "All right."

The skin on the back of her neck prickled, and a picture flashed into her mind of his face in an icy, terror-filled cavern. He bent his head to write in the book, then handed it back to her. Her heart beat hard in her ears, and her hands began to shake.

He leaned forward and spoke softly. "I've never seen you in Domus."

Erin shook her head. "Domus? I don't know what you mean."

Michael frowned and studied her. "I must have been mistaken. It's nothing—my mistake. What's your last name, Erin?"

"Holley."

"Nice to meet you, Erin Holley." He reached out his hand. She clasped it, and his grip was firm, his eyes clear and dark, his face still wearing a touch of a frown. He held onto her hand several more seconds. The skin on her arms rose in goosebumps.

"You, too," she said.

He let go, and Erin turned and rushed to the front of the store where she purchased the book. She quickly walked out of the store and stood still for a few minutes as her heart calmed. She couldn't understand what had happened to her in there. Taking a deep breath, she opened her book and looked at the inscription he had written.

"*Salve Erin, Viator, Tutus somnium*, Michael Woodward."

Chapter 17

Erin paced the street while she waited for Hannah and Aleesha to leave the bookstore. At the corner, she stopped and read the inscription again, then closed the book with a snap. What does he mean "*Salve Erin Viator*?" She walked back to the store just as Aleesha and Hannah walked out.

"Why did you leave so suddenly?" Aleesha asked. "We had a lovely chat. He's not only going to stop by the gallery Monday, he's coming to the dinner party in a couple weeks."

"Wonderful," Erin said. She tried to smile.

They walked down the street toward the car. Hannah touched Erin's arm.

"What did he say to you in there? You looked upset. And then when you left ..."

"It was nothing. I was embarrassed. We saw each other on the ferry to Orcas last weekend, and I spilled a cup of coffee all over him," Erin said. She smiled weakly.

Aleesha stopped. "You spilled coffee on him? I thought you hadn't met Michael Woodward before today."

Erin shook her head. "No, I didn't know it was him. I bumped into him on the ferry."

Hannah grinned. "Was he angry?"

"Not at all. He couldn't have been nicer."

"So why did you run out of the bookstore?" Aleesha asked.

"I don't know. His story kind of spooked me, and I guess I felt strange."

They both stared at her. "Why?" Hannah asked.

"I don't know." Erin shrugged.

They walked the rest of the way to the car and drove to Aleesha's house in silence. She turned to Erin. "Honey, you're a bit shaken. Do you want to come inside?"

Erin shook her head. "I'm fine."

"You're not fine. You're still creeped out," Hannah said.

Erin sighed. "It's these dreams I'm having. I had one last night that woke me up, and I never did go back to sleep. I have so many nightmares, but all I remember is terrifying shadowy monsters. They want to hurt me. And today in the bookstore, Michael Woodward—and his book—made me think of those dreams." Erin frowned and looked out the window, taking a deep breath. "And, well, look what he wrote in my book. Do either of you know what it means?"

She handed Aleesha the book. They were quiet for a minute.

Aleesha read the inscription. "*Salve Erin, Viator. Tutus somnium.*" She shook her head. "It sounds Latin to me. I don't know what it all means. *Salve*, of course, means something like 'good morning.' It's just some kind of greeting." She gave the book to Hannah. "He does write thrillers—of course he'll give you the creeps. Why don't we all go into my house and have a little glass of wine?"

"Thanks, but I should really pick up my kids." Erin said. "It's getting late."

Hannah nodded and said, "Carlos is expecting me any minute—I'll take a raincheck." She handed the book back to Erin.

"All right. But why don't both of you come to the gallery Monday around one o'clock? That's when Michael Woodward plans to drop by. Maybe seeing him in a different setting will chase away those goblins, Erin."

Erin laughed. "Yeah, sure. I'll plan on stopping by on my lunch break."

"I'll try to," Hannah said.

"Good," Aleesha said. She and Hannah got out of Erin's car and said goodbye.

***

"That went well today," Bruce said to Michael as he opened a bottle of beer.

Michael pulled two slices of bread from a plastic bag, set them on the counter, and spread them with mustard and mayonnaise. "Yes, very well. They aren't all as pleasant." He folded several slices of roast beef onto his bread. "Tell me what you thought of the audience."

"Attentive, interested. They're all fans, obviously."

Michael nodded his head. "Sure."

He reached into his pocket and pulled out a business card, which he handed to Bruce. "I've been invited to this woman's art gallery Monday, and to a dinner party in her home in a couple of weeks. Want to go along?"

Bruce took the card and asked, "Is she the thin woman with dark hair—very, umm, elegant? Maybe in her forties?"

"Right."

Bruce nodded, studying the card. "I really need to get back to Portland soon, but I could come back. Yeah, I'd like to go. She owns a gallery, huh?"

"Yep," Michael said.

"The two women we saw while running were there. What is it about them that interests you?" Bruce said.

"Just the small one. You haven't felt it? She's the woman I've seen in my dreams. I'm sure she's a viator," Michael said. He took a big bite out of his sandwich.

"Ahh." Bruce frowned and nodded his head. "A viator. So, have you talked to her in a dream?"

Michael nodded his head and took a long drink of his beer. "Yeah. I was so surprised when she dropped into a cavern that I almost ran her through with my sword. I'm glad I was there. She was outnumbered, and she didn't realize a mortifer was right behind her. I got her out of its way."

Bruce lifted his eyebrows and shook his head. He began making himself a sandwich. "Did you work together?"

"Yeah. She was a big help. But she didn't say much to me." Michael looked out the window. The sun was shining into the kitchen, and he squinted at the backyard. Leaves were just budding out on the trees, and a few blue and white forget-me-nots were blooming under them.

"Was this another one of Arthur's dreams?" Bruce asked.

"No. It was Bagley's. It was bad enough. He needed all the help she could give him." Michael shook his head. "But one thing was odd. Today I mentioned to her that I'd never seen her in Domus. And she didn't know what I was talking about."

"Really? Are you sure she's a viator?"

Michael was thoughtful. "That was my first thought, too, but I don't know. She seemed genuine at the time. But if she's a viator, she should know what I'm talking about, and if she's not, what was she doing in that dream?"

Chapter 18

Erin drove down the highway and took the Deception Pass cutoff, heading toward home. Her thoughts were jumbled; her stomach twisted and her head hurt. This author and his book with the events he described—how could they be so similar to her own experiences? The cemetery appeared on her right, and she slowed her car and turned through the gates. She drove along the narrow gravel road past the neat rows of headstones, past the statue of the angel and the mausoleum, to the one grave she needed to see.

She stopped her car and stepped out. Clouds spread out across the sky in lines of white and pale pink. Sounds of traffic from the highway below mingled with the hissing of the wind. A dog barked in the distance. Erin walked down the hill across the grass until she came to a standing stone, and she dropped to her knees. The yellowed remains of carnations lay on the ground, and she picked them up and kissed them.

"William," she whispered. "What happened when I lost you? Was it just a dream?" She thought back to that day two years before. Their last day. She closed her eyes and could still feel the warmth of the sunshine on her face, still feel the excitement and thrill.

***

The wind whipped through Erin's hair, and she laughed as she and William raced down the freeway. A blue sky, a warm spring day, and they were on their way to the airport for a long-postponed vacation.

She flipped on the blinker, stepped on the gas, and zoomed around a slow-moving truck. She laughed again, and William leaned over and kissed her.

"At last—two weeks with you in Hawaii," he said.

"I was so afraid we'd have to put off our trip again when Gwen got sick. Thank goodness she's better," Erin said.

He grinned and reached out his hand to touch her cheek. "I knew it'd all work out."

Erin's eyes sparkled. "Tomorrow we'll be waking up on the beach at Maui. I know the first thing I'm going to want to do."

"What, go snorkeling?"

"No. That'll be the second thing."

William leaned over and kissed the back of her neck. "I can't wait to see you bathing in sunshine."

"Mmm…" Erin murmured.

"I don't think I can wait till we get to Hawaii," he said. "Maybe we should just pull over right here."

"And miss our flight? Not on your life." She flashed a smile at him.

The car sailed along the freeway with the other fast-moving traffic. Erin and William laughed and talked as they drove along, and the two hours from Anacortes to the SeaTac Airport passed quickly.

Erin checked the mirrors and signaled her lane change to take the exit, when a car from behind swerved into their path. She veered away, but the car struck them, shoving them sideways. Erin and William's eyes met and held for a moment, until they were struck by another car and spun around. Erin froze as the car seemed to move in slow motion. She looked into the shocked face of another driver as he rushed past them and watched as a truck whipped toward her, then raced on by. She gripped the steering wheel, trying to regain control, and held her breath. Another car struck them, and they flew off the freeway, hit a barrier, and rolled.

The crunching and cracking were even louder than the shrieking Erin could hear. The world was a blur, and she realized it was her own voice screaming. She bounced around inside the car, hitting the side, but her seat belt held, and when the car came to rest, she was upside down, hanging in her seat, crammed up against the crunched roof. Her whole body hurt, and she couldn't move. The world was spinning.

"William?" she whispered. It became dark, then light again. Where was he? "William?" she said again.

She turned and he was there, still strapped in.

"William!" she yelled. "We've got to get out of the car. Wake up."

He didn't move.

She caught her breath and reached toward him, felt warm wetness, and saw that the roof of the car was smashed in even further on his side.

"Oh, my God," she whispered. The light faded again, and she fought to stay conscious. "Help him," she sobbed, but blackness overwhelmed her.

Erin felt cold, and when she opened her eyes, all she could see was foggy darkness. The pain was gone. She lay on the cold, soft ground and smelled the damp earth as she rose to her knees and stood up. She peered around hoping to see something, and the fog gradually began to clear. A faint light grew in the distance, silhouetting the tall shapes of the trees and brush surrounding her. Fog drifted away in wisps, curling around the trees; everything was misty and blurred. She walked a few steps toward the distant light and saw William standing alone, facing her. He turned around and walked away.

"Wait for me," she called as she rushed after him. She was barefoot, but the ground was smooth and cushioned her steps. The gray fog swirled around so she couldn't see very far. She followed William for a long time, losing him and then finding him again, but no matter how fast she went she couldn't catch up. Still she hurried on, and her tears mingled with the wet of the fog on her face. Her hair and clothes grew damp. She called out his name over and over. The cold intensified, and she shivered as she walked.

When she heard the gurgling of running water up ahead, she started to run. The fog still clung around her, but William was far ahead, making his way toward the water.

"Come back," she sobbed. "William, come back!"

She reached the river. It was about thirty feet to the far shore, and the water was quick and deep in places, rushing over the rocky bottom. Large stones were scattered across, and the fog had lifted enough so she could see the other side. William was there, already walking away from her.

"Wait for me," she called again as she stepped onto one of the slick stones. Her foot slipped into the icy water, and she almost fell. Carefully she made her way across, balancing on the boulders when she could, fighting against the current up to her knees in places where there were no stones. She finally leapt onto the far bank, wet, cold and shaking. The light was brighter there, but she could no longer see William. She climbed up the bank away from the river and went deeper into the forest.

"Where are you?" Tears streamed down her face. She'd come so far, how could she lose him now?

She strained to see further through the trees, and in the growing light she saw him far ahead. He had stopped and was talking to someone—a man. She called out his name again, and this time he turned around. He saw her.

"Come to me," she called. William hesitated, and she called again. But the other man spoke to him, and William turned from her and walked away.

She ran to catch up with him, but the ground was rough and full of roots and loose stones. She stumbled and fell. As she rose from the ground, looking around for him again, she called out, "Where are you?"

"I'm here," said a hollow voice nearby.

Erin turned toward the sound. "Where is William?"

The shape of a tall man covered in darkness, like a great shadow, grew out of the ground, and the scent of decay wafted toward her. She stepped back.

"Who? William? I don't know William. But you … what can I do with you?" It laughed—a gurgling, hollow sound—and it moved toward her.

The thing was like ice. Erin felt the cold spread from it and creep up her legs. It was freezing her. She shivered, and her teeth chattered. Its stench was nauseating. Hope drained out of her, leaving only numbness. *Where was William?* That question began to lose its meaning. *What did that thing say? What can it do with her?*

She looked at the huge shadow and saw its fiery eyes study her. It murmured, "You killed him. You can't save him now. He's gone forever into torment, and you sent him there. You'll never see him again. You're slow and weak and utterly useless."

Erin's head drooped, and she fell to her knees in the dirt. She had failed. She had lost William. He was gone forever, and she could do nothing to help him now. She felt her strength drain away and her will crumble. She was going to be sick.

The shadow laughed again, low and long, and it moved closer to her. Her skin hurt from the cold. It reached out toward her, and she lifted her head again and saw hunger in its eyes.

"No!" she screamed and struggled to her feet. "Don't touch me. Get away from me."

She backed away from it, but still it came toward her, laughing with its hollow voice.

"Get away," she screamed again, and she struck it with her fist. It staggered back, and she advanced toward it and struck it again and again. Her hands froze, but the creature fell back onto the ground, and Erin turned and ran. When she reached the river, she stopped and looked back but didn't see the shadow following. She scrambled over the ford and climbed up the far riverbank, where the thick fog felt like a blanket of protection. She collapsed onto the grass and lay there for a long time.

Erin felt a hand touch the back of her head, and she jolted upright. A man knelt beside her, surrounded by the swirling fog. His dark brown clothes were the same color as his eyes and hair, and his youthful face was clean-shaven. She backed away from him.

"It's all right," he said, his eyes calm. "I won't harm you."

"Who are you?" she whispered.

"Conn. I'd like to ask for your help. Many need it."

Erin shook her head, and tears washed down her face. "I can't help anyone. I've failed. I couldn't bring William back, and he's lost. I'm lost."

He reached out to her and held her hands. He was warm. "William is gone, but you have not failed. You fought and crossed back over the river. You are strong, Erin. And you can do more. I see so much mercy inside you, stronger than a sword. Where there's mercy, you'll find hope. Come with me now, and I will show you what you can do. Come with me for William's sake."

***

Erin spread her palms over the grave and murmured, "I'm so sorry, William." She closed her eyes and shuddered. "I'm so sorry I left you there. If I made it back, you could have, too." She wiped away the tears from her cheeks and kissed the grass on his grave. A tremor shook her. The wind blew through her hair as she walked back to her car and drove the rest of the way home.

Chapter 19

THE alarm woke her at six-thirty, and Erin switched it off and climbed out of bed. After a night of dreamless sleep, she felt more rested than she had in a long time. She hummed while drying her hair and putting on her makeup. After she slipped on a lavender dress, she twirled around and watched her reflection in the mirror, smiling at how the dress floated around her legs. With strappy sandals and a white jacket, she felt ready for the day and checked to see if the kids were ready, too.

Gwen and Matt were in good moods as well. Erin dropped them off at school and headed to work, and even though it was Monday, she expected a good day.

She unlocked the shop, flipped on the lights, and started dusting the shelves and instruments, humming as she made her way through the building. After everything was tidied up, she entered her studio and began making selections of sheet music for her students. She sat down at the piano and played a few of the songs she was considering. Ed arrived and came in to say hello.

"Erin, you look nice today. I like that piece you were playing."

"Thank you," she said. "It's for one of my students. I think it'll be challenging but not too hard."

He nodded and looked at her quizzically. "You must have had a good night's sleep—or something. You've got a new man in your life, don't you? Is he in town?"

Erin laughed. "I do, but he's not in town now."

The morning passed quickly, and at twelve-thirty Aleesha called to remind her to come to the gallery. Erin pulled on her jacket and started to walk the five blocks to the house Aleesha had converted into her gallery.

A red Lexus pulled alongside her as she walked, and the passenger called out, "Hello there!"

Erin turned. It was the man who had been with Michael Woodward at the bookstore. Michael was driving. She stopped. "Hi. Are you on your way to the gallery?"

"Yeah. How about if we park and walk with you?" he said.

"Sure. It isn't far."

Michael angled his car into a spot, and the two men got out.

"It's nice to see you again." In his jeans and black T-shirt, Michael looked more casual than he had at the bookstore. "I don't think you've met my brother. This is Bruce. Bruce, this is Erin Holley."

"My pleasure," Bruce said as he reached out his hand to hers. She could see the family resemblance. He wasn't as tall and had lighter hair, but he had the same broad cheekbones. He looked as if he smiled often, and he grinned broadly as he looked her up and down.

She laughed. "I'm happy to meet you. Did you move to Anacortes, too?"

"Hardly. I live in Portland—just came up here to see what Michael had gotten himself into. I'll be going back home Wednesday. What about you? Have you always lived here?"

"No, I grew up in Seattle. My grandparents lived here though. When they died, they left me their house, and I've lived here for the last ten years with my son and daughter."

Bruce threw a questioning glance at Michael, who returned the look with raised eyebrows.

"And your husband?" Michael asked.

She pushed her hair back from her shoulders. It had been a long time since she had said the words. She spoke softly. "My husband died two years ago."

"I'm sorry." Michael frowned and looked away.

"Well, I don't have any children," Bruce said. "They must keep you awfully busy. How old are they?"

"Twelve and seven." She looked at Michael. "How about you? Any children?"

Bruce answered for him. "No, his son drowned in a boating accident five years ago."

Erin gasped. "I'm so sorry." She blinked away the tears that filled her eyes.

Michael smiled at her. "Thanks."

They walked the last few steps up to the gallery entrance and went inside. It was well lit, and Aleesha had spread a buffet table full of delectables. Several of her best clients had been invited to enjoy her hospitality and meet Michael, and a few guests were already there, looking around at the art and snacking on finger food. Aleesha came to meet them at the door. Her dark hair was smoothed behind her ears, held in place by a small red carnation.

"Come in. I'm so glad you could make it," she said, reaching out her hand to Michael.

"Thanks for inviting me. I brought my brother, who's visiting for a few days. I hope you don't mind. This is Bruce—Bruce this is Aleesha."

Bruce stepped forward and reached for Aleesha's hand with both of his. He clasped it and said, "I saw you at the bookstore and hoped I'd have a chance to meet you. When Michael told me about your invitation today, I knew I had to come."

Aleesha caught her breath and stood very still. He held tight to her hand, and she said, "My pleasure."

Michael rested his hand on Bruce's shoulder. "Let's see if Aleesha will show us around."

She pulled her hand away. "I'd love to. Please, come over here. I have several pieces by this artist—he's one of my favorites." She led them away from the door, then turned back and said to Erin, "You look divine. I love your dress. Will you come with us?"

"Not yet. I'm going to grab a bite first."

Erin headed to the buffet table where she helped herself to a couple of tea sandwiches and celery. Past her regular lunchtime, she felt a bit lightheaded. As she munched the celery, she looked around to see if Hannah had arrived, but she wasn't there. Some music store customers were there, though, so she walked over to a group admiring several fine antique Native American baskets. Aleesha had already told her a lot about their history, so she passed on her information to the group.

As they began to move to another display, someone grabbed her elbow. She turned and was surprised to see Michael.

"Are you an expert in Indian basketry? You made it sound not just interesting, but exciting."

She gave a short laugh. "Thank you. But I'm no expert. Aleesha likes to keep her friends informed." She glanced around the room for Aleesha and saw her in a far corner talking with Bruce.

"Have you had any lunch? The buffet is excellent," she said.

"No, not yet." They walked together to the table.

Michael helped himself to some of the food and asked her to show him her favorite pieces in the gallery. Erin led him to a painting of a raven she and Hannah had studied a few days before.

"I love this one. It's by Daniel Frank, a Native American artist here in the Northwest. Aleesha has several more paintings he's done, but I like this one best. Raven—he's a trickster, but he's the one who put the sun, moon, and stars in the sky."

Michael nodded and studied the painting. "The power of the raven really comes through in this painting. Raven medicine is like shining a light into another person's head and heart."

"You know the myths," she said.

"A few."

Erin was surprised. She looked back at the painting and studied the eyes of the raven, which seemed to look back at her. A fine mist of sweat broke out on her forehead, and she wiped it away.

"Would you like to see more of his work? Aleesha has the rest of his paintings in this room," she said.

She led him through a nearby doorway into a smaller room. It was filled with paintings, sculptures, and more basketry. Another couple left the room as they entered.

"What are your favorites in here?" Michael asked.

Erin showed him a smooth, nearly white stone sculpture of an owl. She reached out and caressed it, letting her palm and fingers linger on its surface. "It feels wonderful. The stone is so smooth and cold."

Michael slid his hand over its entire surface.

"It feels as beautiful as it looks," he said. "Do you know any Native American owl stories?"

Erin laughed. "Only a few." She was surprised at how easy it was to talk with him. "But come here. You should see these two paintings—the sun and the moon."

They studied the paintings for a few minutes in silence until Erin said, "The inscription you wrote to me in your book—what did you mean? I don't understand."

He studied her face, hesitating, and reached out and smoothed a strand of her hair that had fallen out of place. His touch tingled against her cheek. He stood very close. She noticed he had a fine scar above his left brow. His face looked chiseled and hard as the stone of the owl. "You're a viator," he said.

Just then Hannah peeked into the room. "There you are. I was hoping you were still here. I was finally able to get away from the bakery. Have you seen Aleesha? I can't find her anywhere."

"No, I don't know where she's gone," Erin said. She looked at her watch. "Oh, no, I've got to go. I'm due back at the store in three minutes." She turned to Michael and said, "I'm sorry. I'm sure Hannah will be happy to show you around more."

"Of course, I'd love to," Hannah said.

Erin clasped his hand and squeezed it tight for a moment.

"Thank you, Erin. I hope to see you again soon," Michael said.

"Me too." Her lavender dress swirled around her legs as she turned and almost ran out of the room.

***

Michael followed her to the door and watched as she rushed down the sidewalk toward the music store. He felt an urge to follow her, but instead he turned to Hannah. "I think Aleesha is showing my brother around. Perhaps we should find them."

They found Bruce and Aleesha sitting on a bench in the garden behind the gallery. Aleesha was laughing at something Bruce had just said. Bruce grinned at his brother, and Michael frowned at him, shaking his head slightly.

"Aleesha, some of your guests are wondering where you went," Hannah said.

She stood up and looked at her watch. "Goodness. The time completely got away from me. I'm so sorry, dear." She rushed past Hannah into the gallery.

"What are you trying to do?" Michael asked Bruce as soon as Aleesha was gone. Hannah stood in the doorway.

Bruce's smile grew. "She's charming." He looked over at Hannah with laughing eyes. "Wouldn't you agree?"

"Absolutely," she said.

Michael gave Bruce a little shove on his shoulder and shook his head. They all walked back into the gallery, headed to the buffet table, and loaded some plates. As they munched stuffed mushrooms and crab cakes, they looked at the art around the room. Aleesha soon rejoined them, her red skirt swishing and her face beaming.

"Michael, I'm so sorry I've neglected you," she said. "Did Erin have to leave? Did she show you around?"

"Yes to both questions. She showed me some of her favorite pieces, and she entertained me so well that you have no reason to think I was neglected."

"I'm so glad."

Bruce put his empty plate down and slipped an arm around Aleesha's waist. "Why don't you show us some of your favorites now?" he asked, his mouth close to her ear.

Hannah's mouth dropped open as she looked first at Bruce, then at Aleesha. With a faint smile on his face, Michael watched Aleesha lead his brother away into the next room.

Chapter 20

Erin felt distracted the rest of the afternoon. She wished she had been able to stay at the gallery a little longer. What had Michael meant? He'd called her a viator, as if it were a title. She gave two piano lessons, and at five o'clock she was ready to leave when the phone rang. She picked it up, "Anacortes Music."

"Hi."

"Gary, are you back in Seattle?"

"Yeah. Got in this afternoon. It was an exhausting trip. Glad I'm back. I'd like to see you. Are you working all week?"

Erin shifted in her chair. "Yes, of course."

"Let's have dinner soon."

"Sure. But that's a long way to drive just for dinner. Are you sure you want to do that?"

Gary was silent a moment. "Yes, I'm sure."

She turned to face the window. "I'm busy Tuesday and Thursday, so would Wednesday work for you?" she asked.

"What are you doing Tuesday and Thursday?"

"Matt has a soccer game and Gwen has ballet," Erin said.

"Oh. Wednesday's fine. I'll drive up in the afternoon."

The wind stirred the blossoms in the cherry tree outside the window, and petals swirled to the street and sidewalk.

"Sounds good. I'll see you Wednesday, then. Where?"

"How about your place?"

"All right. I should be home from work by five-thirty."

"I'll be there. Goodbye."

Erin set the phone down. She was flattered and surprised that he wanted to come and see her right away. She gathered her purse and jacket and drove home. As she drove she stopped thinking about Gary, though, and instead she wondered about Michael and what he could have meant by calling her a viator.

***

The sky was growing dark when Erin put down the book she'd been reading to Gwen. They were cuddling together on the couch, and the only light was the nearby table lamp. Outside the sky was clear; a few stars were shining. The kitchen was clean and a load of laundry was in the dryer. Matt was in his room doing his homework.

"Time for bed," Erin said.

"One more story, please."

"Not tonight—it's late."

Gwen sighed. She slowly got up off the couch and started to walk up the stairs just as Matt came running down.

"Mom, I have to talk to you," he said.

"Sure."

Gwen came back down and lingered on the bottom step listening. Matt sat on the couch next to Erin and rubbed his head with his hands. Erin wondered what could be so serious.

"I don't know if you should see so much of Gary."

"What?" Erin was caught off guard.

Matt went on. "He's a lot of fun, and everything, but Jacob thinks he's too smooth, and I think so, too."

Erin reached out and grasped Matt's hand. "Don't worry. I'm not rushing into anything."

"What if he wants to move in here?"

"He's not going to move in."

"You never know. My friend Greg's mom started dating this guy after his dad left, and he moved in. He wouldn't let Greg do anything after that. And Greg's mom was always too busy to notice. Greg can't stand him."

"Do you like Gary?" Erin asked.

"Yeah, I like him all right."

"I like him," Gwen said. "He's so handsome."

"Didn't ask you," Matt snapped.

"All right, that's enough." Erin looked at Gwen. "You need to get ready for bed now."

"I know." She trudged up the stairs.

Matt stood up. "I'm serious, Mom."

"I know you are. Nobody's going to move in." She paused. "I miss your dad, too. I always will."

Matt nodded his head. "Yeah. I know."

Erin grabbed him and hugged him hard. "I love you."

He hugged her back, turned and went back up the stairs. "Night, Mom. Be careful."

"I will. Goodnight."

Erin turned out the lights, walked up the stairs and into her room. She lit one of the candles on the table beside William's picture. She sighed and sat on the floor, and she stayed there until the candle burned out.

Chapter 21

THE cold, wet gray of the fog grew denser, and Erin still hadn't found William. She didn't know if she had wandered off the path, or if the path had just disappeared into the thick forest. She stopped. There were no sounds at all. The fog muffled all the forest noises.

"William," she called. Her voice fell dead in the forest.

She sat on the ground, her head in her hands. What could she do? Maybe she should try to wait out the fog. She felt confused and lost.

"William!" she called again, and this time there was an answering call.

"Mom." It was Matthew.

"Where are you?"

"Here—don't move, I'll be right there."

The fog cleared a little, and Erin stood as Matthew came running to her. He seemed taller and looked older than his twelve years.

"Hey, Mom," he said. "There's a man over there who was calling for someone. I think he needs you."

"Do you know who he is?"

"No, but I think he needs help. Come on, I'll take you to him. The fog is sure bad, isn't it? I'm glad I found you."

They hiked through the forest, and after a while the fog began to blow away in wisps. Beams of sunlight shot through the trees, brightening leaves, and Erin could see they had struck a small path, maybe an animal trail. The underbrush was thick on both sides with ferns and huckleberry, and she heard the gurgle of water in the distance.

"He's just across the bridge," Matt said, pointing to a spot under the oak trees in the distance.

"Okay, Matt, I'll go see what he needs. Go on back home now."

"Okay." He turned around and jogged back the way they had come.

Erin followed the path in the direction Matthew had pointed until she came to a small stream. To reach the bridge she had to turn right and follow the trail for several feet along the top of a steep embankment. The bridge, two narrow boards laid across the chasm, led to another path in the shadows under the far trees. She looked across but didn't see anyone waiting, so she called out, "Is anyone there?"

"Over here," a man's husky voice answered from some distance away.

She sprinted across the bridge into the dark forest on the opposite side. The path continued into a deep gloom, and she saw the man running ahead, stumbling occasionally. He held one arm tight against his body; in his other hand he carried a sword. From the deep forest behind him, she watched as a shadow rose from the ground. She slowed and her whole body grew cold. The mortifer followed the man, and Erin leapt after it, pulling her sword from its sheath. In three steps the mortifer caught up with him and raised a knife to strike him from behind, but Erin reached the shadow first and ran her sword straight through its back. It shrieked and turned around, its gaze on her, but it fell to the ground and disappeared into mist.

The man glanced back but didn't stop. "Wait," she called.

The forest disappeared. The path, now a dirt road, ran through a field of wheat in the blazing sunshine, and she saw him stumbling up the road ahead, holding his body, running away from her up a hill topped with a tall stone tower. He reached the tower, opened the door, and slipped inside.

Erin called after him. "Wait. I'm coming." He didn't answer.

She ran faster, and when she reached the tower, she pulled the door open and followed him inside. She found herself in a dark, damp room just large enough for a circular stairway to hug the walls. The only light came from narrow windows high above, and the dirt floor was muddy around the edges. Erin heard the sound of footfalls above her, trudging up the stairs. She followed after him.

The granite steps were even but grooved from centuries of use, and the curve of the stairway was so tight it was impossible to see far ahead. She climbed as quickly as she dared. Narrow windows were placed too high in the walls to see out, but she knew she was getting close to the top when the sound of the footfalls above slowed to a shuffle and stopped. Erin crept up the last of the steps, hugging the outside wall. The light was a little brighter when she reached the top. She stood on a stone platform surrounded by the curved walls of the tower, a rough granite roof above. No one else was there. All was silent.

Driven into the stones of the wall in front of her, metal bars formed a ladder up the wall. The bars were dirty and damp—damp with blood. She looked up and saw a small wooden trapdoor.

She climbed the ladder, and when she reached the top, she gently pushed against the door. It wasn't locked. She slipped her knife out of her boot, took a deep breath, and pushed the trapdoor open.

Bright sunshine blinded her for a moment, but she climbed out of the passage onto the roof of the tower. A tall wall surrounded the edge, and through gaps in the wall she could see the farmland and countryside for miles in every direction. Lying on the floor in front of her was the man she had followed. Curled up shivering and sweating, he lay pressed against the wall.

She knelt down beside him. "Let me see."

He turned his face to her. His eyes were clouded with pain and his breathing was shallow. His shirt was soaked with blood, and he pulled it open and showed her the slice across his stomach. Blood pulsed from it.

She gasped. "Who did this to you?"

He grimaced. "I thought he was a friend."

Erin pulled her flask from her jacket and poured some of the golden liquid over the wound. He gasped and doubled forward in pain.

"I'm sorry, but you need more," she said.

He sat back panting, and nodded. "It burns."

Erin poured out more of the liquid, and it bubbled up from the wound. She ripped a strip of cloth from the bottom of her shirt and wrapped it around his waist, putting gentle pressure on his wound. The man sat back, leaning against the wall with his eyes closed. Sweat made tracks in the dust on his pale face; his breathing was quick and shallow.

She put her hand on his head and whispered to him, "You'll get better now."

He opened his eyes again. "At first I thought you were someone else. I'm glad you were near, Erin."

"You know me?"

His blue eyes sparkled, but he grimaced again with pain. "Of course."

"Who are you?"

"Don't you remember me? Don't you remember your waking life when you're here?"

She shook her head. "Not all the time—it's so vague. Do I know you?"

He tried to grin. "Yeah. We met not long ago."

She searched his face.

"What's your name?"

"Bruce."

She thought for a moment and her face brightened as she nodded her head. "Of course. Bruce. At Aleesha's gallery. Now just relax and sit still. You should feel better soon. Here, drink some of this." She handed him the flask, and he swallowed a mouthful. He gave it back, and his face regained some of its color.

"Who did this to you?" she asked again.

Bruce shook his head. "A man—I don't know his name."

"Why did he stab you?"

"I don't know. I had chased away the mortifers that were after him, and I was following them. He was running behind me. One of them was waiting in ambush behind some shrubbery, and it leapt on him as we ran past. I turned, slew the shadow, then the man shoved a knife in my gut." He shook his head. "I think he was planning it all along. A dreamer's treachery. After that I ran to this tower, hoping for safety."

Confused, Erin asked, "You're not the dreamer?"

Bruce looked at her, his eyebrows raised. "No. Is that what you thought—that I was a dreamer? Well, I'm glad you were nearby. You saved my life—I wouldn't have been able to fight off the mortifer you took care of, and I couldn't have healed quickly enough without your help. This wound would have been the end of me."

He stood up and slowly straightened to his full height. He was dressed similarly to Erin: dark pants, jacket and boots. He winced as he stood, but the gash had stopped bleeding. She stood also, and he rested both of his hands on her shoulders.

"Thank you. I need to go to Domus. Walk with care."

His image slowly faded until he was gone. Erin stood alone on the tower. Gradually the sunshine dimmed around her, and she felt the cool softness of her bed.

She jolted awake and sat up. *What a dream.* She remembered it as vividly as if she had really been there. The injured man, the tower, the sunshine on the fields, the bridge over the stream—all was fresh in her mind. She had been looking for William. And she had found Bruce. She lay back down and thought about the dream for a long time, then she rolled over and went back to sleep.

Chapter 22

As Erin drove home from work the next day, the purple and yellow wildflowers along the highway seemed brighter than ever. She kicked off her sandals and hummed as she drove, enjoying the warm sunshine on her face. Each of her students had done well that day, she had sold two guitars, and Ed had been in a great mood. And now she was going out to dinner with a fun, good-looking man who obviously liked her a lot.

She drove down the highway to the Deception Pass cutoff. After driving up the hill and around Lake Campbell, she turned down Gibraltar Road and saw Puget Sound sparkling below. When she turned into her driveway, Gary's black Porsche was already there.

He stood leaning against his car, watching her drive down the long driveway. His arms were crossed, and the wind blew through his blond hair.

She parked next to him, and he opened her car door for her.

"What took you so long?" he asked.

She slipped her sandals back on, stepped out of the car and laughed. "I'm early. It's just five-twenty now."

He stared at her for a minute with icy blue eyes.

She frowned. "You're not kidding, are you?"

He looked at his watch. "I thought you'd be here by five."

"No, I said five-thirty. I got off work at five. I'm sorry. Have you been standing here that long?"

"Yeah." He rubbed his forehead. "Let's go inside."

Erin unlocked the door, and they went into the cool, dark house. Gary walked into the living room, sat on the couch, and leaned forward with his head in his hands. Erin watched him for a minute.

"Is everything all right?" she asked.

He looked up at her. "Bad day. It's been a hell of a day."

She sat down next to him and put her arm around his shoulders. "I'm sorry."

He shook his head. "It'll work out. It always does." He looked into her face. "You look good."

"Thanks." She felt her face get warm.

"Where are the kids?"

"They're next door at Edna's. They go there after school every day, and today they're staying for dinner since I'll be with you."

He stood up and walked to the window. He gazed out at the water, and Erin joined him. The tide was out, and a long sand bar full of clam holes stretched out toward the sparkling water of the Sound.

"Is there any place you had in mind for dinner?" Erin asked.

"I made reservations for seven o'clock at Anthony's. We have an hour and a half until then." He slid his arm around her waist, pulled her close, and kissed her hair behind her ear. "What would you like to do?"

She closed her eyes. Gary pressed his mouth against hers and kissed her gently, long and slow. His hands pressed into her back pulling her tightly against him. A thrill raced up Erin's spine. He eased away and said, "The trip was brutal. I've got to get into another line of work." He pressed his lips against her hair. "It's good to see you."

Erin nodded, took him by the hand, and led him out the back door. The breeze felt cold even with the sunshine on her face, and the scent of lilacs lingered in the garden. She led him down the path, across the rocky beach to the sand bar, and took off her sandals.

"Take off your shoes," she said.

He hesitated but did as she asked. She bent down and rolled up his pant legs to his knees, then said, "Come on. When I've had a rough day this always helps."

She took his hand and ran with him over the beach. Their feet sank into the deep, soft sand as they ran, and the clams, disturbed by the pounding of their feet, squirted water out their holes as they dug themselves deeper. Water shot into the sky like a fountain, and Gary stopped just as a clam sent up a spray from directly beneath him. He jumped into the air; his pants were soaked.

"What the hell," he shouted. Erin turned around and laughed. She'd been squirted in the face. She grabbed his hand again and they ran on toward the water. Erin waded into the little waves, and water splashed up around her, soaking her to the waist. Gary stopped with his feet barely in the water. He laughed.

"You're crazy! You're getting soaked."

She laughed and kicked at the water, splashing him. "You're almost as wet as I am."

"I don't think so. You've got mud in your hair."

She felt her hair and pulled out the clump of mud. Then she sloshed back out of the cold water and grabbed Gary's hand again. "Playing on the beach always makes things feel better."

His smile dropped from his face. His face hardened, and he looked out beyond the waves to the south.

Erin looked at him with concern. "What is this about?"

He shrugged. "It's just been a difficult few days."

"Tell me about it?"

They walked back toward the house, weaving their way around the clam holes. They picked up their shoes and sat down on the rocky beach, leaning against a large driftwood log, their bare feet stretched out in front. Erin waited for him to answer.

He shrugged his shoulders and watched a seagull fly overhead. It dropped a clam on the rocks, swooped down and started pecking at it.

Erin tucked her knees up close to her body, wrapped her arms around her legs, and watched him. He took a deep breath.

"I went to New York to try to clear up a problem with some investors. It didn't go well." He watched her face intently and went on. "I'm sure the problems will be cleared up, but they're dragging on."

"What kind of problems?" Erin asked.

Gary shook his head. "You don't want to hear about this."

"Sure. You can talk to me about it."

He rubbed his hands over his face and sighed. "A whole shipment disappeared."

Erin's eyes opened wide. "Really? A shipment of what?"

Gary leaned his head back and looked at the sky. He laughed. "Oh, just some trade goods. But they'll deteriorate if we don't find them soon. Investors don't like that."

Erin turned to him and touched his arm. "Gary, this isn't something illegal, is it?"

He laughed. "No, baby. I'm not a drug dealer. I'm sure it'll turn up. I just hope it's soon. Henry—my partner—he's working on it." He leaned over and kissed her.

She broke away slowly and leaned back against the log. "It's been a long time since I've been kissed like this, you know."

"That's what I thought."

"Oh, you can tell?" She looked at Gary with a smile dancing in her eyes.

"I didn't mean it that way."

"Yeah, sure," she said. She stood up. "We've got to get cleaned up. It's already six-thirty. Let's go back inside."

Erin gave him a towel to wrap around himself while she tossed his pants into the dryer, then she went into her room to clean up and change clothes. She stood looking in the closet, trying to decide what to wear, but she couldn't stop thinking about him. She wasn't sure what it was about him, but her defenses dropped when he was around. She wanted to look her best for him tonight. Riffling through the clothes in her closet, she pulled out a shimmery blue dress with spaghetti straps that would show off the line of her throat and shoulders. She hadn't worn it in a long time—not since William had been alive. A sob rose in her throat and she put the dress back. Aleesha's voice came to her mind, "Don't overthink this, darling. Just have some fun and see where it goes. Spread your wings a little." She pulled the dress back out.

As she walked downstairs, Gary looked up from his seat on the couch.

"You're gorgeous," he said.

"Thanks," Erin said.

She brought Gary's pants back from the dryer, and he stood up and tossed the towel onto the couch. She turned away while he pulled his pants on and pretended to get something from the kitchen. When she returned, he was fully dressed, tying his shoes.

"Ready?" he asked.

"Sure. Let's go."

The evening was warm and fragrant. Gary opened the door of his car for her, and Erin slid in. He jumped into the driver's seat and they rumbled out of the driveway and headed to the restaurant.

Chapter 23

GARY drove the car smoothly over the winding roads into Anacortes, keeping his eyes focused ahead, appearing to be lost in thought. Erin could see how distracted he was. She looked out the window and watched the scenery fly by.

They walked into the restaurant and were seated at a window table with a view of the harbor. The hostess lit the candle on their table, and Gary ordered a bottle of wine. He watched Erin for a few minutes.

"I'm sure your shipment will turn up soon. Is there anything I can do?" she asked.

The corners of his mouth slowly turned up into a grin, and his dimples deepened as he shook his head. "Thanks, but I really can't think of anything."

The waitress brought their wine, poured two glasses, and took their dinner orders.

"Do you really run across the clam beds when you've had a rough day?" Gary asked.

"I've done that on occasion."

He kept his eyes fixed on her as he sipped his wine.

"What other kinds of things do you do when you've had a bad day?"

She thought a moment. "Mostly I play the piano. Or I throw rocks into the Sound."

He shook his head. "You are so different. I've been with a lot of women over the years, and you're not like any of them. You live in the middle of nowhere, in a little house that smells like cinnamon and flowers, and you give piano lessons. And you haven't pulled me into your bed, not even after I spent all day with you and your kids."

Erin gulped her wine and coughed. "Was I supposed to?"

He leaned his head back and laughed. "No, but I've kind of come to expect it."

"You're kidding. That's not how I am."

The waitress brought their food, and they sat back silently looking at each other until she left. Then Gary leaned forward.

"I know you're not like that. I was afraid you were going to be boring. You're not boring, but you're definitely different." He kept his eyes on her as he put a bite of steak into his mouth.

Erin picked up a roll from the basket on the table, tore it in half, and nibbled at it. "I don't want to have a casual sexual relationship."

"I know, I know. I don't either."

She smiled. "Good."

They ate a few more bites of dinner in silence.

"So, how long until it's not casual?" he asked.

"I don't know. I'd have to fall in love with you."

"And you aren't already?"

Erin smiled. "I like you. Are you in love with me?"

"I'm getting closer every minute."

Gary's light blue eyes were so bright Erin loved to look at them. They ate for a few more minutes in silence, Erin looking out the window at the water, the sky, and the seagulls, until Gary asked, "Did you say your grandparents left you your house?"

"Yes. They built it years ago, and when I was a child they decided that I would inherit it. My sister wasn't left out though. She inherited a large chunk of land on the Oregon coast."

"What about your parents?"

"They both died a long time ago. I was in college. First Dad had a heart attack and died, and then Mom died just a year later. That was a hard time." She shook her head and looked at her plate. "But I had William with me then, and he was very good throughout it all."

"I'm sorry. I didn't mean to bring up such painful memories."

"I know—it's all right. It was a difficult time, and I still think of them every day. But somehow I'm able to function as a fairly normal person in spite of everything." She grinned. "Running over the clam beds is a terrific way to cope, you know."

He gave her a quick smile. "And did William leave you well provided for?"

"Oh, he had a little life insurance. I'm saving it for the kids' college."

Gary's cell phone rang. He looked at the number. "I should take this call."

Erin watched his face as he answered his call. His eyes grew icy as he listened, and he glanced around the restaurant.

"I hear you. I'm in Anacortes now. I'll be back later tonight. Yeah, I'll be at the meeting," he said, then listened another minute, shaking his head. "What else did Kenneth tell them?" Gary's face became a frozen frown, his eyes squinting as he listened for a few more minutes. "Like I said, I'll be there tomorrow. Make sure Kenneth is there, too."

He disconnected and put the phone back into his pocket.

"Sorry."

"Kenneth from the art gallery? I didn't know he was involved with your business," she said.

Gary shook his head. "He's not. Only once in a while."

"I hope everything's all right."

"It'll be fine. Dessert?" he asked.

"No, thanks." Erin wiped her mouth with her napkin. "Coffee?"

Gary caught the waitress's attention and ordered them both Irish coffees. After they finished, he paid the bill and they sped back to Erin's house.

The sky was dark with the first stars shining overhead when they pulled into her driveway. She faced him. "Thanks for dinner. Do you want to come in?"

"I should get back—it's a long drive. Henry reminded me I have an early meeting tomorrow," he said.

"Okay."

He got out of the car and walked around to open her door. She stepped out and put her hand on his arm.

"Be careful," she said.

He wrapped his arms around her and pulled her close. He smelled like fresh laundry, and she wondered why she had told him to be careful. He seemed like he could take care of himself.

"I've gotta run," he whispered into her hair. "Next time I'll stay longer." He lifted her chin with his hand and kissed her again.

He let her go and walked around to the other side of the car, paused, and looked back. Then he climbed into his car and left.

She watched him drive down the road, then she turned and looked into the trees on either side of her driveway. The branches rustled in the wind, and a crow landed in a nearby tree, but other than that all was quiet.

Chapter 24

THE glow from a streetlight overhead shone on the wet street in the darkness. A constant drizzle created ghost shapes of mist against the tall, blackened buildings lining the roads. A few derelict cars were parked next to the sidewalks, but no life stirred on the streets: no one, nothing.

Erin stood pressed against a cold brick building in an alley, listening. The drizzle had soaked through her jacket, and her hair hung damp and limp around her shoulders. She thought she'd heard a sound a moment before. It might have been a bird, or it might have been a scream. She reached with her mind again to try to make contact with her dreamer, but she still felt nothing. A crow landed in the street outside her alley, turned its head in Erin's direction, and then flew off again. She brushed her hair from her face and followed it.

It landed on the wrought iron frame of a sign hanging above a narrow door in one of the dark brick buildings. The crow cawed, bobbed its head, and flew away. Erin crept close to the sign, difficult to read in the gloom. *Nocte Intempesta*. Dead of Night. Her mouth curled in a dry smile. She turned the doorknob and slipped inside.

A bit of flickering light from above cast a dim and shaky glow over the bleak entry. The concrete hall led to a narrow wooden staircase; the right side went up, and the left went down. Both ways were silent.

Erin pulled her sword from its sheath and ascended the stairs. Her boots made no noise, and her passing barely disturbed the dust on the floor. Light from the third floor shone down, but when Erin reached the second floor, she left the staircase and crept down the hall.

It was darker away from the stairs, so she moved slowly and listened. The wood floors of the hall were worn and scratched, and there were no pictures on the walls. She came to the first door and pressed her ear against it for a moment. Her heart pounded, and her forehead was damp with sweat. She turned the doorknob and slowly pushed the warped door open. Erin held her breath. All she saw inside the room was a threadbare rug covering the floor. She moved down the hall.

She looked behind the four doors that lined the hallway, and each room was empty. The final door at the end of the hall was different. Made of unfinished wood, it appeared new. Erin turned the knob and pushed hard, but it was locked. She wiped her forehead with her sleeve and listened with her ear pressed to the door but heard only silence. The ceiling above creaked, so she turned and hastened down the hall to the staircase.

The light was still flickering, and Erin stopped to listen again when she reached the stairs. She heard nothing and climbed to the third floor. Taking a deep breath at the top, she crept down the hall to the room where the light glowed. A thick yellow candle rested on the floor, burned nearly all the way down, but nothing else was there. Erin sighed. The floor squeaked nearby.

Holding her sword in front of her, she tiptoed so lightly she nearly floated to the next room. She grasped the doorknob, but the door flew open, and an icy, black shape knocked her over as it raced past. She hit the ground hard, and her shoulder hurt with burning cold from its touch. A man dressed in black raced after it, jumping over her as he ran. Erin was on her feet and after them in an instant. They careened down the stairs, two black figures moving like the wind, and ran down the hall on the floor below. The shadow touched the locked door and it opened. It pushed its way inside, but before the door closed, the man slipped inside as well. The door slammed shut. Erin skidded to a stop and turned the knob. Locked. She heard muted sounds of scuffling and blows from beyond the door, then silence.

Erin retraced her steps to the third floor and went back to the door. A tall woman stood in the doorway, leaning heavily against the wall, dressed in white. Her long black hair tumbled down and obscured most of her face, but Erin knew her at once. It was Franny.

Franny collapsed to the floor. Erin sheathed her sword and dropped to her knees, lifting Franny's head to her lap. She moaned and tried to push Erin away. "I don't know what you want."

"It's all right. It's Erin. Franny, it's me. Look at me."

Recognition lit up Franny's face. "What happened?" She looked around, her eyes wild and wide. "What happened to that monster?"

"It ran away. It's gone." Erin looked in the direction of the stairs and wondered what did happen to it? And what happened to that man?

"Think for a minute. Tell me what happened."

Franny began to cry. "No, I don't know. It was horrible. That thing was so cold, and it hates me. It said it could hurt me forever. It said it had Momma, and it was hurting her. It doesn't have Momma, does it? Did I let Momma go just to have that thing get her?"

Erin hugged her and said, "No, no. Your mother is safe. She is beyond its reach forever now—it can't touch her. It's full of lies. Don't believe what it tells you." Erin smoothed Franny's hair from her face. "Don't be afraid. You're stronger than they are."

"Me?"

"Yes, you are. If another tries to hurt you, tell it to be gone. Don't believe what it tells you."

Franny looked at Erin's face. She nodded and closed her eyes. Erin held her, cradling her head in her arms until Franny finally faded away from her dream.

Chapter 25

Erin helped a customer in the store as two more waited. Ed was late coming in, and she hoped he'd get there soon—she was supposed to give a piano lesson in thirty minutes. The store had been busy all morning, but Erin had been distracted, thinking about Gary's distressing phone call the night before and hoping his meeting had gone well. She wondered what Kenneth had to do with Gary's business.

After the last customer made her purchase and walked out the door, she heard her cell phone ring and ran to her studio to answer it. "Hello?"

"Hi, Erin. It's Aleesha. Come to lunch with me today."

Erin looked out the window. The morning was cool but clear with the promise of becoming a beautiful day.

"I'd love to, but I've got to give a lesson soon. And Ed hasn't even gotten here yet. It's been a busy morning. I don't think I can get away."

"Nonsense. You've got to eat. You'll work even harder if you don't have low blood sugar, darling. We'll keep it short. I'll meet you at Marina Cafe after your lesson—say at noon?"

Erin laughed. "All right. See you then."

She put her phone back, turned around and gasped. Michael Woodward was leaning against the doorframe watching her.

"Hi," he said.

He straightened and stepped into the room, looking even taller than usual in jeans and boots, his dark hair combed back from his face. His eyes seemed to see deep inside her, and Erin trembled, feeling the urge to back away from him, but instead she stood up and reached out her hand. "It's good to see you."

He clasped her hand. "You too. I couldn't help but overhear your conversation, so I know you're busy. If another time would be better, just let me know, and I can come back. I wanted to find some music."

"You've come to the right place. I'm never too busy to help someone find music. What are you looking for?"

"There's a piece by Schubert, I believe. Somewhat melancholy … thoughtful. I'm not sure which one it is. I was hoping you could help me find it?"

Erin looked at him with surprise. "I love Schubert. There are a lot of pieces that fit that description, though. For piano?"

"Yes."

"Do you play?"

"Sometimes, a little."

She pulled out sheet music from the pile of papers on her table. "This is one of my favorites—'Night and Dreams.'"

Erin opened the music and began to play. The melody was a mixture of joy and sorrow, and she couldn't help but be moved by the beauty of the piece. She played for three or four minutes.

"It's beautiful," Michael said. "It's just what I was looking for."

Erin smiled. "Wonderful. I can find you a new copy."

They went into the main part of the store, and Erin thumbed through the sheet music and found the piece he wanted. They continued looking through the music at the different selections.

"Did you enjoy Aleesha's little get-together the other day?" she asked.

"Yes, I did. Thanks for showing me around. I enjoyed you as much as the gallery."

Erin glanced at him to see if he was joking, but his face was as serious as ever.

"Bruce and I stayed and had a very entertaining afternoon. My brother—he and Aleesha seem to have really hit it off. I had a hard time prying him away at all."

Erin hadn't heard anything about this. She wondered what Aleesha thought and was glad they were having lunch together so soon. "Really?" was all she said. Then she remembered the strange dream she'd had about Bruce, and she looked up at Michael.

"How is Bruce?" she asked.

He spoke softly. "He's all right."

Erin felt a wave of relief and nodded her head. "Good. Has he gone back to Portland?"

"Yes, he left this morning." He leaned back against the counter.

Erin pulled out a few more music selections and glanced through them. "Do you think he wants to see Aleesha again?"

Michael grinned. "No doubt in my mind."

"Really? Aleesha never dates."

"She does now."

Erin opened her eyes wide. "Are you sure?"

"Yes, she's seeing my brother this Saturday. He can't stay away from her and is coming back for the weekend."

Erin's mouth dropped. "I can't wait to talk to her."

Michael laughed. His eyes beamed, and his face, which seemed so angular when he was serious, softened. Erin wondered how she could have felt afraid of him when she had first seen him this morning.

"Would you like to try these pieces by Schubert, too?" she asked, handing him two more pieces of music.

"Thank you." His face became serious again. "Thank you very much."

"Anytime."

They both stood there in silence.

"I'll let you get back to work then," Michael said.

"Thanks for coming in." Erin reached out her hand. He grasped it, and for a moment they stood still.

"It was nice to see you again." He turned around and left. Erin watched him walk out of the shop and then went back to her studio to prepare for her next student. After a few minutes, she stopped and looked out the window. What was it about Michael that was so compelling? She saw his eyes vividly in her mind. She shook her head, sighed, and turned back to the piano.

By lunchtime she had finished the lesson, and Ed had arrived. She grabbed her jacket and went to meet Aleesha.

"Here I am," Aleesha called out to her as she entered the cafe. She stood up and kissed Erin on the cheek, then hugged her. Aleesha was obviously feeling good.

Erin decided to jump right to it. "All right, I have to know what's going on with you and Michael Woodward's brother."

Aleesha didn't hesitate. "Darling, he is the most wonderful man. I'm crazy about him."

"I'm amazed," Erin said. "How did this happen?"

"I don't know. I realize I've said many times that I don't want a man to clutter up my life, so this must be very surprising. It is to me, too. But when Michael introduced me to Bruce, I felt like he had just given me Michelangelo's David. I've never been so drawn to anyone before. All I can think about is Bruce. I'm hopeless, Erin."

"Have you seen him since? Does he feel the same way about you?" Erin asked.

"Oh, yes, he does. We spent all day Sunday together, even though he was a bit under the weather. Monday he spent the day with me at the gallery, and we had dinner together that night. We were together Tuesday and all that evening, and then this morning he had to drive back to Portland. He's coming back Friday night."

"Oh, my gosh. It's really true."

"Very true. I had to tell you about it, but I've been so busy with him that I haven't had a chance until now."

"This is so sudden, it has me concerned. Be careful," Erin said.

Aleesha squeezed Erin's hand. "I knew you'd say that. You are always so careful yourself. All I can say is that this is unlike anything I've felt before, and I like it. I'm not worried at all. But I won't do anything stupid, dear."

"Good."

The waitress took their orders and brought them some iced tea.

"Michael Woodward came into the shop this morning," Erin said. "Have you seen much of him these past few days?"

"A little," Aleesha said. "We spent some time at his house and had dinner with him last night. He is a charming man."

Erin sipped her tea. "Hmm. Do you ever feel a little odd around him? As if he can see through your clothes?"

Aleesha laughed. "No. I never noticed that. He's always been extremely pleasant. Much quieter and more serious than his brother, but—maybe it's because he writes thrillers—I understand how he could seem a bit intimidating."

"I've never read any of his books. I don't think that's it. Sometimes it seems like he looks right into me."

Aleesha shook her head. "You always have been more intuitive than me. Maybe there is something strange about him. Or maybe you're feeling an attraction?"

"Oh, no, I don't think so. But tell me more about Bruce."

Aleesha told Erin about all the time she and Bruce had spent together, and how much she looked forward to seeing him again on the weekend. When Erin finally looked at her watch, she saw she needed to get back to work. As she walked back to the store, she realized she should have asked Aleesha about Kenneth and Gary and their business connection, but Aleesha's happy news had driven it from her mind.

Chapter 26

THE last dirty dish was washed, dried, and put away, and Erin sat down at the table with Gwen and Matthew. The sky was growing dark, and she put her head on the table and closed her eyes.

"How are doing with your math?" she asked Matt.

"I only have five more problems. But then I have to work on my science project."

"See my picture?" Gwen said.

Erin lifted her head. "It's beautiful." She picked up the picture to get a closer look. "I love the trees—and the cabin looks so cozy. Who lives in it?"

"No one. It's a vacation cabin. You have to go on a long trail through the woods to get there."

The phone rang, and Erin went into the kitchen to answer it.

"Hello?"

"Hi, Erin." It was Gary.

"How's everything with your friend?" Erin glanced at the children. Matt was showing pictures of stars from his science book to Gwen.

"Who?"

"Your partner, Henry?"

"Oh. He's all right. We'll get it taken care of." Gary paused. "Sorry I had to leave so early last night."

"Don't worry about it. I can't stay up late on weeknights anyway."

"Yeah, well. I'd like to see you again."

Erin paused and lowered her voice. "Are you sure you want to get more involved with a very unglamorous widow who has two children?"

"I wouldn't ask you if I didn't want to."

"All right," Erin said.

"How's Friday night?"

"Friday's fine. What time?" she asked.

"I'll be there around eight. I've got a five o'clock meeting and should be done by six—then I'll head up. Is there any place up there that has dancing?"

"Sure. A few places," Erin said. "It's been years since I've gone dancing." She thought back, trying to remember the last time she'd been dancing. Of course, it was with William—New Year's Eve five months before he had died.

"Then we'll have to do that," Gary said.

He asked her to hold on for a minute, and she heard muffled voices through the phone on Gary's end.

"I've got to go," he said. "I'll see you Friday."

"Okay."

***

The crickets quieted their chirping as Erin approached a small house on a narrow sidewalk edged with boxwood. The dim sky hovered between dusk and dark, and there was no light from the house. A strange prickly feeling came over her. She looked down at her clothes and was puzzled to see them changing from her usual black pants, shirt, and boots, to a short red dress and heels, and then back again. She stopped and felt her arms, making sure the fabric of her jacket was really there. She felt for her sword. It was there as well. *Where had that dress come from?*

She approached the front door, paused and listened. There were voices from inside, urgent but quiet, and she knew the dreamer was there. Without making a sound, she turned the doorknob and went in.

The house was empty—no furniture, bare wood floors. No one was there. Erin looked around at the white walls, holding her breath. Rooms opened to her right and left, and a hallway led to the back. Suddenly, a tremendous crash exploded from the rear of the house, and a man shouted.

Erin dashed down the hall and stopped at the door to the kitchen. The back wall had crumbled to the ground. Dust rose from piles of broken sheetrock and splintered lumber. An enormous man stood there, his fists bloody from the force of knocking over the wall; his breath came in gasps, and as he stood, he clenched and unclenched his fists as if impatient for more destruction. His eyes searched until they locked onto a corner of the room. Erin followed his gaze. Another man cowered on the floor with his hands covering his head, and he moaned. The huge man lunged at him, grabbed him by his throat, and lifted him into the air. The smaller man flailed his arms and legs as he tried to free himself but was flung across the room where he smacked into a wall and crumpled to the floor.

"Where are they?" growled the huge man.

The smaller man groaned.

"What did you do with them?"

"Nothing … I'll get them soon," moaned the small man.

Erin crept behind the giant, grabbed his arm and pulled him around to face her. He towered over her, but she had her sword drawn and at his throat before he could raise his fist. She pinned him against the wall. He stood still and stared at her; his eyes scrunched to narrow points, his mouth drawn down.

"You will leave now," she said.

He laughed. "What is this? You brought a woman to protect you?"

Erin stepped closer, pressing her blade against his throat until a drop of blood seeped from the giant's flesh. "Just a little more pressure, and your throat will split like a burst pipe. You won't take another breath again. Leave."

"All right, all right. I'm leaving. This isn't over, Arthur—you're a dead man, and I'll be the one to do it," he said to the man on the floor and spat on him.

The crumpled man raised his head, sneering with a silver glint in his eyes, "I'll get you first." He looked up. "Erin?"

Her mouth dropped open. "Gary?"

She saw that her clothes had changed back to the red dress and heels. Her sword was gone. The huge man grinned, swung his arm and struck her, sending her flying across the room. She gasped for breath and scrambled back to her feet, the taste of blood in her mouth, but not before he had grabbed Gary again and lifted him off the floor.

He punched Gary in the face, and Erin leapt forward and kicked him in the back, shoving him forward. He threw Gary down as he caught his balance and turned to face her. Again dressed in her usual black, she jumped in close and punched him five times fast to his throat, then kicked him hard in his chest. He staggered backwards, unable to breathe with his throat collapsed and the wind knocked out of his lungs. He fell with a crash that shook the house.

Erin ran to kneel beside Gary who was lying on his face without moving. She turned him over, and he opened his eyes.

"Where is he?" Gary mumbled.

"On the floor. He won't hurt you anymore. Let me help you up."

"What are you doing here?" Gary tried to sit up.

Erin helped him stand. "You're having a dream. I'm just part of your dream."

He looked at the giant on the floor. "What did you do to him?" His gaze scanned the room. "Where's the other man?"

"What other man?"

"He was here before. I don't know his name."

Erin frowned. "I don't know. I haven't seen him. Were you talking to him before this monster crashed in here?"

"Yeah. But how did you get here?"

She looked around the kitchen and through the doorway but didn't see anyone.

"I come when I'm called." Erin grabbed his arms so he would focus on her. "Now I want you to do something. Think of a place you've been that was wonderful—maybe in the Caribbean? A vacation? A beautiful place that you love."

"Fiji."

"Think of Fiji, Gary. The beaches, the sunshine, and how peaceful it was there."

The floor began to turn to sand, and the sound of waves was in the distance.

Gary glanced up and pointed to the doorway. "There he is." Erin looked up and could see a dark figure in the shadows. It turned and ran from the house.

"Think of Fiji," whispered Erin. She turned and followed the dark figure out the door.

Chapter 27

THE man slipped between the trees that bordered the house, the darkness almost obscuring him. Erin followed as silently and quickly as he had done. After striking a path, he ran, and his pace was fast and sure-footed. She could see he knew his way well.

The forest closed around Erin, and she became aware of the night noises: a stream bubbling close to the path, the wind rustling the leaves, the snap of a twig breaking in the distance. In the dark it was hard to keep up with him. Erin followed him through the forest, confident he was not aware of her presence. She was determined to find out who and what he was, and what his purpose was in entering Gary's dream.

His pace slowed, and Erin slowed as well. He had come to a cabin in the forest, small, overgrown and dark, nearly hidden by the shrubbery. No one else was there.

He pushed open the door and entered. Through the window Erin could see him light a candle, then light the fire that had been laid out in the hearth. He stood facing the fire as the flames caught and grew, and he removed his hat, then turned and faced her, placing the hat on a nearby wooden table.

She drew back from the window then cautiously looked in again. This was the first time Erin had seen him in any light. He was tall and lean with dark hair that fell over his forehead to his eyes. Rough stubble covered his cheeks and chin. His dark eyes were deep set. He seemed familiar, and Erin was sure she should know who he was. He took off his gloves and passed through a door to another room. Erin pushed the door open and slipped inside in silence, crouching behind an overstuffed leather chair. She pulled her knife from her boot.

He returned carrying a bottle and a goblet. He poured himself some of the dark red wine, took a long swallow, and set the goblet down, then began to unbutton his jacket. He tossed it onto the chair in front of Erin, then sat in the chair in front of the fire to remove his boots.

Erin leapt up, grabbed his hair from behind to pull his head back, and held her knife to his throat.

"Who are you?" she whispered, looking down into his upturned face.

He sat perfectly still, staring at her with dark, upturned eyes, inhaled a slow breath, and said, "Michael."

She gripped his hair tighter. "What are you?"

He frowned. "A man—a viator like you."

Erin squinted as she studied him. "What? You tried to keep me from fighting the shadows. You threw me against a wall in the cavern."

His eyes widened. "In the cavern? The mortifer in the corner—it was almost on you. I got you out of its way." His nostrils flared. "Remove your knife from my throat; I've seen the damage it can do. I won't harm you."

Erin's heart pounded. She hesitated and studied his face, then let go of his hair and dropped her knife to her side.

He jumped to his feet and grabbed her arms, his eyes flashing. "Why did you follow me? To kill me?"

Erin stepped back. "No. I wanted to find out who you are."

Michael let go of her, rubbed his throat, and grimaced. "Sit down. Put your knife away." He gestured to a chair.

He stepped into the other room again and was back in a moment with another goblet. He filled it and held it out to her with a stony face. "Have some wine."

She took the goblet and sipped. It warmed her thoroughly, coursing all the way to her fingers and toes. She set it down on a nearby table and slipped her knife back into her boot. After she seated herself in a wood chair close to the fire, Michael sat back down.

"How did you find me here?"

"I followed you. You're a viator? Where did you come from?"

"Did you think you were the only one?"

"I … don't know. I hadn't met any others."

Erin suddenly felt exhausted, and tears came to her eyes. She passed her hand over her face and shook her head. "How could I know you weren't evil? The first time I saw you, you were hurting a dreamer."

"What? When?" Michael paused. "Oh, yes. He … was going to do something dangerous. I was trying to convince him it wasn't wise."

Erin stared at him and shook her head. "You're a viator … like me?"

He nodded. "Bruce told me you don't remember much about your dreams." He paused. "Do you remember Bruce? You helped him when he was wounded? You saved his life." He glanced at her and shook his head. "Interesting that you were ready to take mine."

She sipped her wine. "I remember him. But you have frightened me several times."

"Look at me. Don't you recognize me?"

She studied him as he sat nearby holding his goblet. A gold ring on his left hand glittered in the firelight. He stretched out his long legs and drank his wine. His fine features were intense as he turned his eyes on her again, patiently waiting. She finally realized who he was.

"You're Michael Woodward."

He nodded, his mouth curved in a small smile.

She shook her head. "How can that be? I've never seen any other viators before you and Bruce. And now that I have, how can they be people I know?" She frowned and brought the goblet to her lips.

Michael rubbed his forehead. "You're disappointed?"

"No. I just meant I'm surprised. It seems like too great a coincidence."

He gave her a sidelong glance and drained his goblet.

She spoke softly. "You do this in your dreams too? I've been alone since I started, and I always wished there were others. I thought I was the only one who fought the mortifers. How long have you done this? Are there more?"

He leaned his head back on the chair and looked at the ceiling. "I don't know how many of us there are, but there are many. I've been a viator for more than twenty years, as have Bruce and my sister. Our youngest brother was a viator as well. I've met others many times, at Domus or in someone's dream. They always knew what I was, and I knew them. When I first saw you in a dream, right away I knew you were a viator, and I assumed you knew who I was as well. Who was your teacher?"

Erin sipped her wine and pushed the hair back from her face. "I don't know." She thought back, trying to remember. "It's all a fog. There was someone who gave me my sword and my knife." She patted her boot. "He taught me to fight. But I don't remember him very well. When I saw you, I thought you were another bête noir, smarter and more dangerous than mortifers. I was afraid. I am sorry. I hope I didn't hurt you."

"I'll recover, I'm sure," Michael said. He rubbed his throat again. "If I had known you'd never met another viator, I would have been more careful. I wonder why you don't remember more." He paused and looked at her. "But don't underestimate our enemies. They are smart and dangerous enough."

Erin grimaced as she thought about the threats the shadows had made.

Michael continued, "As long as there have been people dreaming, there have been viators. We don't meet each other very often during the day, so I also was surprised when I discovered that you, the pretty young woman who threw her coffee on me, was fighting shadows in people's dreams."

She felt her face grow warm. "I can't believe I did that."

"You're out to torment me, aren't you?"

"No, I'm really not."

He laughed. "You don't remember these dreams after waking, do you?"

Erin shook her head. "Do you?"

"Every minute."

She felt herself grow dizzy and set her goblet down on a table. "I'm fading. I've been gone a long time. Where are we now, anyway?"

"This is my cabin. It was my safe place until you showed up."

"What is Domus? Bruce mentioned Domus, too."

"I'll take you there sometime."

Erin stood up and faded from Michael's cabin.

Chapter 28

MICHAEL shut down his laptop and reached his arms forward, stretching the muscles of his back and shoulders. He bent his head down and rolled it around a couple of times, flipped off the lamp, and walked into the darkness downstairs. The sun was setting, and he'd been writing all day. He turned on the kitchen light and pulled out a bottle of cabernet and poured a full glass. The taste reminded him of Erin in his cabin, and he raised his glass in a silent toast to her. His new book was progressing well, and he had no doubt his new surroundings in general, and Erin in particular, were contributing a great deal to his story, which promised to be faster and darker than any yet.

He hadn't eaten anything since breakfast, so he dug through the refrigerator and found some leftover spaghetti. He took his food out to the front porch.

The sun was down, and the sky was clear and red. He watched for the first stars and listened to the sounds of the birds, the nearby traffic, and the children playing down the road as he ate. His own son would be about the age of those boys by now. He watched them play ball in the street, trying to ignore the heavy sadness that threatened to wash over him. The boys soon went inside, and Michael took a drink of his wine. After he'd scraped the last of the Italian sausage and cheese off the plate, he felt much better. He sat back and put his feet up.

He gazed out toward Puget Sound. A ferry lumbered through the water, heading to the San Juan Islands and Victoria. He thought about his little excursion to Orcas Island and how Erin had bumped into him.

He was glad she finally knew who he was in their dreams, although he doubted she remembered anything about him in waking life. He hoped her memories would grow stronger over time and wondered why she didn't remember them now—could she be blocking the memories for some reason? He was shocked she had distrusted him so much, but he was more concerned that she had ended up in Gary Arthur's dream. Arthur and Erin had recognized each other. And it was obvious he didn't know she was a viator—every time he had looked at her she had lost her strength and even changed to day clothes. That was dangerous for Erin and could have had terrible consequences if Arthur hadn't lost his focus long enough to allow her to do her job. She had done one hell of a good job, too. He had really enjoyed seeing the look on that giant brute's face when Erin had gotten him in the throat.

A car turned onto his street, and Michael leaned forward to look—it was Bruce. He pulled into the driveway, and Michael could see his cheerful face even from a distance.

"I think the whole world is on their way to the San Juans for the weekend," Bruce said as he got out of the car.

"Traffic's always bad on Fridays. It's better to wait till Saturday to come up here," Michael said.

"I couldn't do that." Bruce pulled his suitcase from the trunk. "I want to see Aleesha tonight."

Michael laughed at him. "You've got it bad, don't you?"

Bruce walked up the steps to the porch. "Yeah, I admit it. I'm in love."

"You've been in love a hundred times."

They walked into the house, and Bruce put his suitcase down. His grin dropped from his face. "This is different. Aleesha's very different."

Michael looked at his brother for several seconds. "It's a good thing—I wouldn't want you to hurt her."

"Hurt her? When have I ever hurt anyone? I'm the one who always gets hurt."

"True. But I happen to know that she feels much the same about you. And she's not the type to fall in love every day. She's not the type to fall in love, period. So, be careful with her."

"You don't have to tell me that. I'd never do anything to hurt her."

"Good. Glass of wine?"

"Yeah."

Bruce poured a glass and asked, "How's the book coming?"

Michael raised his eyebrows. "Halfway there."

"I think this place agrees with you." Bruce took a large swallow of his wine. "I know it agrees with me. How about the dreams? Have you run across Erin again?"

"I have. We had our formal introductions just the other night. She tried to slit my throat."

"What? How did that happen?" Bruce sat down.

"She didn't know what I was. In fact, she thought I was evil."

"Hah. I'm not surprised. You scare me sometimes too."

Michael scowled. "Yeah. Erin was afraid of me. But she followed me all along the trail through the forest to my cabin, and I didn't even know she was there. I don't know how she was able to do that—that's my cabin. You can't even get to it unless I let you."

Bruce shook his head. "No, I can't even find the trail."

"Hmm." Michael thought a moment. "She's talented."

Bruce walked to the window and glanced back at him. "You're interested in her."

Michael shook his head. "You're mistaken. I'm only interested in what she does as a viator—it affects us all."

Bruce studied him for a moment, and then he carried his glass into the kitchen. "It's been fun, but I've got a lady to visit tonight."

They both went out the front door, and Bruce got into his car and drove away. Michael sat on his porch in the darkness, an ache in his stomach as he remembered how Erin had pulled a knife on him. She had been afraid of him, thinking he might be evil. If she had felt that way in her dreams, how did she feel about him during the day?

Chapter 29

Gwen rummaged through Erin's closet and pulled out a red sundress. She held it up to herself and looked in the full-length mirror on the closet door, swirling to the right and to the left.

"Wear this one," she said.

"You like this red dress, don't you?" Erin asked.

Gwen held the dress up against her mother. "Uh huh. Can I have it when you're done with it?"

"Maybe. Let me try it on and see if it still fits."

She slipped the dress over her head and studied her reflection in the mirror. It fit very well, and she was surprised at the stunning reflection looking back at her. It had been a long time since she had felt so attractive.

"Okay, I'll wear this dress tonight. It's a good dress for dancing, don't you think?"

"Oh, yes." Gwen twirled around, then plopped onto the floor where she sat cross-legged, looking up at her mother.

"You goofy girl." Erin tousled Gwen's hair.

The doorbell rang. Matt answered it while they walked down the stairs, and Edna came in.

"Hello, Matt," she said. "Are you ready for me to beat you at checkers tonight?" Gwen ran to her and gave her a hug. "Hi, Gwen. How's my favorite ballerina?"

Erin walked down the rest of the steps. "Thank you so much for coming over tonight."

"It's my pleasure. You go out and have a good time."

The doorbell rang again, and Matt swung the door open. Gary stood on the step holding a large bouquet of red roses. He scanned the group in the entry hall.

"Perfect timing—come in." Erin reached out and pulled him inside by his elbow.

"Lovely roses," said Edna.

He handed the flowers to Erin. "For you."

"Thank you, they're beautiful." She went into the kitchen to put the roses in a vase; everyone followed her.

"How's the arm?" Gary asked Matt.

Matt lifted up his cast. "It itches. But it's okay."

"And how are you, sweetheart?" he asked Gwen.

Gwen leaned against him. "I'm fine."

Erin finished with the flowers. "Should we get going?"

Gwen hugged her, and Matt said, "Don't stay out late."

"You two behave yourselves," Erin said. "Thanks again, Edna."

"Have a good time." Edna gave Erin a quick hug.

Gary opened the car door for her and then climbed in himself. He stopped the car at the end of the driveway.

"I like your dress," he said, facing her. "And you smell irresistible."

"Thank you. So do you."

"I hope so." Gary's smile stretched over his whole face and his dimples deepened. He reached his right hand out, caressed Erin's cheek, then slid his hand behind her head and pulled her closer. His lips brushed hers. He pulled back and looked at her face, then kissed her again, a deep, fiery kiss. She forgot everything else—all she knew was his mouth on hers, his desire thick in the air. She felt swept along by it. It felt good to be desired, to be beautiful, to be alive.

But then it hit her: his kiss was different, his lips were a stranger's lips. She pulled back from him. No one would ever be the same as William. He looked at her with half-closed eyes, his breathing hard.

"What is it?" he asked.

Erin sat back in her seat and looked out the window. How could she compare Gary with William? Of course they were different. She looked back at him and shook her head. "Nothing. That was nice."

"Nice isn't quite what I had in mind," Gary said as he put the car in gear and sped out of the driveway.

They drove to the Wharf, a newly remodeled trendy restaurant on the waterfront. The decor included rough-hewn gray timbers, ropes, fishing nets and floats, and the seafood specialties were very good. Friday nights were busy, especially after the dancing started. As they pulled into the parking lot, they noticed the crowds of customers loitering outside. They walked inside to see many young men and women celebrating the end of the workweek.

Erin had never been part of the singles crowd since she had married and started a family when she was twenty-one. She wasn't any older than many of the patrons at the restaurant, though, and a few of the young men glanced at her as she stood waiting. Gary rested his hand lightly on her shoulder and pulled her closer to him. Their wait wasn't long, and soon the hostess led them to a booth.

The dim light from the candle cast a flickering shadow on the wall behind Gary as they sat at their table. He ordered a bottle of Pinot Noir. Erin drank a sip and let herself relax into the soft cushions of the booth. Gary's eyes were dark as he watched her.

"When I was a child, we would come here for dinner with my grandparents," she said. "Of course, it's been remodeled since then—I'd never recognize the place. But they served great food back then."

He smiled slightly. "We never went out to dinner when I was a kid."

"Really? Where did you grow up?"

"L.A."

Erin's brow creased, and she dabbed her mouth with her napkin. "What was your childhood like?"

He stared at her for a minute. "Here's the short version: Mother worked hard, Dad left when I was three. I had two older brothers who got their kicks trying to see how much abuse one kid, me, could take. I got out of there as soon as I could."

Erin reached across the table for his hand. "I'm sorry."

"Don't be. I had the last laugh. I got out of there and never looked back. Graduated from UCLA, got a great job, and the rest is history. I can have anything I want. And it's been a long time since anyone beat up on me."

Erin shivered. "You've never been back?"

"Well, actually I have been back to see my mother. She's still alive, and she's in a retirement home now."

"She must be proud of you."

Gary shrugged. "Maybe. I suppose so."

They both sipped their wine, and the waitress brought them a basket of bread and took their orders. "At Aleesha's dinner party I heard that you go to the Caribbean often," Erin said.

He nodded, a smile on his face. "Yes, I do. It's the best place in the world for scuba diving. I've been to several islands."

"Which is your favorite?"

He thought for a moment. "I'd have to say Grand Cayman. I've had a lot of fun in Georgetown. I go there at least once a year on business."

"William spent a couple months in the Caribbean long ago. He liked Cozumel best. He learned to dive in Fiji, though. He spent two weeks there before going to the Caribbean," Erin said.

"Fiji. Yeah, Fiji's a lot of fun. I've only been there once, but it was for four weeks. The first week I got so sick—I think it was the food—but after that I felt like I'd gone to heaven. Incredible beaches and friendly people." Gary's eyes seemed to gaze onto a faraway scene. "I didn't know William had gone there. Why didn't you go with him?"

"I was in college. He had finished and took some time off. We weren't engaged yet, and I think he wanted to have a few months of complete and total freedom."

He nodded. "It seems like that's what I've been doing for years."

Gary poured them each another glass of wine, then reached out and took both of her hands in his. "You're a beautiful woman. William must have loved you very much."

Erin felt a sob rise in her throat, and she swallowed hard to keep it down.

He gazed at her for a minute in silence, then went on, "I hope he left you well provided for."

"We never considered that anything would happen to him or to me either," she said. "The kids and I need every cent of what I earn at the music store. I'm lucky I own my house outright."

He studied the table, his brow slightly furrowed. "Money problems make everything harder. I never thought …"

"You never thought what?"

He shook his head. "I just never thought about it before … that you might be left without enough money."

Erin twirled the wine around in her glass and took a sip. "We do all right. I take care of us just fine."

Gary tipped back his glass of wine and drained it. He set it down on the table, raised his eyebrows, and said, "I imagine you do."

Erin ran her forefinger around the rim of her glass. Gary's eyes were grim and cold, he flared his nostrils and let out a deep breath.

"What is it?" She leaned forward.

The waitress approached with a tray of food. "Here you go. The halibut with mango for you, ma'am, and the swordfish picata for you, sir." She set down their plates, and her gaze lingered on Gary for a few seconds before walking away. He kept his eyes on Erin.

Erin leaned back in the booth, waiting.

"There have been a few problems with the client Henry and I are dealing with," Gary said. "That lost shipment. It's taking a little longer to resolve the situation than I thought. You're right. It has been bothering me." He picked up his fork and took a bite of the swordfish. "But we've got other things in the works, too. There's a different investment that seems very promising. I should know more about it tomorrow."

Dancing had begun in the next room, and the whole place seemed to come alive. Everyone became more animated. People were talking louder, and Gary's mood seemed to brighten.

He refilled their glasses, emptying the bottle. His eyes had regained their usual twinkle, his dimples deepened. Erin felt the wine going to her head, and she knew her face must be a little flushed. She put her glass down.

"Would you like dessert tonight?" Gary asked.

"No, thanks—maybe some coffee."

When the waitress reappeared, Gary ordered two Irish coffees. Erin protested, but he said, "Irish coffee's a tradition with me."

She relented. The smooth, hot liquid was delicious. Gary became very talkative, and as they sipped their coffee, he told her about his travels through Eastern Europe and Russia. He'd also spent a lot of time in China, and she was entranced by his descriptions of Beijing. Her attention encouraged him to talk more, and he charmed her with his laughter and stories. He ordered them both brandy to sip after their coffees were finished and told her details about sailing through the Mediterranean. She was feeling very relaxed when Frank Sinatra's Summer Wind began to play.

"I love this song. Let's dance," she said.

Gary drained his glass and handed Erin hers. She tilted her head back and finished her brandy in one large swallow. They walked to the dance floor, and he held her close. Erin's head was light, and she had to hold onto him to keep from feeling dizzy as they danced.

"I'm not used to drinking this much," she whispered.

"Are you all right?" he asked, resting his mouth on her hair.

"I think so."

When the song ended, they went back to their table. Gary ordered her a black coffee, and she sipped a little of it, then laid her head on his shoulder and immediately fell asleep.

"Erin," Gary laughed. "Erin, are you all right?"

"Yeah, sure." She lifted her head and looked around. "I'm sorry."

"I think I'd better take you home."

She leaned heavily on his arm as they left the restaurant. He opened the car door and helped her in. She wrapped her arms around his neck.

"Thank you," she said.

"For what?"

"Everything."

"You're welcome."

He helped her into the car, and they drove through the empty streets and along the quiet highway to her house. A few clouds streamed across the starry sky. The moon hadn't risen yet, and the world seemed hushed, almost as if it were moving in slow motion. Erin wondered what time it was—it couldn't be too late—and she hoped Edna wouldn't notice what kind of condition she was in. Gary pulled into the driveway and slowly drove up to the house. Erin rested her head on the seatback with her eyes closed and listened to the crunch of the tires on the gravel. She opened the door when they stopped, and Gary rushed around to offer her some support. He took her key and unlocked the front door.

Edna stood up to greet them. "You're home earlier than I expected."

Erin's face flushed with embarrassment. "I'm not much of a partier, I guess."

Gary turned to Edna. "Why don't I walk you back to your house?"

Erin thanked Edna and collapsed onto the couch fighting to keep her eyes open. She couldn't believe she'd let herself drink so much—so much that Gary had to bring her home early. She'd spoiled their plans for dancing.

Gary returned in a few minutes and sat down next to her. He picked up her hand and held it to his mouth, watching her. He leaned over and kissed her lightly on the cheek, then kissed all around her face, her cheeks, her forehead, her mouth. Erin leaned her head back with a little smile and closed her eyes. When he kissed her mouth, she kissed him back, and he reached his hand behind her neck and kissed her more deeply. He trailed his fingers to her shoulder and slipped the narrow strap of her dress off. Erin opened her eyes, her heart beating fast.

"Don't do that." Her head was spinning.

He bent down and kissed her shoulder, then traced his fingers along the top of her dress, right above her breasts. She felt her nipples harden, and heat pulsed through her body. Gary's breathing was ragged, his eyes dark, and his face intense. She sat up straight.

"No, wait," she said.

"What for? Now is a good time."

"I'm not ready for this. And the kids are upstairs."

He slipped the other strap down and slid his hand over her breast.

Erin pushed his hand away, pulled her dress back up, and whispered, "Gary, no."

He leaned away from her, studied her face, and reached his hand out to caress her cheek with his fingertips. She closed her eyes and sighed.

He kissed her mouth gently. He kissed her face again, her ear, her neck. She relaxed back onto the couch. His voice whispered, "Don't my kisses feel good, Erin? On your throat? On your shoulder?" He kissed her just under her ear. "Wouldn't you love to feel me kiss you everywhere?"

He kissed her throat and made a slow line of kisses along her collarbone. Erin's skin tingled, her heart pounded. She knew his kisses would feel very good all over. But even with her foggy thoughts, she knew she wasn't ready for this, and she didn't want her children to see her like this either.

He stood up and lifted her from the couch. Her eyes opened wide, and she grasped hold of him.

"What are you doing?"

"Shh," he said, and he carried her upstairs to her room. Her head reeled. He laid her on the bed and quietly closed the door.

Erin sat up. "Let's talk about this."

Gary gave a short laugh and pulled his shirt off over his head. His body was perfect—tanned skin pulled tight over his muscled frame, no little bulges of fat at his waist. He sat on the bed next to her, lifted her in his arms, and kissed her hard. He slipped his hands to the back of her dress and pulled the zipper down. Erin pushed him away.

He sat back and looked at her, his eyes, still dilated, were full of questioning amusement, his mouth a thin smile. He reached out and touched her face, tracing his fingers over her cheekbones, her forehead, her lips. She closed her eyes. His gentle touch felt so good. He kissed her lips lightly again and then grasped her hands and put them around his waist. His skin was warm—almost hot—and so smooth. She slid her hands over his back, and he kissed her mouth over and over. He pulled the straps off her shoulders again and slid her dress off. She tried to sit up, but he pressed her down onto the bed and kissed her again, holding her close. He tossed her dress onto the floor. She hardly felt like she could stop this and wasn't sure she really wanted to anymore. He seemed so urgent and alive.

"You're beautiful," he said.

"Gary, we shouldn't do this now," she whispered.

"Now is the best time." He kissed her breasts, sliding his tongue over and around her nipples. Erin gasped as the tingling went through her.

"Doesn't it feel good if I do this?" He lowered his head and made a trail of kisses down her stomach. He looped his fingers through her bikini panties and pulled them down and over her feet. She started to sit up again, and he pushed her back, holding her head down with a kiss. She relaxed back on the bed and shivered as his hands caressed the length of her body. He pushed her legs apart and lowered his head, kissing and tasting, and Erin twined her fingers in his hair and closed her eyes.

He unhooked his belt and pushed his pants down. She watched him with her half-open eyes but didn't try to stop him any longer. He threw his pants on the floor, pressed against her, and pushed himself inside. She felt him as if he burned inside her, and then she exploded with pleasure. It had been so long. She hadn't realized how much she had missed this.

When they were finished, Gary lay next to her, holding her close and tight, her head on his chest, the blankets twisted at the foot of the bed. Erin fell asleep in an instant.

Chapter 30

THE white sand glowed in the brilliant sunlight. The air itself seemed to shimmer. Erin had never seen so much light. Brightly dressed people and umbrellas dotted the long expanse of beach, all the way down to the shores of the wide, slowly flowing river. Across the water, Erin could see a misty city of pastel buildings that climbed from the far shore up the hill to the hazy horizon beyond.

Some boys wearing red and yellow shorts ran past her, tossing a ball and laughing. A young mother sat with her toddler, helping her fill a bright blue bucket with white sand. Most of the people sat in small groups, some in beach chairs, some on blankets, and a few lay alone on towels soaking up the warmth of the day. Sea grass grew beyond the sand, silvery green and swaying in a gentle breeze. Erin's black pants and jacket contrasted with the brightness around her like the dark shadow cast by a bird overhead. She knew she must look very out of place, but no one seemed to notice. She walked down the beach toward the river, smiling in the sunshine among the happy, laughing people. She sat down on the sand and took off her boots, then waded out into the water as she carried them. The water felt warmer than bathwater on her feet.

A woman called out, "Hey, you can't go into the water. Come back."

Erin looked at her and glanced around. She realized no one else was in the water. No one was even close to it. The woman stood watching her, and several other people turned to see what the commotion was about.

"Why?" Erin asked.

"It's not our time," the woman said, and she walked back up the beach toward her family. Her orange sundress flounced as she sat down on a blue and green striped blanket.

Erin waded back to the shore and sat cross-legged on the sand. She gazed across the wide river and felt a strong desire to go to that glowing city on the far shore. Its pull felt like a fish on a line. She had to find a way. A crow flew low over the water, coming from the opposite shore, and landed on the sand nearby. It took a few wobbly steps toward her and cawed, then it lifted its wings and flew high overhead, back over the river until it faded from view.

If only I could fly like that crow. There must be a way for me to get across. After brushing the sand from her feet, Erin put her boots back on and stood up. A group of boys played nearby, trying to skip stones on the water, and she walked over to them. She picked up three well-worn, flat stones and threw one. It skipped four times before falling into the water. One of the boys stopped to watch. She tossed the second, and it skipped five times. The rest of the boys looked over at her, and she threw the third stone, which skipped six times before it dropped into the water far from the shore. She turned to face them.

"Do you know if there's a way to cross the river?" she asked.

"Why would you want to do that?" asked one lean, tanned boy in green shorts.

"I just need to go over there."

"People say if you go far up that way," said a short, dark-haired boy pointing upstream, "the banks of the river get closer together, and you can get across. But I don't know anyone who's ever done it."

"Thanks," Erin said. "I'll give it a try." She waved to them and started to walk up the beach.

The boys looked at each other and followed after her. "We want to see if you can do it," the boy in green said.

Erin welcomed their company, and they all marched up the beach through the crowds of sunning people, over the sand until it merged into the tall grass, leaving the other people behind. The banks of the river rose gradually, and they climbed the hill further and further, until they were high above the water.

Erin enjoyed listening to the boys as they joked with each other, but they grew quieter the further they went. The sun stayed high in the sky, brightening the air around them just as it had at the beach, as they walked on for what seemed like hours. Finally, Erin saw the far bank of the river grow closer, leaving a deep, narrow gorge where the river wound far below.

"I think we're almost there," she said.

"Look up ahead," the boy in green said. "It really does get narrow up here."

They drew near the edge, and Erin guessed the far bank must be only about ten feet from where she stood. It still looked like a long distance.

"Can you jump across that?" the blond boy asked.

"I'll just have to do it," Erin said. "Thanks for your help, guys."

She backed away from the cliff, paused, and then ran for it. At the edge she leapt, and seconds later she rolled across the grass on the other side. The boys cheered, and Erin stood up, brushed herself off, and bowed low to them. They waved and headed back down the long hill to the crowded beach and the rest of their friends.

Erin scrambled down the hill on the far side of the river toward the village, its attraction stronger than ever.

Soon she came to the outskirts of the town. A cobblestone street wound down the hill, and a few small houses and outbuildings rested among flower and vegetable gardens. White sheep grazed in a pasture in the distance. Crumbling stone fences divided the pastureland, and she saw cows in a field further away. She passed an apple orchard, and branches of the trees overhung the road, the fruit giving a delightful fresh scent. Gradually the houses nestled closer together and more roads branched off, leading to more houses and several small shops. Soon Erin walked through a town of small, gleaming buildings—pink, green, blue, and yellow—and gardens bursting with tall flowers. Some houses appeared hazy and were difficult to see clearly. Sometimes children played in front; at times men and women sat on their front porches or tended their gardens. They smiled or waved at her as she walked past, and a few greeted her, "*Viator, salve.*" She waved back and said, "*Salve!*"

The streets and bright houses all felt familiar, and she walked with confidence. Though she felt pulled in a certain direction, she didn't know what she would find when she got there.

As she turned the corner into a narrow lane, Erin felt she was nearing her destination. Seven houses lined each side of the street before it came to an end. The houses were pale blue, or pink, or yellow, and their gardens were all enclosed with short, white walls of stone overgrown with trailing vines and flowers. More flowers peeked over the fences, and the gates were painted bright white. The third house on the left was butter-yellow, the gate wide open. A small copper sign embedded in the wall read, "Domus Viator."

Erin entered the garden and walked up the path beside a pool of water. Inside the pool stood the statue of a young woman pouring water from a pitcher she held with both hands. As Erin walked past, the statue stood up straight and stepped off her stand. Startled, Erin stopped.

The statue spoke. "*Salve, Viator. Quid agis?*"

"*Bene,*" said Erin. The statue smiled at her and returned to her place on the stand where she stood motionless, and the water poured again from her pitcher. Erin stared at her for a moment, then walked up to the open door of the house and looked inside. The front room stretched out before her; it was filled with chairs, sofas, tables, bright paintings, and brilliant sunshine. Amid the furniture people were talking, laughing, eating, drinking, singing, and dancing. Erin heard a flute's melody from a distant room and violins from another. Vases overflowed with enormous blossoms, and their sweet fragrance filled Erin's senses. But what she noticed most were the people themselves: men and women of all ages, sizes, shapes, and races, dressed in many different fashions. Many were dressed as she was—dark pants, shirts, and boots.

As she stood in the doorway, a tall man dressed in dark brown and green approached with a wide grin spread across his face. "Erin, I'm so glad you found your way. I was just telling my brother here … oh, where did he go? That we should find you and bring you here."

Erin stared at him. "Bruce?" she asked.

He laughed, "Yes, it's me. You had a hard time recognizing me? No matter—it takes practice in this place. I must thank you again for saving my life. I am in your debt." He put one arm around her shoulders and gave her a friendly squeeze.

"Are you completely better?" she asked.

"This visit will have me as good as new."

"Don't let him fool you—he's too worn out to ever be as good as new."

Erin turned to see Michael. He looked as he always did, dressed in his black clothes with his dark hair combed away from his face, his arms folded across his chest.

"Look who's talking," Bruce said. "He's got years more wear and tear than me."

"Hah," Michael said. He smiled at Erin. "I'm glad you found Domus."

"Michael told me you two have worked together?" Bruce asked.

Erin nodded. "Yes, in a way."

Michael laughed. "Yes, we've fought together." He rubbed his throat. "Erin carries a sharp blade."

Bruce laughed. "Oh, yes. She thought you were evil. Doesn't surprise me one bit." He turned to Erin. "So, where did you get him? He hasn't shown me any new scars."

Erin blushed. "I … I didn't really hurt him …"

"She skillfully kept her knife from actually slicing through my throat," Michael said.

"He wasn't so kind to me. One of the first times I saw him he threw me against the wall of a cavern—almost knocked me senseless. I think I still have a lump on the back of my head," Erin said.

Concern showed in Michael's eyes, and he frowned. "I'm sorry. I didn't mean to throw you so hard."

"My two favorites." A very tall young woman walked up to them, and her long white gown seemed to float over the ground. Her dark hair was piled on top of her head, held in place by silver cords and gems that glittered like stars. She reached out and grasped Michael's and Bruce's hands in her own, leaned forward, and brushed a kiss across each of their mouths.

"*Salve*, Salina," Michael said.

Bruce draped one arm around Salina's shoulders. "It's good to see you."

She caressed Bruce's cheek with the palm of her hand. Then she looked at Erin. "What is this, this little one dressed as a viator?"

"My name is Erin." She almost took a step back, away from the penetrating gaze of the woman's silver-blue eyes.

Salina laughed, her voice almost musical. "Are you a viator?"

"Erin is a worthy viator, Salina. She's the one who helped me," Bruce said.

Salina opened her eyes wide and looked at Erin more closely. She tucked her hand into the bend of Bruce's arm and pressed herself against him. "What would we have done if we had lost Bruce? But tell me, little girl, how did you manage to help him? How were you there at just the right time?"

"What do you mean?" Erin asked.

Michael laid a hand on Erin's shoulder. "Erin has fought with me, too, and I was happy for her help. I am sure of her motives. Come, Salina, she has only been here once before, and she may not remember that visit. We want her to be willing to come back again."

Salina leaned toward Michael and kissed him. "You are so charming, dearest Michael. Come, Erin." Salina took Erin's hand. "Let me show you around Domus. There are people here whom you must meet."

Without looking back at Bruce or Michael, Erin followed Salina, who kept hold of her hand and led her to a table laid out with refreshments. She picked up a silver pitcher and poured golden wine from it into two tall, delicate crystal glasses. Picking up both, she handed one to Erin and raised hers. "*Virtute et veritas.*" "Courage and truth."

"*Ita vero,*" said Erin as she raised her glass to Salina's, then drank a sip. The wine tasted like fresh pears, crisp and light. She immediately felt its effects, becoming more alert, more aware, as well as more relaxed. It truly did seem to give her courage and the ease to express the truth. She took another sip while Salina watched her over the edge of her own glass, smiling as if to herself.

"So, little viator, you are truly the one who saved my dear Bruce?" Salina asked. "Tell me about it. Were you there when he was attacked and wounded?"

Erin shook her head. "No. I was far away from him, looking for someone else. My son told me Bruce needed me, so I went after him but found a mortifer stalking him, ready to attack. I destroyed it before it reached him. But Bruce had already been injured, and I followed him to a tower, where he stopped and I was able to help him."

"Who stabbed him?" Salina asked.

"I didn't see. That happened before I got there."

"What did Bruce tell you? Did he tell you who it was?"

"He said it was a friend—a dreamer. He said it was a dreamer's treachery." Erin frowned. "I am shocked. I don't understand how such a thing could happen."

Salina paused a moment, regarding Erin. "After the loss of our beloved Sean, nothing surprises me. But come, let me introduce you to a few of the others here today."

She looked around, her blue eyes bright and intent in her fair face. A dark curl had come loose from its silver cord, and she casually brushed it out of her eyes and tucked it back into place.

"And you, are you a viator?" Erin asked.

Salina looked at her, a slight smile curling her rosy lips. She said, "No, I'm not a viator. I have never been in the world as you are."

"You've never … what?"

"Ah, *veni hic*," Salina said. She had spotted someone in the crowd.

She led Erin toward a group of people standing around a fire blazing in an enormous fireplace. A dark-skinned, herculean man was speaking enthusiastically, swinging his muscular arms over his head as they all laughed. They were dressed similarly to Erin, with long, dark pants, jackets, boots, and some with hats in their hands. They all held full mugs.

Salina stood at the edge of the group. "I rejoice to see you again, Ariston," she said.

The large man turned to her and bowed low. "Salina! Your beauty and grace overwhelm me."

Nearly as tall as Ariston, Salina rested her hands on his shoulders and kissed his mouth. "My dearest," she said. She turned to the others seated there. "*Salve*, Eric. *Quid agis*? *Et tu*, Camille? Are you well after that surprise attack? Frank, it is good to see you here again. *Quid agis*, Elsie; is your daughter well?" Salina kissed each of them, and they all greeted her in return.

"Have any of you met Erin yet? She has not been here before—or maybe once?" She turned to Erin with a questioning glance. "Erin, here is a handful of our finest: Camille has helped hundreds of dreamers over the years, and Frank has spent every night of the past seven years doing our work. Elsie was injured recently, but is now healed and fighting again, and Eric has fought steadily for more than twelve years."

"And what will you say about me, my lady?" Ariston asked, grinning broadly, his arms folded across his massive chest.

"What can I say about Lord Ariston that he hasn't already said more eloquently himself?" laughed Salina, caressing his arm. She kissed him again slowly this time. When she broke away, she turned to Erin. "This is Lord Ariston."

Erin bowed slightly. "I am very pleased to meet all of you. I have been fighting for only two years now, and until recently I didn't know there were any others. This is a real pleasure."

Salina smiled. "Erin saved Bruce's life when he was knifed. She has fought alongside Michael as well."

They murmured to each other, and Elsie said, "I am glad you were nearby to help him, Erin. It is a pleasure to have you here."

"Yes, it is always good to meet another viator. There are too few of us these days," Eric said. "You are most welcome here."

Salina, who had been whispering into Ariston's ear, now began to move away. "Erin, enjoy your visit. *Vale*, my friends." She glided away, shimmering as the sunshine fell on her.

Ariston pulled up a chair and sat down. He looked Erin up and down and said, "And what brought you here, little one?"

"I ... I don't know for sure. I was on the beach across the river, and knew I needed to come here."

"No, I mean the first time. Who brought you here the first time?" asked Ariston again.

"The first time?" Erin paused. "I don't remember the first time."

"Hmm. You don't remember anything?"

The others exchanged glances.

"Who brought her here?" Eric asked.

"When did you say you started fighting?" Elsie added.

"It has been about two years now."

"It is strange that you don't remember your call," Elsie said.

"I do remember speaking with someone, but it was very dark, the night my husband William was killed. I ... wandered far across a river trying to find him and bring him back to me. I wasn't fast enough, though." It all came back to her as if it had just happened. Sorrow washed over her, and she bowed her head.

"We all remember who first called us and brought us here," Ariston said. His face was angry, his voice harsh. "Since Sean, one of our own, was betrayed, we've seen others ambushed, and we know it was through deception. But who?"

Erin stared at him with horror. The group was silent as they watched her.

"And you think I may not be who I say I am … that I may be responsible?" She shook her head. "No, no, I fight those creatures. I destroy them. That first night—the night my husband died—I remember this: I was attacked by a mortifer, fought him, and made my way back across the river, where a young man came to me. He was dressed in brown. I think his name was..." She paused, looking up as she concentrated, and then she closed her eyes. "He said his name was Conn."

They stared at her.

Camille whispered, "Conn. It was Conn."

The others nodded.

"There you are, Erin. I wondered what Salina had done with you." Michael strode up to the group. He turned around in front of the fireplace, leaned his back against the mantel and spread his arms out across its width. He was as tall as Ariston. He frowned as he eyed them, and finally he looked at Erin.

"Have our friends been entertaining you?" Before she had a chance to answer, he went on, "They are naturally cautious. As you have seen, sometimes when we trust, it comes back to bite us. But come with me. More time has passed than you realize, and I can show you an easier way home than the one by which you came."

"I am very glad to have met all of you," Erin said as she looked at each and paused to hold Ariston's eyes with her own.

He touched his lips with his fingers and bowed slightly. "May the light go with you, little one."

Michael led her through the room, filled with people now, and greeted those he passed with a smile or a quick hello. Some wore long robes similar to Salina's, and possessed the same translucent beauty, but most were dressed plainly, in simple pants, jackets, and boots; some of the women wore long skirts, many with knives or swords fastened to their belts. Erin noticed Bruce and Salina sitting on a small couch somewhat apart from everyone else. Salina sat next to him, their heads were close together, and they spoke quietly. Then she kissed his face as she unbuttoned his shirt. Erin saw a huge red gash on his stomach, and Salina spread her hands across it. Erin turned away to catch up with Michael, and they continued weaving their way through the crowd.

When they reached the front door, Erin turned around to look once more at the people in this strange room. Sunshine poured through the windows, and in the distance a tenor's voice rang out in song. She wanted to stay.

Michael had stopped, waiting for her. She looked up at his face. "Must we go?"

His eyes softened. "Yes, you've been here a long time. You need to get back."

She nodded, and they turned to leave.

"Salina must keep very busy with so many viators to caress," she said.

"What?" He looked at Erin and knotted his brow. "Salina has her own work to do, and she does it well. Things are not always what they appear to be."

They walked down the street the way Erin had come, past the pastel houses and lovely gardens. The sky blazed red and purple as the sun set, and a slight breeze carried the fragrance of honeysuckle and stirred the leaves on the trees.

"What is she?" Erin asked.

"Who? Salina?"

"Yes, she told me she had never lived in my world—our world. Where does she come from?" Erin asked.

"Salina and the others like her live here between the branches of the great river. They help us with our work and help others in different ways as well. I've seen her heal a deep gash on a man's arm with a song. Her touch is even more potent."

"Michael, why did the others distrust me so?"

He slowed his pace. "We have all become wary, and you should be wary, too."

"Of treachery?"

"Yes. Here we are—we can take this boat across."

They had walked down to the river's edge where a small pier jutted from the shore into a little bay. No houses stood nearby, only a few trees in the grass and the rocky shore of the river. A boat was tied up to the wharf with oars resting in the bottom. Erin stepped into it while Michael untied the line and jumped in after her. He picked up the oars and started to row while she turned around and watched the shore fade into the twilight.

Michael's strokes took them out into the middle of the river, and all was calm. The first stars glittered in the dark sky above. He stopped rowing.

She couldn't see his face in the shadows, but she could tell he hadn't stopped to look at the stars; he was looking at her. Her heart beat faster. She looked back at him even though she couldn't see his eyes. He was black in the shadows and sat very still.

"You went to Gary Arthur in his dream. Do you know him?" Michael asked.

Erin was startled. "Gary? I know him in day life. Why? Do you know him?"

"I know him only in his dreams."

Erin's heart beat several times in the silence.

"What is it?" she asked.

"Will you remember this in the waking world?" he asked.

"Probably not. I try to remember these dreams, but they fade quickly. I get so frustrated."

"You don't know who you are."

She waited for him to explain, and he finally said, "You would be wise not to visit Gary in his dreams. He puts you at risk because he doesn't allow you to use your power. His beliefs prevent it."

Erin nodded. She didn't like it but knew it was true. "Why don't I remember these dreams?"

He began rowing again and shook his head. "I don't know. Maybe you want to forget."

She frowned. She barely remembered Conn. The memory was as faint as her memories of being a toddler. A pain stabbed through her chest—William died the night she had met Conn.

Michael stopped rowing. "Are you all right?"

She caught her breath. "Yes. I was trying to remember more, but it's painful."

"Just give it time." He resumed his slow, rhythmic rowing.

There was so much more Erin wanted to ask him, and she remembered something Salina had said.

"Salina and the others mentioned someone named Sean. What happened to him?"

He was silent for a moment, and she felt his eyes on her. "Sean was my youngest brother. A dreamer led him into an ambush. He was killed by mortifers."

"Killed? How? Surely not really killed." Erin's heart pounded harder, and her stomach felt queasy.

He whispered, "Yes. In life, he suffered a brain aneurysm and never awakened."

The night was suddenly icy cold, and Erin shivered. She bent her head to her hands and covered her face, crumpling with exhaustion. Michael pulled out a blanket and handed it to her, and she gratefully wrapped it around her. The rough warm wool helped calm her trembling. She wanted to try to stay awake, though. She had so many more questions, but she lay down on the bench and held the blanket close.

The sound of Michael's rowing soothed her, and her consciousness drifted with the rise and fall of the boat. Time didn't seem to matter any longer, so she was surprised when the hull of the boat finally scraped against rocks. Michael shipped the oars and reached over to touch her shoulder. She could barely open her eyes as he tucked the blanket more firmly around her and picked her up. Her head rested against his shoulder and neck, and she felt the roughness of his face. He smelled like pine trees in the evening, and it made her think of camping, warmth, and firelight. A sense of intimacy with this man rushed through her. She wrapped her arm around his neck and turned her lips to his warm skin. She pressed her face closer to him.

"Are we already there?" she whispered.

"What is it?" The voice sounded like Gary.

"What?" she asked and opened her eyes. Gary was lying next to her, leaning on his elbow, his eyes drowsy. The room was dim and the blankets had fallen onto the floor. He smiled at her. "You were talking in your sleep."

She still felt as if she were in her dream, still felt as if Michael were carrying her. She could almost feel his arms, his face, and smell his scent.

"I was dreaming," she said. She pulled the blankets over them.

Gary pulled her closer to him and buried his face in her hair. He relaxed and dozed off again, but Erin woke up completely. The dream had vanished. She was in bed with Gary. How had she let this happen?

She waited a few minutes until she was sure Gary was asleep, and then she eased herself out of his embrace, slipped into her robe, and tiptoed down the stairs. Without a sound she went out the kitchen door and ran barefoot to the beach.

Chapter 31

THE high tide lapped against the shore, and a cutting wind sent shivers through her body as Erin climbed onto a large driftwood log and sat down. The clouds hid any possible light from moon or star, but Erin welcomed the dark. Waves slapped against the log, splashing salty water into the air. She pulled her bare legs up close to her body and let the wind whip her robe around while her skin became a mass of goosebumps. She sighed and rested her head on her knees.

How foolish she'd been to drink so much. And then to be so swept away that she slept with Gary in the same bed she'd shared with William, and with her children sleeping in the next rooms. Her stomach ached. She looked out over the water at the dark swells bringing in the tide. How did she feel about Gary? He was intelligent and fun. She liked him, and she was sure he cared about her. That was a start. He had been wonderful during the fiasco of a day on Orcas Island. His attention and obvious attraction to her were as intoxicating as the wine she'd had with dinner. Her grief had left her parched, and he had come into her life like a rainstorm.

The sky grew lighter, the tide began to ebb, and Erin climbed off the log and stood still on the rocky beach. The cold wind had made her stiff and numb, and she felt chilled through to her bones. She picked up a handful of rocks and threw them one by one into the water.

Pieces of her dream flitted through her mind—she saw the pastel houses, the sunshine, the laughing people. She saw Michael's face and remembered his soft pine scent. She stood still on the beach, her heart pounding.

She turned around and looked up at her house. A light switched on upstairs in her bedroom. Gary must be awake. Erin ran back into the house and up the stairs, where she could hear him talking to someone. He was on his phone. She quietly opened her bedroom door.

Gary's face looked twisted with shock as he listened to the caller. He was sitting up on the bed, his feet on the floor, a sheet draped across his lap. He glanced at her.

"No, no, there's nothing you can do," he said into his phone and paused, listening. Erin sat beside him cross-legged on the bed. She could hear the voice on the other end of the line. It was a man's voice—shrill and loud.

"You think he knows who it was?" Gary asked.

Again Erin could hear the shrill voice, then both Gary and the voice were silent. Gary covered his face with his hand and combed his fingers back through his hair. He looked at the ceiling.

"Shit," he whispered. Then louder, "I'll head back now. Where is he?" A pause. "I'll be there as soon as I can. About an hour and a half." He disconnected and looked at Erin. The color was drained from his face, and his eyes were hard and cold. He looked away again.

"I've got to go. My partner Henry was shot. He's in the hospital. I've got to get down there."

"Oh, my God. He was shot?" Erin was horrified. She reached her hand out and rested it on his knee. "Of course. Go see Henry. Is there anything I can do? How about if I make you some coffee for the road?"

"Yeah," he said. "That'd be good." He stood up and pulled on his pants and shirt. Erin jumped off the bed and went downstairs to start the coffee. It was just about ready when Gary came down, fully dressed, hair combed and face washed. Erin filled a tall travel mug and handed it to him. He took a sip, put the mug on the counter, and pulled her close.

"I don't want to leave," he groaned. He crushed her close to him and kissed her hard, then picked up his coffee and rushed out the door.

Erin poured herself a cup and looked at the clock; it read five forty-five. She sat down at the dining table. Henry shot, one of Gary's close colleagues. How horrible. She wondered if Gary was in any danger. She'd never seen him so upset before; he'd looked outraged.

***

Michael opened his eyes to the darkness of his room and checked the clock on his nightstand—four-ten. He rolled onto his back and lay there staring upward with his hands behind his head, thinking about the dream. Someone must have awakened Erin to pull her away so abruptly. Maybe one of her kids. He hoped everything was all right.

He smiled thinking of their visit to Domus. Salina could certainly stir things up. But Erin had held her own. Ariston was even impressed in the end. The work had become so much more interesting since he'd discovered Erin there, and he found himself always watching for her to show up in whatever dream he entered. He hadn't wanted her to leave so abruptly from their dream tonight. When he'd picked her up, she had embraced him and pressed her lips to his neck, stirring feelings in him he hadn't felt in a long time.

He heard the soft voices of Bruce and Aleesha in his guest room. Apparently Bruce was awake now too. After his visit with Salina, Bruce should be feeling much better, and he'd be even more amorous with Aleesha. Besides being a wonderful healer, Salina also enhanced sexual desire. Michael rolled over, covered his head with a pillow, and drifted back to sleep.

Chapter 32

"MOMMY, can we have pancakes?" Gwen's voice stirred Erin to consciousness. She had fallen asleep with her head resting on the dining room table. She lifted her head, and her neck and shoulders ached.

"Sure." She looked at the clock. Half past seven.

"Can I help?"

"All right."

They woke Matt and ate pancakes together. Erin made another pot of coffee and joined her children on the couch for Saturday morning cartoons.

Her head still hurt, but watching cartoons with her children was a welcome distraction. After a while, though, her thoughts drifted back to Gary's friend. Finally, about ten o'clock she dragged herself off the couch, went upstairs, and called Aleesha. She might know something about Henry's background and why someone would want to shoot him, or maybe she could find out something from Kenneth.

"Hello?"

"Hi, Leesh, it's Erin. Are you going to be around today at all? Could I stop by?"

"I'm at Michael Woodward's house, dear, but we'd love to have you stop by," Aleesha said. "Is everything all right?"

Erin paused. "You're where?"

"Bruce is in town."

"Oh, of course. Everything's fine—I'd just like to talk with you." Erin brushed her hair away from her face. "Gary was over last night."

"That's great. I'm so glad you two are hitting it off together," Aleesha said.

"Do you know his friend Henry?"

"Umm, yes, I have met him once or twice."

"He was shot last night and is in the hospital," Erin whispered.

"What? Shot? Who shot him?"

"I don't know. I don't know any details. Gary got a call from someone, and he left right after to go see Henry. I haven't heard any more."

"That's horrible."

"Yes. What do you know about Henry? What's he like?" Erin asked.

"He's a lawyer. A decent-enough man, so far as I know—divorced, middle-aged, drinks too much. I really don't know a lot."

"Gary called him a business partner."

"Yes, they work together. I believe they make good money. Kenneth has done some work with them in the past. Darling, I've got to run now, but will you come to Michael's?"

"Are you sure I won't be in the way?" Erin asked.

"Of course not—we'd all love to see you and the kids. You and I can wander off by ourselves for a tête-à-tête."

"Where does he live?"

Aleesha gave her directions, and Erin was getting ready to step into the shower when the phone rang.

"Hello?"

"Hi."

"Gary, how's Henry?"

"He's okay. Right now he's asleep. They finished surgery, and he's pulling through."

"Thank God," Erin said.

"Yeah."

There was a little silence.

"I'd like to come see you tomorrow," Gary said.

"Oh. Yes, do come. I've promised the kids a picnic by Deception Pass. Come with us." Erin lay back on her bed and gazed out the window.

"What time?"

"Can you get here by noon or one?"

"Yeah. I'll be there."

She sat up. "Do they know who shot him?"

Another silence. "They've got some leads but nothing for sure."

"I'm sorry."

"Hold on a minute."

"Sure." Erin heard the muffled sound of a man's angry voice speaking to Gary. He snapped back, and there was more heated conversation, but Erin couldn't hear what was said.

Gary came back on the phone. "Sorry. I'd better go. I'll see you tomorrow."

"All right. See you then."

Erin stared at the floor for a few minutes wondering about Henry. She shuddered, then got up and looked out her window at the Sound. The sun was shining, but the wind blew the water into whitecaps. A small sailboat rushed past, heeled over so its gunnel nearly touched the water. Erin watched it sail past, then she got into the shower.

Matthew went to visit Jacob for the afternoon, leaving just Erin and Gwen to drive to Michael Woodward's house. Erin found it easily and parked on the street. Surprised by how small his house was—no larger than her own—she smiled at its welcoming appearance: the lawn was trimmed and the gardens well-tended. She felt a little uneasy about intruding into his home. She rang the doorbell.

Michael opened the door. "Erin. And this must be Gwen. Come in."

He held the door open wide, and they walked into a small entry hall with a slate floor and a suit of armor in the corner. A faint scent of pine trees lingered in the air, and Erin was struck by its familiarity. She took a deep breath.

"It's good to see you again," she said.

"You too." He stepped forward as if to embrace her, then stopped short.

Aleesha came from the living room and slid her arm around Gwen's shoulders. "I'm glad you could make it, sweetie, and thanks for bringing your mom."

Gwen took Aleesha's hand. They went into the living room, and Bruce came down the stairs.

"Good morning." He looked at Gwen. "I'm Bruce."

"I'm Gwen."

Erin gazed around the room. Her eyes widened as she studied the medieval weapons and gargoyles, and she reminded herself that Michael wrote horror stories and thrillers. A tall upright piano was in a corner of the living room with photos on top, many of a young boy. Aleesha sat down on the arm of Bruce's chair.

Erin smiled at Bruce and asked how he was feeling. His eyes sparkled with a smile. "Much better." He slipped his hand into Aleesha's, brought her hand to his lips and kissed it.

Michael sat down next to Gwen, and she scrunched closer to Erin on the couch. "We've got lunch just about ready," he said. "Would you like to join us?"

"Thanks," Erin said. "That would be nice."

Aleesha got up. "Would you two gentlemen finish fixing lunch while Erin and I go outside for a few minutes? Gwen, dear, how about if you set the table for us?"

"For lunch?" Gwen asked.

"Yes, for lunch."

"All right." Gwen sighed. "Show me the silverware."

Aleesha grabbed Erin's arm and took her outside onto the back patio.

As soon as the door closed Erin told her, "I heard from Gary right after I talked to you on the phone. Henry's had surgery, and he's going to make it. They have some leads on the person who shot him but nothing definite. That's all I know."

Aleesha led her down a gravel path through the garden, further into the backyard. "Was it a random shooting?"

"I really don't know—but somehow I don't think so."

Aleesha frowned. "That's frightening." She shook her head. "What do you think of Bruce?"

"How could anyone not like him? He's great."

Aleesha held Erin's eyes steadily with her own. "I want to marry him," she said.

"What?" Erin grabbed both of her friend's arms. "But this is so sudden."

"I know, but it's what I want."

"Don't rush. You haven't known him long, and there are so many differences between the two of you. I hate to point this out, but he is a lot younger than you. How do you feel about that?"

"I don't care. I'm happy with him—happier than I've ever been."

"Have you two talked about getting married?"

Aleesha sat down on a wrought-iron bench under a birch tree. "He asked me. I said yes."

Erin sat down next to her. "I'm stunned. You just met him."

"I feel like I've known him forever."

Erin stared at Aleesha's eager face, so full and open, and she hugged her. "I never thought you would want to marry, but I think you've found the right person. Bruce is a great guy. Where will you live, though? And have you talked about when?"

"We're not sure just when. We're going to look at our schedules and decide the details later. That goes for where we'll live, too. We'll take our time to decide."

They walked back to the house. The short time Erin had known Bruce had already convinced her of his worth, and she couldn't have been more thrilled for Aleesha. They went inside, and Bruce, slicing bread in the kitchen, looked at them expectantly. Aleesha kissed him, and Erin gave him a hug.

"I'm so happy for you both."

"Thanks. We're pretty happy ourselves," Bruce said.

"Is there anything I can do to help with lunch?" Erin asked.

Bruce put the bread into a basket. "No, thanks, Erin. I think we're about ready. Michael ran upstairs to change his shirt—he spilled his drink. But he'll be back in a minute."

"I'll just go use your bathroom. Is it this way?" Erin pointed down the hall.

Bruce nodded. "To the right."

Erin went down the hall and around the corner. She passed the laundry room and saw Michael standing inside with his back to the door. He had taken his shirt off and was reaching for a new one hanging from a rack. His body was lean, his muscles carved like a statue's, but when she saw him, Erin almost gasped. Down the entire length of his back Michael's flesh was crisscrossed with long red scars. Round shiny patches of purple skin showed the trauma of past burns. She rushed past the doorway and into the bathroom nearby, her heart pounding.

She took a few deep breaths as she washed her hands and closed her eyes as if that could erase what she had seen. What could have done that to him?

When she rejoined the others in the kitchen, Michael was washing strawberries, but he stopped and watched her as she came in. "So Aleesha's told you about her whirlwind romance with this scoundrel?" he asked.

"There's only one scoundrel in this family, and it's not me," Bruce laughed. He wrapped his arms around Aleesha, and she kissed him.

"I feel like an outcast," Michael said.

"Oh, sorry. We wouldn't want that." Aleesha gave Michael a hug and kissed his cheek. "You're both a couple of wily rascals."

Erin smiled at their playfulness, and when Michael glanced at her with his eyebrows raised, she laughed and brushed her lips across his cheek. The scent of pine and spice on his face brought back more memories of her dream: Michael picking her up from inside a boat and holding her tight. The feeling of his warm, rough neck against her lips. She sucked in a breath and stepped away from him.

Michael watched her, frowning. "What is it?"

Her head felt light. A sudden dizziness came over her and she swayed.

Aleesha stepped forward and put her arm around Erin's shoulders. "Are you all right?"

Erin shook her head. "It's nothing. Just a little dizzy spell. A dream suddenly came back to me." She looked up at Michael again. The memory was there, powerful and clear. In his eyes she saw recognition and a sense of anticipation. *Did he know somehow? How could that be?*

"You've had a difficult morning. Come sit down," Aleesha coaxed her.

"I'm better now, really."

Gwen stepped into the kitchen. "Is lunch almost ready?"

"Yes, we're ready. I hope everyone's hungry," Michael said.

The five of them sat down at the long dining table. A small fire burned in the hearth. Erin studied the swords and spears on the wall as she ate her salmon bisque and salad. She was quiet, overwhelmed with her thoughts about the shooting of Gary's friend, her own foolish lapse of judgment in sleeping with him, Michael's scarred body, and now, this vivid memory of a dream.

Aleesha was openly affectionate with Bruce while he was just as devoted to her. Michael tried talking with Gwen who was shy at first, but she opened up to him as he gave her extra strawberries for dessert and asked her about her friends and what activities she enjoyed. Erin ate in silence unless one of the others asked her a question.

When they finished lunch and Erin and Gwen were getting ready to leave, Michael pulled Erin into the hallway. He held onto her elbow and said, "Thank you for coming today."

"Thanks for lunch. It was delicious."

His eyes were intense as they searched her face. "The dream you remembered earlier, was I part of that dream?"

Erin blushed and lowered her voice. "Yes. There's a lot I don't remember, but you were part of it."

He let out his breath and smiled. "Don't you ever remember your dreams?"

"Not very often," she said. How much should she say? "Sometimes I'm awakened by nightmares, but I don't remember them. It's terrible. I lose a lot of sleep because of them."

He nodded slowly, still holding her arm. "I might know something of your nightmares."

"What do you mean? How?"

"It's a long story. I know you have to leave now, but we could get together sometime and talk about it."

Erin hesitated a moment. "Sure."

"Are you busy tomorrow?"

"Yes, actually I am. But what about lunch during the week?"

"All right. Monday?"

"Okay."

He stood looking at her for a moment in silence. Erin hesitated, then pulled her arm away and squeezed his hand.

"See you Monday then," she said.

Chapter 33

THE waves slapped softly against the side of the rowboat as Erin sat still on the seat. She scanned the shoreline. The fir trees lining the shore were black silhouettes against the clear twilight sky. It was a small lake; Erin was sure she could swim across it if she needed to. Stars began to glimmer, but no moon was out to give its light.

As she gazed around the lake, a low moan from the shore behind her spread until it encompassed the entire lakeside. It grew louder and echoed from the trees. She sat still, waiting.

There it was. A flash of light in the forest to her left, and Erin's oars hit the water. It took only minutes to reach the shore, and she leapt out, her bare feet splashing in the icy cold water. She tied the line around a nearby tree branch, and her eyes searched the darkened forest for the source of the flare. The moaning stopped, and she heard no sound except her own breathing and the gentle lapping of the water.

Another light blazed in the forest. She was close, and she crept carefully toward it, trying to keep from making any noise in the underbrush. The ground was soft and yielding, but she still wished for her boots. Immediately they were on her feet. Shrubs and trees grew crowded the further she went, and it was hard to see more than a few feet ahead. The air became musty, and the moaning began again, this time on the other side of the lake. It spread around the entire lake again, but Erin ignored it, intent on reaching the source of the flare.

Another flash of light, nearby and to her right. A very tall, black shadowy shape stood there holding a long staff, its back to her.

Where was the dreamer? The twilight sky helped Erin see a little under the darkness of the trees, but she couldn't see the dreamer anywhere.

She inched toward the mortifer, but it spun to face her and laughed—a hacking, low, wicked laugh. She drew her sword and leapt toward it.

It blocked her thrust with its staff and swung it around to hit her on the other side. She blocked that blow, sending the shadow back a few steps. She closed on it and struck again, but it leapt to the side, swinging its staff low and fast. Erin stopped it and pressed it back, further and further into the forest. She fended off every blow it struck, but it blocked every thrust of her sword, even as it retreated.

Several lights flashed around her, and Erin saw the trap. Five mortifers charged forward with staffs raised, ready to strike. She stopped and swung her sword high, shouting, "Leave! You have lost." They hesitated, and Erin felt their uncertainty.

She grasped her sword with both hands and swirled in a circle to send them tumbling backwards. They wavered as she crouched and leapt at the closest one, swinging her sword to slice across its face. Its cry filled the air, and its black shape melted into vapor that flowed across the ground and dissipated.

She whirled around to face the rest, but they turned and ran, heading deeper into the forest. She listened for a moment and called out, "Where are you?" She hoped the dreamer was nearby.

The only sound was the wind in the trees. She called again, "Where are you?"

Still no answer. Erin shivered. She sheathed her sword and ran, following the path the mortifers had taken. They had a head start on her, and she feared an ambush, but she had to find the dreamer. The trail grew darker, but her senses were alert, on guard for any sound or smell out of the ordinary. Tightness grew in her chest as she ran, her stomach tensed with fear as she remembered Bruce with the knife in his gut. He had been chasing a mortier, too.

A cry filled the forest, and Erin's skin rose in gooseflesh. She stopped and drew her sword again. The dreamer. She trembled as she stood, her heart pounding, but still she could see nothing but the darkness of the trees. She kept going along the path in the direction of the cry. The faint stench of decay grew as she headed deeper into the forest.

A sharp blow whacked her across her shoulders and sent her flying into the trees. Her sword flew from her grasp, but she was back on her feet in an instant. She pulled the knife from her boot just as another blow struck her across her back and threw her forward onto her face in the dirt. She rolled and jumped to her feet, but her knife was gone.

A low laugh rumbled nearby. Erin faced it and could see the mortifer there in the dark, its staff raised above its head, ready to strike her again. She ducked from its swing, rushed toward it, and grabbed the staff. Caught off-guard, it let go, and Erin slammed the staff across its head. The blow threw it down, and its blackness melted into the ground, but the stench grew.

Again she was hit from behind, and two more blows smacked her from the side and dropped her to her knees as more mortifers emerged from the forest. Icy trembling swept through her whole body, and her eyes stung with tears. She staggered to her feet and swung the staff at the mortifers on the path, when a blade from behind skewered her low in the back and pain like fire shot through her body. The searing agony overwhelmed her. She cried out and fell to her knees again just as another staff struck her. She heard it crack, and she collapsed forward face down on the ground. A crow cawed overhead.

She squeezed her eyes shut, coughed, and tasted blood and dirt. She heard more blows being struck and a loud wail, and when she opened her eyes she saw two men storming through the shadows, their savage swords cleaving through the mortifers. She tried to focus on the men, on their swords, on the light around them, but the agony in her back was more than she could bear, and she began to slip into oblivion. She turned her head to the side and was sick.

"We've got to get her out of here," shouted one of the men.

Erin squeezed her eyes shut and wiped her mouth.

"Cover me!" shouted the other.

He scooped her up off the ground, and she cried out from the wrenching pain. Her eyes shot open. He was running, holding her and running. She closed her eyes again and buried her face in his jacket, the scent of pine strong on his skin.

His running finally slowed to a walk, and Erin heard his footsteps pounding on wood. She struggled to open her eyes again and saw the lake. They were on a dock, and the man stepped into a boat moored there. He took her into the small hold in the bow and laid her down on the bunk. She focused on his face; it blurred and then cleared. It was Michael. Bruce stepped inside as well.

"How is she?" he asked.

Shaking his head, Michael answered, "Don't know yet."

"Erin, can you hear me?" he asked.

She whispered. "My back."

Michael turned her over and pulled up her jacket. He pulled her shirt away from her skin, and she cried out as blood pulsed from the wound.

Michael groaned. "We need some water."

Bruce turned and left the hold.

"I need to take care of your wounds. Hold on. Stay with me, Erin," Michael said.

She was afraid she was going to get sick again.

Bruce came back with a pan of water and some cloths.

"This is going to hurt," Michael said. He pulled off her jacket, and Erin gasped and shrank away.

"Wait. The dreamer? Where?" she asked. Shivering, she could hardly speak.

"We had already sent him back before they attacked you. It was a trap."

She closed her eyes.

"This is going to hurt. You're cut open, and your back is covered with black welts."

He washed the wound and pulled a flask from his jacket. He poured a little of the liquid over Erin's injury, and she cringed.

"We've got to go. They'll be after us," Bruce said.

"Let's go to my cabin. It'll be safe. We have to keep Erin with us for a while—we can't let her wake up like this. She needs more time," Michael said. "I need to bandage this first."

"Be quick."

"Stay with us, Erin." Michael wrapped a bandage around her and left the hold. She lay on her stomach on the bunk, barely hearing what they said.

Erin fought to stay conscious and listened to their footfalls as they worked the boat, the flapping of the sail as it was raised. The hull creaked as the wind caught the sail, and the boat lunged forward. She lay in the darkness trying to calm her breathing and control her pain. The sound of the water flowing past was soothing, and the boat sailed smoothly for what seemed like a long time before she heard Michael call out. The boat slowed and came to a stop.

Michael came into the hold as Erin struggled to sit up. With his help she was able to stand. She was shaking, her teeth chattering.

"Thank you for coming to me. I … I wouldn't have made it back," she said.

"I know," he said. The boat was tied to a small dock on a slow-moving river with sandy banks and a dark forest beyond. Michael helped her off the boat, then he and Bruce half-carried her along the path to Michael's cabin.

She looked up at him beside her. His face was filthy and sweaty, with blood splattered and smeared on his clothes, face and chin. She realized it was probably her blood. His gray eyes almost glowed in the darkness, and they looked hard and angry as they stared ahead.

Once inside they helped her lie down on the couch. The cabin looked just as she remembered from her first visit there, the time she had confronted Michael, thinking he was evil. It seemed like years ago. Michael lit the fire in the hearth and brought out three goblets and a jug of wine. He filled them and handed one to Bruce and one to her, then turned to face the fire with his back to them. He took a long drink. Erin sipped her wine. It went to her head immediately but helped ease some of the pain. Her body ached all over, and the wound on her back throbbed and burned.

Bruce sat down beside her and gently brushed some hair out of her face. "Any better?" He was dirty, too, splattered with mud and blood.

"I'm getting there," she said.

He drained his goblet and set it down on a table.

"I hope I don't look as bad as you two," she whispered.

Bruce let out a big laugh, and Michael turned around and stared at her, his eyes wide. "You look like hell," he said.

Bruce nodded, concern on his face. "You do, Erin. You're as white as death."

Michael frowned. "You were too close to looking like death permanently. What the hell happened out there, anyway? How did you end up trying to find that dreamer?" He paced to the window and back. "How did they all know you'd be there?"

Bruce stood staring down at Erin. She looked from one to the other, shaking her head. "I have no idea. I was just there. That's the way it always is. I'm just there, and I know what I'm looking for. The dreamer. But this time I couldn't find him." She felt faint and dizzy, the pain came in waves, and her words came slowly. "I started in a rowboat in the middle of the lake. When I saw a light on shore, I knew I needed to go that way." She drank again, and tears welled from her eyes. "I have no idea how they knew."

"Hey, it's all right. You'll be all right," Bruce said.

"I don't know how this could have happened," Michael said. "The darkness is too close. The mortifers know what we're doing, where we're going. Bruce, we've got to go to Domus about this."

"Right. How much night is left?"

"Probably not enough. We have to help Erin recover first. She can't go back with this wound still open." He sat beside her and brushed some of her hair from her face. "You don't look any better. Let me look at your back again."

Erin spread herself out face down on the floor. She couldn't stop shivering, even close to the fire. Michael took the bandage off.

"That's an evil wound. Your whole back is battered."

Michael pulled out his silver flask and poured more of its golden liquid over Erin's wound, filling the room with a faint aroma of peaches. Then he poured some onto his hands, rubbed them together, and smoothed them gently over Erin's back beneath her shirt. The aching of her bruises began to ease, she breathed a deep sigh, and her shaking began to subside. He continued to lightly caress her back. "This should help some."

"I'm going to Domus while I still have some time," Bruce said. "You can stay with her, Michael?" He rested his hand on Erin's head for a moment, then was gone.

Michael sat beside her on the floor and continued to slowly rub her back. His warm hands eased much of the pain. She let out another sigh and opened her eyes.

"How did you find me?" she whispered.

"I felt you there."

She nodded and closed her eyes again. "That feels wonderful."

He poured more of the golden liquid over her wound and smoothed his hands over her back again, and then rested his warm palms flat on her back for a few minutes in silence. Erin's breathing relaxed, and her back tingled where his hands touched her.

"Is it getting better?" he asked.

"Yes, so much." She opened her eyes and rolled over to look at him.

He pulled his hands away and nodded his head. "Are you cold?"

"Yes."

He picked up her jacket and helped ease her into it. As he fastened her buttons, she watched his face. His eyes were dark and serious, without the trace of a smile. She tried to stand but stumbled, so Michael helped her to her feet. He smoothed her hair back away from her face, and his hand continued through her hair to the back of her head. He pulled her to him and pressed her head against his chest. Erin closed her eyes and wrapped her arms around his waist. She could hear the pounding of his heart and felt his body fill her with warmth.

"You'll be going soon," he said.

"Not yet," she answered. "I don't want to go."

He kissed her lightly on her forehead. "Walk with care."

The cabin seemed to fade into the darkness, and Erin felt her pillow under her head. She was aware of her smooth, easy breathing and the comfort of the cool, soft cotton sheets. For a while as she lay there she felt both Michael's warm arms around her and her own blankets. She awakened gradually and finally opened her eyes. She remembered Michael, his warm electric touch, and his cabin. She searched her memory for more, but the rest of the dream faded away, vague and frightening, beyond her grasp.

Still dark out, Erin glanced at her clock, just three-thirty. Her body ached as she climbed out of bed. She shuffled into the bathroom, turned on the light and looked in the mirror. She had a faint bruise on her cheek. Pulling off her shirt, she looked at her body more closely. Remains of yellow bruises covered her torso, and on her lower back was a bright red wound about three inches long. A fresh, new scar. Fragments of the battle flashed into her mind, and all the hairs on her body rose as she trembled. Was she losing her mind? Where had that injury come from? Drops of sweat glistened on her forehead, and her breathing grew quick and shallow. *What was going on?* She stood still for a long time before shuffling back to lie on her bed.

Chapter 34

Erin woke to the sun's warmth on her face, and the sounds of Matt and Gwen eating breakfast downstairs floated up to her. She looked at her clock—already nine, so she rolled to get out of bed, groaning in pain. Her back ached. She went into the bathroom and looked at her face in the mirror, remembering her middle-of-the-night visit; it seemed like just another dream. She pulled on her robe and went downstairs.

"Morning," she said, and she started a pot of coffee. She sat down with the kids and ate some breakfast while they talked about the day they had planned.

"Jacob wants to come along. Is that all right?" Matt asked.

"That's fine," Erin said. "What about you, Gwen, do you want to bring a friend?"

"Yeah! Can I bring Julie?"

"Sure. We'll give her mom a call. Gary's coming today, too, so we'll all have friends with us," Erin said.

"What about that man from yesterday?" Gwen asked. "He was nice."

"He is a nice man. But Gary asked first," Erin said. "I thought you liked Gary."

"I do like him. He's so handsome," Gwen said.

"Do you want to walk across the bridge today, hike on the trail, or what? Should we backpack our lunch and spread a blanket out on the big knoll?"

"Yes!" both Gwen and Matt said together.

"We can do it all," Matt said.

"Okay. I'd better get things ready."

She climbed upstairs to her room, still feeling sore, and turned on the shower. When she glanced in the mirror, she was surprised to see several faint yellow bruises on her shoulders and arms. She stared at her reflection and slowly turned around as the skin on the back of her neck prickled. More bruises covered her back, and the scar was really there, nearly three inches long, glaring at her. She ran her hand over it.

"How?" she whispered. Michael's face flashed into her mind. Running through a black forest, the taste of dirt and blood. She held her breath and tried to remember more, but the memory slipped away. She shook her head and stepped into the shower.

***

"Let's get in the car, kids," Erin called. They piled into the back of her SUV, and Gary got into the front beside her.

"We're going to Deception Pass? Is it a cool place?" he asked the kids.

"You've never been there before?" Erin asked. She pulled out of the driveway and turned left onto the street.

"No. What's it like?"

"It's scary," Gwen said.

"No, it's not," said Matt. "There's a tall bridge that connects us to Whidbey Island. The pass is the water below—it's called Deception Pass because the explorers who discovered it thought they found the Northwest Passage, but it wasn't."

"Why is it scary, Gwen?" Gary asked.

"The bridge is so big. And the water swirls fast way down below. If you fell, you'd be dead," she said.

The highway wound its way through the dense forest of fir trees and climbed the hill that led to Deception Pass Bridge. Trees blocked most of the view of the water until they reached the top, where they had to slow to a crawl because of the many tourists walking on the side of the road. The bridge crossed to a small island, and from there, a longer section stretched across the pass to Whidbey Island, a narrow ribbon high in the air. It was crowded, so they drove across to a large parking area on the far Whidbey side. High above the Sound, cliffs on both sides of the long stretch of bridge plunged far down to meet the rushing, churning water. They parked, loaded up their backpacks with lunch, and took off. The plan was to walk across the bridge to the small island for a good look first, then return to the Whidbey side to hike the trail and find a good spot for their picnic.

Gwen and Julie were hesitant about walking out onto the high bridge, so Erin held their hands. Matt and Jacob ran on ahead to the middle and stood there looking down. When Erin, Gary, and the girls reached them, they all stopped and looked far below. The waters of the Sound swirled through the narrow channel of the pass—the current boiled, swift and dangerous. A small boat motored through, fighting the current to stay in the center.

As Erin gazed at the water below, a scene flashed into her mind of a bridge cracking beneath her feet and a young man's face full of fear. She gripped the handrail and looked around. Tourists wandered in the sunshine, and she peered at them, wondering if she would see that face again, and where it had come from to begin with. Was it from another dream?

"You okay, Mom?" Matt asked.

Erin realized her hands were white from gripping the railing so hard. She made an effort to relax.

"Yeah, I'm okay."

Gary looked at her. "Where's your house from here?"

She pointed out the direction.

"This is amazing. I had no idea something like this was here. It's so powerful—it's almost frightening," he said, putting his arm around her.

They continued walking to the far side of the bridge, then turned around and walked back across to the Whidbey Island side.

The trail was shady and cool under the fir trees. They strolled in silence, and Erin enjoyed the peaceful forest after the crowds on the bridge. A few other people wandered along the path, but most of the visitors stayed near the bridge or in the park on the other side. After they had walked about a mile, Matt, who had been leading the way, stopped and put his finger to his mouth. "Ssshh."

He pointed to the right. Five deer stood under the trees. They were munching leaves, and they turned their graceful necks to look. Two fawns, two does, and a buck. They took a few steps across the forest floor. More people approached on the trail, and the deer stood still as statues, then flicked their ears and leapt away. They were out of sight in seconds.

Matt took the lead again, and they walked on until they came to a high knoll where the sun shone on the green grass, and a few flowers bloomed along the edge of the forest. Erin could see Puget Sound far below and Hope and Camano Islands in the distance. The water glittered in the sunshine, and the islands were covered with the dark green of fir trees down to their rocky shores. Erin looked up at the sky and pointed out two bald eagles flying directly overhead.

"How's this spot for lunch?" Gwen asked.

"It looks good to me," Erin said. "What do you think, Gary?"

"It's perfect."

They dropped their packs, spread out the blankets, and Erin brought out the lunch containers. She had brought thermoses of iced tea and lemonade, plus fried chicken, potato salad, grapes, cheese with crackers, and chocolate chip cookies for dessert. They all sat down on the blankets and filled their plates.

When the kids finished their lunch, they wandered off to explore. Erin called out, "Don't go far. Stay in earshot."

Gary pulled off his shirt and lay back on the blanket in the sunshine while Erin put away the lunch things. Then she lay down on the blanket next to him.

"How's Henry?" she asked.

"Pretty well," Gary said. He put his hands behind his head and closed his eyes.

"Have they found out who did it?"

"No. Not yet."

"Any ideas?" Erin asked.

He opened his eyes and gazed at the sky for a minute, then leaned on his elbow to look at her. "I don't want to talk about Henry today. Let's just enjoy each other."

Erin nodded. "Sure."

Gary moved closer to her. He trailed his fingers lightly over her face and kissed her.

"You bring me to beautiful places."

"I'm glad you like it, but you've been all over the world. You've been to many more exotic places than this."

"Maybe more exotic. But when I'm with you … well, this is the closest to heaven I'll ever get." His smile was teasing.

Erin shook her head. "What do you mean?"

His grin widened. A crow landed in the tree above them, nodded its head and cawed several times.

Gary picked up a rock and threw it at the crow. "Annoying bird."

It cawed once more before flying off.

Erin frowned; she felt an urge to follow it and started to get up. Gary put his hand out and held her arm. "Don't go."

She lay back down and closed her eyes. Gary leaned back with his hands behind his head. "I never intended to fall for you so hard. I'm falling in love with you, Erin."

She sat up. "Oh, Gary. I enjoy being with you—I like you—I more than like you. But I'm not sure I can fall in love with anyone yet."

He frowned. "It's been two years—don't you think that's long enough?"

Erin gazed at the sky. She could see the crow flying away from them, and she sighed. "I know it seems like a long time." She was quiet for a few moments as William's face came to her mind. She turned her head away, pulled her knees up and wrapped her arms around her legs. The sun beat down on her head and back. She turned to face him again.

"I love being with you," she said.

"That's a good start."

He reached for her and pulled her close. His arms felt strong, his skin so smooth. She ran her hands over his muscled back, and then stopped and listened for a minute. She pulled away, stood up, and looked around for the children, but couldn't hear them, so she called out, "Matt! Gwen!"

"Over here, Mom, we're all here," Matt called from further down the trail. Satisfied, Erin sat back down on the blanket, picked a long piece of grass and put the end into her mouth. She lay back on the blanket and closed her eyes.

Gary leaned up on his elbow and traced his fingers lightly over her face. The tingling feeling of his touch made her smile.

"Someday I want you to marry me," he said, still running his finger around her face. "And I always get what I want."

Erin's eyes shot open, and she saw his amused smile. "Are you laughing at me?"

"No," he said. "Just relax. Enjoy my touch."

She closed her eyes. The warm sunshine made her feel dreamy, and his light caresses made her feel beautiful. She didn't know how she could ever say no to him.

The sun began to sink into the west behind the trees, and a cool wind blew from the south. The children wandered back to the picnic spot and were ready to head home, so they gathered their blankets and headed back down the trail, winding through the forest as the twilight deepened under the trees. Erin felt strangely subdued, and Gary was quiet as they hiked down to the car.

They emerged from the forest and crossed the highway to the still-crowded parking lot, and Erin saw that two men were standing beside her SUV. Gary noticed them too, and he slowed his pace and glanced around, scanning the area.

"Wait here," he said.

"Who are they?" she asked.

"What's going on?" Matt asked.

Gary's face was like stone. He ignored their questions, and they stopped while he walked toward the men. They were dark-haired, dressed in dark pants with shirts tucked in. One of them flicked a cigarette away and spat on the ground. They watched Gary as he walked with confidence toward them. A few other people in the parking lot eyed the men warily and hastened away.

"Who are they, Mommy?" Gwen asked.

"Shh. I don't know," Erin said. "Stay here." She slowly followed Gary and stopped a few feet away.

"So here you are, Arthur," one of the men said, a burly, whiskered man wearing a gold bracelet. Erin thought his accent must be from somewhere in Eastern Europe.

"Yeah. I'm not hard to find."

The men laughed. "Your woman isn't hard to find either," the burly man said as he looked at Erin.

She caught her breath—anger flared inside her, mixed with a trembling fear.

Gary's voice was as cold as his eyes. "What is that to me? There's no problem here." Erin could see how every muscle in his body was tensed.

The men laughed again. "Is that what you think?" the man said. "We have the ship. The cargo is …" he laughed a sneering laugh, "… worse for wear."

Gary stood still.

"So you see, we have a problem here," the man said. His eyes slid to Erin again, lingering on her.

"Did Grekov send you?" Gary said.

"He is angry."

"I know. But Grekov knows I always make good. And I make him a lot of money." Gary's voice grew louder. "And Grekov knows he needs to keep me happy."

The burly man stepped closer. Erin could see the tendons standing out on his neck; his face was turning purple as he shook with anger. "Fuck you. Grekov wants you to take care of this NOW."

Gary laughed. "Tell Grekov I feel his pain. Tell him if he's patient—IF HE'S PATIENT—he'll be remunerated for his trouble. But if he's not, well, remind Grekov that there are consequences if anything happens to Gary Arthur."

They both stood still, eye to eye, staring at each other. Erin felt the hair on the back of her neck rise. Gary didn't move a muscle, but the other man clenched and unclenched his fists. Finally, his companion broke the silence. "Fuck this. Let's get out of here."

Gary didn't move. The other man, his eyes still locked with Gary's, spat on the ground. Then he turned around and the two men walked to a black car parked nearby and climbed into it. The car started, and the men took off out of the parking lot, forcing several people to dash out of their way.

Only when they were out of sight did Gary turn around to face Erin and the children. His face was a frozen mask, his eyes hard and unreadable. Erin's heart was beating fast, but she called to the kids. "Go to the car."

Gary stood still, watching her.

"What was that about?" she asked.

He looked away and his nostrils flared as he breathed. He clenched his fists and shook his head, then looked back at her with blazing eyes. "I'll take care of it. It doesn't concern you—it's not important anyway."

"What do you mean it doesn't concern me? Those brutes came here to hurt you."

He laughed and shook his head. "No. They had no intention of hurting me. They wanted to scare me. They're bullies and don't know how to behave. I've seen their kind often enough."

Erin was shocked. He laughed again. "It's okay." He put his arm around her shoulder and started to walk to the car, but Erin stopped him. "What was that about? What was the cargo?"

"The cargo? It was from that shipment I told you about—the one that was missing. Mechanical equipment from the Ukraine." He put his finger under her chin, lifted her face to his and whispered, "It wasn't drugs. I don't have anything to do with drugs." He kissed her lightly and his dimples deepened with his smile.

Erin let out a sigh. "Gary, I'm frightened. What are you going to do?"

"I knew I was going to have to deal with Grekov as soon as I found out the shipment was late. I've got it figured out. Everything'll be fine—don't worry. Let's go back home."

Chapter 35

Erin felt exhausted and achy after the long day at Deception Pass. Gary left to drive home after a light supper at her house, and her emotions were frayed and raw. She felt a little better with Gary's reassurances, but the whole scene had been terrifying.

Her back hurt. After the kids were in bed she examined it in the mirror again. There were no longer any signs of bruises, but the red scar was still there. She tried to think of any time when she had cut her back but couldn't. Pieces of last night's dream floated through her mind, and strongest of all was the memory of Michael carrying her through the forest.

And then she remembered—she was supposed to have lunch with Michael the next day. She needed to call and find out where he wanted to meet. A glance at the clock showed nine-thirty, so she called Aleesha's cell phone to get his number.

"Hello, Erin. We were just talking about you," Aleesha said, laughing.

"Who?"

"I'm sitting here with Bruce and Michael. Bruce is packing up to go back to Portland tonight. He's got a class to teach in the morning."

"Oh, what does he teach?" Erin asked. She tucked the phone under her chin, sat on her bed, and took off her sandals.

"Latin and math at Portland U," Aleesha said. "Plus he coaches basketball."

"Really?" Erin laughed. "When I think of a Latin professor, I think of a stern old taskmaster armed with a cane and a pipe. Bruce sure doesn't fit that image!"

"No, definitely not."

"I called to see if you had Michael's phone number, but since he's right there, do you suppose I could have a word with him?"

"Certainly."

Erin set down her phone, pulled her shirt off, and slipped a blue camisole on. She picked up her phone and overheard some muffled talking and laughter on the other end of the line, then Michael came on.

"Hello, Erin. I hope you felt all right this morning?" he asked.

She caught her breath.

"Not terrible." She tucked the phone under her chin, unzipped her jeans, and slid them off over her feet.

"I'm glad to hear that," he said.

"What makes you ask me that?"

Michael was silent for a moment. "You told me about your bad dreams. I thought you might have had another one last night."

An image of Michael with his face splattered with blood flooded into her mind. "Oh … I did."

"Do you remember it?"

"Only a little." She didn't want him to know she'd dreamed of him.

"Is that why you called?" he asked.

"No," she exclaimed. "No. I just wanted to make sure you were still on for lunch tomorrow, and to find out where you want to meet."

She lay down on the bed, wincing a little from the pain.

"I'll pick you up at the store."

"You don't have to do that—I'd be happy to meet you somewhere."

"No, I'll pick you up."

Again there was silence on the line. Michael spoke quietly. "Is your back feeling better?"

This time it was Erin's turn to be quiet. "Yes." *How could he know?* Her scalp prickled; if he had some answers, she wanted to learn more without saying too much out of the ordinary herself. She walked to her window and looked out across the water.

Michael continued, "What do you think happened?"

What did he know? "What do you mean?"

He laughed. Erin felt a little dismayed at that. "Why don't we talk about it at lunch?" he asked.

"Sure," she said. She realized how exhausted she was. She threw herself down on top of her bed and laid her head on her pillow.

"Have a good night's sleep, then," Michael said.

"I hope so. It's been a long time, though," she said with her eyes closed and her left arm draped across her forehead.

"Do your dreams wake you in the night?" he asked. His voice soothed her tired mind.

"Yes, then I can't get back to sleep."

"It'll get better once you start remembering more."

Erin opened her eyes. "It will?"

"Sure. Say, Aleesha's about to leave so I'd better give her phone back. I'll see you tomorrow," he said.

Erin sat up straight. "Wait. What do you mean?"

"Just let yourself remember."

"I try."

"We'll talk. Walk with care—safe dreams," he said.

She sighed. "*Et tu.*"

Chapter 36

"COME on, kids, it's time to go," Erin called up the stairs.

Matt came running down, grabbed his backpack from the floor, and said, "Ready." He went out the front door and got into the car.

"Gwen!" Erin called.

"Here I come." Gwen's muffled voice came from above. Erin waited another ten seconds and then bounded up the stairs just as Gwen hustled out of her room, pulling her sweater on.

"It's about time." Erin ran down the stairs after Gwen. "Did you brush your teeth?"

"Yeah. I'm all done," Gwen said. She stopped. "Is that dress new?"

"Yes, it is new. Do you like it?"

"Yeah. You look pretty."

"Thank you." Erin had chosen her new blue dress to wear to work that day. She had even spent a little more time on her hair but told herself it wasn't to look good for lunch with Michael. A feeling of discomfort had settled in her stomach, and she convinced herself that looking her best would cheer her mood.

Erin dropped the children off at school, and when she got to work, she dusted and polished the instruments and counters as usual. The sidewalks were wet with drizzle, and the morning sky hung low with dark clouds. She glanced at the people walking past the store with their open umbrellas and looked at her watch. She had some time before her next lesson, so she went into her studio and played a few songs on the piano. As it neared eleven o'clock, she worked on finishing the lesson plans for her afternoon students and started putting away the new sheet music. The phone rang.

"Anacortes Music, this is Erin."

A man's husky voice said, "Erin Holley?"

"Yes? Can I help you?"

Silence.

"Hello. Can I help you?"

Erin heard a click as the caller hung up.

She hung up the phone and frowned. *Who was that?* She looked around the store, opened the door, and scanned the street. Two women were window-shopping, and a man was walking his dachshund a block away. A white Subaru drove past.

She shook her head as if to shake away her fears and went back to her studio. She needed to concentrate on going over new music for her students. After a while she sighed and looked up. Michael stood watching her, one shoulder leaning against the doorframe. She clapped her hand to her mouth. "You startled me. How long have you been standing there?"

"Only a minute. Can you break free from work?"

His eyes were warm and his mouth curved in a small smile, and although every time Erin saw him she felt a thrill of fear, she also felt a sense of warmth and familiarity.

"I can go as soon as Ed gets here. He should be here any minute. I'm starving. I didn't realize how late it was," she said.

"Good. I have lunch ready for us at home—I thought we might like more privacy than a restaurant can offer."

Erin took a step back.

He saw her confusion and smiled. "For a good conversation."

She felt her face grow warm. "I hope it wasn't too much trouble."

"Not at all. I love to cook."

Ed arrived, and they left the store and walked the half block to where Michael had parked. He opened the door, and she slid into his car. The now familiar scent of spicy pine greeted her. Michael eased himself into his seat and pulled out onto the road. Erin glanced at him; the scent brought to mind the feeling of his neck against her face. She tried to shake the feeling away.

He kept his eyes on the road and asked, "Did you have a good night?"

"Yes, I did. It was all quiet."

They sat in silence for a few blocks.

"How is your book coming?" she asked.

"Very well. My agent is excited about it, and of course, I am, too."

They reached his house, got out of the car, and went inside.

"I've got lunch nearly ready—would you like some iced tea?" Michael asked.

"Sounds good."

Erin looked around while he went into the kitchen. The weapons on his walls were fascinating, but she walked to the piano to look at his sheet music. The pieces by Schubert were there, as well as a few other classical compositions. She sat down on the piano bench and played part of a melody. Arranged on top of the piano were several small photos, and she stood up to look at them more closely. One photo was of a wiry boy, maybe five years old, with dark hair. Another photo was of a younger Michael, a big grin on his face, holding the laughing little boy when he was about three. A photo of a cabin in the woods leaned beside another picture with Michael, Bruce, a tall, slim, dark-haired woman, and a younger man with lighter hair. The family resemblance was obvious.

Michael came back into the living room with two glasses of iced tea.

"Are these your brother and sister?" she asked.

He looked at the picture. "Yes, that's Elizabeth and Sean. Elizabeth's married and lives in Portland. She's a couple years younger than me, then Bruce next. Sean was the youngest."

Erin smiled. "You all look alike. I have one older sister, and we don't look anything like each other. She lives in Spain with her husband. I don't get to see her often."

She picked up the photo of the boy. "Your son?"

He nodded, his eyes on the boy. "Yes, that's Colby." He glanced at Erin. "This was taken only a week before he died."

"I'm so sorry."

Again, he nodded his head. He picked up the picture of both him and his son. "Portland Zoo. Colby fell in love with elephants that day, and after that, all he wanted was toy elephants. His mother loved elephants, too, so that was fine with her."

Michael picked up the last photo, the one of the cabin. "This is the cabin I built near Mt. Hood."

She took the photo from him and studied it. "It looks so familiar."

He raised his eyebrows and said, "Maybe you've seen it." He started to walk back to the kitchen.

"What?" she asked.

He glanced back at her with a grin. "Let's eat lunch."

Michael brought the food to the dining room—a huge seafood salad, rolls and butter, and slices of cantaloupe.

"This looks wonderful," Erin said. "You didn't have to go to so much trouble."

Michael sat opposite her at the large cherry-wood table, and they served themselves. They ate in silence for a few minutes. She eyed him curiously. "Do you always fix such great food?"

"Only when I want to impress someone."

"You want to impress me?" The thought hadn't occurred to her before.

"Of course. But more than that, I want you to be comfortable. I want you to feel free to talk to me."

She ate another bite of salad. "I don't know you very well."

His eyes clouded over.

"You invited me here today because you said you might know something about my dreams." She frowned. "But I don't understand."

"What don't you understand?" His voice was quiet.

"How you could know anything about my dreams. And why you think it's important."

Michael helped himself to another serving of salad. "You've told me how your nightmares wake you. Have you ever woken with an injury or scar?"

Erin's fork paused in midair, and she didn't feel hungry any longer. She wasn't sure what she should say. She was afraid he'd think she was losing her grip on reality if she said too much. She nodded her head.

"Tell me what you remember about the dream you had when you woke with a scar. That's a good place to start."

She frowned and looked out the window, debating what she should tell him. She looked back at him. His face looked expectant, patient, accepting, and she felt reassured. She took a deep breath and said, "I don't remember much. I was running through a forest, searching for someone. I don't know who. Then I was attacked by some dark ..." She paused, her eyes searching. "Monsters. In my dream they hurt me. One of them stabbed me through my back—it hurt so much."

"Do you remember anything more?"

She didn't want to tell him she had dreamed about him. "Only a little."

"Do you remember how you got away?"

She stood up and walked to the window, looked out at the garden. "I don't want to talk about that."

"Try, Erin," Michael said.

She faced him. "I am trying."

"So did you wake up with the scar? Right where you were pierced with a sword?"

Erin nodded her head slowly.

"Is there any possibility that you were with someone who hurt you, but you just don't remember?" Michael asked.

She frowned as she looked at him and punched out her words. "No, I wish that were the case, but it's ridiculous. I don't forget what happens to me when I'm awake. I went to bed alone and woke up with bruises and a scar. Even stranger, by the end of the day the bruises were almost gone. The scar—I still have it—but I know I didn't have any scar before I went to sleep that night."

"Just wanted to rule out that idea."

"I didn't tell you it used a sword."

He raised his eyebrows. "No, but it did, didn't it?"

Erin felt a shiver run through her, and she took a step back. *How did he know?* "Yes."

Michael got up from the table, stood beside her and gazed out the window at the garden. "When did you start having these nightmares?"

She groaned inside. "Around the time my husband, William, died. They wake me up in the middle of the night. I don't remember much of them, but I can't get back to sleep—they leave me shaking and shivering. Lately, though, I'm remembering more. Are you sure you want to hear about this?"

Michael nodded, a small smile on his face, and she felt easier about telling him.

"I do remember more of the dream I had that night. Please don't think I'm crazy. The … monsters outnumbered me, and they … beat me with long poles, until one of them ran me through with a sword. I fell." She paused and closed her eyes.

"Then what happened?" Michael whispered. He reached out his hand and grasped hers. Erin opened her eyes and studied his face as she continued.

"In my dream, you and Bruce appeared. You fought them, and you picked me up and carried me away. You took me to your cabin. And you healed me." Her eyes strayed to the picture of his cabin at Mt. Hood, and she looked at Michael's hand holding hers.

Michael didn't take his eyes from her. "Do you think the dream was real?"

She looked at him like he was crazy and pulled her hand away. "What do you mean, real? Sure, it was a real dream, but dreams are, well, all in your head."

He turned around. "The other night Bruce dreamed that he was stabbed with a knife and you helped him. He still had a scar when he woke, too."

Erin's mouth dropped open.

"This doesn't make sense, Michael. You told me you might have some answers—that you might know something about these dreams. I was really hoping you would tell me something. I was hoping you could help me. But you're just giving me more questions."

"I'm not sure you want to hear my answers," he said.

"Are you telling me you have answers, but you won't tell me what they are?" She turned around and walked toward the door. "I have to get back to work."

He crossed the room and stood in front of the door, blocking her way. "Stop, Erin. It's not that easy. You've had the answers all along, and for some reason you won't let yourself see. If I tell you, you might just think I'm nuts. You might not believe me. It might not help."

His eyes were earnest, almost pleading.

"Tell me what you think," she said.

"I'll just tell you this, and you can come to your own conclusions. When you dreamed I picked you up and carried you to the boat away from the shadows, I also dreamed I did that. I remember everything that happened in your dream, because I was there, too. When you dropped into the cavern to help Bagley and first met me, I dreamed that, too. I remember when you followed me to my cabin and held a knife to my throat."

Erin backed away from him. She thought back, trying to remember those dreams. "How? How can that be?"

"It's the way it is," he said. He walked back into the living room and sat on the sofa.

She followed him. "Why?" she breathed.

"Fear, anger, hatred, guilt—these can become monsters inside of people. We are open to a whole different world in our dreams, and these shadows—mortifers—prey on the vulnerable. To put it simply, we help other people overcome their monsters."

Erin sat down on the chair facing him. "We? Who? Does everyone do this?"

"No. There are many of us, but not enough."

"That's the answer?" she asked.

"Yes."

She shook her head. "Then why the scar?"

"There's a lot more to the dream world than imagination."

"Are you saying it's real?" she asked. This conversation was starting to seem surreal. It was frightening.

"It has its reality," he said slowly.

She shook her head and closed her eyes.

"Most people who do what we do remember their dreams and know who they are. It doesn't change daily life—at least not much. At least not often. I don't know why you have such a difficult time remembering."

What Michael was saying sounded ridiculous. They sat in silence again while she thought. If this were true, then Bruce really was injured a couple weeks back. And Michael actually had saved her life.

"Do you have any scars from your dreams?" she asked.

"Yes."

Erin's skin crawled as she thought about Michael's scarred back. This couldn't be true. She looked at him and shook her head, remembered his scent and the feel of his neck against her face. Did he remember how she had embraced him in her dreams?

She stood up. "I have to go."

Michael looked at his watch and said, "You still have fifteen minutes. You're running from me."

She turned away. "I should get back."

"Will you think about what I told you?"

She looked up at him. "It's so strange."

"Just think about it. I'll take you back to work."

They were silent in the car on the way back to the store as Erin grappled with what he had told her. He parked the car on the street in front of the store and turned to her.

"Anytime you want to talk, just give me a call," he said. He smiled a twisted smile. "Even if it's in the middle of the night, after a bad dream."

"Thanks. But how do you know what you've told me is true? Don't you question it?"

"I've lived this for years. There are many of us. You're not alone."

Erin's brow knotted into a frown. "You might be crazy," she murmured.

"That's always possible," Michael said. "You'd better go. Now you're late."

"Thank you for lunch." She leaned over and embraced him, kissed his cheek.

He smiled. "Walk with care."

"*Et tu*," she said as she opened the door and stepped out of the car. She realized that was the second time she had said that to him. "*Et tu*?" Where had that come from? She walked into the store.

"Long lunch, baby?" Gary said from where he stood leaning against a counter. He grabbed her arm and pulled her into her studio, kicked the door closed, and kissed her.

Chapter 37

When he let her go, Erin stepped back and bumped into the wall. This was too sudden.

"I didn't know you were coming," she said.

"Obviously." He turned away and played a few notes on the piano. "Who was with you in the car?" He faced her; his eyes looked sharp, his smile forced.

"A … friend—a local author and customer—he invited me to lunch today," she said. She sat down at her table.

Gary rested his hands on the table and leaned toward her. "Was it a date?" he asked.

She looked him straight in the eyes. "No, it wasn't a date. He is simply a friend."

He held her eyes for a minute and then sat down on the piano bench. "I was a little worried there."

Erin raised her eyebrows and said, "I could tell." She slid out of her chair and gave him a brief kiss, then opened the door. Ed called out to her, "Erin, are you back from lunch?"

"Yes, I'm back."

She sat down again. "What are you doing here today?"

"I had some business in Anacortes, and I thought I'd stop by and say hello. I was hoping to take you to lunch, but I guess I missed my chance."

"I'm sorry. I wish I had known you were coming. How long can you stay? Can you come over for dinner after I'm off?"

Erin saw his face relax. "I could do that," he said.

"I've got a student coming in a few minutes. You could stay here or go shopping or something until I get home. Or you could go ahead to my house, if you want."

"I'll meet you at your house later. I'll let you get back to work."

"Okay." They stood up, and she took his hand and squeezed it. "Bye."

He kissed her. "Mmm. You smell good."

He went out the door to his car. She watched him from the window, and after he drove away, she collapsed into the chair. She picked up some sheet music and stared at it but didn't even know what she was looking at. What a shock—Gary waiting in the store. He must have seen her in the car with Michael. He must have seen her kiss him. No wonder he was upset. And what about that strange lunch with Michael? She didn't know what to think about all he had said, and she didn't know what to think about him. He made her feel on edge. One minute he was soothing, the next he unsettled her again. What he had said about their dreams was so farfetched; did he really believe it? But if he was right, if these dreams were in some way real, then they were doubly frightening. And what other explanation could there be for her scar?

When the workday finally ended and she was on her way home, Erin took a few minutes to turn off the highway into the cemetery. She drove to William's spot and got out of her car. She sat on the grass covering his grave and stared at the cold gray headstone. His face came into her mind, laughing, teasing, joking. A tear slid down her cheek, but she didn't brush it away. The wind rose and blew her hair away from her face, and she closed her eyes. The face of a little boy came into her mind from the photos at lunch, Michael's son, Colby. She could easily imagine Michael's grief-stricken face bending over his son's grave. She looked out over the horizon, then got back in her car and drove the rest of the way home.

Erin saw Gary's black SUV parked in her driveway as she drove up the street toward her house. A large black sedan was parked further down the road, a little past her driveway. There were two men sitting in it, but she couldn't see who they were.

She pulled into her driveway, bouncing over a few potholes as she made her way through the apple trees toward the house. Gary wasn't in his car, and she didn't see him outside. Matt and Gwen should still have been next door at Edna's. She parked and looked around. Seeing no one, she passed through the hedge to Edna's.

Edna opened the door. "Hi, dear," she said. "Is everything all right?"

Erin frowned. "Aren't Matt and Gwen here?"

"No, they went home when Gary got here. He came over, and I let them into the house. He said you knew he was coming."

"I did. I was expecting him—I didn't realize he would get the kids, though."

Edna's face grew concerned. "I hope it was all right for me to let him into your house like that. I just assumed ..."

"It's fine," Erin hastened to reassure her. "Of course it's fine. I'll just go back home—I haven't even been in the house yet."

Edna breathed a sigh of relief.

Erin walked home and looked up the street at the black car. It was empty now; the men must have gotten out. She looked around but didn't see where they had gone. Her heart beat faster and she rushed back to her house.

The front door was locked, so she got out her key and went inside, calling out, "Anybody home?"

"We're in here," Matt answered. Erin walked down the hall to the dining room and saw Gary, Matt, and Gwen sitting at the table playing cards. "Hi, Mom," the kids said, looking at her expectantly.

"Hi, guys," she said. "What a surprise."

Gary stood up. "I hope you don't mind me getting the kids and coming inside." He grinned. "How was your afternoon?"

"It was good."

He turned to the kids. "Are you guys getting hungry? Now that your mom's home should we put the pizza in the oven?"

"Yeah!"

Gary walked into the kitchen. "I picked up a take-and-bake pizza on my way over. I hope that sounds good." He glanced at her face, opened the oven door, and put a large pizza into the oven. "Want a glass of wine?"

"Yes, I'd love one." Erin watched as he got a wine glass from the cabinet and poured her some red wine from a bottle on the counter.

"Gary's teaching us how to play poker," Gwen said. "It's really fun—I already won a game."

"Oh, great." Erin laughed.

When the pizza was ready, they took it outside and ate dinner in the garden. The sun was setting, but the air was calm and not very cold. Afterward, Matt and Gwen washed the dishes while Erin and Gary walked the short trail to the beach. The tide was high and small waves lapped against the driftwood. They climbed onto the uprooted stump of a large tree that had washed ashore years before. The wood was whitened and polished smooth from the salty wind.

"I've got to get back to Seattle soon," Gary said. "I shouldn't have stayed this long—Henry's got some documents he needs me to look at before morning."

"How's he doing?" Erin asked.

"He'll be all right."

"Do the police have any leads?"

Gary looked at her with a glint in his eyes and answered her slowly. "Not that I know of. I think Henry was just in the wrong place at the wrong time."

Erin frowned. "And what about those men we saw yesterday? Any sign of them?"

He grinned, his dimples deepening. "Don't worry about them." He bent down and kissed her slowly. She wrapped her arms around his waist, and he put his hands on her shoulders, then around her back, pulling her tight. He slid his hands down her back and pressed her backside close. He kissed her again, and her heartbeat quickened.

She whispered, "It's getting late. I'd better get those kids to bed."

"Yeah." He kissed her again. They climbed off the tree stump and walked back to the house.

Matt was finishing his homework at the dining room table, and Gwen was playing with her dolls. The kids wanted to play one more game of poker with Gary before bed, so Erin let them while she tidied up the living room. She built a fire in the fireplace and poured two glasses of brandy, and after Matt won the game, she walked upstairs with the children to say goodnight. She felt warm and safe—she hadn't felt such a sense of calm since William had been alive, and she savored it. What a wonderful evening it had turned out to be.

Gary was standing facing the fireplace, his brandy in one hand, when she came back downstairs. His blond hair gleamed in the flickering light, and he turned around and smiled at her. He put down his drink and pulled his shirt off over his head. Erin gave him a questioning glance and sipped her own brandy.

"Are you too warm?"

"No. I'm very comfortable."

She bit her lip.

He approached her and took her glass from her hand, setting it on the table. He touched her cheek with his fingers and kissed her softly. "I want you more than ever," he whispered.

Erin closed her eyes and slid her hands over the smooth skin of his chest and around his back. He was so warm. He took a deep breath and let it out again.

"Let's go upstairs," he said.

She hesitated.

He pulled away from her and studied her face. His eyes were sharp, but when he spoke again, his voice was gentle. "It's all right. I want you more than anything … you are beautiful and luscious. And … mmm … you want me, too." He kissed her and whispered, "Feel me."

She did want him—his smooth skin and the strength of his whole body. She knew she wanted him. He took her hand and led her up the stairs to her room. He sat on the bed and watched as she took off her shirt, her pants, her bra and panties. His eyes, the blue barely showing behind his huge black pupils, stayed on her, his smile faint and his breathing ragged. He touched her tentatively, gently, and kissed her body slowly. She was entranced, caught up in each minute sensation, every nerve alert and sensitive to each breath, every touch of his lips, his tongue, his hands.

She unfastened his pants and pulled them off, then kissed him slowly. He lay back and moaned as her long hair caressed him while she spread kisses along his body.

Suddenly he sat up, grabbed her arms and pushed her flat on the bed, pressing his own body on top of hers. In an instant he was inside her, and she cried out. He kissed her. His urgency was overwhelming, and she was overcome as her own desire reached its peak, and she grasped him harder and tighter. He groaned and pressed ferociously into her, knocking the breath from her.

He slowly stopped, his breathing rough, heart pounding. Erin gasped, and he eased from her. He wrapped his arms around her and held her close. They lay still for a few minutes. A breeze had arisen outside, and Erin listened to the sound of the wind through the trees and the waves on the shore. Some crows called in the distance.

Gary sat up. "I've got to go."

Erin was startled. "Right now?"

He smiled as he looked at her. "Yeah. I should have left a long time ago. I've got to meet with Henry tonight, and it's a long drive."

He pulled on his clothes, and Erin stood up and wrapped her kimono around herself. They went downstairs, and Gary kissed her once more before he dashed out the door. Erin stood outside and watched him as he drove away. She glanced down the road, and saw that the black sedan was still there, empty. She shivered and went back inside, closed and locked the door. After turning out the lights, she climbed the stairs and stopped in front of the picture of William. She lit the candles and sat on the floor for several minutes before getting ready for bed.

Chapter 38

Erin peered over the edge of the hole that opened into a cavern deep below, but she was unable to see anything in the scattered twilight. Ragged clouds raced across the sky. She drew her sword and dropped down to the floor ten feet below. Landing softly, she crouched low, holding her sword out to the side. She stayed low and listened. All was silent except for the sound of water dripping deep in the cave.

This was familiar. Erin knew she had been here before, and she remembered the tormented dreamer—a man chased by far too many shadows. *Was he here tonight?* She straightened up and searched the gloom of the cave, where she had first encountered Michael. But that night there had been five mortifers hiding in this darkness. She strode around the edges of the chamber, sensing its emptiness tonight. The dreamer must be in one of the many tunnels branching away, so she paused to allow her mind to reach out to him. His fear leapt toward her, and she nearly staggered from the blow of his terror but knew which way she had to go. Choosing her path, she ran through the tunnel in the dark.

She hadn't gone far when she heard scuffling and murmuring ahead. Slowing, she continued without making a sound. The air became very cold, and the voices grew louder.

"I'll get it, I'll get it," said a trembling voice. "If you kill me I can't get it."

A rumbling voice answered, "If I kill you, your friends will make sure we have it. We're tired of waiting."

Erin clung close to the wall. This was no mortifer—this was another man.

"No! I'll get it. Arthur has it."

A blow was struck, and Erin moved. She rounded the corner into the room and saw an enormous man lift up the dreamer by the front of his shirt. His feet kicked helplessly in the air, and he gasped and choked. The giant flung him to the corner of the room where he crumpled and cringed against the wall. As the huge man turned, Erin recognized him—the same man who'd attacked Gary in his dream. He saw Erin, and with a loud growl he lunged at her and tackled her to the ground. She smacked her head on the floor and lay there, stunned. With a snort, he sat on top of her, knocking the air from her lungs. She gasped and coughed, and clenching every muscle she told herself to move. She curled her knees and feet to her body and thrust her hips upwards. As the giant tumbled over her head, she rolled away, grabbed her sword, and rose to her feet, gulping for air. He staggered up. Erin whipped her sword around and pressed the point against his throat. He stopped.

"It's time for you to leave," she said through gritted teeth, and pressed her sword tighter against the skin of his throat. "We've met before, remember?"

His face twisted in a snarl, and he lunged sideways, reaching out to grab her. Erin ducked and swung her sword upwards, slicing his torso open. His eyes went wide as he watched his blood spill out onto the floor, hovering for a moment as if held up by strings, before he collapsed in a heap.

Erin ran to the dreamer who was sitting on the floor against the wall with his mouth hanging open.

"Are you all right?" she asked.

"No, no." He buried his face in his hands.

Erin rested the palms of her hands on top of his head for a moment, then took hold of his hands and helped him stand.

"Let's go," she said. "We've got to get out of here."

He sobbed. "I can't. I'm afraid."

"We're in danger here." Erin grabbed his arm and pulled him out of the little room.

"No, I can't go. They'll find me out there."

"They'll find you in here, too. Come on."

She dragged him through the tunnel into the large cavern and turned to face him. Moonlight cast a cold glow on the rough cavern walls, illuminating piles of crumbling stones and the man's ashen face. He cowered away from her and held his hands out as if warding off a blow. She studied him as he crouched against the wall. He was definitely the same man she'd helped in this cavern before. His eyes darted around, avoiding her gaze.

"Who are you?" she asked.

He flinched as if she had struck him.

"What is your name?" she asked again.

"Henry," he whispered.

Erin took a deep breath. "Henry Bagley?"

He frowned. "How do you know me? Who are you? Are you one of them?"

Queasiness grew in Erin's stomach.

"Do you know Gary Arthur?" she whispered.

"What if I do?"

"Don't play games with me. Do you know him?"

He sneered and turned away from her. "Yeah. I know Gary Arthur. This is his fault. He got us into this mess. If he were here, I'd have you slice him up like you did to Lehman back there."

"What did Lehman want?" she asked.

Henry snorted. "To hurt me, couldn't you tell?"

"What does he want from you?"

"Go to hell. I'm outta here."

"No," she yelled. She reached out to grab him, but Henry had disappeared.

***

"Mommy, wake up."

Erin rolled over and murmured, "Get back here."

"I'm here," Gwen said. "Wake up."

Erin felt Gwen's warm body snuggling next to hers in her bed, and she woke completely and put her arms around her. "What is it, sweetie?"

"I'm afraid."

In the dark, Erin could still see the cavern, still feel her anger. The twisted, insolent face of Henry Bagley was fresh in her mind.

"Afraid of what?"

"Big, bad men coming into my room."

Erin reached over to turn on the bedside lamp and cuddled her daughter again. "No big, bad men are going to come into your room. You're safe. Everything's all right." Her own heart was still beating too fast.

"I want Daddy."

Erin closed her eyes, and a sob filled her up inside. "Me, too."

She caressed Gwen's hair. She remembered the dream clearly and wondered if all those forgotten dreams in the past were similar. In her dream, Gary's friend was a miserable jerk. Was it true? She shuddered, remembering how the big brute had smacked her to the floor like a beanbag, but then she'd gutted him. His sticky blood had run all over the floor—she even remembered its metallic smell. It made her feel sick to her stomach.

Her thoughts drifted back to Henry Bagley. He had said he wanted her to slice Gary open like she had that giant. Anger grew inside her again.

Erin turned out the light, then pulled the blankets to her chin, keeping one arm wrapped around Gwen.

CHAPTER 39

THE buildings facing the dark street were shades of leaden gray and black. Michael stood with his back to the edge of the wet concrete walls, and the rain poured over him, drenching his cloak and hat, seeping into his boots, and splashing from his collar into his face. He wiped his eyes and mouth with his hand and turned his head, looking up and down the street. Nothing moved except the crow that flew overhead. It landed on top of a burned out streetlight and cawed. Michael retreated into the hollowed-out doorway of the building where he blended into the darkness of the shadows.

He heard the faint sound of running feet approaching from a distance. The sound grew louder until he could hear the splash as each step hit the water pooled in the street. He tensed, his hand on his sword hilt, and pressed against the wall. The footfalls grew louder and echoed down the street as the running man passed right in front of him and kept on going.

Michael peered out and watched him recede into the distance. When he turned a corner, Michael raced after him, his boots making no sound in the pounding rain. The crow flew overhead, seeming to follow as Michael hurtled down the street, careful to keep the runner in view.

When the man turned into an alley, Michael slowed and trailed him close to the buildings. The crow flew ahead and stopped at the place the runner had turned. It landed on the ground and drank from a puddle of water, then cawed and flew on, following the new route the runner had taken.

Michael quickened his pace and saw him turn into a doorway, push the door open, and step inside. The crow rested on an overhang above the entry, and Michael slowed, edging his way close to the walls until he reached it. The building was made of concrete blocks, but many were cracked, and all were drenched. Water ran down the walls and poured over the gutters.

He turned the knob and silently pushed the door open. Icy air flowed out. He stepped inside and closed the door, shutting out nearly all the light. When his vision adjusted, he saw the hallway and crept down it toward the first room. A sweet, rotten stench hit him in the face. He pressed his back against the wall of the passage.

"What have you brought us?" a thin, hollow voice asked from inside the room. A mortifer's voice. The sound of a chair scraping against the old wood floor pierced through the voice, and Michael shivered. His stomach tightened.

The silence from the room felt like ice, frozen and immovable. Michael held his breath.

The chair scraped across the floor again. Michael nearly jumped.

A man's voice croaked. "Information."

"What is it?" the hollow voice hissed.

"I … I know where he'll be."

The deep, hollow voice laughed. "Who?"

There was silence for a moment, then the man whispered again, so quietly Michael barely heard him. "The viator."

The scornful laugh was louder. "And what do you want for this information?"

"Kill Grekov—destroy him."

"We've already killed one man for you. You haven't yet paid us for that." The hollow voice was menacing.

Again, there was silence.

"This information will fulfill that debt," the man said. "And I brought you one viator already."

The mortifer's voice was harsh. "That was not part of our bargain, fool. You had to prove yourself. But I see we may need to require further proof from you."

"No, no you don't. I understand. And I can get you something more." The man's voice quavered.

"What do you have for us?"

"Not yet. I can get it, though, if it is valuable to you. A flask."

Silence stretched out like a frozen river. The mortifer spoke again. "That might have some small value. You must let us see this flask."

The man's voice was calm. "I can possibly do that."

Again, the mortifer laughed. "Aaah … We'll see. Well, we'll take care of Grekov, but only after you destroy the viator."

The chair scraped over the floor again, and Michael heard the man scramble and fall to the floor. "No, I can't."

Michael felt frozen to the wall, listening. His heart was pounding. He'd heard enough. He slipped back down the hall and out the door into the rain. He crept into the shadow of the doorway of the closest building and waited.

The man burst out of the building and started to run back down the street. Michael stepped out of the shadows and grabbed him as he ran. He threw him against the wall. The man screamed and crumpled to the ground. Michael picked him up by his shoulders and held him up high, pressing him against the wall.

"What the hell are you doing, Arthur?" Michael said through gritted teeth.

Gary's eyes were wide. His face was twisted, spittle on his chin. "Fuck. What are you doing here?"

Michael shook him, banging his head against the wall. "What are you doing with them?"

"Nothing." Gary's voice was a squeak. "Nothing."

"Like hell, you stupid shit. You didn't think I'd find you."

Gary stared at him. Michael put him down but still held a tight grip on his shoulders.

"They're trying to make me do things, but I told them no," Gary said in a shaking voice.

"Don't lie to me. What man did they kill for you?"

"No one," Gary yelled. "I didn't."

Michael still held him, his face twisted with anger. "And you led a viator to them?"

"No. They're lying."

"Was it Sean?"

"I didn't. I don't know what you're talking about."

"Dreamers don't bargain with mortifers unless they choose to."

"Go to hell. You don't know everything," Gary swung his arms up and around, breaking Michael's hold on him. He shoved Michael back. Michael grabbed him by the throat and pressed him to the wall again. Gary choked, his eyes wide, face turning red. He flailed his arms, grasped Michael's hands, trying to get free, but Michael pressed him harder.

"What the fuck are you doing?" Michael whispered, teeth clenched. "I would kill you now if I could."

He let go of Gary, and Gary staggered, coughing. He rushed at Michael and took a swing at his face, but Michael moved and took the hit in the shoulder. Michael shoved him away. Gary stood still for a moment and sneered. "Why are you even pretending to threaten me? You can't hurt me. Isn't it against your rules?" He spat on the ground, wiped his chin, turned and ran down the road.

Michael stood for a long while in front of the building in the shadows while the rain poured over him. He finally closed his eyes and faded from the street until he felt the warm softness of his bed. He opened his eyes to the darkness and lay awake, staring at the ceiling until dawn.

Chapter 40

Erin looked out her bedroom window at Puget Sound. The early morning fog still hovered in a thin layer over the calm water, blue sky above. She had lain awake for a long while with her arm around Gwen before finally falling to sleep again herself.

Gwen's eyes opened and she looked up at Erin and smiled. "Mommy, did I sleep in here with you?"

"You did. Do you remember you came in here in the middle of the night?"

"Yes. Is it time to get up?"

"You can stay in bed a little longer. I'll go take a shower. Then you'll need to get ready for school."

After dropping the children off at school, Erin tried to focus on work, but the memory of her dream lingered, leaving her feeling taut and preoccupied. Her first student was due to arrive soon, and as she gazed out the window, she noticed an empty black sedan parked across the street. The sight made her heart race and sent a jolt of adrenaline through her veins. She chided herself for being so jumpy. It was only a car.

When the lesson was over, she walked her student to the door, noticing with relief that the car was gone. She grabbed her coat and headed out to Hannah's bakery.

The bell jingled when she opened the bakery door and Hannah looked up.

"Erin. It's good to see you."

"I know—thought I'd stop by and get a quiche for lunch. Do you have any?"

"Sure, we have a couple left." Hannah pulled one out of the case and placed it on a plate. "Glass of water?"

"Thanks. Can you take a few minutes and sit with me?"

No other customers were in the shop, so Hannah joined Erin at one of the small café tables. "I could use a lunch break now anyway." Hannah called out to the back room, "Katie, could you watch the store for half an hour?"

"Will do." Hannah's part-time helper came out of the back room for a minute. "Can I get you two anything?"

"No thanks, we're good," Hannah said. She turned to Erin. "Is everything all right?"

"I have too much on my mind lately." She looked sidelong at Hannah. "I've been seeing quite a bit of Gary, for one thing, and I'm concerned."

Hannah looked puzzled and reached out her hand, resting it on Erin's arm. "Why?"

Erin sighed. "Well, the other day we had a picnic at Deception Pass—Gary, me, and the kids—and when we got back to the car, a couple men were waiting to talk to him. They were threatening."

Hannah's eyes widened. "What did Gary say?"

"He said there was nothing to worry about. He explained that a shipment he was responsible for had been missing but now it's found, although some of it's damaged. He said these guys were just bullies who wouldn't really hurt him."

"What was in the shipment?"

"I don't know. Gary assured me it had nothing to do with drugs."

"I'm sure it doesn't," Hannah said. "He was a good friend of William's, and I think William would have had some idea if his friend was into anything illegal. And these men—I'm sure Gary's right—I'm sure there's nothing to worry about." She sipped her coffee. "How do you feel about him?"

Erin smiled, thinking of the night before. "I can't help but like him … more than like him. But this is moving so fast. He told me he wants to marry me."

"What? Why didn't you tell me?"

"I didn't tell him yes."

"I had no idea you two had become so serious," Hannah said. "It's natural to feel some hesitation, but if it feels like the right thing, well, you need to let yourself move on."

"Yes, I know … and I really am trying to. He was at the house last night, and he played with the kids, and we had a wonderful evening."

"Good."

The bakery door opened and Michael stepped inside.

"Hello, Hannah, Erin." His stance was relaxed, but his face looked tentative.

"Hi. It's good to see you again," Hannah said.

Erin felt her face grow warm, and she smiled. "How are you?"

"All right. I was walking by and saw you. Can I join you?"

"Of course," Hannah said. He pulled up another chair and sat next to Hannah. Katie brought him a cup of coffee, and he poured in some cream and sat stirring his cup, looking across the table at Erin.

"Is Bruce in town?" Hannah asked.

"No, but he'll be back Friday. He'll be here for the weekend." He sipped his coffee. "Your new girl seems like she's learning the ropes. How's she working out?"

"She's wonderful. It's nice to finally feel all right about taking a break or leaving the shop for a little bit. I know the place won't fall apart without me."

Erin watched him, noticing the sharp line of his jaw, his cheekbones, his straight nose, the dark gray of his eyes. She thought about what he'd said about her dreams and remembered how he'd looked in the laundry room with the scars covering his body. She felt a sudden urge to reach out and touch his face, to get up close and hold onto him.

He looked across and held her gaze. "I've been trying to learn the Schubert you got me—it's hard work."

She relaxed and smiled. "Yes, I know. Just let me know if you need a lesson."

"Maybe I'll do that." He looked back at Hannah. "You and Carlos are coming to Aleesha's Saturday?"

She laughed. "Of course we'll be there. Aleesha would never forgive us if we didn't."

He took a drink of his coffee, leaned forward and put his hand on Erin's arm. "And you, too?"

"I'll be there," she said. The pressure of his hand sent tingles up to her scalp. He sat still, holding her arm for a moment.

He pulled his hand away and gulped down the rest of his coffee. "Good. I'd better run. Nice to see you two."

"Bye, see you Saturday," Hannah said.

"Bye," Erin said.

He rushed out of the bakery and was soon out of sight.

"For a minute there, I thought he was going to eat you up," Hannah said.

"What? What do you mean?"

"Couldn't you tell? I could feel it like electricity. He's very attracted to you."

Erin looked out the window in the direction Michael had gone. "Do you really think so? To tell you the truth, I've always been a little afraid of him."

Hannah nodded. "He is a little frightening. He seems very complex."

"Exactly."

"Is Gary going to dinner Saturday, too?"

Erin's eyes slid over to her friend's. "Yes. We'll be there together."

"That should be interesting."

***

Erin helped at the counter with sales until her next lesson—a sixth grade boy who showed some real talent. The lesson went well, and after he left, Erin saw that Gary had left her a message on her cell phone. She called him back.

"Erin. You got my message?"

"Yes. Did you get back in time to see Henry last night?"

"Yes, I kept him up late looking at paperwork."

"How's he doing?" Erin asked.

"All right. He's back to his old annoying self."

Erin laughed. "Good. I had a dream about him last night."

"What? I didn't think you remembered your dreams. And you've never met him. Should I be jealous?" Gary asked.

"I wouldn't worry about it. In my dream, Henry was an overweight, frightened, middle-aged coward. Please don't tell him I said that."

"Hah. You just described him perfectly," Gary said.

Erin shivered. She felt her back where she still had a faint scar. Her legs felt wobbly.

"Is everything all right?" Gary asked.

"Yes, yes. Fine," she said. "It was such a strange dream. There was another man—a huge man—named, um, Lehman. He was trying to hurt Henry, and so I, um, I killed him."

Gary was silent. "Erin, that is weird. A man named Lehman is a suspect in Henry's shooting."

"What?" Erin sat down. Her head felt light.

"Are you okay?" Gary asked.

She rubbed her forehead. *Get hold of yourself. It was just a dream.* "I'm fine. I was just startled at the coincidence. It's pretty amazing."

His voice was cold. "Yeah, it's strange."

Erin sat still and silent. She heard an angry voice speaking to Gary in the background.

"Hold on a minute," he said. There was more muffled talking, and then Gary got back on the line. "Sorry."

"Who's there?" she asked.

"Oh, a client just got here. I've got to go."

"I'll see you later then."

"Yeah. Bye."

Erin walked out of her studio and looked out the window as an uneasy feeling settled in her stomach.

Chapter 41

Dinner was done and the kitchen cleaned up, and Erin sat on the couch in the living room reading a few stories to the children. Her mind kept traveling back to Gary and to Michael. She didn't know what to think about Michael's explanation of their dreams, and she was anxious about the men confronting Gary, in spite of his reassurances. A gust of wind blew hard outside, shaking the little house.

"Is a storm coming?" Gwen asked.

"I don't think so. It's just a bit of wind for now," Erin said. She looked out the window, and the dark water of the Sound was covered with whitecaps.

"Darn. We haven't had a storm since winter," Matt said. "They're exciting!"

Erin laughed. There was nothing like one's own children to lighten the mood. In that, she was much luckier than Michael. Although she had lost her husband, she still had her children. Even though his ex-wife was still alive, he had lost her just the same. His child, then his wife. She shuddered.

"Are you cold, Mommy?" Gwen asked.

"No, just had a little shiver. Okay, time to get ready for bed."

"One more story?" Gwen asked.

"All right, just a short one."

After the children were both in bed, Erin took off her clothes and wrapped her kimono around herself. Barefoot, she slipped outside into her garden and walked down to the beach. The wind almost tore the robe from her, and the cold raised her skin in goosebumps. She shivered and hugged herself tightly as she stood on a driftwood log, looking out over the wild, rushing waves. The half-moon was hidden by ragged clouds that raced across the sky, like a mirror of the rushing water below. Erin stood there for a long time, allowing the wind to empty her mind, allowing the wind to blow her clean.

When she went inside and got into bed she was icy cold, but she slipped under the blankets naked. She felt fresh and free.

As Erin drifted off to sleep, the fragrance of cherry blossoms filled her room. She found herself standing at the edge of a forest, looking across a gently sloping field that ended abruptly in a bluff. Beyond the cliff, she could see a sparkling sea, spreading out to the horizon. The light was pink and dim. As the sun sank toward the water, it turned the sky red and purple, and the silhouette of a man stood dark at the edge of the bluff. The cherry trees nearby filled the air with their sweet scent, and she saw that she wasn't wearing her usual black pants, jacket, and boots. Instead she wore a long, white dress, and her feet were bare.

The peaceful surroundings filled Erin with a sense of tranquility. She walked toward the man, the grass soft and cool under her feet, and as the sun sank lower in the sky, she recognized Michael. He wore his normal black pants and shirt, his jacket and boots lying on the ground nearby.

He turned as she drew near. "I thought you'd find your way here tonight."

"Did you want me to come?" she said.

"Yes."

Erin stood next to him, her arm brushing against his. They both looked out over the bluff at the sky and the water below. Although the breeze was from the water, she could still smell the sweet cherry blossoms.

"Why?" she asked.

"I want you to see this sunset."

The sun slowly sank as the sky blushed red. As it neared the horizon, the sun appeared to drip, fiery and blazing, into the water, spreading out until it was lost from view. Then it reappeared, a shimmering orb, as the water cast the sun's reflection back into the sky. It slowly faded until all that was left was the blood-red stain on the horizon. A few stars glittered above in the darkening sky.

"Beautiful," Erin whispered.

"Yes, now be very still and listen."

She watched and listened as the stars began to light up the sky. After a few more became visible, she heard faint music, like singing. More stars appeared, and the music grew louder, until there was a chorus of voices, the intricate melody graceful and pure.

She whispered, "I've never heard the stars before."

He smiled. "You've been a viator for two years now. It's time you heard the stars sing."

They stood and listened for a while.

Michael reached out his hand and clasped hers. "How long were you married?"

Erin was surprised and tears came to her eyes. "Twelve years."

"And it was a car accident? You were there?"

"Oh, yes." She turned away. "I was driving."

Michael put his hand on her shoulder, holding her still. "You followed him."

"I followed him as far as I could. I called and called for him. I tried to catch him. I tried to get him to come back. But I failed."

Michael held both of her shoulders, bringing her around to face him. "It wasn't your fault. You couldn't have brought him back."

Erin shook her head and looked at the ground. "I wasn't fast enough. I couldn't do anything right. I failed him."

"Who told you that?"

She thought for a minute. "The mortifer."

"Their greatest power is fear. Their greatest weapon is despair. Don't listen to them."

She turned back to face him. The stars had filled the sky, and Erin listened to their song again.

"Is that why there's so much you don't remember? Oh, Erin …" Michael wiped her tears from her face, and they stood silent.

"Will you dance with me?" he asked.

She nodded. He placed one hand around her waist and held her hand with the other, and they danced while the stars sang. She closed her eyes and held him tighter. The fragrance of cherry blossoms mingled with the pine scent of his skin. The grass under her bare feet was soft and yielding, the breeze gentle, and his arms were strong. The light from the stars was so bright it lit the ground and sparkled on the water. When she looked up at his face, she saw he was watching her, his eyes darker than ever.

"Whose dream is this?" she asked.

"Ours."

She pressed herself closer to his warm body. He wrapped both his arms around her waist as they danced tight in each other's embrace.

Suddenly Michael stopped, still holding her. "I have to go, Erin; a dreamer is calling." His lips brushed the top of her head.

"Do you want me to come?"

"Not this time. But stay here a while longer. I'll think of you here."

"All right."

Michael reached his arm up into the sky and scooped his hand across the stars. His hand held a bunch of small blue and white flowers—forget-me-nots.

He gave them to her. Then he was gone.

Erin lay back on the grass and listened to the stars for a long time. No dreamers called for her that night, and she slept deeply.

She woke before the alarm went off and looked at her clock. Little blue and white faces of forget-me-nots greeted her from a vase on her nightstand. She sat straight up and jumped out of bed, pulling on her robe. Her door opened a crack, and Gwen peeked in. She was carrying another bunch of the flowers. The ankles of her pajamas were wet and dirty.

"I'm making bouquets," Gwen said.

"Yes, I see," Erin answered. "They're lovely, thank you. But it's a little early for you to be going outside."

"But it's not dark."

"No, but it's too early when I'm still asleep."

"Well, it's time for you to get up now, or you'll be late for work," Gwen said, and she left the room and closed the door.

Erin shook her head and looked with wonder at the flowers. She picked them up and inhaled their subtle fragrance, then went into the bathroom to take a shower.

Chapter 42

THE clouds were low and dark as Erin drove to work that morning. Gwen had carried a bunch of forget-me-nots to her teacher, and Erin took some to work. She looked at the bundle of little flowers on the seat beside her. Michael had said these dreams were in some way real. Had he really been with her in her dream last night?

She pulled into the parking lot and went into the music store carrying her purse in one hand and her flowers in the other. She had just put the forget-me-nots into a vase when the outside door opened, and a man carrying a stunning bouquet of red roses walked in.

"I've got flowers for Erin Holley," the man said.

"That's me. Thank you so much."

She took the roses, set them on the front counter, and opened the card. It read, "Erin, What are you doing to me? I want you all the time. Can't wait to see you Saturday. All my love, Gary."

Erin felt a rush of pleasure.

Ed came in the shop. "Those are gorgeous!" he said with a grin. "Are they from Gary?"

"Yes. He does things well, doesn't he?"

"I'll say. He makes the rest of us guys look bad. Who gave you the forget-me-nots?"

"Gwen picked them for me."

"Nice."

When Erin drove home at five o'clock, big drops of rain splattered on her windshield. Clouds darkened the sky, and she turned on her headlights. Lightning flashed in the distance to the west. As she drove down her driveway, she could see the whitecaps on the black water of the Sound.

After retrieving Gwen and Matt from Edna's, Erin put some leftover soup on the stove to heat when the phone rang.

"Hello?"

"Did you like the roses?" It was Gary.

"I love them. Thank you." She sat down on the couch.

"Good. Are we still on for the dinner party Saturday?" he asked.

"Yes. Aleesha would be very upset if we weren't there."

He laughed. "I'm sure that's true." He paused a moment. "I've got a meeting Saturday afternoon, so I won't be able to get there until about five-thirty. Hold on a minute."

Erin heard Gary talking to someone but the sound was muffled. She waited.

He came back on the line. "Sorry. What was I saying?"

"You can't make it here until five-thirty."

"Right."

"That's fine," she said.

"Good."

"Aleesha's very excited."

"Hold on again."

Once more, Erin heard muffled voices as he spoke to someone else. She walked to the stove and stirred the soup, and nibbled a cracker. When he came back on the line, she asked, "Anyone I know?"

He laughed. "No. It's nothing—just some business. I've got to get back to it, so I'll see you Saturday."

"Yes. Thanks again for the roses."

"My pleasure. Bye." He hung up.

Erin sat still for a few minutes. She couldn't get rid of her anxiety about his business and those men from sent by Grekov. She helped Matt put their bowls of soup on the table, poured three glasses of milk, and they sat down to eat.

The wind and rain blew past that night and by morning the sky had cleared. A few clouds hurried across the sky, and the breeze kicked up whitecaps, but the sun shone. Erin had slept well, and her day was busy. It was nearly six o'clock, and she was cleaning up for the weekend when the store phone rang.

"Anacortes Music. This is Erin."

There was silence on the other end of the line.

"Hello?" Erin said.

"Erin Holley?" said a man's husky voice.

"Yes. Can I help you?" Erin said.

"You live on Gibraltar Road?"

Erin stood up. "Who is this?"

"Relax. You have nothing to worry about … as long as your friend fulfills his obligations."

"What? What friend? Who is this?" Erin asked.

"Give him my message."

Erin heard the click of the phone as the caller disconnected. She hit the button to retrieve the last incoming phone number. It didn't look familiar at all—even had a different area code, so Erin punched the numbers into her phone. It rang ten times before she gave up. She replaced the receiver and sat wondering. Could this be one of those men Gary had spoken to at Deception Pass? She dialed Gary's office number and left a message on his voice mail, left a message at his home, and tried his cell number. He answered.

"Arthur here."

"Gary, it's Erin."

"I'm just about to go into a meeting. Can I call you back?"

"Do you have just a minute?" She frowned and sat in her chair facing the window.

He paused. "Sure. Go ahead."

"I just received a phone call from someone who wants to make sure my friend fulfills his obligations. Do you have any idea what that's about?"

He was quiet for a minute before answering. "Why would I?"

"You're the only person I'm seeing."

"You have other friends. It could be anyone."

Erin grew angry. "My first thought is that it's one of those men working for Grekov. They did not strike me as being overly ethical."

Gary laughed. "You have a good imagination, baby. That's just business—they're not going to call you. They're certainly not going to threaten you. I really don't know anything about this."

"They seemed pretty threatening at Deception Pass."

"You're making a big deal out of nothing. Look, Erin, I've got to go. We can talk about this more tomorrow."

"All right. I'll see you tomorrow."

Gary disconnected. Erin drove home as quickly as she could, keeping an eye on her rearview mirror. *Was Gary telling the truth?* She hoped so. She was afraid for him.

Chapter 43

THE streetlamp threw a faint, cold light onto the ground, barely illuminating the sidewalk and path up to the little house. The still air smelled heavy and damp. Erin stood on the sidewalk shivering in the cold, staring at the pale house. A boxwood hedge bordered the walk to the door, separating it from the dry lawn. There were no stars or moon. The sky above seemed murky and dense, and Erin's gaze wandered from it to the silent house. She felt the presence of a dreamer inside.

Erin took a step up the path and stopped. The still air felt tense as a bowstring, almost as if her movement would cause it to snap. She sucked in a breath and held it, her heart beating fast. Standing still, she scanned the house with her mind, reaching into every corner, searching for the dreamer and the possible presence of mortifers. She sensed the icy cold inside the house, but all she could find was the dreamer. *No. What was this? Two dreamers? Strange.*

After taking a long look into the edges of the darkness up and down the street, Erin silently drew her sword and walked up the path. Each step was a struggle, and when she reached the door and put her hand on the knob, she felt the cold through her glove. She turned the handle and cracked the door open.

Pale light from the streetlamp lit up the room, revealing a dusty wood floor and an old sofa covered with a blanket facing the doorway, empty. Beyond was a hallway. Erin crept past the sofa and into the hall, and her teeth began to chatter from the cold. Several rooms opened off the passage. The house was much larger than it had appeared from the street. Erin scanned each room as she passed, but she felt drawn to the door at the end of the hall.

The silence and cold were numbing her, and her steps slowed as she neared the door. She turned the handle and looked down a stark wooden staircase into complete blackness. She stared into the dark until her eyes adjusted and she could see the shape of the bannister, then she started down the stairs.

Her feet were silent on the steps, but her ragged breathing was loud in her ears, and she crept slowly into the cold basement. The stuffy air smelled faintly sweet like rotting fruit. She clamped her teeth together to keep them from chattering, but she couldn't stop the loud pounding of her heart. No sound came from below.

When she reached the dirt floor, she slowly turned around and tried to peer through the darkness. The dreamer should be here, but where? She stepped away from the stairs.

A hand grabbed her hair, jerked her head back, and a knife pressed against her throat. Her sword hit the ground with a dull thud. She gasped and felt the knife graze her flesh; a trickle of blood ran down her neck. She froze.

"Erin, is that you? Shit." Gary's voice boomed out into the dead air. A match flared and a candle was lit. Gary's face shone in the yellow glow. "Dammit, Bagley. It's Erin. Let her go."

The knife was pulled away, and Bagley let go of her hair. Erin whirled around. "What the hell are you two doing? Look at this—you've cut my neck." She wiped the blood off her throat and showed them the wet crimson on her glove. She looked from one to the other. Bagley just stared at her, but Gary sat down on a chair with a smile on his face.

"Don't you realize this is a dangerous place? I can feel it. You're in danger here," Erin said.

Gary stood up and walked toward her, still smiling. "This is just a dream. Except for you." He put a hand around the back of her neck, pulled her to him, and kissed her.

She pushed him away. "This isn't a joke."

His brow knotted into a frown as he looked at her. "No. But you took me by surprise. I wasn't expecting you." He looked her up and down. "Baby, you look good. I like your dress."

Instead of her usual black pants and jacket, Erin was now wearing a short, slim red dress, cut low in the back. "This is obviously your dream," she said.

"Oh, is that how this works?" Gary said with a grin. "I just couldn't resist." He turned around, and Erin felt the warmth of her own clothes wrap around her again. She picked up her sword, sheathed it, and grabbed Gary's arm.

"Let's get out of here. Come with me—we'll go where it's safe," she said.

He glanced at Bagley. "All right."

"Arthur," Bagley said.

"What?"

"This'll be a problem."

"I'll deal with it."

They followed Erin up the stairs and out of the house. She held them each by the arm. "Think of another place—a peaceful, safe place. Remember what it was like in Fiji, Gary. The sand, the sun, the incredible blue water."

He smiled at her. "We'll have to go there together some day." He reached out to touch her but faded and was gone.

She paused and turned to Bagley. "Tell me about a wonderful place you've been—someplace you'd love to go back to someday."

"I don't have a place like that."

"Then think of home. Think of your own bed, of being at peace. Feeling safe."

A few minutes later, Bagley was gone.

Erin frowned. *Gary and Henry Bagley? Who had they been waiting for?* She walked down the street and faded into the darkness.

Chapter 44

Erin leaned toward the mirror to watch closely as she smoothed the ruby lipstick over her mouth. She blotted her lips on a tissue. Aleesha liked it when her guests looked their best. Erin's white silk pants and blouse made her look cool and breezy, and with her hair piled on top of her head, she felt elegant. She walked downstairs to wait for Gary.

Gwen and Matthew were already at Edna's, so Erin poured herself a small glass of white wine and stepped outside into the garden. The air was mild, and she slipped off her sandals as she walked down the path to the beach. The sun had warmed the rocks, and she stood on them at the edge of the beach to look out across the Sound. Gary would arrive soon, and Erin struggled to keep herself composed. Bits of her dream of the night before were vivid in her mind, and she felt a chill of fear when she remembered the knife at her throat. She didn't want to believe these dreams had any connection to reality, but she couldn't be sure. She had enough questions to frighten her.

She heard the crunch of gravel on her driveway. She gulped the rest of her wine and walked back to the house, arriving as Gary got out of his SUV.

"You look ravishing," Gary said. He kissed her lightly and grasped her elbow, leading her to the back of his car.

"Thanks," Erin said. "How was the drive?"

"Not bad," he said, smiling. "Where are Matt and Gwen?"

"They're at Edna's already."

"I brought them some presents."

Gary opened the back of his SUV. Inside were two new bicycles. Erin's mouth dropped open as she stared at the bikes. The boy's bike was silver, and there was a smaller purple girl's bike. Gary's grin was as big as she'd ever seen.

"Matt's bike was wrecked—he needed a new one. Of course if I got one for Matt, I had to get one for Gwen. I had a lot of fun picking them out. Do you think they'll like them?"

"Do I think they'll like them? Are you kidding? They're going to be thrilled—but Gary—you shouldn't do this."

Gary pulled her to him, wrapped his arms around her. He spoke softly. "I want to do this."

Erin kissed him. "You're wonderful. What can I say?"

He squeezed her close. "Mmm … I like hearing you say that. Let's get the kids so they can see their new bikes."

Erin laughed. "All right."

Erin went to Edna's while Gary unloaded the bicycles. She came back in just a few minutes with the children and Edna.

"Awesome! Mom, did you see this?" Matt said as he looked over his new silver bike.

"It's a princess bike!" squealed Gwen as she clapped her hands.

They both hopped on their bikes and rode them around the driveway for a few minutes. Erin slid her arm around Gary's waist, giving him a quick hug.

"I didn't know when I was going to be able to get a new bike," Matt said. "Thanks, Gary. It's awesome."

"Thanks, Gary," Gwen said, and she hugged him.

"I'm glad you like them," Gary said.

Erin looked at her watch. "Let's put the bikes in the garage for now, kids. Gary and I have to go. You can ride them more tomorrow."

After the kids put the bikes in the garage and Edna took the children home, Erin and Gary walked into the house to get her purse, and he went to the refrigerator and pulled out the bottle of wine. He poured himself a glass and refilled Erin's.

"Thank you," she said. "What a surprise. I never dreamed you would do something like that."

Gary peered at her over the top of his glass as he drank his wine. He put his glass down. "I'd do anything for you, you know."

He walked to the window to look outside. She followed him and stood beside him to gaze at the water.

"Did you get any more scary phone calls today?" he asked with a grin.

"No." Erin frowned. "Are you making fun of me?"

His eyebrows shot up as he looked into her face. He kissed her then, long and slow. When he stopped, Erin pulled him close and kissed him again.

"Mmm," he said. "Are you sure we have to leave soon?"

"Yes."

Gary laughed as she grabbed her purse and pulled him out the door.

Cars lined the street in front of Aleesha's house, and they had to park in the next block. Aleesha opened the door as soon as they knocked.

"Erin, you look like an angel in that white silk," Aleesha said. "And Gary, it's so good to see you again. I think the last time I saw you was at dinner here."

"It's been too long."

Bruce approached them and wrapped his arm around Aleesha's waist. He smiled at Erin. "I'm glad you finally got here. Michael was afraid you might not come after all."

Erin blushed and glanced at Gary, who frowned slightly and looked at her. Aleesha laughed at Bruce and kissed him. "What do you mean, darling?"

Bruce shook his head and winked at Erin, then turned to Gary. "You look familiar. Have we met? I'm Bruce."

Gary shook Bruce's hand. "Gary Arthur." His brow was still knotted, and Bruce's smile dropped from his face. He glanced back at Erin.

"Aleesha, your house is packed. How many people have you invited?" Erin said.

"Nearly twenty tonight, dear. With the nice weather we can eat outside, and I've borrowed some tables for the patio. It'll be so much fun." Aleesha turned to Bruce. "Would you get something for Gary to drink? I've got to talk to Erin in private for a minute."

Bruce looked at Aleesha with wide eyes and nodded. He asked Gary what he'd like and led him to the bar that had been set up in the living room.

"I don't know what's gotten into Bruce," Aleesha said. "Come into my room where we can have a word in private."

She grabbed Erin's hand and led her through the crowd. Erin tried to squeeze past a large woman who moved into her path, and she tripped over the woman's shoe, falling hard into a man standing nearby. He turned and grabbed her arm to keep her from falling to the floor. It was Michael.

"I'm so sorry. Are you all right?" Erin said.

"I'm fine—you?" He held onto her arm.

"Yes." She straightened her hair as Aleesha came back to see what had happened. She grabbed Erin's hand again. "I need to talk to her first, Michael, but I'll bring her back."

"I'll hold you to that."

They finally reached Aleesha's room, and she closed the door behind them and stretched her arms across it. "At last—I've been dying to show you." She opened a small chintz-covered box on her bed and pulled out a card, which she handed to Erin.

"Your wedding invitations. Oh my God. You've set the date. You're really getting married." Erin hugged her and looked at the invitation again. "October. You're getting married in October. That's so soon. Leesha, I'm so happy for you."

"I'm happy for me, too."

"Who else knows?"

"No one. We're going to announce it tonight at dinner."

Erin hugged her again. "Congratulations. I know you're going to be so happy."

"There is one more thing. Will you be my matron of honor?"

"Of course." Erin's eyes filled with tears. "Of course. Thank you."

They hugged again. There was a knock at the door, and Bruce stuck his head inside. "Did you tell her?" he whispered.

Erin pulled him inside and hugged him. "Congratulations."

Aleesha slid her hand into Bruce's and pressed herself close to him.

They rejoined the crowd in the living room, and Aleesha began to guide people outside to the patio. Erin looked around for Michael but couldn't find him, so she looked for Gary. He was standing in the middle of a crowd, entertaining them with a story about a visit to Morocco. Bruce followed and stood behind her.

"Are you here with Gary Arthur?" he asked in a quiet voice.

"Yes."

He took a deep breath. "How long have you known him?"

"He was an old friend of my husband's. But I didn't know him well then. We ran into each other again a little more than a month ago." She looked at him. "Do you know him?"

"Not personally."

"What do you know about him?"

Bruce studied her face and shook his head. "Nothing, really."

They stood silent for a few more minutes listening to Gary tell his story. Erin glanced out the French doors to the deck and saw Michael sitting there, talking with a pretty blonde Erin didn't recognize. He laughed at something the woman said, and then glanced up, catching Erin's eyes. He smiled at her, and then turned back to the other woman. Erin looked away, but when she looked back he was gone.

Gary finished his story, and his listeners began to ask him questions.

"Do you want a drink?" Bruce asked.

She nodded, and they walked over to the bar where he mixed two vodka martinis. He handed one to her. "*Veritas vos liberabit.*"

She looked at him with a question on her face. "Truth will free you," he said.

She nodded, touched her glass to his, and drank a sip. A hand touched the back of her neck and gave it a little squeeze. She turned, thinking it was Gary, but it was Michael. He left his hand on her neck and leaned over her toward Bruce. "I'll take one of those."

His body was pressed against hers, and Erin caught her breath as she inhaled his subtle pine scent. It brought back memories of him carrying her, holding her close—memories from her dreams. His hand was warm on her neck, and she stood very still.

Bruce mixed another martini and handed it to Michael, who took a swallow and stepped away from Erin, dropping his hand to his side. His eyes seemed to laugh as he looked at her, and she felt her face grow warm, afraid he could tell how much his touch affected her.

"There you are." Hannah strolled up to the group, Carlos at her side. She wore a long blue skirt with an embroidered peasant blouse, her blond hair in a braid down her back. Carlos, black hair slicked back, kept his arm around Hannah's waist.

Again, Erin felt a hand on the back of her neck. Everyone was silent as she turned around. "Gary, have you met everyone here?" she said. "This is Hannah and her husband, Carlos, and you met Bruce at the door, and this is Michael Woodward, the author."

Michael stood still and stared at Gary. His eyes blazed in his stern, frozen face. Gary stepped away from him as his eyes widened. Michael slowly exhaled and reached out his hand, and Gary straightened, lifting his head high. His eyes narrowed. "I think we've met." He reached forward and shook Michael's outstretched hand. Both men glared at each other.

"Yes, we may have. Gary Arthur, is it?" Michael said.

"Yes," Gary said, and he slid his arm around Erin's shoulders, squeezing her tightly against him. She took in a quick breath and held it, the sudden tension holding her still. She looked from one to the other.

Michael raised his eyebrows. His eyes flicked back to Gary.

Hannah grasped Michael's elbow and pulled him away. "Carlos is dying to hear about your latest book. Why don't we go outside and you can tell him about it?"

His mouth formed a half-smile, and he glanced back at Erin as he let Hannah lead him away. Carlos shrugged his shoulders and followed.

Bruce watched them leave. "Anybody want a drink?"

"Yeah," Gary said. "I could use another." He banged his glass down on the bar and let go of Erin.

She watched Michael as he walked outside. "I'm going to find Aleesha and see what I can do to help."

She made her way through the crowd. What had happened back there? Gary and Michael knew each other? She found Aleesha in the kitchen directing the caterer.

Aleesha turned to Erin. "I'm so glad you're here. Could you light the candles on the tables outside? Thanks, dear."

Aleesha dashed after the caterer. Erin hesitated. She wanted to tell her about Michael and Gary's confrontation, but it would have to wait. She grabbed the matches and went onto the patio, taking a quick look around to see if Michael, Hannah, and Carlos were nearby. She didn't see them, so she went to each table and lit its candle, then came back inside and found Aleesha again, who was heading outside with the caterer.

"I'd like you to place the salad plates out now, and I'll gather the guests to the tables," Aleesha told the caterer. She turned toward Erin. "Thank you, darling. We're going to seat everyone now—could you find Gary? You two are sitting at the table beside the rose trellis."

The crowd started to take their seats for dinner, and Erin joined Gary at the table with Hannah, Carlos and several other friends from the area. Michael sat at the table with Aleesha and Bruce, and a number of others. Hannah caught Erin's gaze and pointed to Michael. Erin saw that he was watching her. His face was serious, frowning, but he held up a tiny blue flower for her to see—a forget-me-not. Gary kissed her behind her ear, and Michael turned away.

After the dinner dishes were cleared, coffee was poured, and Bruce stood up and tapped on his wine glass with a spoon.

"Friends!" he called out. "Friends, we are honored to have all of you join us tonight. We hope you're having a good time."

The crowd clapped, and some shouted, "Yeah!"

"Wasn't that a fabulous feast? Thank you, Aleesha." He nodded to her.

More applause and some whistles.

"Aleesha and I are especially happy you are all here tonight, because we have some news we are excited to share."

He paused, and the guests were silent as they focused their attention on him.

"I fell in love with Aleesha the moment I first saw her, and I knew then that I couldn't live without her. After begging and pleading, she has finally consented to becoming my wife. We've set the date for October third. We'll be inviting all of you to the wedding, and to the huge party afterwards."

Everyone clapped and shouted, "Congratulations!"

Aleesha stood up and kissed Bruce. "Don't you believe him when he says he begged and pleaded—I wanted him just as badly as he ever wanted me." She kissed him again.

People laughed and clapped.

Michael stood and raised his wineglass. "A toast—to Bruce and Aleesha!"

Everyone stood, held their wineglasses in the air, and called out, "Bruce and Aleesha." They drained their glasses.

Dessert was served, and Erin nibbled her poached pear with chocolate for a few minutes, then excused herself for the bathroom. She headed to Aleesha's bedroom, slipped inside the door, and closed it behind her.

The bathroom door opened and Michael stood there, looking as surprised to see her as she was to see him.

"Hi," she said.

"Hi." He stood in the doorway to the bathroom, blocking her way. "Delicious dinner."

"Aleesha always serves the best food."

Michael nodded. "I didn't know you were involved with Arthur."

"I ran into him at a gallery with Aleesha right before you moved here."

He frowned. "And when you dream, how often do you go to him?"

Erin covered her mouth with her hand. "I've only seen him there a couple times, I think." She remembered Bagley with the knife at her throat, and Gary's amused attitude. She moved her hand to her throat.

Michael stepped closer to her. "And have you thought about what I told you?"

"Yes, I've thought about it. I still don't know what to believe."

"I see." He sighed. "Erin, be careful. Gary Arthur has problems."

"How well do you know him?"

Michael shook his head. "I don't know him well. Only through his dreams."

"Through his dreams? Then how can you know he has problems?"

Michael's brow creased and he put his hand on her arm, sending a shiver through her body. "He'll bring you grief."

"How can you say that? He's been so good to my kids, and to me. He's a good man. And he was one of William's friends."

His eyes squinted in thought. "He knew your husband? I wonder how much he's let you know. Beware of him."

"Beware of him? He loves me, and I know he'd never hurt me." She paused. "He wants to marry me."

He pulled his hand away and stepped back. "All right then." The muscles in his jaw clenched as he stood still with his eyes on her, then he walked out of the bedroom and closed the door behind him.

Erin's stomach ached and tears came to her eyes. When she returned to the table, the party was breaking up, and people were saying their goodbyes to Aleesha and Bruce. Michael was standing in a corner of the garden speaking to another man. Gary seemed anxious to leave, so they said thank you to Aleesha and headed out to the car. The evening had already grown dark. Gary was silent as they walked, and after they got into the SUV and had driven a few blocks, he turned to Erin. "Why didn't you tell me about him? Was he the man you went to lunch with?"

Erin was startled. "Who? What are you talking about?"

Gary took a deep breath. He almost spat out the name. "Michael Woodward."

"He's a friend. There's nothing more to it than that. And I had no idea you two had met before."

His voice grew louder. "Yeah, we've met. And your friends think there's more to it than that. It's obvious. He couldn't keep his eyes off you."

"Gary, that's not true. And you know how I feel about you."

"Do I? What are you up to? You were in my dream last night—what were you doing there?" He stopped the car in the middle of the road and looked at her with a fierce light in his eyes.

"What? Your dream?" Erin couldn't believe what he was saying. "What does your dream have to do with any of this?"

His glaring eyes searched her face. He was gritting his teeth, breathing hard.

Erin frowned with alarm. "Let's pull over so we can talk."

He nodded, drove a short distance further and pulled into the parking lot of a small park. Trees sheltered the park from the road, only one dim streetlight shone from a distance. Erin turned to face him, shaking her head. "I don't know what you could be thinking—I'm not up to anything."

He sat still, his breathing fast and shallow, staring into her eyes. He slowly shook his head and rubbed his hands over his face. After a big sigh his gaze washed over her body. Erin could see both anger and hunger in his eyes.

He pulled her toward him and kissed her hard. She felt his heart pounding, his muscles tense. She kissed him back, kissed his face, and he nuzzled her neck and ears with his mouth. She was confused and anxious. What was he thinking she could be up to, something that would make him so angry?

He let go of her and pulled himself away. His voice was forceful as he said, "You are mine. I don't know what you know, but you are mine."

Chapter 45

Erin brushed her hair as she looked down from her bedroom window, her thoughts skimming over the events of the evening. She watched the light from the moon as it shone like a pathway across the water, glimmering over each swell of the Sound. She felt a sharp sense of anxiety deep in her stomach.

When they had reached home, Matt and Gwen were already in bed, and Edna went home next door, but Gary said he had a meeting early the next morning and had to get back. She was relieved that he had gone; she wanted time to think.

What had set him off like that—so angry and intense? He remembered that she had been in his dream? Was it the same dream she had last night? What did he think she knew? Michael's warnings came back to her mind. Could these dreams be real, just as Michael had said?

She put down her brush and climbed into bed, leaving the blinds open so the silvery moonlight could shine into her room. As soon as she lay down, her body relaxed and her eyes closed. She hadn't realized how exhausted she was.

***

The light was dim and cold as Erin looked around at the bleak city street. Beyond the weak light of the streetlamp she could see very little in the gloom. Not even a little moonlight lit the mists. Wispy fog floated up to the brick buildings, pressing against them as if trying to get in. The silence was as thick as the fog, and the dark windows and barren sidewalks suffocated any hope of life.

She recognized this place. She'd been here before.

Wings flapped above and she looked up to see a crow fly past. It soared in a loop above her, and then continued on its way. She followed it, running to keep up.

She ran down several empty streets until the crow landed on the roof of a two-story brick building with no windows in the front. One dark door faced the street, and Erin turned the knob and pushed. The door slowly opened, and a blast of cold air hit her. Pulling her sword from its sheath, she stepped inside and entered a large foyer. A hallway led to the back of the building and a staircase. Holding her sword in front, Erin crept up the stairs in the dark.

When she reached the top, she heard the crow caw from the roof of the building. The cold, pale glow from a streetlight shone through the grimy windows, casting shadows throughout the large room, which was filled with sheet-covered furniture. A tall, dark figure leaned beside one of the windows, arms crossed, watching her. It was Michael. He stood very still, nearly invisible in his black clothes, his sword at his side.

She sheathed her sword and took a deep breath.

"Hello, Michael," she whispered.

"Hello."

"This is a little different setting from the one you chose last time we dreamed together," Erin said. She walked over to a sheet-covered chair and sat down.

"I didn't know if you even remembered that. It's not surprising I would bring us somewhere else."

"Why are we here?" she asked.

"Several reasons." He looked out the window to the alley below. "You haven't been honest with me."

"What are you talking about?"

"You're involved with Gary Arthur."

Erin frowned. "In my day life."

"It's all one life, Erin," he said. His face was in the shadows, his voice grim. "And you've seen him at least once in his dreams. Maybe more."

Her stomach lurched, and she thought back, remembering the dream she had just the other night, with Bagley holding the knife to her throat. She shuddered. Who had Gary and Bagley been waiting for? "Yes, I have. I told you that."

Michael pushed away from the wall, pulled up a chair close to her, and straddled it. "I warned you before about the danger of going to him. He has control in his dreams, not you. And since he knows you during the day, he will limit your abilities in his dreams. You may not have any strength."

"I know this," Erin said. "I've handled it. Besides, when I last saw him, he seemed to know my strengths. I think he knows how to use the dreams."

The crow on the roof cawed twice, and Michael lifted his head to listen a moment.

His voice grew angry. "Why do you say that? What did he do?"

"You don't need to get upset. Gary purposely changed my outfit, and he laughed about it."

"What? How did this happen?"

"I think he was just joking around. I was drawn to the house where he and Bagley were hiding in the basement. They were waiting for someone and had mistaken me for that person. Fortunately, they realized their mistake before they slit my throat." She rubbed her neck.

Michael's eyes flashed. "Damn it, Erin. Do you think they were playing a game? Who do you think they were waiting for?"

She shook her head.

"They were waiting for me. It was my throat they were going to slit."

Erin's mouth dropped open, and she stood up. "You're crazy. Why would they want to harm you? They don't even know you."

"They know me very well. I have been a viator for both for more than a year now."

"What? I didn't know that. But it doesn't make any sense—why would they want to hurt you?"

"Sometimes a dreamer will bargain with mortifers against us. Mortifers can grant some benefits for a dreamer in the waking world—they can help people get what they want. And when people conspire with those demons, they open the doors of darkness into our world. It threatens everyone. The other night when Arthur and Bagley ambushed you, I felt called to that dream but didn't go. You must have felt his call because of your relationship with him, and so you went instead." Michael scowled and looked away.

She shook her head. "You're saying that Gary is in league with mortifers? He wanted to hurt you? I can't believe that—I know Gary—he wouldn't do anything like that."

"You don't know him as well as you think you do."

"This is ridiculous." Erin started to walk away. "He's a good man. What you say is impossible. What do you have against him?"

Michael jumped up and pulled her around to face him. "Don't be a fool. I've been dealing with his nightmares for more than a year. I know what's in his soul."

Erin pushed him away. *This couldn't be true.* Her mind flashed back, remembering Gary holding Gwen, his help when Matt was hurt, his tender kisses, his thoughtful gifts. "You only see one side of him. You haven't seen how he helped my kids when they were hurt, how concerned he was when his friend was shot. You haven't seen how good he is and how much he cares for us. I know him, and he loves me."

Michael winced. "You're only seeing what you want to see. What he wants to show you. You know why he was so upset when Bagley was shot? He knew he'd be next. His business is corrupt and he's in trouble."

Outside the crow cawed again.

"You don't know this. You don't even know him in real life. How can you say these things? I don't believe you."

"Shit, Erin—are you so infatuated with that fucking liar that you've lost your reason? Don't be such a fool."

She struck him across the face. Michael's cheek turned red, and he stood still for a moment, eyes wide staring into hers. He turned around and strode toward the window. At that moment Erin caught a whiff of a sweet, rotting smell, and she pulled her sword from its sheath.

Tall and cold, five mortifers burst into the room, and their harsh laughter crashed like waves in front of them. Erin whirled around and thrust her sword at the first shadow. It wavered, and another brought its sword down, meeting her blade. Cold air hit her in the face and filled the room. She staggered back.

Michael rushed at them with his sword ready and pushed them back. Erin held her breath and swung her blade hard, slicing a shadow's neck. Its high-pitched wail echoed through the room and it slumped to the floor, dissipated, and was gone. With her sword in both hands, she lunged and struck one that was attacking Michael. It twisted around and thrust its sword into her face just as she ducked out of its way. She slashed her blade straight up through its body, and it shot apart and disappeared while its shriek filled the room.

Michael's sword flashed through the air, and another shadow was gone. He pulled out his knife and fought with both hands. A mortifer's blade darted through his defense and sliced him—blood oozed from his arm and soaked his ripped jacket. The shadow laughed and attacked again with its blade overhead. Erin threw herself at his attacker, and it turned and brought its sword up against hers, wrenching it out of her grasp, sending it flying beyond her reach. She kicked it in the gut, and it staggered backwards, while Michael thrust his sword through its back. It lingered in the air a moment, then screamed and was gone. The last mortifer rushed at Erin, swinging its sword—she jumped back, but its blade grazed her torso and sliced through her clothes and skin. Fiery pain burned through her, and the room spun. It thrust again and she staggered away, struggling to keep standing. Michael leapt onto its back, and it threw him over its head and he crashed to the floor. It turned toward Erin and she ducked, then danced out of its reach. Michael was up in an instant. The shadow swung its blade at Erin again, then turned and slashed at Michael who stopped its thrust and pressed it back with his sword. It broke free and lunged, knocking Michael's sword into the air. He dove to the floor so the next blow went wide. The mortifer turned to attack Erin as Michael scrambled after his sword. He rose from the floor, jumping on its back, and pulled his blade across its throat. It fell forward on top of Erin, its cold blackness flowing around her. The rotting smell was overwhelming, numbing her and filling her with nausea before it blew away, as the shadow's wail of despair faded to an echo.

Erin struggled to her feet and doubled forward, shaking, trying to protect the sliced skin across her stomach with her arms. She tried to catch her breath, and cold sweat dripped into her eyes. Michael rose from the ground. He was breathing hard and fast, and his dark eyes were filled with fury. He stepped toward her with his sword still tight in his hand. She backed away from him until she hit the wall. His eyes were black as he stared into her, blood splattered across his face and clothes, dripping from his arm. Fear pounded through her, and she stared back into his eyes, shivering and gasping. His sword clattered to the floor. He grabbed her arms, pulled her tight against him, and kissed her.

She tasted salty blood from his mouth and felt his heart pounding as hard and fast as hers. His pine scent filled her, driving out the sick sweet stench of the shadows. She stopped shaking. When he finally pulled away, he picked his sword up off the floor, turned around, and strode to the door.

"Damn it all to hell!" he yelled, and he threw his sword through the air. It hit the far wall and stuck. He ran out the door, down the stairs, and was gone.

***

Erin opened her eyes to darkness. The moon had set, and no light shone through her window. She lay still, filled with grief, her body aching. All her pain blended together.

Finally she rolled over to look at the clock on her nightstand and gasped as she moved. Her stomach. She eased her way out of bed, flipped on the light, and pulled up her shirt. A bright red wound stretched horizontally across her abdomen. She sucked in a breath, her eyes wide.

"Mommy?" Gwen whispered as she opened the bedroom door and peeked inside. "Can I come in?"

"Of course, come in," Erin said. "What are you doing awake?"

Gwen climbed into the bed, and Erin snuggled against her, wincing at the touch against her body. "I had a bad dream," Gwen said.

Erin caressed her daughter's hair. "Tell me about it, honey."

"Matt and I were at the fair, and we were on the rides. I wanted to go on the Ferris wheel, and he didn't want to, but he said if I went on the roller coaster, he would. So I went on the roller coaster, but I fell out. And I fell and fell, and then I woke up." Gwen snuggled closer and rubbed her eyes.

Erin was grateful it was such a simple dream. She kissed the top of Gwen's head. "It was only a dream, sweetie. Everything's all right. Let's think of something happy to get your mind off of it."

"Okay," Gwen said. "Julie's getting a new kitten tomorrow. Can I go over and see it?"

"Yes, of course." Erin started to gently rub Gwen's back, and Gwen was quiet for a few minutes.

"Did you have a bad dream, too?" Gwen asked.

Tears filled Erin's eyes. "Yes, I did."

"Tell me." Gwen's eyes were closed, and Erin was sure she'd be asleep in a minute.

"All right. I went into a big building and went upstairs. Michael Woodward was there, and we had an argument. Then some bad guys came and we fought them. We won, and then Michael left."

"Hmm. It's good you won. Was he still mad at you?" Gwen asked.

"Yes."

"That's too bad. But it was only a dream. It'll all be better in the morning," Gwen said.

"Yes, you're right."

Gwen closed her eyes and was soon asleep. Erin watched her daughter breathe peacefully.

She made sure Gwen was covered with the blankets and tried to sleep. But the fury in Michael's eyes and the bloody taste of his mouth came back to her mind as soon as she closed her eyes. He had kissed her. And he was so furious with her that he had thrown his sword away. It made her sick to think of his anger. She wanted to sob.

It was only a dream. She touched her stomach, feeling the stinging pain of the wound. *This was more than just a dream.*

Gwen murmured in her sleep, and Erin stroked her hair. Could these dreams be real, as Michael had said? Memories of her other dreams began to flood back to her: The time Michael rescued her and carried her to the boat, when she first met him in his cabin and had held a knife to his throat, the feeling of his rough face against her cheek, dancing with him under the singing stars. Tears filled her eyes.

She remembered following William at his death and the mortifer that had attacked her there. If only she had been able to bring William back. She had run away, and she had left him to his death. If she could find her way back, surely she could have helped him, too. She had utterly failed him.

She imagined Michael's face again: blood splattered, eyes black with anger. So much sorrow washed through her she could hardly bear it.

More dreams came to her mind: rescuing Carolyn, helping Franny and Paul, and many more. She remembered Bruce in the stone tower, healing him with the golden liquid from her flask. She remembered the man who had soothed her on the riverbank after she had fled William and the mortifer: a small man, brown hair and eyes, and so very kind. She remembered how he had taken her hand and led her to a bright garden in the sunshine, with fountains and birds singing in blossoming trees. She realized now that it was Domus—he had brought her to Domus for the first time and taught her to fight the mortifers and how to care for the dreamers. Why had she never remembered this before?

What about Gary?

Could what Michael said be true? Gary waiting in ambush to kill him? She didn't want that to be possible.

She opened her eyes and stared at the dark ceiling. Gwen breathed softly beside her. In the morning, she would call Gary and tell him they needed to talk. She needed to find out the truth. And she would go see Michael.

Chapter 46

"Arthur here."

"Gary? It's Erin," she said into the phone. Matt and Gwen were at the kitchen table finishing their breakfast, and Erin was on her third cup of coffee already. Her thoughts had kept her awake the rest of the night.

"Erin? Jeez, what time is it? I overslept. Shit. I'm late. I'm glad you called. I've got to go," he said.

"Wait," she said. "I need to talk to you for a minute."

"What about?"

"I need to see you soon. Today, if you can get away. I'll come there."

"Hey, I'd love to see you today, but I can't. I've got to catch a flight to New York at noon."

"I didn't know you were going to New York."

"It was sudden."

"When do you come back?"

"Friday. Friday afternoon. Why don't I drive up straight from the airport, and we can have dinner?"

"That sounds fine," Erin said.

They were both silent for a minute.

"I've got to run," Gary said.

"Yes. Have a good trip."

"See you Friday."

Erin tossed out the rest of her coffee and sat down next to Matt. "I've got to run an errand in town, but I won't be very long. We can do something fun when I get back, okay?"

"Sure," Matt said.

"Okay, Mom," Gwen said. "Let's go see Julie's kitten later."

Erin pulled on a denim jacket, grabbed her purse and went out the door. Cold dew still covered the grass, and fog swirled in wisps across the ground.

She drove along the highway into town and debated about going to see Michael. Her midnight resolve had faded into doubt—doubt about the dreams and doubt about him, with more than a little fear of facing him again. But she needed to talk to him and decided not to turn back.

She pulled to the curb and walked up the path to his porch. The flowers blooming in pots beside the door gave the house a friendly atmosphere, and Erin's courage rose. She rang the doorbell and waited. Bruce opened the door.

"Hi, Erin," he said in obvious surprise. "Are you looking for Aleesha? You just missed her—she's on her way to the gallery."

"No, I'm actually here to see Michael. Is he here?"

"No." He frowned. "I'm not sure where he is. He left sometime in the early morning, and I'm not sure when he'll be back."

"Oh." Erin's eyes searched the ground as this information sank in. "What did he say? You don't know where he went?"

"Come in and sit down," Bruce said, opening the door wide.

"Thanks. He left in the early morning?"

Bruce led her to a couch and sat beside her.

"He left me a note, so I think he left some time during the night. He didn't wake us. Here it is." Bruce retrieved the note from the side table and handed it to her.

Bruce—Am going away to finish the book. Not sure when I'll be back. When you go to Portland, would you ask Aleesha to water the plants? M.

"It sounds like he plans to be gone a long time," Erin said.

"It's hard to say. He knows I have to drive back to Portland for classes tomorrow," Bruce said.

"Do you know where he would go?"

"No. He's gone off to different places when he wants time to be alone to write, so there's no way to know. But he'll let his agent know soon. His agent usually knows where he is."

Erin felt like crumbling. "I really wanted to talk to him. What about his cell phone?"

"I already tried to reach him on his cell, but it's shut off."

She sighed. "If you get hold of him, would you tell him I stopped by?"

"Sure."

"Would you ask him to call me?"

"Of course."

Erin stood up and walked to the door while Bruce followed. She tried to hold them back, but a few tears ran down her face.

"What happened? Was it a dream?" Bruce asked.

"You know about the dreams?"

"Was Michael hurt?

Erin looked at the ground and brushed her tears away. *Bruce knows, too. These are not ordinary dreams at all.* "How do you know about these dreams?"

"I thought Michael talked to you about them. You still don't remember them?"

"It seems crazy."

He shook his head. "Believe me, it's not crazy. Those dreams are as real as you and I standing here right now. Was Michael hurt?"

"We argued and he was angry. Then we had to fight five of them—five ... mortifers. He was hurt but not badly." She shook her head and frowned. "He threw his sword and left it there."

"He left his sword there?" Bruce grasped Erin's arm. "Why?"

Erin turned away, the knot in her stomach growing more painful. "He was furious with me."

"Oh. Well. I'll go get his sword. Tell me where this happened."

"I don't know where it was—on a deserted city street somewhere, on the second floor of a concrete building. How will you find it?"

"I'll focus on the sword. Well, now I understand why he left. I'll try to find him as soon as I can and give him your message."

"Thanks," she said. She went to her car and the sick feeling grew inside her.

After driving home she took Matt to Jacob's house, then spent the rest of the day with Gwen making cookies and visiting Julie's new kitten. All day she hoped for a call from Bruce or Michael that didn't come.

That night she searched for Michael in her dreams, but instead she lost her way traveling through a murky forest. She felt the cold dread of a mortifer following behind, but it never came close enough for her to see. She woke with a start, sitting straight up in bed, sweat dripping from her face.

***

Bruce crept through the dark city street, avoiding the occasional glow of a streetlight overhead as he passed shattered windows in crumbling empty buildings. He studied each building he passed, pausing at every doorway to sense the right direction.

When he reached a two-story concrete block building, the skin on his scalp prickled and his stomach lurched. He knew at last he'd found it. But how many mortifers lay in wait?

Without a sound, he pulled his sword from its sheath, yanked the door open, and slipped inside. Icy air hit him, knocking his breath away. He crept forward heading for the stairs, and a sickening stench grew as he approached.

A black shadow grew in the hall beyond the stairway—a mortifer. Bruce rushed it, slashed straight across its torso with his sword in both hands, and it blew apart. Another one was behind the first, ready for him. It swung its blade over Bruce's head, brought it down hard. Bruce lunged to the side and forced his sword up, but the mortifer twirled around and the stroke fell wide. It laughed and charged, swinging its blade. Bruce danced backwards, feinted to the left, and cut upward, slashing the shadow. Its eyes burned bright red, then shattered like crumbling coals as it dissipated.

Bruce stood alert listening to the silence, then sprinted up the stairs.

Pale light from the windows cast shadows around the room, making ghostly shapes of the toppled sheet-covered furniture. Bruce surveyed the room and ran to the nearby wall. He pulled the sword from where it was stuck.

"To Domus," he said and faded from the room.

Chapter 47

THE week dragged by with no word from either Michael or Bruce. Each day brought Erin closer to her meeting with Gary, and her dread for that meeting grew. Thursday evening, after the children were in bed, Erin tidied the kitchen and folded a load of clothes from the dryer. She made herself a cup of peppermint tea and threw the teabag into the trash. The garbage was full, so she picked up the bag to take it outside.

As she stepped out the back door, a dark form rose slowly from the ground in the bushes in front of her. She dropped the garbage. An icy gust of wind blew, and she pulled her sweater tightly around her body; her bare feet hurt from the sudden chill. The shape grew taller until it blotted out some of the stars. Was this a man, or a trick of the shadows? She peered up at it, and its searing eyes stabbed through her. Terror spiraled through Erin's body. Could this be a mortifer escaped from her dreams?

She cried out and dropped to her knees on the gravel driveway, blackness almost overwhelming her, and the creature stretched out its icy claws. Erin felt its bitter touch. She recoiled, and it laughed—a high, hollow sound that was frigid in the night air. When a crow landed in the fir tree overhead and let out one loud caw, the shadow hesitated. It stood motionless while the crow flew to the ground nearby and called out, "Caw, caw, caw," as it hopped toward Erin.

She knew she had to get up. As if in slow motion, she lifted herself from the ground and was almost overwhelmed with nausea. Fight it, she thought, keep moving.

The crow drank from a nearby puddle, and the shadow stretched taller, looming over Erin. Taking a deep breath, she turned and ran across the soft lawn of her garden and down the pathway toward the beach. *Could that thing swim?* She wouldn't last long herself in the frigid water. A faint groan escaped her as she turned to see if it had followed her.

The tide was out and the rocky shoreline glowed faintly in the light of the moon. Erin scanned the beach and the pathway, her heart pounding. *What was that thing? Where was it? Was it gone?*

The crow cawed, and the hair on the back of her neck rose as she felt the air become icy cold once again, and the shadowy creature emerged on the path—a darker black than the woods behind it. Erin turned and fled along the beach without looking back, with no idea where she could go. The sharp rocks and barnacles cut into her bare feet, but she kept running, while the beach grew narrower and rockier as the tide rose.

A large boulder blocked her way, stretching from the forest to the water, so she stopped, her heart racing, her lungs about to burst. She whirled around and saw the shadow a distance away, slowly gliding toward her. The rock face was too steep to climb, so she thrashed into the woods, searching for a path to the road. She stumbled over tangled brush and a small rowboat covered with vines. Pulling with all her strength, Erin dragged and pushed the little boat out of the woods. She could find only one oar. She pulled the boat over the rocks to shore, and pushing hard, she got it into the water.

The brittle voice of the mortifer called out behind her. "You will never get away."

The stench gagged her, and she stumbled.

"Go away." Erin tried to yell, but her voice faded to a whisper.

The thing mocked her with its high-pitched laugh. "You are weak."

She felt like she would be sick.

"It amuses us that this viator has taken a lover."

Erin's head jerked up. The sound of its words hurt her to her bones.

The glint from a knife caught her eye as the shadow bent toward her. "Such irony. The very man who paid us to put an end to your William. Wretched fool. You are so easily seduced."

She fell to her knees, cringing in the face of the mortifer's scorn. The crow flew overhead and landed on top of the rock behind her. It cawed one time, and the mortifer took a step back. Erin looked up. A salty breeze blew off the water, and she breathed it in.

"No," she yelled. "Your words are lies."

The mortifer stood motionless with its flaming eyes piercing through her. Erin got up and grabbed the oar from the boat. She lunged forward with the oar over her head and struck at the shadow. The oar seemed to pass through it.

It mocked her with its hissing laugh.

Erin screamed at the shadow again. "No!" She struck harder. "Go back to your hell."

It laughed once more, but it vanished into the ground, jeering as it left. "You are ours, viator."

Erin dropped to the ground as the crow flew away. Blackness overwhelmed her. When she could see again, her body felt like ice, and she couldn't stop trembling. Her bare feet were cut and bleeding from rocks and barnacles, but she had to get back to the safety of her home, back to her children. She struggled to stand and hobbled the long way back down the beach to her house. The only sound she heard was that of the gentle waves.

Erin's house was in darkness as she limped up the trail from the beach. She went straight to the kitchen door—it was closed but unlocked just as she had left it when she had taken the garbage out. She was too cold, too dazed, and in too much pain to think about what had happened. All she wanted was to get inside, make sure the children were safe, and crawl into bed.

Once inside she slipped on the flip flops left by the door and went to look in on the children. Both Matt and Gwen were sound asleep and safe in their beds. Erin stumbled to her room and approached the small, cloth-covered table. She struck a match with trembling hands and lit one of the candles, gazing at William's photograph. She bowed her head and sank to the floor.

That had been no dream. That was real. How had a mortifer from her dreams come into her waking life? Its scathing accusations made her nauseous, and she grabbed hold of William's photo and hugged it close. *Its words had to be lies. How could she believe anything it said?*

She went into her bathroom and filled the tub with steaming water, took off her clothes, and lowered herself into it. Her feet stung, but she needed to get them clean. The warmth helped stop her trembling. She knew she had to face it: the mortifers were real. Her dreams were real. More than ever she wanted to talk to Michael.

After stepping from the bathtub and bandaging her feet, Erin tried to call him, hoping he had turned his phone back on. No answer, and she groaned. She blew out the candle, eased herself into bed, and stared at the ceiling for a long time before drifting into a troubled sleep, haunted by the voice of the mortifer.

Chapter 48

WHEN Friday morning finally arrived, Erin felt worn out and ready for the week to end. She put on a T-shirt and didn't bother with much makeup. Breakfast and two cups of coffee revived her a little, and after kissing the children goodbye at school, she drove to work. She had arranged for Matt and Gwen to go directly to Edna's after school, so if Gary showed up early, she wouldn't need to go home.

The music store was bustling that morning, and Erin was grateful. She wanted to stay busy to keep from thinking about the night before. Her feet were very sore. In the daylight, the idea that a mortifer from her dreams had actually been at her house was almost unbelievable. Thinking about it made her skin crawl. One thing she had no doubt about being real, though, were her scars. The wound across her stomach was still healing. She had a quick lunch at the café with Hannah, who expressed concern about how tired Erin looked.

"It's been a tough week," Erin said. "I haven't been sleeping well."

"Is it your dreams?" Hannah asked, her face anxious.

"That and too many things going on right now. I'm seeing Gary after work, and I'm really looking forward to a relaxing weekend." She didn't want to tell Hannah any more than that—Hannah would worry too much.

Hannah nodded. "I'm sure you'll feel better soon." She reached across the table and squeezed Erin's hand.

Erin had just returned to the store after lunch when two men walked in. She recognized them as the men who had confronted Gary at

Deception Pass, and she felt a shiver of fear. One had greasy brown hair slicked back from his face, and the thick black eyebrows on the other gave him a permanent frown. Both of their eyes were cold and dull. Ed was in his office upstairs.

She greeted the men cautiously. "Hello. Can I help you?"

The men exchanged glances. The one with the thick eyebrows said, "You are a friend of Gary Arthur?"

"Yes."

"We would like to talk to you."

"I'm listening."

He smiled scornfully at her. "In private, Ms. Holley."

She startled at his use of her name. "We can go into my studio."

"We would prefer to go outside."

Erin did not want to go anywhere with them, and she called out to Ed. "I have to take a couple minutes to talk to these two men. We'll be in my studio."

Ed walked down the stairs. "Okay, Erin." He looked the two men over. "Everything all right?"

"Yes." She looked at the men and was determined to maintain some control. "We will talk in my studio, and it should only take a couple minutes, right?"

They exchanged glances. Erin led them into her studio. She sat on the piano bench and motioned for them to take the chairs. One of the men sat, the other pulled the door closed and remained standing.

"What is this about?" she asked.

The man in the chair looked her up and down. "Arthur owes us. And you are going to make sure he pays."

Erin's heart pounded. "Why would I do anything to help you?"

The man by the door stepped toward her and raised his hand. But the other man briefly shook his head and his eyes squinted. "Because you will, and you know you will."

She looked back and forth between the two. "What does he owe you?"

He leaned closer and grasped her chin in his hand. "A healthy shipment. He didn't take care of things the way he should."

Erin slowly, deliberately moved his hand away from her face, holding his gaze with her eyes. "What? What didn't he take care of?"

"If he transports cargo, but there are delays, there can be losses. And losses lead to consequences."

"Drugs?"

The man raised his eyebrows. "No. More family. Much more profit."

Family? Erin drew back with a sharp intake of air. Then the man in the chair leaned forward. "You will make sure. Tell him if he does not take care of this now, we know where you work and where you live. We know where your children are. But that would not be enough. He would still owe more."

Erin felt dizzy.

The men opened the door and left the music shop, but Erin stayed seated on the piano bench for a moment, too stunned to do anything. She shook her head … more family, he had said. People. He's trafficking in people. She stood up and walked out of her studio to where Ed was working. "I'm not feeling very well. I think I need some fresh air. Would you mind if I took fifteen minutes to go outside?"

"You're white as a ghost. Are you all right?" he asked.

Erin nodded. "I just need some air."

She pushed open the door, turned right, and almost ran down the street. Her feet hurt, but she didn't care. She didn't notice any of the people she passed; her mind was a blur. She couldn't think clearly and felt smothered by all her thoughts. *People? Human trafficking? Oh no, no.*

She walked to Hannah's bakery and went inside. Hannah's new girl beamed at her from behind the counter.

"Good afternoon, ma'am. Can I help you?"

"Is Hannah here?"

"No. She just left for Seattle and won't be back until late."

"Thanks," Erin said, and she whirled around and headed down the street to the gallery. It was only a quick ten-minute walk, and when she got there she went inside and looked around. No one was up front. She glanced in the various rooms, but they were deserted. The raven painting by Daniel Frank caught her eye; she hadn't seen it since the time she'd shown Michael. She remembered his face as he'd looked at it, how his eyes had danced with amusement as he talked about the raven myths. His sharp interest in her had been frightening at the time, and now she realized he had remembered her from their dreams. And now he was gone. Her stomach ached.

She wandered out to the garden in the back, and there she found Aleesha's assistant with a customer. He looked up at her, and she asked him if Aleesha was there.

He frowned. "No. She went to Seattle this afternoon. I thought she went with you. But maybe it was just Hannah."

"Thanks."

She walked back through the gallery and to the music shop again. Sitting in her studio, she was thankful she didn't have any lessons scheduled. *What was she going to do? Could Gary really have done those things?* The rest of the afternoon passed slowly.

Erin was putting music away and cleaning up her studio at five o'clock when she saw Gary come into the shop. He wore a finely tailored charcoal Italian suit that fit his muscular body perfectly, and his blond hair was trimmed and neat. As he entered the store, he loosened his tie and took it off, said hi to Ed, and went straight into Erin's studio. He looked her up and down.

"A little casual today?" he said.

She frowned slightly. "I wanted to be comfortable."

He grinned and his blue eyes sparkled. "I can help you get comfortable." He wrapped his arms around her and kissed her lightly. "Miss me?"

She nodded. "Yeah. I did."

He pulled back from her a little, looking into her face more carefully. "What's wrong?"

"We need to talk—but not here—let's go."

She grabbed his hand and pulled him out of the shop with her. His Porsche was parked next to the curb only two cars away, so they climbed in.

"Where to?" His face was serious, concerned.

"Do you want a drink?" she asked. Now that he was with her, she wanted to postpone the discussion as long as she could.

"Yeah." He studied her from the corners of his eyes as he pulled the car onto the street. "Let's go to The Wharf."

They drove the short distance to the restaurant. The sky was clear and still bright, but it was cold in the convertible. Erin had forgotten her jacket in the store and hugged herself to keep warm. Gary parked and got out, coming around to open her door. They walked into the restaurant bar where they sat in a booth in the corner. Erin ordered a glass of merlot, and Gary ordered scotch on the rocks. It was still early—the bar nearly empty.

"What is it?" he asked with a frown.

Erin took a sip of wine. "I had a visit from some friends of yours today."

His face froze—his eyes like ice.

"The men we saw at Deception Pass came into the store today." She glanced up at him—his eyes were intense, watching her. "They wanted to speak to me. I made them go into my studio." She frowned and tears came to her eyes.

Gary's eyes softened. He reached one hand toward her face and caressed her cheek. "Oh, baby."

"Don't." She continued in a quiet voice, "They told me that I have to make sure you fulfill your obligation. That you owe them. They know where to find me and the children, but—you would still owe them more."

He lifted his eyebrows and gave a short laugh. She stared at him.

"Erin, why did you even listen to them? You should have called the police. They're a couple of thugs."

"They told me the merchandise that was lost was more profitable than drugs." Erin's heart was beating fast.

Gary narrowed his eyes. "What are you thinking?"

Her voice was a whisper. "Were they people? Were you trafficking people?"

He took a gulp of his drink and his nostrils flared. "For Christ's sake, is that what you think of me?"

"I don't want to, but what is going on?"

Gary stared at the far wall, his jaw clenched. He looked back at her and threw back his scotch. He waved to the bartender for another.

"Nothing's going on. They're trying to scare you and get to me. They're full of empty threats."

Erin frowned as she finished her wine. The waiter brought them both fresh drinks, and Gary told him to bring him another as he gulped half of his fresh one.

"Does this have anything to do with Henry getting shot?"

"Henry has his own demons."

"What do you mean by that?" Her dream came to mind with Henry cowering from the horrible shadows. Henry with a knife at her throat. And Gary there too.

He hesitated before answering. "Henry's made enemies—the same as anyone. Look, I'll take care of those thugs. You don't need to worry about them."

"Don't patronize me. There's something going on, and you don't want to talk about it. Are you involved in what they said? I've heard your business is … I've heard there are issues."

"What did you hear? I didn't think William ever talked to you about my business."

"William? Was he involved?" Erin felt dizzy with shock.

Gary shook his head. "Shit, Erin, what have you heard?"

She remembered what Michael had told her in her dream. "That your business is corrupt," she whispered. "Was William involved in your business?"

"No, he had nothing to do with it. I was selling him parts for the nav systems they built. Does that sound like a corrupt business?" His voice grew louder.

"What was the shipment you lost? Were they people? What happened to them? Did William know you were doing that?"

Gary's eyes widened. The waiter brought him another drink, and he picked it up and stared at the wall. When he turned back to her his voice was icy calm.

"You need to stop asking questions."

Erin felt a wave of fear and anger surge through her. She sat back, breathing hard. "I need to know the truth." Her heart was beating so hard she could almost hear it.

Gary gulped the rest of his drink, stood and grabbed her arm, pulling her up and toward the door. He tossed a few twenties to the bartender as he rushed out, still holding Erin's arm until they got to the car.

"What are you doing?" she yelled.

"Shut up. Listen to me." He stopped at his car, his breathing ragged. "I can't believe this. First Grekov with his damn lost cargo, then Lehman and his threats, then Bagley gets shot. And I thought with William gone I had no worries." He grabbed her arms and looked into her eyes. "And there you were—William's goddam widow. What did he tell you? Fuck!" He paced away, then came back and kicked the tire of his car. He reached for her and grabbed her again. "You seemed so innocent. And then you showed up in my dreams. You're one of those viators."

She gasped.

He stared at her, his jaw clenched, pulling the keys from his pocket and unlocking the car. He opened the door and pushed her into the passenger seat, then climbed in and backed the car out. He peeled out of the parking lot and onto the road.

Erin found her voice. "You know about the dreams?"

He looked at her with disbelief. "Are you kidding?"

"It's true then. What else? Do those shadows help you get what you want? Were you and Bagley planning to kill a viator when he almost slit my throat? Is that how you pay them for helping you?"

Gary stared straight ahead, and Erin could see that every muscle in his body was clenched as he sped down the main street heading to the highway. Fear and anger pounded through her. The terrifying words the mortifer had spoken the night before haunted her—was Gary responsible for William's death?

A bitter wind blew through the convertible, and Erin shivered in her T-shirt. Gary drove furiously, passing every car. They turned onto the highway to Mt. Vernon.

"What did you do?" Erin shouted.

Gary shook his head. "Shit. Henry warned me about you. But I had to know what William told you." He looked over at her and his voice grew louder. "He kept asking questions. He couldn't leave well enough alone."

"So you arranged his death?" Tears ran down Erin's face. "With mortifers' help? William was your friend."

He threw her a glance. "I did what I had to do."

Erin hit him across the face. The car swerved into the other lane. Another car honked, and Gary leaned over and grabbed her arm. She pulled free, and the car careened into the other lane again. The oncoming car honked and hit their rear fender. Erin lurched to the side as the car spun around and the other car flew off the road. Her head flew forward as another car rammed them from behind, shoving them off the road and over the embankment.

The car bounced down the hill, each bump jolting Erin, forcing her to cry out. The rear of the car hit a ridge, bouncing it up and over, flipping them upside down, metal crunching against metal, and they finally stopped. The roll bar held, leaving a little room, but the car was crushed. Erin heard a loud rushing noise in her ears and struggled to get out. She felt desperate and panicked, claustrophobic and hurt all over, and she could taste blood in her mouth, felt it seeping into her eyes. A deep blackness covered her, soft as a blanket, muffling her pain. As if from far away, she heard Gary moan.

Chapter 49

Erin smelled damp earth and shivered in the biting cold. She lay on the hard ground and opened her eyes but could barely see the trees overhead in the dim light. The sound of running water was in the distance, and she could hear the rustling of someone moving in the bushes nearby.

She sat up slowly. Her T-shirt and jeans were dirty, but she had lost her shoes and her feet were bandaged. She couldn't remember what had happened to her shoes and looked around for them. Where were they? Why were her feet bandaged? *What had happened? Was this a dream?*

The nearby underbrush rustled again, and Gary stood up about ten feet from her. She watched him look around, spot her, and look away again. He looked as if he didn't know where he was either. "Where are we?" she said as she stood. "Do you know what happened to my shoes?"

He glanced at her and mumbled, "I don't know." He frowned slightly and wandered in the direction of the running water. Erin followed him and saw he had lost his shoes too.

The shadowy forest was dense with underbrush, and the trees were close. They followed a small trail, and the light ahead grew brighter, making it easier to see the way. Erin sensed the place was familiar, but she had a hard time remembering when she'd been there before. She grew anxious and struggled to think back to where she and Gary had been before they came to the forest. All she recalled was being at the restaurant. She focused on that and tried to follow the events in her mind. She remembered they had argued and that she was very angry but didn't know why. Her thoughts were so confused. The ground was cool and soft under her bandaged feet. She was certain she had hurt her feet running on the beach. Her memories started to return—there had been a mortifer on her beach. She remembered the men in the music store and what they had said—how they had threatened her. And riding in the car with Gary—she had been so angry. Why? Then she remembered—Gary was responsible for William's death. She stopped. Her anger flared as her memory returned, and she wanted to scream at him, hit him, hurt him. He had taken her husband from her, destroying her life, her hopes and dreams.

Gary kept walking through the forest, heading to higher ground along the winding trail. Erin scrambled after him. He seemed focused on the path ahead and didn't appear to notice that she was there, following him. She didn't try to talk to him.

The sound of rushing water grew louder, and just ahead a river cut through the forest. The moment she saw it she stopped. She knew where they were. The river was about thirty feet wide, swift and deep in places, shallow in others, with boulders scattered across. Some of the stones were nearly submerged, and they looked slick and treacherous. She felt a sharp pain in her chest at the realization: This was where she had followed William the day he'd died. Gary walked up to the shore and watched the torrent rush past.

Erin knew he was going to cross the river, just as William had done. She hadn't been able to save her husband, and now Gary would cross, and he would die, too. She couldn't save him. There was no hope for him, and he was corrupt. She knew that now. There was nothing she could do.

She heard a whisper in her mind. "I see so much mercy inside you, stronger than a sword. Where there's mercy, you'll find hope."

She didn't feel any mercy. He could go to the devil.

A chill wind blew, and Gary groaned. He looked around, and Erin saw the fear on his face. When he saw her his eyes widened as if he hadn't realized she was there. He shivered and took a step into the river. If he crossed, would mortifers find him and take him, as they had tried to do with her? Mortifers would give him no mercy. Could she simply stand by and let him die in torment?

She grabbed his jacket sleeve. "Gary, no. Don't go across."

"What?" Trickles of sweat ran down his face. She knew he was disoriented and terrified.

"Gary, let's go back—we can go back that way," she said, pointing back the way they had come. "We can make it."

He looked at her with confusion and shook his head. "No, I've got to get over there." He pointed to the other side of the river.

"You don't know what's over there. I've been there before, and I'm not ready to go there again. You don't want to go. Stay here—the way out is down that path." She pointed back the way they had come.

He shook his head again. "I have to go across." He stepped onto a rock and jumped from it to the next stone without difficulty, making his way across the width of the river. When he reached the opposite shore, he leapt onto the bank and looked back at Erin for a moment, his face white and filled with terror, then he turned and walked into the forest on the other side.

The ache in Erin's stomach gnawed at her and her head throbbed. If Gary could make it back, might there be some hope for him? *There will be no hope for him if a mortifer takes him.*

Erin watched as Gary walked away. *I am a viator, and I fight those demons.* She leapt to the nearest rock in the river, slipped and almost fell, and stepped to the next. She struggled to make her way across, sliding on the wet stones, finally leaping to the opposite bank, where she pushed her way through the woods. She wished she had her sword. The memory of the mortifer that had found her there before was vivid in her mind, and she trembled, her stomach queasy as she looked around. She rushed to catch up with Gary and finally saw him in the distance ahead. He had stopped and was standing still with his back to her. A mortifer was facing him.

"No!" she screamed.

The shadow fled into the forest.

"Gary," she called.

He turned around just as she reached him.

"Are you all right?"

His face was pale and drawn, and sweat ran down his cheeks. "I'm okay."

"Come back. I'll show you the way."

"I'm finished. There's no hope for me."

"Is that what the shadow told you? It's full of lies. Come back," she said.

His eyes pleaded with her. "I need to go this way now."

"Think of Fiji, Gary. Of dancing and scuba diving. Think of warm sunshine and running on the beach."

He hesitated, his eyes searching hers.

"Come with me." She took his hand and he let her lead him back to the river. The way was rocky and treacherous, and dense undergrowth scratched them and tore at their clothes as they struggled to get through. By the time they reached the river, they were dripping with sweat, their feet cut and clothes torn. They stood at the shore, watching the icy water rush past. Erin found the ford, but Gary drew back, trembling. She coaxed him to go in front of her onto the first rock, and they made their way to the middle of the river together, when Gary stopped and turned around. His face was white, and he was shaking, his breathing labored.

He reached into his jacket and pulled out a long knife. A mortifer's blade.

She looked at the knife and looked up at his face.

His eyes pleaded with her.

"I'm sorry. I have to do this."

He shoved the knife into her belly.

Her eyes opened wide and she stared at him as she gasped. The sharp pain pierced through her, spreading through her whole body. She clutched her hands to her stomach and felt her blood pulsing out. Gary pulled out the knife and threw it into the river; his face twisted with horror.

He shook his head and whispered, "I had to."

Erin tumbled into the rushing water, and Gary scrambled across the rest of the rocks, reached the other side, and ran back through the forest the way they had come.

The icy water caught her, rushed over her, and pushed her downstream. She saw her blood mix and swirl with the water. Huge rocks that jutted out of the river caught and slowed her, but the water flowed over her face pushing her down, and she gasped for breath. Her strength was draining away. She was in agony and cold and too weak to stop herself. The river pulled her away from the rocks, and she swirled downstream again.

She held her breath as long as she could, then gasped and choked. The rushing water battered her against more rocks as she swept past until a low-hanging tree branch finally caught and held her in a shallow pool. Forcing her legs to move, she crawled up the shore on the far side, where she dragged herself into the shelter of some fir trees, coughing water and blood. She tried to stand.

Dizziness overwhelmed her, and she collapsed onto the hard ground. A gray haze settled over everything, and the forest grew cold. Erin felt like such a fool. She lay on her side and curled her knees up to her chest, covering her face with her hands. Her body shivered and her teeth chattered. How could she have allowed this to happen? She had been so blind. Michael had tried to warn her, and she had pushed him away. *Oh, Michael.* She felt so much agony, and now she was dying here, alone in the dark forest where no one could find her, and her children would have no one.

She moaned. Her stomach was on fire, and she was utterly alone. She had failed completely. The blackness surrounding her was spinning, and she felt herself spiraling down, further and deeper into the darkness, full of thorns and ice that pierced her again and again. Pain spread from her wound and shot through every part of her body. She smelled a sick, sweet odor, and terror filled her mind and her heart. She was lost.

Chapter 50

THE drive from Portland was grueling on a Friday night, but Bruce finally made the turn into Anacortes and drove up to Aleesha's house. The house was in darkness; he wondered if she had gone to Michael's to meet him there. He pulled into her driveway, hopped out of his car, and sprinted up to the door. It was locked, so he pulled out his key and let himself in. No one was there. He flipped on some lights and saw the note on the message board: *Bruce—Erin was in a car accident. I've gone to the hospital in Mt. Vernon. I'll call you when I can. Love, Aleesha*

Bruce sat down. A car accident. Must be bad if they were at the hospital. He got up and went to the refrigerator and pulled out a bottle of beer, popped it open and took a drink. The phone rang.

It was Aleesha. "I'm so glad you're there. They're airlifting Erin to Seattle—they don't know if she's going to make it." He could tell she was crying; it was hard for her to speak. "Gary's pulling through—he's going to be all right. But Erin …"

"Do you want me to come and get you? I can take us there," he said.

"No, you don't need to—Hannah and Carlos are here, and they're driving. I'll go with them. But Bruce, try to reach Michael, okay?"

"I will," he said. "I'm sure she'll make it. She's a strong woman."

"She's been through so much already," Aleesha started sobbing. "Damn it. I don't want to cry."

"Babe, she'll be all right."

"Okay. I'll call you from Seattle."

"Try not to worry," he said.

Bruce dialed Michael's cell phone, but there was no answer, so he left a message. He tipped back his beer and drank half the bottle, then went and lay down on the couch. If Erin were wandering in the dream world, maybe he could find her. He had to try something. She had saved him before, and he had to do what he could, but he wished he could find Michael.

He closed his eyes and relaxed each muscle in his body, one by one, taking his time. When he relaxed his face and eyelids, he felt himself slipping away, and he took a deep breath and let it out slowly. He imagined Erin's face. He took another deep breath, opened his eyes and found himself in a forest. It was twilight, and he could see the silhouette of the fir trees against the sky. The air was icy but smelled fresh and clean. He found a narrow path and followed it toward the distant sound of running water.

The sky was a little brighter in the direction he was heading, and the brightness grew as he walked. He was dressed in black with his sword at his side, and he moved silently through the forest. The sound of the water grew steadily louder, and he finally came to the bank of the river.

He frowned. He knew this was a dividing line, and if Erin was on the opposite shore, he didn't know if he could reach her. "Erin Holley!" he called out. There was no response.

He saw the ford in the river, and he stepped out onto the first stone. His foot slipped off into the water; he caught himself and tried again. The rock was so slick he couldn't stay on it, so he took off his boots. The water was biting cold, and he still couldn't gain a secure footing. He put his boots back on and scrambled along the rocky shore, heading downstream, looking for any sign of Erin. Finally he saw a figure in the shadows of the fir trees on the opposite shore. He drew closer; it was a tall man with brown hair dressed in khakis and a blue shirt. He was standing still watching Bruce approach.

Bruce stopped and called, "I'm searching for a woman!"

The man said nothing, but his brow creased, and he pointed to the ground at his feet. The dense undergrowth hid whatever was there.

Bruce's heart pounded. "Is she there?"

The man pointed at the ground again.

"I can't get across," Bruce called out. The man made no sign.

"Shit," Bruce said under his breath. A crow flew overhead.

"What?" said a voice behind him. Bruce whirled; Michael stood there.

"When did you get here?" Bruce said.

"Just now," said Michael. "The crow led me, and I came as quickly as I could. What's happened?"

"I think Erin's across the river. She was in a car accident. I don't know how bad it was, but she's not answering."

***

Michael's stomach twisted as he scanned the opposite shore. "Who's that?" he asked, looking at the man standing in the forest.

"Don't know. I asked him if he'd seen Erin, and he pointed to the ground at his feet. I think she's right there."

Michael lowered his voice to a whisper. "I think I know who that is."

He walked to the edge of the water and called out, "William."

The man looked over at him.

"Is Erin there?"

William pointed to the ground.

"I'm coming."

"There's a ford upstream, but I wasn't able to cross it," Bruce said.

"I'll try." Michael didn't know if he could get across, and if he did make it, he didn't know if he could get back. They made their way upriver to the stony ford, and Michael took off his boots and stepped onto the first rock. His foot slid off, but he caught himself and tried again. This time he kept his footing and stepped to the next stone. Bruce watched him from the shore. Michael carefully stepped from one stone to the other, and was more than halfway across when he slipped and fell into the rushing water. The current pulled at him and started to wash him downstream. He came up, gasped for air, and reached out to grab onto a boulder. His grip held; he got his feet underneath him and stood, braced against the pull of the water.

"You all right?" Bruce yelled.

Michael coughed. "Yeah," he shouted, feeling for his sword and knife, finding them both still tight against him. He readied himself to force his way across the remainder of the river against the current. He pushed against the boulder and kept his feet on the rocky bottom as he struggled the rest of the way across. He reached the shore and lay down on the grassy bank.

He caught his breath and stood up just as Bruce called out, "Mortifer!"

Michael smelled its putrid odor before he saw it, and he drew his sword and whirled around. The shadow rose out of the forest floor and pulled a staff from its black robes. It swung the staff, preparing to hit Michael across the head, but he dodged and thrust his sword to slash at the shadow. It laughed and jumped away. "You are out of your world, viator. I have the power here."

Michael gritted his teeth. "Show me."

The shadow howled, and another mortifer rose out of the ground beside it. It lunged at Michael with its sword while the other one leapt forward with its pole and brought it smashing down. Michael countered with his own blade, and blocked the pole with his arm. He heard a loud crack and intense pain shot through him. He swung his sword fast, advancing on the mortifers before they could ready another attack. He slashed through one, and it let out a screeching wail before it blew away on the breeze. The other dodged his blade and thrust its own sword back and forth. Michael leapt aside and brought his sword down on its head, cleaving it in two—the shadow shrieked and was gone.

Gripping his injured arm, Michael dashed away to find Erin. Soon he could see William through the trees, still standing in the same spot, and he slowed his approach. When he got closer, he saw Erin lying at William's feet, pale, wet, and still, huddled on the ground, her bloody arms hugging her body. He gasped and looked at William's face—he was expressionless and said nothing; he just pointed to her again.

Michael dropped to his knees beside her and felt her face and hands. She was icy cold. He pulled her arms away and saw her stomach had been ripped open and blood still pulsed out. He swallowed hard. She was already so far gone. He pulled out his small flask, opened it, and poured some of the golden liquid over her wound. Erin's face was almost blue and she didn't move. Holding the flask to her mouth, he poured a tiny amount of the liqueur between her lips, but it ran down her face. When he picked up her body, cradling her on his lap, she was limp, and he held her close and caressed her cold, wet hair and kissed her pale face and bloodless lips.

There had to be something he could do—he couldn't let her go like this. Where had she gone if she wasn't here? He laid Erin back down on the ground, took off his jacket and shirt, wrapped the shirt around her body, and covered her with his jacket. He sat on the ground with her head in his lap and held her face in his hands, then closed his eyes.

"Let me follow you," he whispered. He pictured her face, alive, laughing. He imagined her dancing in his arms, warm and close. He felt himself sink into blackness, following her path, chasing after her. The way grew colder and more desolate than anywhere he'd ever imagined. He cried out, but kept going, racing after her. Pain pierced him like knives as he fell into a spiral of despair where his path descended into catacombs of darkness and terror.

Chapter 51

Guitar—someone was playing a slow melody far away. A tenor voice rose in song. Erin listened to the music, wondering, and its beauty broke her heart.

How could she hear those things? The cold voice had told her nothing was left—no light, no warmth, no life.

Soft voices spoke nearby, and she gradually became aware of comfort and softness, warm hands on her shoulders. She felt cradled in peace.

A woman's gentle voice, as light as crystal bells. "Ah, little one."

"She's awakening at last?" a man's voice said.

Erin opened her eyes. She lay on a soft couch with her head resting in Salina's lap. Salina's radiance glowed clear and bright as sunlight. A small man stood beside them, his eyes brown as obsidian.

"It's good to have you back, Erin," he said. "You gave us quite a fright."

She couldn't take her eyes from him. "I know you."

He smiled. "Yes. It's been a long time since I first brought you here. Now rest a while longer."

Erin struggled to sit up, but had no strength for it. "How did you find me? Did you bring me here?"

"Not this time." His eyes seemed to look deep inside her. "Rest now. This is the time for healing."

Salina squeezed his hand. "Thank you, Conn."

He turned and left the room.

Salina soothed her face with a cool, fragrant cloth, and the guitar began another melody. Erin looked around the room, which was filled with sunlight and strewn with several pale yellow chairs and a few small tables. The French doors opened to a garden with bright blossoms and fluttering green leaves. Above, candles in a chandelier emitted a soft, powdery fragrance.

"How did I get here?" Erin asked.

"Michael brought you."

Erin closed her eyes and took a deep breath. "Michael. How did he find me?"

"The crow led him to you. But Michael had a terrible time getting to you once he found you. You were almost beyond reach, little one. It took all his strength to pull you back."

Erin frowned. "Where is he?"

"He's already left Domus."

Erin listened to the guitar in the distance. The tenor sang with the melody, but she didn't understand the words. "Conn was my teacher," she whispered.

"Yes."

Her brow creased. "Why did I have such a hard time remembering him? Why couldn't I remember my dreams?"

Salina sighed. "Your husband's death was a terrible loss, and you blamed yourself. Conn came to you in the midst of that immense pain. Remembering your dreams brought all that pain back, so your mind closed the door to those memories." Salina wiped Erin's forehead with the soft, cool cloth. "Conn felt he should have waited to ask you to join us until your grief was lessened, but our need is great, and he saw the strength inside you."

"I have no strength."

Salina raised her eyebrows. "Is that what you think? You have won the hardest battle, risking yourself for someone else—someone who has done you so much harm. You are strong."

They were silent as they listened to another song. A light soprano voice joined the tenor, singing strange, soothing words.

"How did I begin to remember?"

"Other viators. Being with them helped awaken your memories—especially Michael."

More voices joined in the song, adding an intricate harmony. Erin realized she must have been gone a long time.

"How long do I need to stay?"

Salina spoke gently. "You can leave whenever you like. You will bear a scar if you go back now, but it will fade some. The scars on your heart will take longer to heal, of course, and they will never go away completely. You will feel much grief from your ordeal."

"How long have I been here?"

"A few days."

Erin tried to sit up and winced at the pain in her stomach. She sat up anyway. "My children must be worried about me."

"Yes."

"How will I get back?"

"Lord Ariston will take you. He's waiting right outside."

The large man entered the room and bowed to Salina, then bowed to Erin. "Are you ready to go back now?"

She gazed at him—he was dressed in shorts and a wide belt; he looked even more powerful than before. He grinned at her.

"Erin may need some help getting to the boat, my lord," Salina said.

Erin stood up and felt very weak. The room began to spin, so she grasped Ariston's arm and leaned against him.

"Take good care of her." Salina kissed both of Erin's cheeks. "Come back soon, my dear, so I can see how you are."

Erin nodded. "As soon as I can. How can I thank you enough?"

"My joy will be to see you fight again, little viator. *Tutus somnium*. May your dreams bring you safely to our shore again."

Erin leaned against Ariston as they walked through the restful house past many small groups of viators speaking softly together. Sunlight and candles cast a warm, flickering glow on their faces, and they smiled and greeted Erin and Ariston as they passed. When they reached the door her legs gave out, and he picked her up and carried her the rest of the way to the rowboat in the nearby harbor. He set her on a cushion in the bow, covered her with a blanket, and pushed off. The day was still bright, and the water glimmered in the sunshine. He rowed slowly and steadily out into the wide, slow moving river. They left a shimmering wake behind them as they made their way across.

Ariston kept watching Erin, and she finally asked, "What is it? Do I look strange?"

"No. I've just never known anyone who's gone so far. You were on the far side of the distant river—we don't go there. And you had fallen even further from there, into blackness. Michael said it was a long and evil journey."

"You talked to Michael?"

"Yes, after he brought you to Salina. It was quite a tale he told."

"Is he all right?"

"He's all right. He was injured too, but not badly. He was shaken, though, by where he had to go to finally reach you—he was shaken to his soul. You were severely hurt." He paused. "Your attacker made it back."

Erin thought about Gary and began to tremble under her blanket. "Yes, I remember seeing him cross back over the ford." He had made it back, and he was alive. Horror welled up inside her as she remembered what he had done.

"He was the one, wasn't he?" she asked Ariston. "The dreamer who led a viator to his death."

"Yes." The big man's nostrils flared and his brow creased so tight his eyebrows became one line across his face.

"And the shadows caused the accident that killed my husband. A mortifer told me himself—they did it for Gary."

Ariston nodded, and they rowed on in silence. The only sound was the dip and splash of the oars as they hit the water.

"You were lucky in one way, though," he said. "If a mortifer had found you in your state, I don't think even Michael would have been able to help you. You would have been destroyed. But it was a strange thing. Michael said there was a man standing beside you as you lay injured. He stayed until Michael had finally reached you and could carry you back, then he walked away, deeper into the forest on the other side. Never said a word. But Michael was sure he kept the mortifers away."

She stared at Ariston, unable to speak. Who had guarded her? She could think of only one person it might be, but it seemed too amazing. "Did Michael know who it was?"

"He thought it was someone named William. Do you know him?"

Erin's eyes filled with tears. "He was my husband," she whispered.

Ariston stopped rowing and shipped the oars. He went to her, wrapping her in his huge arms, and held her while she cried.

"Michael was sure it was him," he continued. "He guarded you both the whole time and only left after Michael brought you back across the river."

Erin nodded, and Ariston went back to rowing. They didn't speak again until they reached shore. He tied the boat to the dock and lifted Erin out. When he set her on her feet, she embraced him.

He said, "May we meet in our dreams again soon."

"Thank you, my lord. Walk with care."

Chapter 52

THE nurse wrapped the blood pressure cuff around Erin's upper arm and began to inflate it, listening to the pulse of her blood flow. Erin lay back on her hospital bed and looked at the sunshine streaming through the window, coloring the room bright gold. The nurse jotted down the readings onto a chart and smiled.

"You're doing better today," she said.

Erin's gaze wandered to the window. "I need to go home."

"I heard you'll be able to go home tomorrow."

"Good." Erin gave the nurse a faint smile.

"You have some beautiful flowers."

Several colorful bouquets sat on the counter, their sweet fragrance filling the air, and get-well cards were propped open beside them. Erin's stomach ached as she thought about the fear and worry her friends and children had felt. So many regrets—she had been so blind. "My friends are wonderful. They do so much for me."

The privacy curtain was closed, shutting off the view to the hallway, but Erin's door was open. She heard footfalls approach from down the hall, and the curtain was pulled aside. Gwen stood there.

"Mommy!" Gwen rushed to Erin but stopped short of the bed, her eyes wide.

Matthew followed and stopped when he saw her. "Mom." Tears ran down his cheeks. He hugged her, and Gwen came close to hug her, too. Hannah followed them into the room.

"My darlings," Erin whispered. "I'm so sorry. This has been terrible for you."

Matt stood up straight and studied her. "Mom, are you all right? How's your head?"

Erin's head was bandaged and her face was bruised. Her left arm was in a sling. Her body was bandaged tightly around her waist, and she was glad Matt couldn't see it.

"It still hurts, but I'm okay. Soon I'll be good as new," Erin said. She fought back her tears. She was determined to reassure them—to make sure they knew she would be all right.

"Gwen picked these for you." Hannah approached, carrying a vase of tiny blue and white forget-me-nots. "She said they always make you feel better."

Gwen nodded. She took the vase from Hannah and showed the little flowers to Erin. "I picked them this morning. You should see the garden—all the flowers are blooming now." She leaned on the bed and grabbed Erin's hand.

"Thank you. They're just what I wanted," Erin said. "Good news, kids—the nurse just told me I can come home tomorrow."

"Wonderful," Hannah said.

"I know you two might not want me to come home so soon since you're having so much fun with Hannah and Carlos, but you'll have to put up with me again," Erin teased, her eyes crinkled in a smile.

"We want you home!" Matt and Gwen said together.

Erin and Hannah exchanged grins.

Aleesha walked into the room with a vase of yellow roses. "Darling, you look so much better." She set the vase on the counter and kissed Erin's cheek.

"Thanks, Leesh. I'm feeling better today. More flowers? You're spoiling me. These roses are lovely."

Aleesha studied Erin's face. "Are you going home tomorrow?"

"The nurse said yes."

"Just give me a call when you're ready and I'll pick you up. I'll come over as often as you need help, too. Don't worry about a thing," Hannah said.

"Thank you. I don't know what I'd do without you—all of you."

They were silent for a minute, then Gwen told Erin about her last day of school before summer vacation, and Matthew told her about the new fort he and Jacob had built on the beach. They talked about the delicious dinner Carlos had fixed for them, and how they were able to stay up late and watch movies. Gwen laughed about Hannah's and Carlos's silly games and how they made up funny stories. Erin began to relax.

The children talked for over an hour. Time passed so quickly Erin was shocked when Hannah said it was time for them to go. Matt and Gwen kissed and hugged her, and Hannah squeezed her hand before they left, promising to come back the next day to take her home.

When they were alone, Aleesha sat down on the edge of the bed. "You were right not to let the kids see you until now. Even yesterday they would have been frightened."

"Yes, even so, I'm not a pretty sight."

"It won't be long." Aleesha squeezed Erin's hand.

"But you, Leesh—I was shocked to wake up and see your face—red and swollen from crying. I've never seen you like that. I was sure you must look worse than I did," Erin joked.

Aleesha laughed. "I hope you never see me look like that again. But you looked a lot worse than me, darling. I never want to see you like that again either."

Erin smiled and looked at her cards and flowers. "Is Bruce in Portland?"

"Yes, he'll be back in a few days."

"Is … Gary still here in the hospital?"

Aleesha shook her head and frowned. "No, he left the day after the accident. His injuries weren't nearly as bad as yours. He wouldn't talk to me, though. Just told me to go away. And then he left. I'm sorry." She was silent a few moments. "What happened, Erin? How did the accident happen?"

Erin's stomach ached again and she closed her eyes. "I found out about Gary's business," she whispered. She looked at Aleesha's puzzled expression, unsure how much she should say. "He's involved in human trafficking."

Aleesha's mouth dropped open, and she shook her head. "Are you sure of this?"

"Yes. I confronted him, and he admitted it. We argued in the car—I've never been so angry, and he was furious. He lost control of the car. I was a fool. I didn't let myself see until it was too late." That was all she could bring herself to tell Aleesha. She felt the pain welling up inside her, remembering how Gary had admitted so much more than that. He had taken William's life. Taken him from her.

Aleesha stood up and paced the room. "That is horrible. You poor dear. I'm so sorry. That explains his behavior."

She sat down on the bed again and took Erin's hand. "This morning I called Kenneth to ask him if he'd seen Gary, and he told me Gary had left the country—he went to Amsterdam. I didn't know how I was going to tell you."

Erin gasped. "He's gone?"

Aleesha nodded.

"He's lucky to be alive. I hope he turns his life around, but I also hope I never see him again," Erin said. "Leesh, the week before the accident I was trying to reach Michael Woodward, but he was gone somewhere. Did he come back?"

"Yes, he did, but he's gone again. He's got a cabin near Mt. Hood. Bruce said he went there."

Erin looked down at her hands resting in her lap and fought back tears.

"He was here for a few days," Aleesha said. "He showed up the day after the accident, and he practically camped here by your side until you started to wake up. Then he told Bruce it was time for him to go."

Erin lay her head back on the pillow, the pain of her injuries throbbing, and she desperately wished Michael was still there.

Chapter 53

GWEN ran into the house waving a picture in her hand. "Mommy, look what I made at Mrs. Edna's."

Erin put down the dishcloth and took the picture. It was a drawing of a small butter-yellow cottage with a fountain in front.

"This is beautiful," Erin said. "You're becoming such a good artist. This house looks familiar—did you make it up or have you seen this before?"

"I made it up. I want to live in a house like that when I grow up."

"That would be fun."

Matt got up from the table where he'd been building a Lego castle. He looked at Gwen's picture. "I think we've seen that house somewhere before. It looks familiar." He turned to Erin. "You look pale, Mom. You'd better lie down for a while. It's only been three days since you got out of the hospital."

"Maybe I'll go sit on the beach with a book."

"I'll help you."

He ran upstairs and grabbed a blanket and Erin's book and brought them outside for her. He told her not to worry about him and Gwen—he'd keep an eye on Gwen for a while.

Erin sat on her blanket on the beach and leaned back against a driftwood log. She closed her eyes and let the sun warm her face. She was still very weak.

Her thoughts drifted to her time in Domus, to Salina and Lord Ariston. She thought about what Ariston had told her—that William had been there, protecting her.

Her thoughts moved on to Michael, and she could see him vividly in her mind—his dark hair falling into his eyes, his cheekbones and angular jaw, his black clothes. She hadn't seen him since they had quarreled, both awake and in the dream—that terrible dream. She shuddered to think of the things she had said, and she could still see the anger in his eyes. She had treated him so badly, and yet he had come to her. And he had kissed her. Why had he left the hospital? He must have stayed only long enough to know she would be all right—to know he had done his job. She couldn't blame him. Sadness made her stomach hurt, and a cool breeze raised her skin in goosebumps.

The sound of a boat motoring past woke her from her thoughts, and she looked out over the Sound. The water sparkled in the setting sun, and the breeze mingled the scent of the salt water with the fragrance of the flowers in her garden. She opened her book but couldn't concentrate on the words. Glancing at the rocky beach beside her, she sorted through the stones, selecting some creamy white ones and gathering them into a small pile.

The crunch of tires pulling into her driveway made her turn around. She wasn't expecting anyone, and she was shocked to see Michael's Lexus.

She turned around again and looked out at the water, her heart pounding. His car rolled to a stop. The car door slammed. She stood up to go back to the house, but Michael had seen her and was walking to the beach, the breeze blowing his hair away from his face.

He was close enough for her to see his serious expression—his eyes searching. She didn't know what to say to him and looked down at her feet.

He walked to the steps that led down to the beach and stopped.

"You look well," he said.

She felt her face flush and looked up at him. "Thank you." She seemed frozen in place. He stood still and kept his eyes on hers. A seagull flew overhead and dropped a clam on the rocky beach, then swooped down to grab it up again.

Erin was finally able to move. She walked the few short steps toward him. "I mean thank you," she said. "Ariston told me all that happened."

Michael stepped down to the beach and touched her cheek with his fingers, a question in his eyes. "You remember?"

She nodded her head slowly. "All of it. How can I tell you how sorry I am? Or thank you enough?"

He wrapped his arms around her and pulled her close. "You don't have to say anything."

He leaned down, and his lips found her mouth. His kiss sent a thrill through her whole being. She turned her head and looked into his dark eyes.

"Thank you for taking me to Domus. I think I've seen a bit of heaven," she whispered.

He smiled at her. "And I followed you all the way to hell."

She closed her eyes and took a deep breath, inhaling his warm pine scent. "I'll have to make it up to you."

Michael laughed and kissed her again, long and leisurely, his mouth tender and warm. The tide was out, and the first stars glimmered in the eastern sky. He took her hand, and they walked up the steps to Erin's little house.

A Note from the Author

Thank you for reading *Viator*. I hope you enjoyed reading it as much as I enjoyed writing it!

As the first installment of The Viator Chronicles, *Viator* has told you the story of how Erin Holley first joined the ranks of dream warriors. The second book of the series, *Mortifer*, will delve deeper into the realm of evil that Erin and Michael struggle to overcome as the demons finally gain access to our world. In the final book, *Domus*, Erin will have to fight an ever more powerful evil as it grows to threaten the survival of her loved ones, her world, and the world beyond.

If you'd like to hear about new releases, please visit my website at JaneRalstonBrooks.com or my Facebook page at Facebook.com/janeralstonbrooks. You can also reach me by email at jane@janeralstonbrooks.com. I welcome your feedback!

Made in the USA
Thornton, CO
07/16/23 16:26:45

82503331-06a2-4549-b41d-f820d64c39b3R02